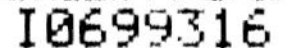
I0699316

Praise for C. A. Farran

A tantalizing treat and an epic escape.

> — INDIES TODAY ON THE BALLAD OF
> THE LAST DRAGON

It pulled at my heartstrings and I didn't even know I had heartstrings.

> — D. H. HOSKINS, AUTHOR OF THE
> COUNCIL OF ATHYZIA

If you love romance and you love fantasy and you love cozy taverns and bards and ale and knights and quests... please PLEASE pick up this book.

> — KRISTEN MOORE, AUTHOR OF
> THROUGH THE WICKED WOOD

The Ballad Of The Last Dragon

T. A. Farran

To everyone who's ever hidden their pain behind a smile. Just because you make it look easy, doesn't diminish how hard it is.

The Ballad of the Last Dragon is an adult fantasy romance that contains mature content that might be troubling to some readers, including but not limited to, strong language, explicit sexual content, depictions of and references to death, graphic depictions of violence, and attempted sexual assault.

Chapter One

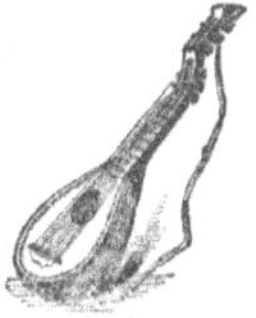

I t's a slow night at the Rusty Nail, but I bend in a deep bow and straighten my cap as if the queen herself is in the audience. I claim the stool center stage and begin plucking the familiar tune, "While the Fisherman's Away." It's one of my bawdier songs and doesn't require much effort with my vocal range. It isn't my finest work, but it's a crowd pleaser.

Not that there's a crowd tonight.

Summer nights usually draw in stray travelers and traders —the folks eager to wet their whistles and listen to my songs. But my talents are wasted on my employer, Kingsley, and our regular, Petey, who's well into his cups.

No matter. The show must go on.

My lute is smooth beneath my hands as my fingers dance over well-rehearsed melodies. I might not perform in Lindale, where bards like myself are swimming in riches and treated like nobility, where one's ears is but a footnote in an extensive collective of attributes, but I take pride in my work. It takes a certain level of artistic flair to entertain the likes of Hollowden. Salt of the earth people, they are, without all the fancy trappings of city life. Even if they find me a bit odd, a bit unsettling. It matters not, because a true artist transcends these obstacles and relates to the masses. And I—

Petey slumps over, fast asleep.

For fuck's sake.

My fingerpicking takes on an agitated edge. My callouses can handle it, but I'm not sure my strings can.

"I'll probably close up early, eh, Syl?"

I halt my playing. Kingsley frowns at a spotty tankard and wipes it with vigor. The hanging candelabrum adorned with melted wax highlights the grays dotting his black hair and beard. Kingsley and his wife, Brigitta, are just about the only people in town who never balk at the sharp point of my ears. He's never asked for more than professional courtesy, and he's always been kind to me. A giant of a man, and when he laughs, his entire body shakes, but I'd bet every coin Petey owes to the gamemaster that he's killed a man with his bare hands. I've tried to get him to spill his secrets, but he knows me well enough to be wary. Secrets don't stay secret very long with me. I have songs to write, inspiration to find, and all that.

"What about my set?"

Kingsley abandons his quest for the cleanest tankard in town to glance around the empty tavern.

Point taken.

"Someone might roll in, pockets heavy and throat parched." And easily plied with enough alcohol to part with their coin. My cup is looking rather desolate. Is that a cobweb on the rim?

Kingsley shakes his head. "I can't pay you to sing to Petey in his sleep."

"But you enjoy my playing, don't you?"

I take his silence as humbling awe of my talent.

With a sigh, I pull my velvet cap from my head. My hair, neck, and forehead are damp with sweat, and the relief is instantaneous. But I'd rather play sweaty and uncomfortable than go hungry, and when seeking coin, it's best if my ears remain hidden. Their shape is the most obvious trait of my elven heritage, a fact, I've learned, that isn't well-received in most places. Even in Tarrgein. Superstition about the ancient elves of old might not have followed me too closely across the sea to this country, but that hasn't prevented ignorant prejudice from taking root. Normally I wouldn't dare remove my cap mid performance. Even around here where I've stayed long enough people have finally accepted I won't use my "evil she-elf magic to bewitch them," I always get more appreciation when I keep my ears safely tucked away. That and my red cap made of crushed velvet with a large black plume is gorgeous. Since our only customer is fast asleep, I bundle my long blonde hair into a knot and cast another glance at my empty cup. "When will the season pick up again?"

Kingsley shrugs, stacking the now spotless tankard with the rest and wiping the bar top, carefully avoiding Petey's unconscious form.

Summer has its ups and downs in patrons. The larger cities have festivals, and with First Fruits Day right around the corner, everyone has probably headed for grander accommodations. Still, it wouldn't kill our patrons to show loyalty to their local tavern, would it?

I abandon my stool and march across the faded wood of the stage, avoiding the loose board that always creaks under foot. Slinging my lute onto my back, I fan myself with my cap. I've grown used to this town, or rather, I haven't been booed off stage yet, and so long as I keep my ears covered, no one hassles me.

I don't ask for much. Food in my belly, recognition of my work, a bevy of adoring fans. Shades, I'd settle for food in my belly. Kingsley won't let me ever truly go hungry, but he isn't exactly swimming in riches. He and Brigitta manage and try their best to include my needs, but I know it puts a strain on their coin purse. Sometimes I imagine how it would feel to know my next meal was all but assured. As it is, I must swallow my pride and accept the charity each time Brigitta "accidentally" makes extra. This tavern doesn't have a kitchen, so no sneaking off plates here. I can't complain. Two years back, I played in Birchfield for a time, and when the owner caught me eating abandoned scraps, he tried to arrange what he claimed to be a "mutually beneficial arrangement."

I have a good thing going here.

My belly grumbles as if in rebuttal.

"We could host themed events." I sit on the stool next to Petey, leaning my elbows onto the freshly wiped bar top. "Draw in some customers."

"What sorta events?"

"Hmm... what about poetry readings?"

Kingsley laughs, his whole body shaking.

Evidently, he doesn't appreciate my suggestion.

"What if we host competitions? Like testing strength and stamina?"

He raises a graying brow at me. "Stamina?"

"Sure!" Now that I have his attention, I need to reel him in. He's always so opposed to new ideas. "We could have drinking contests."

He snorts and waves toward Petey. "Every night is a drinking contest one plays with themselves."

"But we could offer incentive." I'm losing him, I can feel it. Jumping atop the bar, I pace back and forth. His grunt is the only indication of his displeasure, despite just wiping it down. He probably loves every chance he gets to clean the bar top. For a tavern in the middle of nowhere, it's absurdly clean.

"The incentive to drink is drinking," he says, crossing his massive arms. "Let it go. Business will come. It always does."

There's nothing inherently wrong with the simple structure of this establishment. The daily hook for my hat, so to speak. But as I glance around the empty tavern, noting the mismatched wood of the chairs Kingsley built, the pitch in the floor from where the ground softened, creating a slanted effect that makes dropped bottles roll to the other end of the room, I can't help but imagine the potential if we only drew in more coin to cover expenses.

"This place could be more. The Rusty Nail could be the crowned jewel of Tarrgein! Warriors and nobles from the Western Isles, Dwarven merchants and architects from Hawthok, they would all flock to our establishment. Lindale would be a thing of the past while Hollowden takes center stage. Just imagine"—I drop to sit on the bar, wrapping an arm around his shoulders as if showing him the path ahead—"your tavern, swimming with patrons. You could retire and hire some cocky young-blood to tend the bar. You'd have more time at home with Brigitta, and, oh look! She's swathed in silk, samite, the finest fabrics this side of the Jürdan Sea. A proper lady!"

Kingsley chuckles and disentangles himself. "Brigitta is no lady, and I like it that way." A suggestive smile curves against his mouth.

Ew. I don't need to picture whatever he's thinking to plant that expression on his face.

"You're missing the point—"

"Sylvaine." He only ever uses my full name when he's annoyed... which is most of the time. "I'm not changing things."

I should let it go. He's made up his mind, and that's that.

"If you would just listen—"

"Enough. Go lock up."

Rolling my eyes, I trudge to the door, dragging my feet with every step. It might be a bit dramatic, but hunger and neglect of one's art will do that to a person. "May Welkin's guardians bless my weary soul."

"No prayers until you lock up."

I bite my lip to keep from laughing. Kingsley has little patience for talk of religion, even going so far as to prohibit it from the tavern during working hours. Says it causes too many bullshit arguments he hasn't the time nor energy to deal with. It's just as well; I tend to blaspheme according to the sentiments of most faiths in these parts. My goddess, the mother of wisdom and strength, is a false idol, Welkin's guardians are demons, and any mention of nature's energy earns a hiss and spitting in my direction.

When I reach the open door, I lean against the threshold and stare off into the darkness. The summer night is thick with the lingering heat of the day, but at least there's a breeze. We'll lock up and let Petey sleep here. He doesn't crash here every night but often enough that if he wakes before we open, he'll help himself to a recovery drink, equal parts liquor and bad habits, and wait for one of us to add it to his tab.

Before I can shut the heavy door, a light bobs into view, far in the distance. It swings back and forth in the dark forest, a beacon in the night. The *clip-clop* of horse hooves meets my ears.

Riders. That means customers.

I spin around just in time for Kingsley to sigh and toss me my hat.

Ducking my chin, I place my cap just right, hiding my ears and letting my finger graze the large black feather.

It's showtime.

Chapter Two

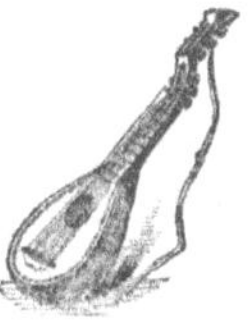

Perched on my stool, lute in hand, I await my audience. I pluck a gentle tune, something inviting, and glance at my cup.

It'll be full in no time.

A tall man skips through the door. *Skips.* As if his excitement propels him. He wears his long red hair loose and spilling over his shiny armor. Custom made, I'd wager. His broad grin lights up his whole face, straight white teeth on display. I find myself smiling back. He's handsome, but the eagerness he wears with abandon makes him utterly adorable.

"I'll have a bottle of your finest brew!" he calls out loud enough to startle a snore from Petey.

Kingsley raises his brows but sets to work pulling from his most expensive reserves. It's Bjovian wine, and I've only tried it once when he was in a particularly good mood.

It tastes like shit.

The red-haired man notices me, and his grin widens. He dips his chin in acknowledgement and leans against the bar to watch me play.

I might show off a little with an extra flourish of my finger-picking.

"Ye could have tied yer own horse," a woman calls out in a thick brogue. A portion of hair above her ear is shaved to the scalp, the rest hangs down in a dark curtain. Rather than sit at the bar, she tugs a chair out with her boot and sits at the table in the center.

When she glances my way, a thick scar cuts down one side of her bronze face, from forehead to jaw. It does nothing to dim her beauty, but a scar like that, and on the same side where she keeps her head shaved gives me insight on this stranger. She's survived the edge of a blade, and she wants the world to know.

I've been accused of inventing stories. In my line of work, an active imagination is an asset, but I'm certain I've pegged her accurately.

"You know I'm dreadful with knots." The red-haired man takes a swill from his wine, trying desperately to hide his grimace. "Are they coming in?"

She juts her chin toward the door just as two men appear.

One wears an easy smile on his umber face, dimples creasing his cheeks. Hair cropped close to the scalp, the chiseled lines of his cheekbones and jaw are on full display. He gives me a wink and runs his hands together as he saunters across the tavern, his wiry frame moving with smooth elegance. A bow and quiver are strapped to his back, and his green cloak billows behind him, revealing the set of glinting daggers at his hips.

Hm. We have a crew of well-armed folk. Best be sure they enjoy my songs.

"I owe you five silvers," he says, clapping the armored red head on the back and flagging Kingsley down. "I thought for sure this was a private residence."

We get that a lot. To be fair, this was little more than an alehouse once, but Kingsley expanded his home, built the bar, changed the layout, and turned it into the Rusty Nail. When I first found this place, there wasn't even a stage for me to play on. It only took six months of begging and odd jobs to get him to build it for me.

So lost in my memory of the time I had to coax Kingsley's cow, Honeysuckle, back into her pen, I almost forget the fourth stranger in the tavern.

Broadly built and nearly as tall as Kingsley, the man is huge. His black hair cuts just above his wide shoulders, most of it pulled into a knot at the back of his head. A tight beard hides his jaw, and the floorboards groan under his heavy steps.

He doesn't so much as glance my way, sitting beside the woman and scowling at the wall.

Well, my keen ability to read people tells me this is a right bastard.

When I end my song, three sets of polite applause greet me. I bow my head in thanks and kick out my cup toward the edge of the stage just in case they need the reminder.

I begin my new song, "When Night Calls." I haven't sung it for anyone apart from Kingsley, but I have a feeling it's my best work yet.

"When Night Calls
Will you be there to answer?
When it's all quiet
Will I be alone there?
In the dark, can you trace my scars?
Close your eyes, can you feel my heart?"

I glance toward my audience. It's important to connect with my soon-to-be fans. The woman has her head tilted, a posture I recognize as intently listening. The men at the bar whisper to each other, occasionally taking a drink. Some people prefer to listen while engaged in activity, I understand.

It's less intimate than being in the moment with me. Petey still slumbers at the end of the bar.

But the dark-haired man, the scowling one, refuses to look at me. His sights remain fixed on the wall. His hands curl into fists atop his thighs, and I trip over the next pluck pattern. His expression darkens, like thunder clouds rolling in.

Does he really hate my song that much?

I sing even louder. He can pretend he can't hear me, but I won't make it easy for him.

When my song ends, he stands abruptly, scraping his chair across the floor. His large frame towers in our little tavern, and I get the urge to knock him over to see how hard he'd fall.

"Are we done, Aeron?" His voice is deep with a gravelly edge. I hope it's because his throat is sore.

My stomach sinks and the tips of my ears burn. I'm used to rejection by now. The way of an artist is to bleed for the masses while thickening one's skin. It's a precarious balance but one I'm sure I've struck.

Most days.

"Patience, Jaromir. The dragon will wait."

The bastard, Jaromir, heaves a gusty sigh and stalks out of the tavern.

I'm about to start my next song when curiosity overtakes me. He said dragon, didn't he? There hasn't been a dragon sighting in over a century. There have been tales of the dark times when they prowled the land and soared through the skies. One of my favorite stories is about a bard and his wayward brother who slayed a dragon, but they've long been hunted to extinction. I have heard rumors of a lost hoard from a few travelers. But no one has ever found such a thing, and maps forged for trickery are a copper a dozen.

The way this man speaks... it's as if he knows something I don't, a fact that doesn't sit well with me. If there's a story, I want to commit it to memory. Perhaps the dragon is nothing more than a moniker or code for something else, but I itch to know for certain.

"Dragon?"

Aeron, the red-haired delight of a man, gives me another of his heart stopping smiles. "Oh, yes. We've embarked on a dangerous quest. Fraught with peril! I'm sure a lady such as yourself wouldn't want the details."

I hop off my stool, leaning my lute against the wall. I'm a storyteller, and this sounds like a story worth telling.

"You're hunting a dragon?" I don't tell him it's impossible because dragons don't exist anymore. Anything is possible if you spin your words just so.

He waves his hands as I approach. "Oh, no. I can't bear to subject you to such horrors. It's too perilous for delicate ears."

I laugh. He has every intention of telling me, but I play along. "Please, tell me." Some men need to feel like they're important enough for begging. His over-embellished gestures and demanding volume ring of a man who loves to hear himself talk.

"If you insist." Aeron leads me to the table where the scarred woman sits. "May I introduce you to Neith." She studies me with a wry smirk. "And Cadoc."

Cadoc waves to Kingsley for another round and drops in the chair beside me. "Here we go," he mutters.

Aeron leans forward. His eyes are brilliant blue with gold around the edges, and he has a smattering of freckles along the bridge of his nose. "There are whispers of fathomless wealth, deep in an unnamed mountain. All who have sought the hidden riches have perished, lost to flame, because a dragon—the last dragon of our age—guards its entrance. Few dare to believe such a place exists anymore, but it's real. The one who defeats the dragon and claims the treasure will be immortalized. A legend long after he's gone." He sits back, watching me carefully.

I try not to let my opinion show on my face. Where were the details? Something to slam me into the moment. He didn't even draw out the tension!

"What do you think of that?" he asks.

"I'm thinking when I tell this tale, I'll take some dramatic license with the details."

"Huh?"

"How do you even know they were lost to fire?" It's utter nonsense and poorly constructed. But I've worked with less. I snap my fingers as an idea comes to me. "I know! Scorched armor! Maybe someone went searching for a loved one who left in pursuit of the treasure and found their scorched armor! Oh, but then that begs the question of how close one can get without the dragon attacking. If the armor is where the loved one can find it, why didn't the dragon attack them, too? Unless it can sense greed, and our hero is pure of heart! Oh, I love where this is going. Should the loved one be a lover or their child? I recognize the value of a lover, but there's a beautiful symmetry of a child following their parent's legacy. Maybe even growing up with thoughts of finding their parent's resting place?"

I leap from the table and reach across the bar to the cubby beneath where I keep a spare vellum and quill.

"This is good. This is all very good." I scribble furiously. When I'm satisfied I have the initial forms of this story down, I return to their table.

Aeron eyes me with raised brows. Neith fights a losing battle against her smile, and Cadoc appears torn between delight and confusion. His dark eyes are crinkled while his white teeth and dimples are on full display.

"What are you doing?" Cadoc asks, and his voice has a pleasing quality. Smooth and elegant. Hmm... does he sing?

"I collect stories," I say by way of explanation. "You spoke of heroics immortalized." I fan my hands out over my vellum.

"This is how it's achieved. You think it's the heroes who tell stories of their exploits? No one believes a story one tells about themself. People lie, especially in pursuit of fame. But a story whispered in taverns around the world?" I point to myself. "People like me make your legends. Now, is it a lover or a child who discovers the armor?"

Aeron's eyes widen, and his knee-weakening grin returns. I can't help but smile back. He has a cleft in his chin, and I hadn't realized until this moment what an attractive feature it is.

"What's your name?" he asks.

"Sylvaine Abelan," I say with a flourish. "Syl among friends."

"Syl," he repeats, beckoning me with a wave of his hand as he leans in. "How would you like to go on an adventure?"

Chapter Three

The sun is a hint on the horizon, and I've been up for hours. There was no chance for sleep once I agreed to accompany Aeron and his group. Cadoc, Neith, and Jaromir are all blades for hire. They're on his payroll for this venture. And now, so am I.

The hours following our agreement have afforded me time to wonder. His quest seems a far-fetched notion, but I can't pass up the opportunity to travel from tavern to tavern with both coin and protection. This is how I can make a name for myself. If I can make a name for him, too, all the better.

Do I really think he's found the fabled hoard of the last dragon?

Doesn't matter what I think. What I can convince others of... that's what matters.

Swiftly, I pack up my meager belongings. I've changed out of my performance clothes, tossing my stockings, short pants, and vest into my pack. I wear sturdy breeches, a light-weight tunic, and my brown linen vest. It's too warm for my travel cloak, so I fold it up and pack it away before I sling my bag across my chest.

It's lighter than I thought.

Leaving my hair loose, I carefully place my cap. There are other ways to hide my ears, Brigitta once showed me how to plait the front section of my hair to create a barrier around them, but I prefer my cap. I might not risk ruining my finer clothes, but donning my hat feels like a statement.

I'm off on a quest.

A knock at the door announces Kingsley. He frowns as he steps into my room, hunching to avoid hitting his head against the sloped ceilings. He and Brigitta gave me the small dwelling abutting their barn when I first started working for him and he found out I was sneaking back into the tavern to sleep.

With my bag packed, all evidence of my living here has vanished.

He keeps the door open, a medium-sized leather satchel hanging from his massive hands. "You're off then."

My lungs are tight, so I nod. It isn't forever. I'll be back before winter.

"Well, here." He holds the satchel out to me. Hesitantly, I take it from his grasp. Inside is enough salted jerky, apples, and carrots to feed me for a week. There's even a pouch full of my favorite mushrooms, witch's butter and king bolete. Brigitta must have foraged and raided their larder to stock me so fully.

I find his face, but his features have started to blur behind my unshed tears.

"And, uh, this." He hands me a small, wrapped parcel. I peel back the cloth, and the familiar scent of black currant hits my nose. Kingsley is the only person I know who adds black currant and mulberries to his mixture of beech ashes and goat fat to make divine smelling soap.

I try to thank him, but the words get stuck somewhere between a laugh and a sob. Instead, I throw myself into his arms.

He pats my head and clears his throat. "I just thought, you might want the simple comfort on the road."

He always thinks of my comfort. I used to wonder after his intentions, but I realized he would do it for anyone.

Nodding, I step away and rub my eyes. "I'll be back before Winter Solstice."

Kingsley smiles, and damn if it isn't the most bittersweet thing I've ever seen. "Take care, Syl." He turns to leave—he must open the tavern without me—but hesitates. "You know, it's okay if you don't come back. Here, I mean. So long as you're safe."

The tears I've only just mastered fill my vision once more. "Of course I'm coming back. We haven't finished our conversation about themed events to draw in more customers."

Kingsley laughs, but this time it's a quiet sound contained to his chest. "We're not hosting competitions."

"Not yet."

He shakes his head and leaves.

I pack the food and soap, careful to keep them separate, and adjust my cap once more.

Time to get an early start on the first day of the rest of my life.

I'M ALMOST SURPRISED to see Aeron's crew waiting for me. I round the side of the Rusty Nail to find them and their horses as they ready for travel.

Aeron is resplendent with the dawn illuminating his fiery mane. Hands on his hips with his spotless armor gleaming in the sun's rise.

Neith picks her nails with her dagger, casually leaning against the side of the hitching post. Examining her in the daylight affords me a better look. Her eyes and hair are dark, that scar along the side of her face on full display with how she shaves the side of her head. Her full lips and the delicate shape of her nose indicate how comely she'd be all done up like the noble ladies I used to see passing through Birchfield. She's still striking—a dangerous sort of beauty I could write ballads about.

Cadoc murmurs and strokes his horse. When he catches me staring, he pauses and gives me a knowing smile. "I like to tell her of my dreams each morning." Dimples crease his dark skin. With his large eyes, sharp cheekbones, and strong jaw, he possesses a handsomeness I'm sure makes anyone caught in his attention blush.

"You talk to your horse?"

"She's a good listener."

Fair enough.

A loud thud nearby jolts me out of my skin. Jaromir drops another satchel from his saddlebags onto the dirt, pointedly ignoring me.

Well, that simply won't do.

"I hope you don't have anything valuable in there," I call out to his retreating form. He stiffens at the sound of my voice but says nothing.

"He's just salty this morn," Neith says, pushing off the wall to come stand by me. "Dinnae pay him any mind."

Warmth floods me at the unexpected comment. At least she likes me.

"He'll be right as rain as soon as we get underway." Aeron claps me on the back, and I flinch. If he damages my lute, I'll make sure the only song written in his name is the Ballad of Lost Bullocks.

Jaromir drops another satchel unceremoniously at our feet. A metallic clang hints at pots and pans in that bag. "She shouldn't be coming."

Right. He doesn't want me along. What a surprise.

Though what I've done to offend him is lost on me. Has he spotted my ears? Is he one of *those* humans? I can't decide if I should call him out on it or simply needle him. Perhaps both.

"Your reaction to disappointment is to throw things around?" I ask. "What an evolved response." This is the second time I've addressed him, and I'm sure he'll ignore me again.

Instead, he exhales a harsh breath. "I've been informed you'll be riding with me. I'm the faster rider should we encounter any danger." He doesn't say it like he's boasting but relaying a mundane fact. He glares at Aeron. "I won't kill my horse so you can bring someone to feed your ego."

Indignation spikes through my chest, hot and quick. "My artistic integrity comes first. I'm here to complete a job, not offer false flattery." It's bad enough he insulted me during my song, but how dare he openly dismiss my work?

Jaromir continues as if I haven't spoken. "If I'm carrying the extra weight, I'm not taking these supplies. You'll go without, or you'll find a way to manage them."

Aeron nods to the others, and they quickly divide the supplies between their horses. Once everything is set, Aeron turns to me. "Ready?"

My gaze finds Jaromir. He's standing beside his horse, scowling off into the distance. He turns as if he feels my eyes on him, and the crease between his brow only deepens. If he takes issue with me, I shouldn't be his ward. As much as I loathe to have this conversation, it needs to be done.

"If it vexes you so greatly to have me along, now's the time to air your grievances. I won't worry for my life and wellbeing, not at the hands of my supposed allies."

"You should worry for your life and wellbeing. That you don't proves you shouldn't come with us." He continues unburdening his horse, indicating just how much unwanted weight he believes I add to the journey. "You needn't fear my actions, only my ability to keep you alive."

I study him intently. His words ring of truth, and yet, I can't let this go until I'm sure. "Would you let a blade by you, allow my death, and claim it was an accident?" With a steady hand, I pull the cap from my head and tuck my hair behind my ear. It's a statement, and a challenge.

Jaromir turns to meet my stare, and his expression doesn't change. Not even a flit of surprise. "No." He mutters something under his breath. "Satisfied with your questioning?"

I glance around. Aeron studies my pointed ear with an expression of interest, Cadoc gives me a grin, and Neith has already moved on from this exchange.

No one cares about my ears, and this fact is enough to stoke the excitement in my belly once more. I give Jaromir my best stage smile before plopping my cap back atop my head. "Absolutely."

Aeron gives me a nod and ruffles my hat. I fix it quickly and step up to the hulking tower of disapproval. I'm close enough to see Jaromir has dark eyes, almost black. Behind his beard, his mouth is a tight line.

I hope he gets a jaw ache from clenching.

"You'll ride in front so you don't slip off when we encounter steep terrain. Give me your lute."

My hand flies to the neck of my instrument. Over my dead body. "I've seen the way you handle supplies. Forgive me if I'm disinclined to trust you with my livelihood." I spent years scraping enough coins together to afford one. I'm not letting him toss it away like rubbish. "Perhaps if I need a rock smashed, or expert level sulking, I'll consult you."

Cadoc laughs and smothers it with a cough.

"Are you done?" Jaromir asks, arching his brow.

"Nearly. If I need tips on how to throw an adult-sized

tantrum, I'll defer to your judgment. If I need advice on how to make a poor first impression, I'll rely on your expertise. If I wish to master the art of stomping and grunting to make my feelings known, I'll look to you." I lift my chin in triumph. Also, because it makes it easier to meet his gaze. "Now I'm done."

He rubs his forehead as if this conversation is giving him a headache. "I'll damage the lute if I ride behind you while it's strapped to your back."

Oh. That makes sense. Sometimes I might benefit from listening *before* unleashing my mouth.

Alas, nobody's perfect.

"Fine." I hand off my most prized possession. To his credit, he positions it on his back, the leather strap tight across his broad chest. It blends in with his hardened leather armor. I haven't seen many folks dressed like this in these parts. There's something pleasing about the way it fits his form like a glove. I don't need to see what's underneath to know he's built like a warrior. When my thorough stare finally finds his face again, he's narrowed his dark eyes at me, and a bit of color seems to have flared high on his cheeks as if he knows what I'm thinking.

Evidently, he doesn't appreciate being ogled. That's fine. A man who doesn't smile holds no interest of mine.

Without warning, he lifts me up, and I let out a shrill shriek. I mean... a battle cry of outrage. Granted, I can't reach the height of his mount on my own, but he could have asked. Once he swings in behind me, I scoot forward as much as possible, so his thighs aren't against my backside.

Aeron waves at us. "Are we off?"

Jaromir kicks off without answering, and I'm flung back against his firm chest.

He was right, my lute would have been crushed by the impact.

I sigh and turn my thoughts to more pleasant things. Like how I'm going to write the most epic ballad of pursuing a dragon.

I might even have an adventure of my own along the way.

Chapter Four

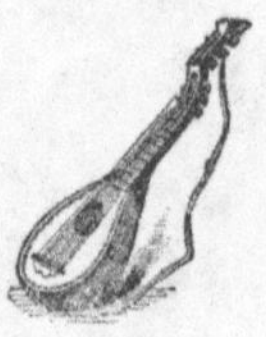

I jolt awake. A warm, solid body is pressed against my back, and the earth is moving.

Jaromir.

Aeron's quest.

My aching back.

I stretch, wincing at the way my neck twinges. I must have drifted off as we rode. Serves me right for not sleeping the night before. Now my daily rhythm is going to be off kilter.

"You never stop speaking," a deep voice growls in my ear. "Even as you sleep."

I roll my eyes. He is not very pleasant to wake up to. "Did I say anything interesting?"

He pauses. "No."

Prick.

"That's it," I say with a groan. "When I write Aeron's ballad, I'm leaving you out."

"That would be preferable."

Would it now?

"You know what, I'm going to write you your own ballad. The song of..." My brain stalls. I'm barely awake and having a hard time forming a clever insult. "The grumpy one."

To exactly no one's surprise, he doesn't quip back. He merely grunts in response.

I rub my eyes. The sun sits low on the horizon, barely peeking through the dense forest. We're still on packed road, so at least the journey hasn't taken any interesting diversions. Aeron leads the group, while Neith and Cadoc ride side by side, and we take the flank.

"Remove your hat."

I half turn, not realizing how close Jaromir's face is to mine. Up close, he's almost handsome with an elegantly sharp nose and a strong jaw beneath his beard. But the perpetual scowl ruins it. A pity.

"What's wrong with my cap? I'll have you know this is the height of fashion in Lindale." Probably. I mean, I like it.

"The feather keeps assaulting my nose." He says it so seriously, that I can't halt the laugh that erupts from my chest.

"*Assaulting* you? My good sir, I apologize for the violence of my headwear." I pull the cap from my head and run my fingers through my matted hair. The breeze feels good against my scalp and ruffles through my newly freed tresses.

Aeron calls back to us. "We should make camp while we still have the light."

There isn't much light left to be had. The ever-encroaching gloaming darkens the trees, and the shadows have long since stopped growing under the sun's pass. But I can't begrudge the sight of fireflies twinkling in and out of view among the ferns.

"We should have stopped when Cadoc noted the day's end," Jaromir answers. "It will be dark before we finish setting up camp."

"We stop on my command, as you all agreed when I hired you." For the first time since I've known him, which admittedly isn't very long, Aeron sounds annoyed. "Come, now, off the road."

Cadoc turns back and shrugs. Neith holds up a dagger as if she's going to toss it toward Aeron's back but puts it away with a sigh.

Jaromir urges his horse to follow, and I twist my fancy cap between my hands.

It would be wise to make sure I develop a good rapport with all of them and not rely on Aeron. Coin and social capital will only get one so far, but piss off the wrong person? Anyone can wind up with a knife in their back.

THE HEAT from the fire stings my face and dries out my eyes, but I huddle closer, desperate to use the light. I'm chronicling our journey as we travel while everything is fresh.

Unfortunately, I slept through most of the first day.

The road-wary adventurers found a secluded spot to make camp. Unbeknownst to them, they weren't the only ones in the shadowy forest that night.

Hm. I quite like that. It adds an air of mystery. Is it a threat? Will we survive the night? I add that last bit about surviving the night to my vellum.

A mosquito buzzes in my ear.

The creatures of the forest were curious.

No, too whimsical. I cross it out.

The creatures of the forest were drawn to the band of travelers like moths to a flame.

"What are you writing?" Cadoc's voice breaks through my thoughts. His brow is raised, but a warm smile claims his mouth. He's amused, but it doesn't feel cruel so much as interested.

I hold up my scroll. "Just jotting a few notes. It helps me organize my thoughts and keeps my muse close by."

Jaromir snorts, actually *snorts*. He reclines across the fire, propped up by his elbow. His considerable size seems ridiculously at ease, as if roughing it in the forest is his idea of a luxury retreat.

I've been to the finest bathhouses. Well, outside the walls. But I've peeked through. This is not luxury, though I admit, there is something soothing about spending the evening under the trees, leaves shaking in the wind, and stars glimmering in the expanse of sky between branches. Like a piece of me has nestled back into place after being locked away for so long.

Oh, that's a good line. I should write that down.

"Ignore him," Aeron says, ignorant of the fact that I'm doing just that as he studies his map with a frown. "He knows nothing of artistic pursuits." He holds up a hunk of Bjovian cheese and shoves the entire piece in his mouth so it bulges out his cheek.

"But you possess such knowledge?" I ask, baiting him. I'm going to need this information at some point; might as well let him think it's his idea to share his life story. He'll embellish either way, but it'll feel more organic if he volunteers it.

Aeron inclines his head, flaming-red hair tumbling over his shoulders. He tucks his map safely beside him, turning fully to face me. For once, he isn't wearing his armor, only a light tunic and breeches. He's left the strings untied, baring his smooth chest. I make note of the way the firelight dances over unblemished skin. Just in case it enhances his ballad.

"I hail from the noble house of Fowler," he proclaims.

I've heard that name before. They own half the Trevett countryside just beyond Lindale. What is he doing out here?

He must recognize my bewildered expression or have encountered it enough to know what I'm wondering. "I have to make a name for myself. I'm the youngest of five brothers with no interest in the family legacy. I don't care for the dragon's hoard, nor my own. But for my name to last the ages?" His blue eyes shine with such excitement, such fire. "Why, that would be worth everything I own. Down to the last copper."

In a world so vast, it's easy to get lost. To be swept away with the tide and blink out of existence as if you were never born. But to carve out one's place? To demand immortality? This, I get.

"Which is why he's using said wealth to pay us." Cadoc lifts his cup before taking a deep swill. "Even to follow a useless map to a fabled hoard no one can locate."

"Useless?" Aeron's voice hits a high-pitched shriek. "How can you call it useless?"

"You can't even read it." Still holding his cup, Cadoc points to the map in question with one finger. "Like you said, it doesn't make sense."

"I know the path takes us through Marshwood Forest." Aeron's cheeks turn scarlet, and he glares at the ground. "I only said the margin notes don't make sense."

"The notes are the directions."

Don't tell me we're following a faulty map. I'll have to title his ballad The Time Aeron Led Us in a Circle. Curiosity and an inability to accept this could be a waste of my time fuel my words. "Mind if I take a look?"

With a shrug, Aeron hands the old parchment to me, carefully avoiding my gaze. I unroll the map and send a silent prayer to the goddess not to find obvious signs of trickery. A hand-drawn depiction of Targgein stares up at me. Mountains and valleys all called by names I don't recall, but the layout is very much the same as the maps I've seen spread across tables and held down by mugs of ale when travelers came through Hollowden. I study every feature, detecting nothing amiss, apart from archaic names of known landmarks. My eyes snag the scrawled notes in the margin. Directions to find the dragon's lair. It's written in a combination of old Common Tongue, dwarven runes, and a language I've never encountered in Targgein: Ancient Elvish. Even in Smarighad, Ancient Elvish was a dead language. The language has changed, sifted through generations of hiding the written word, adopting some of the Common Tongue, and decaying morphology.

Not in my household, though. My da used to have me practice my alphabets before he'd let me play in the forest. I'd trace my letters in the dirt until he was happy with my progress. Ancient Elvish, Dwarvish, Common Tongue, even the forgotten human languages—I was required to master it all. And I loved knowing I gained access to even more stories this way.

But that seems like lifetimes ago.

"Everything appears to be in order." I hand the map back to Aeron, taken aback by his wide eyes.

"How can you say that? Some of the words are utter nonsense."

I snort, shoving down any hint of irritation at his ignorance. "No. Some of the directions are written in other dialects. Someone went through a great deal to make this map difficult to read. But it's all right there." It's been years, but I haven't forgotten how each letter appeared, carved into the earth.

"You can read this?" Aeron's hero smile is back, wiping away any lingering shame. "Truly?"

"Of course I can," I say with a laugh. "I'll translate it for you."

What would they have done if I couldn't translate their map?

Aeron leaps up with a hoot of joy, running around the fire to hug me. I endure his attentions for a moment before shrugging away. My gaze finds Jaromir's, and his thorough stare is difficult to read.

"I knew having a bard would be a brilliant addition to our group. Didn't I tell you? I knew it!" Aeron is now forcing his affections on each member of his crew, pressing a sloppy kiss to Cadoc's cheek before pulling Neith into an embrace she maintains at full arm's length. When he skips over to Jaromir, not even the force of his scowl can deter him. Aeron leans his head on his shoulder, sighing happily while Jaromir pats his back.

I'm still trying to sort out the dynamics here. There's a familial fondness and annoyance between these people, and I find it utterly fascinating.

"How did you all meet?" My question can't be helped, not when my hands itch for my quill to begin jotting notes, but I leave it where it rests on the ground beside me.

Cadoc answers first. "I got a tip there might be a job that served my interests. When I got to the Rutting Goose, all I found was the bottom of a few bottles. But I saved Aeron from getting killed when he waltzed in announcing he needed skilled fighters and he was willing to pay handsomely."

The Rutting Goose is the seediest tavern this side of the Jürden Sea. A place of black-market deals and unsavory ventures. Only two kinds of people survive a trip to that place. Those who are dangerous enough to be a threat and those who are invisible.

Aeron is neither.

"I suppose either luck or fate stepped in," I say with a laugh.

"Fate? Blimey, I don't know about that, but I will say he was lucky I was nursing a massive hangover that morning or I woulda been at the docks, prepping The Jaunty Loon for voyage." Cadoc grins at Aeron and gives him a light shove. "And you woulda been gutted and hung in the market square, emptied of your full and fancy purse."

"How else was I supposed to find the seasoned fighters I sought?" Even chagrined, Aeron manages to appear charming with only a slight flush high on his cheeks and the bridge of his nose.

"By parading your naivety and your brimming purse, clearly."

I laugh and hug my knees. "So, you saved him from an assured death?"

"Indeed. I pretended he was my drunk cousin and led him out of the tavern. He needed blades for hire. I get antsy staying in one place too long, and I'd already missed the ship's departure, so it was an easy decision to make." Cadoc offers a shrug as if agreeing to help slay a dragon, real or metaphorical, is a typical appointment.

Fascinating. Utterly fascinating. I turn to Neith who is drinking straight from a filmy, brown bottle. "What about you?"

She takes another gulp before wiping the back of her hand across her mouth. "Cadoc dragged me along. Said it was easy money and time on th'road." She tilts her head, so the light catches the scar slashing down her face. "I always enjoy an extended trip that pays for travel."

"How did you and Cadoc meet?"

"On a job a few years back. I got him out of a nasty scrape."

"That's a kind way of putting it," Cadoc says. "She saved me from the noose when our transport mission landed me in a dungeon."

Neith shrugs. "He'da done th'same for me. After that, I kept a correspondence at The Oak and Leaf Inn. Cadoc doesn't stay in any place for long, so it was the only way t'stay in contact if he found a job I might be interested in. Or in case he needed another jailbreak."

"And Aeron?"

"I knew Aeron afore all 'is." A strange look comes over her, but she smothers it with another deep pull from the bottle.

Aeron glances over at her, biting his lip like there's something he refuses to share. Strange, since the man seems keen to shout his business like a town crier.

Neith trusts Cadoc but doesn't trust me with the details of her and Aeron's meeting. No matter, I'll get them sooner or later. Or I'll make some up.

Jaromir still hasn't spoken, not that I'm surprised.

"And that leaves you." I turn to him, stunned to find he's watching me with razor sharp focus. But as soon as I catch his eye, he's turning away.

"What about me?" The rough scrape of his voice rings harsh against the quiet night.

"How did you land this job?"

"Heard about it."

"Articulate as always."

Jaromir blinks at me before glancing away to stare at the trees. It's a dismissal; I've faced enough of them to recognize it as such, but I'm not so easily dismissed.

"Let me guess"—I hold my hands out as if sensing the air—"you owe a substantial debt to your local gamemaster, and he threatened to turn you over to the guard."

Jaromir exhales an exasperated sigh, refusing to answer.

"No? Let me try again. You're trying to prove yourself to a lady far above your station, but so far, you've only been able to communicate with grunts and beating your chest, so you thought a big jewel-shaped gesture would bring you together!"

He scoffs his distaste at that particular guess.

Aeron laughs, loud and bright. It echoes in the night, rupturing the stillness and calm of the evening. "That would be quite the tale! As it is, I'd already hired him for a separate venture. He spotted one of the advertisements I placed on the noticeboard and found us the morning we embarked!"

Cadoc shakes his head. "I told you not to post those."

"Well, I was right in doing so! If I hadn't, Jaromir might

have left for Kalinia before he realized what a clever opportunity awaited him. Now we have a merry band of adventurers." Aeron gestures to me. "And a real bard to sing of our exploits! This is coming together better than I planned."

I smile as warmth spreads through my chest.

"Would anyone care for a song?" I'm already reaching for my lute, so it's happening whether they want it or not.

"Splendid!" Aeron claps his hands.

Neith shakes her head and settles back, amusement curling her mouth. Cadoc shifts to get comfortable.

I begin plucking a soft tune, one I haven't named but I play to keep my hands busy while my mind roams. A red fox scurries out from the underbrush, pausing to watch me. Neither the fire nor my companions deter him as he creeps closer. When he's close enough to touch, he rasps out a bark before scampering off into the woods.

I'll take that as a sign of good fortune.

I continue playing, letting the notes wash over me. Cicadas hum and peeper frogs call. I almost forgot how loud it is in the forest after dark. I keep plucking, harmonizing with the night. There's freedom in this, playing with no thought as to how many coins may or may not rattle around in my cup at night's end. I can give way to music without pressure—apart from the pressure to craft an epic ballad that is assured to launch me to fame. As excited as I am for this opportunity, a constant dull ache resides in my gut. When my thoughts drift to the Rusty Nail, to Kingsley and Brigitta, my throat gets tight.

My gaze travels over my temporary companions. Over Neith, who stares up at the pieces of sky between the trees. Cadoc, who even relaxed looks like his mouth could break into a smile at any moment. Aeron, who keeps his chin up in his "heroic expression" at nearly all times.

My stare wanders over Jaromir, who now lies on his back, hands tucked behind his head, eyes closed. His dark hair hangs out of his face for once, and I can appreciate the full scope of his profile. He really does have an elegant nose, both strong and straight, like it was carved from marble. His short black beard does nothing to hide the strong jaw beneath, and from here I can see his pulse jumping in his neck.

As if he can feel my gaze, he opens his dark eyes and turns. We stare at each other for half a stanza before he turns away and closes them off to the world again.

Chapter Five

S ince I stayed up far too late translating the map, morning comes faster than I would prefer.

The directions eluding Aeron's understanding detail a path through *Glas Fian*, now known as The Veridian Wilds. Through here, we're instructed to travel with the sun on our left shoulder until midday for three days. We'll need to venture away from the road, over the river, and to the base of the mountain pass. The valley on the map is called *Bealucwelm*. That isn't the name anymore, but I can't remember what the humans call it now. We'll travel through Bealucwelm, and rather than take the mountain pass, we climb the western peak to a cave where the dragon awaits.

I hope they realize what a credit to my profession I've proven to be.

I stretch my stiff joints, a soft whimper escaping my lips. I'm not used to riding, especially not for so long. Every muscle aches its reminder, and the thought of another day on that horse makes me want to cry.

I grab my vellum and quill.

The pain of a new road traveled pales in comparison to the pain of a life spent waiting in the wings.

There. That's better. I stretch again with newfound verve, reveling in the twinge in my hips and the pricking behind my eyes. Dragging myself out of my bedroll, I untie the flaps to my tent.

Jaromir douses the fire while the others ready their mounts.

I missed breakfast. Would have been nice to receive a wakeup call.

I crawl out into the bright light of a new day. The sun is high in the sky, midmorning if I were to guess. The notes of birdsongs trill through the air.

Cadoc and Neith have already packed their mounts and are watering the horses before we depart.

"Good morning!" Aeron is bright and cheery with his armor buckled into place and beaming like a beacon.

"Morning," I say back with a yawn. "I assume you already broke fast."

"Afraid so, but Jaromir said not to wake you."

Did he now?

I spin around to find the man in question has already emptied out my tent and is now breaking it down. My lute rests neatly against my pack, and my bedroll is already rolled up nice and tight.

I'm no fool, I can recognize a favor when I encounter it, but I don't want any favors from him. He'll likely use it against me, claiming I can't pull my own weight.

"I can pack my own items." I snatch my lute from the ground. It swings and nails me square in the shin.

Jaromir finally glances at me.

I will not reveal how much my leg hurts. No, I will not.

"You woke late. I wish to make up the time." He nudges

past me, pausing to grab my lute. His large hand claims the strap, brushing against mine. I disregard the way my nerves buzz from his touch and rip my hand away.

"Only because I spent half the night making your map legible, *and* you didn't wake me."

Jaromir ignores me and trudges past.

"Did you really?" Aeron bounds over to me, and I pass off the parchment complete with my translations and explanations. "I could kiss you!"

Jaromir scoffs, the sound impressively filled with derision for only a single syllable.

I ignore Aeron's praise for the moment. I'm too angry at the way Jaromir behaves. I storm after him, frustrated that he won't halt his movements to engage in a fight with me. "I'm assuming you didn't save me anything to eat."

"You have apples in your bag," he calls over his shoulder and continues toward the mounts as if I'm nothing more than another item to pack.

I reach into my sack, yank one of my apples out, and hurl it as hard as I can at his retreating form.

I don't know why I do this. Maybe I'm cranky from hunger, or maybe I'm sick of the way he acts like I'm a burden. Perhaps I just want to see the look on his face. But the apple sails through the air and lands square between his shoulders with a loud *thump*!

Jaromir stills, slowly turning to face me.

I'd be lying if I said it wasn't terrifying to receive a death glare from such a massive man. But I don't lie, I inform the truth. Instead of terror, I decide this is the rush of facing down my foe. I'm sizing up my opponent. My very large and angry opponent. I lift my chin and pull another apple from my bag.

His eyes blaze, and a preternatural stillness comes over him.

Since I'm decidedly not afraid, and we're apparently facing off in a pissing match, I stride right up to him and take a bite of my apple. Loudly and inches from his face. The juice from the fruit squirts onto his chin and neck. I'm sure there's a filthy joke about that somewhere in the back of my mind, but for now I'm content to revel in the flash of surprise on his face. His nostrils flare, and his dark brows draw together. His gaze dips to where I'm still chewing, and his mouth tightens.

I take another bite. "Sorry," I say around a mouthful of apple. "I meant to say, catch." I push past him, pleased with the exchange.

I've always been adept at making new friends.

WITH REST COMES CLARITY, and with clarity—inspiration. Too bad I can't write while we ride, not legibly, at least. But I marvel at life on the road. The sun streaking through trees and dancing along the dusty road, the trill of songbirds in the morning, the rhythmic clopping of our horses' hooves in a steady trot.

Aeron peppers me with questions, and the more I answer, the more Jaromir tenses up behind me. It's a game. Aeron asks me about my life, and I make sure to answer in the most verbose, long-winded manner I possibly can, and with each word, I seep beneath the skin of the man at my back. And here I thought I wouldn't be able to find entertainment.

"How long were you at that tavern—what was it called? The Broken Horseshoe?"

"The Rusty Nail," I say, laughing. "It'll be two years come winter. Originally, I hailed from Smarighad. But you know how it goes..."

Namely, the elven raids forced thousands of us from our homeland. I maintain my chipper demeanor and shove thoughts of childhood away. "I managed to stow away on one of the merchant vessels, and I spent the better part of five years living in Bridgebarrow before scraping together enough coin to travel from town to town in Mysture proper." Nothing I've said is a lie, but the unspoken truth coils in my chest. "I spent some time in Elmwood and Birchfield before I settled in Hollowden. For a temporary reprieve, of course. I needed to refill my artistic well before tackling a city like Lindale."

"I see. And what about those years traveling? You're no stranger to adventure, it would seem."

Adventure. That's one way to put it. Another is uncertainty, hunger, and pickpocketing. "Quite right. I made a name for myself in the local taverns. You're lucky you caught me when you did, otherwise I might have been moving on to bigger venues. Then where would your map have taken you?"

Jaromir sighs, his warm breath tickling the back of my neck. If he doesn't stop breathing so damn heavily, I'll put my cap back on. I don't care if it bothers him, it's gorgeous.

"I should say so! We'd be utterly lost without you. It was fate, our joining." Aeron grins at me, and my answering smile feels easy and unrehearsed.

Something tightens around my waist. I glance down to find Jaromir's arms have closed the gap above my hips, his hands clenching the reins.

I turn, taking in the hardened lines of his face. "Do you need to relieve yourself?"

Confusion steals his expression. It's a nice change from the surliness. "Huh?"

"Do you need to relieve yourself? You're tensing, and the leather is all twisted in your grasp." Memories of a particularly unpleasant night resurface. "It reminds me of the time I went berry picking. Kingsley told me the red ones were fine but to avoid the purple ones—but he didn't stipulate the magenta berries. Imagine my surprise when *those* were the ones to avoid. Well, it was too late. I'd already eaten several fistfuls, and I suffered some of the worst stomach cramps of my life, shedding my trousers for the night, otherwise I'd have soiled my smallclothes for sure. I made it a point to discuss the differing shades of colors with him. One man's purple is another man's—"

"No, I don't need to shit."

"Fine, fine." I wink at Aeron, who has been watching the entire exchange with a strange expression. He urges his horse to the front.

I lean my head to each side, stretching out my stiff neck. Next time we stop, I'll take some time to stretch out every kink in my poor body. I'd kill for one of Kingsley's shitty grogs. It burns going down but numbs by the time it hits the stomach. Once, I drank two cups, and it was as if I was floating.

"You're sore." Jaromir's deep voice scrapes out from behind me.

"Riding nonstop, preceded by never at all, will do that to a person."

I reach back to squeeze the ligaments connecting my neck to my shoulders. He transfers the reins to one hand, and with the other, he nudges my hand out of the way to massage my neck.

I freeze, unsure how to respond, until gradually the tension melts into relaxed pleasure pricking at my sore muscles.

His touch is warm and firm as he applies the perfect amount of pressure to the spot that aches. My eyes slip closed, and I don't even care that an embarrassing groan escapes my lips.

His voice ruins the magic of his hand. "This is the first time you've been quiet."

Prick. Utter prick.

He wishes for silence? I'm a bard, not a djinn. I clear my throat and prepare one of the bawdiest tunes I know.

"Way up in Lindale
there once was a lass
with cornsilk for hair
and a shapely ass
the menfolk adored her
she possessed great aplomb
for all of her bedfellows
got a thumb up their bums!"

Cadoc begins singing along, waving his arms in the air as if conducting an entire troupe. I'm not surprised he knows this song; it's rather popular. Neith tries to hide her smile, and Aeron laughs loud enough to drown out my voice.

Jaromir drops his hand, and I almost miss his touch. But not even temporary muscle relief is worth giving him the satisfaction.

The day is far too beautiful for his nonsense. Dappled sunlight dances along the path, verdant leaves forming a canopy above. Bright yellow flowers dot the grass, and I want nothing more than to snatch them from the earth to carry with me.

"Buttercups," I say. "I was told they tasted like butter. I'd collect them up, stuffing my cheeks as if it were the finest delicacy. I was convinced I just I hadn't found a 'ripe' one yet." I laugh at the memory of explaining to my da how Tanniv said I had to chew them up to release the flavor when I suffered a bout of painful stomach cramps after eating them. "Even if they don't taste like butter, they are pretty."

Jaromir says nothing, of course, because the man has a stick lodged so far up his arse, he's choking on it.

Aeron's horse rears up ahead. He's stopped in the middle

of the road. I crane my neck, trying to see beyond Cadoc and Neith.

Four riders trot up the path. They're dressed awfully light for travel, no saddlebags or supplies. But their swords catch my eye. One man, the one with his blond hair tied in a knot, even has two swords, their hilts jutting out over his shoulder. Weapons aren't what put me on edge. Everyone carries a sword or dagger or bow. Survival extends beyond fighting, and some need to hunt their own food. No, it's the look in his eye that gives me pause. The narrow glint of hunger I've seen on the face of many a man.

The hunger for a fight.

Instinctively, I shrink back into Jaromir's chest. His hold on the reins and around my body tightens.

"Good morning," the blond man says, a cold smile cutting across his mouth. He glances back at his companions, as if weighing their reactions.

Three men flank him, forming a tight-knit circle behind what I can only assume is their leader. Or at least, the man they want us to believe speaks for them. It's a well-rehearsed maneuver, all four of them fitting together as if they've done this a hundred times.

My mouth goes dry, and without thinking, I thread my fingers through Jaromir's. I know he'll shake me off, but I need something to hold on to.

He lets me squeeze his hand and makes no move to pull away.

"Where might you all be headed?" the blond man says, letting his gaze rove over each of us, assessing. When his stare snags on me, he pauses before shifting Jaromir in his sights. It's a subtle thing, an upward flick of his gaze over my shoulder, but the way his grin spreads across his face sends a chill down my spine.

I squeeze Jaromir's hand hard enough my own aches.

"We are embarking on a noble quest." Aeron's using his hero voice again, and he thumps his fist against his spotless chest plate. "A quest for—"

"—the finest drinks this side of Mysture." Cadoc cuts Aeron off, shooting him a look I can't see from back here, but I can guess is a warning to shut his mouth.

"Are you now?" The man is watching Jaromir again. I want to turn around and ascertain what he's doing to draw his attention, but I'm afraid it will signal something I don't intend. "Where you coming from?"

"Hollowden," I call out. Why I do such a thing, I can't say, but it's out, and once I start speaking... "A bit small for my taste. I'd much prefer to explore Lindale. I've heard they boast the finest taverns in the country. But really, any will do. I can appreciate the rustic feel of The Rusty Nail, but I heard their swill can burn a hole in your gut and the proprietor once killed a man using nothing but a spoon."

I might not have heard that rumor so much as started it, but the way the man winces tells me my tale has made the rounds. I have a tendency to talk when new customers and travelers visit, and what better way to pass the time than to share all my theories about Kingsley. He's killed a man with his bare hands, I just know it.

Jaromir shifts behind me, one hand still clasping mine as the other reaches for the hilt at his hip.

"I heard about that tavern owner. Said to be seven feet tall and strong enough to lift a horse."

Oh, I forgot about that rumor. I tighten my lips to keep from smiling.

"Seven feet? At least that." I pretend to shiver. The image of Kingsley—massive, but I wouldn't say seven feet—and his tiny Brigitta dancing around the tavern last Winter Solstice, fills my mind. She had wrapped her arms around his neck as he spun her, her feet dangling and never reaching the floor.

"You seem to speak quite easily from the back of your group. Why don't you come closer and tell me more of your travels?"

Ice runs through my veins.

Jaromir tightens his arm around me. "We're done talking."

I don't know if he's speaking to me or the man, but I clamp my mouth shut.

The man arches his brow, rubbing his jaw. "I thought we were having a pleasant conversation. There's no need for any misunderstandings."

"I understand just fine." Jaromir grips the hilt of his sword now. My heart punches against my ribs so hard I can feel it in my throat. There's an energy to his stillness, it vibrates through me. As if at any moment he's about to spring into action.

After a moment, or an eternity, the man chuckles and nods. Waving his friends to follow, he slowly rides down the middle of the road, through our group. When he comes to Jaromir and me, he pauses.

"Enjoy the day." His mouth wears a smile but his eyes remain hard. He kicks off, and it isn't until he and the others disappear that I finally release my hold on Jaromir's hand. His skin bears the bite of my nails, and my palm is sweaty.

Jaromir wordlessly urges his horse into a canter, and we plod down the road. Aeron and the others follow suit, seamlessly shifting back into our typical riding formation—Aeron at the helm, Cadoc and Neith claiming the middle, and us taking up the rear. No one seems to want to break the silence, and we push forward, putting that bend in the road and those strange riders behind us. The tension in Jaromir's arms grows tighter with each passing moment, caging me in and closing around me as his horse kicks up a cloud of dirt beneath its hooves.

Whether Jaromir's issue is the threat of danger, or the dissatisfaction of a fight avoided, he hasn't let up his grip on the reins. I don't know how much time passes, but by now the sun has sunk in the sky and trickles through the lower branches of the forest.

Aeron glances over his shoulder, his mouth quirking to the side as if debating his next words. Finally, he speaks: "They seemed like decent enough folk."

Perhaps he should have taken longer to deliberate.

"Fuck," Jaromir says. He halts our horse and slides down, nearly toppling me. "Truly, Aeron?" He runs his hands over his face.

"We don't know what they wanted, not really," Cadoc offers. He turns to Aeron. "Though I'll advise you again to stop telling everyone we meet what we're doing."

"How else will we make history if no one knows of us?" Aeron asks with a shrug, as if we hadn't just encountered that tense standoff.

I slide off the horse, wobbling when I hit the ground. "That's what I'm here for! Allow me to decide when and where we spout our stories. I know what I'm doing."

"You?" Jaromir turns on me and advances. Everything in his gait is agitated, aggressive. I back away, stumbling over the dip in the road. "You are the last thing we need. You shouldn't even be here."

Bastard. I've proven my worth ten times over, and still he treats me like a burden. He doesn't even deserve the energy it would take to argue. I'll simply ignore him, so he knows how insignificant he is. "Everything was fine until you started your little glaring contest with the man." Well, I almost ignored him.

"My—" His words stall, and his face turns red as a beet. "I'm the reason you're still standing and not face down in the dirt."

"That's balderdash, and you know it!" I prod him in the chest hard enough my finger aches. He catches my hand before I can do it again, drawing me in close. His eyes never leave mine, and my stomach flips.

"You're a liability." He drops my hand.

The tips of my ears burn.

"You're a hotheaded prig and most likely to die by the sword, if I don't strangle you first."

He blinks at me, his jaw clenching against whatever insult he's holding back. It only now occurs to me how closely we're standing. Warmth radiates from his body. Waves of tension roll off him as if every muscle in his body is pulled taut.

I can't tell if I feel hot or cold. Cold, I think. It's a tingle through my legs and a sinking in my stomach. Yet caught in the force of his dark stare, my cheeks burn.

"Jaromir, walk it off," Neith calls from her mount, rupturing the silence of our staring contest.

He glares at her, and suddenly I'm free from whatever spell we were caught in. I turn my attention to Neith, a much safer sight. Jaromir is a bulwark of anger, but she doesn't even flinch under his hard gaze.

Finally, Neith rolls her eyes. "If ye wish t'behave like a child, so be it. Syl can ride wi' me."

It takes a moment for my legs to move. Warmth thaws out my previously frozen posture—the warmth of gratitude for Neith in the moment. I reach a hand up to her, and in my periphery, Jaromir stands in the middle of the road, watching me with an unreadable expression. The strap of my lute cuts diagonally across his chest, and for some reason, the sight of it is enough to make me hesitate.

His mouth doesn't move, and yet I can sense he's holding something back. Probably another insult.

I grasp Neith's arm, and she swings me into the saddle behind her.

Problem solved.

As we ride, I glance over my shoulder. Just once. Jaromir

sits atop his mount, indecision stealing his composure. His dark eyes meet mine, and for a second, I think I might see regret. But that would be ridiculous.

I turn my eyes and thoughts to the horizon. To what lies ahead.

Chapter Six

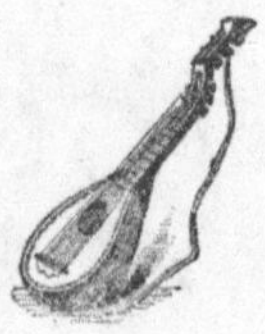

When morning comes, I'm ready for it. Rising before the sun, I sit by lantern light—surely a fire hazard within these tent walls—and scribble away. I long to see all the world has to offer. To sing on every stage in front of hundreds of people. To bear witness as the sun hits the highest peak of The Hoarfrost Mountains or lie beneath the glittering stars over the flatlands. But sometimes, all I want is the familiar scratch of my quill against parchment. Here, the world fades and words spring to the surface. Words have always been easy. They're both the bridge and the great divide. Words bring me into stories—into worlds I might never have known. They give me strength—a shield against what lies out there. Behind words, I can disappear until all that remains is a faint whisper. A flicker of a story spoken in hushed tones.

Words can be a boisterous tune or a quiet confession.

In the darkness of my tent, my words come to life.

The adventurers faced down a nameless threat. For greed knows no limits. Greed of wealth, of power, and even greed of suffering. It can lurk in any shadow of any man's heart. The watchful demon waiting to pounce. But Aeron's crew was unafraid, for any danger they encountered, they would fight together.

I stare at the page until the words blur before my tired eyes. It sounds better than, *We came across some strange folk. Possible veiled threats were launched. Jaromir yelled and hasn't spoken to me since.*

I sigh and lower my quill. The first rays of dawn bleed through the gaps in my tent, and it's time to greet the day.

I won't miss breakfast again.

Shoving my vellum and quill into my satchel, my knuckles brush against something soft. I feel around until my fingers close around my target.

It's a small, crumpled yellow flower. A buttercup.

How in the bleeding shades did this end up in my bag? Perhaps it's another sign of good fortune. I spin the flower between my fingers, and tuck it behind my ear. It will likely fall out, but it seems as good a place as any to keep it.

Pulling my tent flaps back, I find Jaromir already seated in the middle of our camp, a fire burning in the center stones. His broad back faces me, and I take a moment to admire the way the orange light frames his form.

He turns. "You were up early."

Of course, he heard me. The man has the ears of a wolf.

I disentangle myself from my tent and straighten my filthy tunic. What once was stark white has faded to a beige-brown, covered in dust and grime. I desperately need a bath. Kingsley's soaps are calling to me. With as much dignity as I can muster, I saunter to my place across from him.

I feel his gaze on me, and it burns like a brand. But I don't meet his stare until I'm sitting. He's examining the flower tucked behind my ear, his jaw tightening. The full force of his dark eyes makes something flip in my stomach.

I clear my throat. "Yes, well. You made it abundantly clear yesterday that I held up travel."

His brows draw together as if in confusion, and he gives a little shake of his head. He seems to start several sentences judging by the way his mouth opens and closes, but no words break through.

"What's for breakfast?"

He reaches for the sack at his side and tosses it to me. Though the canvas is pulled taut as if full, its contents are light. I reach in and pull out a loaf of bread. It's been baked in the Bjovian style, its crust is a glossy sheen from the honey and butter that was painted on before it baked.

Kingsley makes this for special occasions, and my stomach gives a pang at the thought. Or at the hunger gripping me.

I glance in the bag. There are several more just like it.

"We had these all along?"

Jaromir pokes the fire with a stick and nods.

"And why am I just finding out about it now?"

He runs a hand through his dark hair, pushing it out of his face. For the first time, I notice the small circles of onyx in his earlobes. He doesn't seem the type to wear any sort of adornment, and I've never seen such simple pieces as these, but they're oddly becoming on him. Again, my stomach leaps. I must be starving. "Do you want the bread or not?"

Rolling my eyes, I take a large bite. The taste is just as I remembered, and I nearly moan. "So," I say around a mouthful of the best damn bread I've ever eaten, "how many days 'til we reach the next town?"

"Three days at the pace we're going." He watches me with an unreadable expression, so I take another bite large enough I can't close my mouth to chew. His brow puckers. "Two if we can move at the pace I'd prefer."

"Sounds like you've got it all mapped out." My words are garbled by the massive bite I've taken.

His mouth twitches. "Not really but I thought I could make it up as I go and pretend it was all intentional."

I cough as a bit of bread gets lodged in my throat. Pounding on my chest, I ask, "Did you just make a joke?"

Jaromir shrugs, and this time it's more than a twitch curving against his mouth.

It's an actual smile.

It's small, and a little lopsided. His face must be a bit rusty. I'll endeavor to earn a few more of those.

"Welkin above," I say, placing a hand on my chest, "you've scandalized me. Now, if you pissed on the fire to put it out, or got so drunk you danced the Hawthokian jig naked, I wouldn't bat an eye, but an actual joke?"

He sighs, and on its edge, I detect a growl. "You always fill the air with chatter."

I laugh. "Of course I do. And you fill the air with contempt. I'm merely bringing balance to nature. Two sides of the same coin, we are. Perhaps you and I were meant to share the same fires all along."

He eyes me with an expression I can't put my finger on. "Perhaps."

THE DAY SETTLES into a haze of riding, endless trees, and scorching sun. The air seems to tremble with the heat. Sweat rolls down my back, and I bundle my hair into a knot. Neith doesn't sigh or growl or make any sound to draw my attention. She's a quiet rider, unless Cadoc drums up a conversation, which she's more than willing to carry with him.

I didn't ask to ride with Jaromir, and he didn't offer.

I glance over my shoulder. His gaze darts away, too quickly for me to know for sure if he was looking at me.

Aeron is wilting upon his horse. That armor must be boiling. He's been reminded numerous times to take it off, lest this summer heat cooks him from the inside out. But he's remained steadfast in his decision.

"When they tell this tale, they shall marvel at my strength of will and fiber. Not even the elements could sway me."

Even though I am quick to remind him that I can say whatever I want, he has a determined commitment to realism.

I respect that.

The buzzing hum of the cicadas is near constant, and somehow the sound makes the air even hotter. I mop my brow with a spare kerchief. Dusk can't come soon enough.

"Once, I wished to be a juggler." Aeron's voice is weak, faded.

What a random thought. I love random thoughts. "You what?"

He flashes me his hero smile—the one that's all teeth and dimples. If he didn't have that glazed look in his eye and the threat of heatstroke reddening his cheeks, I might have felt its effects. "Once upon a time, I wanted to be a juggler. I practiced for days. I even purchased my own set of balls—"

Cadoc's laughter cuts through Aeron's story. He shoots him an exasperated look and continues. "I wanted the eyes of a crowd. To be that which they marvel at. An image they carried with them long after they'd gone."

"You wished to accomplish all this through juggling?"

He shrugs, and the metallic clang of his suit is a reminder of how far he's willing to go for glory. "When I've returned to the earth, I want something of me to remain. I suppose that's why some people have children. But even the bond between parent and child is precarious at best. I wanted to find a way to connect with strangers. One is less likely to face rejection amongst strangers than with one's own family."

I don't know about that. But there must be personal truth to such a statement. While he is overheated, that much is clear, there's an honest clarity to his words. I blink the stinging sweat from my eyes. "Again, through juggling?"

He laughs. "I'm afraid I'm not a very talented performer. I can't carry a tune, I gag at the idea of swallowing swords, and learning an instrument seemed too difficult." His expression turns sheepish. "Turns out juggling was too difficult for me as well."

Is that all it was? Is the life of a performer, an artist, simply a scream into the void? The fear of being forgotten made flesh.

No. It's more than that.

I recall the day I knew my life's purpose. I'd stowed away on The Maiden's Revenge and been in Bridgebarrow for three days. My stomach was raw with hunger, a sharp ache that cut deep. I stumbled into the market square, and the most beautiful sound carried over the rumble of the crowd. Perched atop a stack of crates, sat a woman with deep umber skin. Golden hoops ran the length of her ear peeking out from beneath her velvet hat of cornflower blue. A large violet feather swooped out from her cap. The rest of her ensemble complimented the color, but I remember that giant feather swaying with every strum of her lute.

Though the city guards sneered at her and made a few remarks I didn't understand, she ignored them and even earned a few coins from passersby. Her voice was thick and soulful, and the words she sang were in a language I didn't know. But I felt her melancholy. I felt the weight of sorrow and loss. When she plucked the last note, a wide grin spread across her face. She leapt up onto the crates and began strumming a jaunty tune. How she was able to slip into a completely different persona, a different feeling—it was like shedding a cloak.

It was simple and magical.

I knew that was for me.

I did what I had to do to survive. The rusty knife I slept

with became my means to opening pockets and collecting enough coin to eat. Most days. And with my time, I watched. I watched her play, how she angled her fingers, the pattern of strumming, and committed it all to memory. When she stopped appearing in the market, I assumed she moved on to a new town.

I shove memories of the unnamed bard from my mind and flash Aeron an eager smile. "If you still wish to learn to juggle, I could teach you."

Aeron's smile grows so wide, his nose and freckles crinkle. Utterly adorable. "Really? I admit, I'm rather hopeless at it."

"I'll keep my hopes safely diminished to avoid disappointment."

He laughs, loud and bright. Everything about the man is bright. Like the sun fighting its way through a keyhole.

I should write that line down. I twist, searching for something I might be able to reach in the saddlebags, when I feel it. It's a prickle of a thing. I lift my gaze to find Jaromir staring at me. This time, he doesn't look away. His dark eyes, intense and thorough, are fixed on me. Something hardens in his stare, and a crease appears between his brows.

"Something troubling you, Jaromir?" I can't help it. He's just staring, and it's making my skin flush. Worse than it already is.

Before he can respond with what I'm sure would be a symphonic series of grunts, a thrumming noise vibrates through the trees.

Jaromir tilts his head, listening. It almost sounds like the cicadas, but louder and... *angrier*.

There is a rustling in the trees, and it grows more frantic. The buzzing is overwhelming now, and even my teeth are vibrating. Something breaks through the trees, branches snapping and leaves shuddering.

Now the buzzing is all-consuming. I can feel it against my skin and in the over-firing of every nerve.

Of course I've heard the tales of forest beasts. Oversized creatures one only uncovers when deep in the woods where man has yet to settle with any permanence. I've even told a few of those stories.

This is different.

This is real.

A swarm of giant beetles—the size of wild hounds—surrounds us. The sun glints off their shiny black shells and the noise they make shakes my ear canals. A shiver runs down my back, and my throat burns. It's a high-pitched drone, and it's settling over me like a thousand pricking needles.

Neith yanks me to the ground and shoves me behind a hollow log. She stands, positioning herself in front of me, and draws a sword and dagger from her back and hip. She cuts and slices with expert finesse, never appearing winded as she wields her longsword. It reminds me of how Kingsley would chop wood, namely whenever Brigitta was watching. He'd cut the axe through the air swiftly enough to create his own wind. The force of Neith's strikes blows the hair back from my face as she cuts down a beetle flying dangerously close.

The others are fighting, swords flashing in the midday sun. Cadoc wields dual daggers. His reach is limited, but his speed is incredible. His weapons spin, slashing and slicing, but with the grace of a choreographed dance. Like the gamemaster switching and rearranging the cups to hide the ball from view. Once he's dispatched the beetles surrounding him, he yanks his bow from his back. His hand flies to his hip quiver, fast as lightning, and he turns to face us. A nock of an arrow, a pull, and *whoosh*. It sinks with a loud *thwack*, a giant beetle landing hard and heavy beside me.

The beetle's mandibles open and shut a few times, pincers clicking, and I'm sure that honeyed loaf is going to make another appearance. I cover my mouth, eyes watering against the gagging of my throat.

Jaromir holds his sword steady, turning and twisting steel with the ferocity of a warrior. His face is tightened, a pucker of concentration between his brows, but in his eyes there's a glint of... amusement? Pleasure? As if he was honed for this. He's still wearing my lute strung across his back, and though for a moment I fear it might get damaged, I quickly squash that thought. He'd stripped his leather jerkin, so beneath his thin tunic, his hard muscles ripple with each pass of his blade. He cuts and conquers with an exquisite grace.

Now this, I could write a ballad about.

"Have at you!" Aeron calls out, dueling against a trio of giant beetles. His footwork is tentative, and his sword is too heavy. It trembles, casting a shaky beam of light on the ground.

Neith follows my line of sight and groans. "Stay down."

Her command rings in my ears as she leaps over the log to assist Aeron. I peek out from my hiding space, excuse me, my surveillance spot, and I spy Jaromir once more. His dark hair is matted with sweat as he bares his teeth against the onslaught. A beetle creeps up behind him, pincers snapping. He's too busy with the four he's facing to turn and cut it down.

I feel around, hands shaking until I find a rock the size of my fist. Leaning up, I throw it with every ounce of strength I have. It lands with a sickening squelch, black blood spurting out of the beetle's body. It doesn't fall, but it lets out a blood-curdling screech which is enough to get Jaromir's attention. He turns and slams his sword down, bisecting the creature. It falls in a pile of mangled bits.

A sharp cry rings through the trees. I turn to find Neith gripping her shoulder, biting down on her lip. Red blood spills between her fingers. Jaromir surges forward, lopping the last beetle in half.

Silence fills the packed dirt road, nothing but the sound of a slight breeze whistles through the trees. Insectoid carcasses litter the path, and we're all coated in varying amounts of black blood.

Except Neith, who grimaces at the wound in her shoulder.

Cadoc is already at her side, pulling out supplies and bandages. "We'll get this cleaned up in no time," he says.

She nods and keeps her stare fixed on him while he works.

It's much too quiet, much too bright in the forest now. I can still feel vibrations in my teeth.

A shadow dots out the light, looming over me. I glance up to find Jaromir, his face a mask of concern. He crouches and examines me. Running a hand along my jaw and chin. "Are you hurt?" His voice is both harsh and soft, somehow.

"No." For once the words don't tumble out of my mouth. The place where my words usually lie in wait, ready to spring forth without my permission, is hollow. Despite the heat, my limbs feel cold and tingly. I touch Jaromir's face, if only to see if he flinches.

He doesn't. He holds my stare, and I want to look away, but I can't. "Are you hurt?"

"No." Jaromir gently takes my hand from his face before pulling me to stand.

"Neith, are you all right?" Aeron's voice rings out, far too loud in the heavy silence. He extends his hand as if reaching out to touch her.

"Your incompetence could have gotten her killed." Cadoc shakes his head, a muscle feathering in his jaw as he wraps Neith's shoulder.

Aeron's mouth falls open, a sputtering noise escaping. "Me?"

"You can barely hold that bloody sword, and you're wearing heavy plate armor in the middle of summer. She wouldn't have had to cover you if you cared less about playing hero and more about being smart."

Aeron's face falls, and his gaze upon Neith turns desperate. "Neith... I would never—"

"Dinnae fash," she grinds out between gritted teeth, refusing to meet his stare as Cadoc finishes dressing her wound. "It's just a scratch."

"It's a blooming miracle you haven't been killed for your witlessness," Cadoc says, glaring at Aeron.

Several heartbeats of awkward silence fill the air. Aeron's cheeks are bright red, and his eyes are glassy. Finally, he speaks. "The risks were made clear. This is the job you signed up for." He marches up to Cadoc, his armor clanking with every step. "No one is forcing you to follow me. You're being paid handsomely, and if the coin isn't enough to command your respect..." He lets his voice trail off and spreads his arms wide.

A line drawn in the sand.

Cadoc clenches his jaw and firms his lips, fighting against whatever unsaid words dance on his tongue.

Jaromir tugs me gently toward his horse. "Neith, ride with Cadoc. I can tether your horse to mine." He lifts me up as if I weigh nothing, and I scramble to grab ahold of the reins. "We can travel far enough from the nest to camp safely but call it an early night. Neith needs to preserve her strength." He gives her a nod, and she answers with one before allowing Cadoc to help her to his horse.

They are behaving rather strangely. Sure, it's a deep gouge of the flesh, but Neith looks like she can handle herself. Why are they treating it like a mortal wound?

Jaromir settles in behind me, and my heart kicks into double-time.

Aeron frowns and opens his mouth as if to speak.

"Do you take issue with this?" Jaromir beats him to it. He's far more observant and diplomatic than he seems.

Aeron sighs and nods, mounting his horse without another

word. His shoulders carve in on themselves, and he keeps sneaking glances at Neith.

"She can't ride with her shoulder injured?" I can't help but ask, but I keep my voice low enough for Jaromir's ears only.

"It isn't the wound but the venom."

Venom? "Oh."

"She'll be fine," he says quickly. "But she'll face a night of fever dreams and disorientation. Depending on how much she was struck with. I didn't want to risk her falling from her horse."

Giant beetles. Venom. Fever dreams. These are the types of things I'd kill to write about with enough detail to enrapture an audience. But stories are so much safer when they live in your head. Out in the world, it's too real. It's been ages since the reality of the world was impossible to ignore. I've lived quite comfortably in the safety of my own stories for far too long.

We make camp while the sun is still high. Neith disappears into her tent as soon as it's set up, and Cadoc follows closely behind. Aeron casts a longing glance at their departure, his stare lingering long after the tent flaps flutter closed.

At dusk, it's only Jaromir, Aeron, and me who sit around the fire. Cadoc appears long enough to retrieve food for him and Neith before once again disappearing behind the flaps of her tent. Embers float high in the sky as the three of us sit in silence.

I don't reach for my lute. I let the quiet wash over me. Fill me and rattle me. Until finally I can't stand keeping my eyes open any longer.

Chapter Seven

"All right, company, listen up!" Aeron saunters into camp, holding a dark leather-bound book high above his head. He's forgone the armor, thank the goddess, but his approach is just as conspicuous as he stomps over twigs and leaves. Everything about him is loud and draws one's attention, even if they don't wish it.

I break off another small piece of bread and shove it in my mouth. The crumb has taken on a chewy texture. We're almost out anyway, but we've finally hit the more populated roads where traders frequent. If someone is willing to barter food, it would be a blessing. But if not, the town of Astervale isn't far off—our first major stop along the way where we can resupply —and I can begin my work spreading news of Aeron's quest.

I glance around the camp. Everyone is dutifully ignoring him. Perhaps his presence slowly fades to the background the way the audience fades when I'm lost in a song.

Jaromir sharpens his sword, and for once, his face is smoothed of his perpetual scowl. He runs the whetstone over steel, the sharp ring almost musical.

Neith's complexion has a greenish hue as she sips from her

mug. We agreed the last of our water should go to her. She shivers beneath a blanket despite the heat. Cadoc studies her with his ever-vigilant gaze, always assessing, and never far from her side. But she's clear eyed and far better this morning than she was last night.

Whatever she saw during her venom-induced hallucination judging by the screams and soft murmuring that drifted from her tent, it wasn't pleasant.

I hope if I'm ever struck by visions, they're at least enjoyable. Like swimming in a sea of coins while an adoring audience cries out for an encore. Or a bakery all to myself, stuffed with the finest cakes and breads. Maybe with a handsome, muscular man feeding me. An unwelcome image of Jaromir, wind blowing through his dark hair as he leans over suggestively, caressing a perfectly baked loaf of honey bread fills my mind. I snort and shove it away.

I'd much prefer a man who smiles and doesn't treat conversation like a poisonous snake to be avoided.

As if he can sense my thoughts, Jaromir looks up from his blade. His face is relaxed, almost curious, and a flutter of warmth fills my chest. I smooth a hand down my emerald-green tabard, the one with the embroidered sunflowers Brigitta added for me.

"This guidebook here," Aeron calls out, and good goddess, is the man still speaking, "will prevent us from ever getting caught unawares again!" Though he's addressing all of us, his stare remains fixed on Neith, a muscle feathering in his jaw.

Jaromir sets his blade down. "We don't need a book. We need to move quickly to the next town. And next time, we factor in the elements."

"Never mind that. This survival guide has taught me more than I could ever learn in one lifespan."

"That sounds more like a personal failing than the strength of one book." I bite my lip, but the words have already flown from my mouth. When did I turn on Aeron, my ally and likely the only one truly excited to have me along for the trip? I glance over at Neith, a fine sheen of sweat dots her brow. Oh, yes. Now I remember.

Jaromir laughs. *Laughs!* Well, it's more of a short exhale, but it bears amusement rather than exasperation. I will make the man laugh one day so I might hear what it sounds like.

Aeron rolls his eyes. "Yes, very funny. But listen to this. 'Humans are interlopers in the wilds. To traverse unnoticed, one must blend in with their surroundings.' Don't you see? We must conceal our human nature so as not to disturb the delicate balance of the forest."

"How exactly are we to achieve this?" Cadoc's question rings detached with feigned curiosity as he rummages through his pack.

"Ah, there is a clever method of utilizing nature's abundance and merging with the masquerade it offers."

It takes a full minute for me to register that my mouth is hanging open. "You mean," I begin, trying my best not to laugh, "you want us to cover ourselves with leaves and branches to walk through the woods?" I glance over at Jaromir to assess his reaction.

His mouth twitches, and he resumes sharpening his sword.

"You make it sound silly. This is scientifically proven to work."

"I'm not playing nymphy dress-up with you," Cadoc says. His tone is softer than the day before, but a hint of an edge remains. Especially when he says, "No matter how much you're paying me."

Aeron's face flushes, red creeping all the way up to his hairline. "Yes, well. Things were said in anger... I'm not proud of how I behaved. Nor how Neith bore the brunt of my mistake."

His words just hang there. And for a moment, it seems Cadoc will reject his apology. But he sighs and nods.

"Neith"—Aeron runs a hand over his mouth, two lines forming between his brows—"you know I'd rather die than let anything happen to you."

That's a rather bold proclamation if I've ever heard one.

Neith tugs the blanket tighter, shrugging. Never so much as lifting her gaze from the ground. "Nae harm done."

Aeron's throat bobs, his eyes boring holes into the top of her head. He blinks and flips to the middle of his book, peering down at it with concentration creasing his brow. "I need to find a good mud hole."

"A what?"

But he's already off in search of 'a good mud hole.' Whatever that means...

THE SICKLY PALLOR and greenish hue has finally fled Neith's face. A healthy flush creeps in, and when her laugh rings through our packed up camp, I know she's feeling better.

Now is as good a time as any to thank her for protecting me. I leave Jaromir to finish loading the saddlebags and approach her. She meets my eye before she busies herself with checking the straps of her bags.

"You look well," I say, and she nods without a word. It strikes me, she probably doesn't show weakness very often, and for me, practically a stranger, to bear witness must discomfit her. "Thank you," I add quickly. "I was useless yesterday and were it not for you..." I let my words trail off without their destination. She knows full well without me saying it.

Neith nods. "I'd do it for any o' us."

Us. Boy, do I like the sound of that.

She turns back to her horse, done with the conversation. But I'm not quite finished.

"Can you teach me to fight?"

My stars, did those words spring forth from my lips? Judging by the way she lifts her brows in surprise, they must have. Do I even want to fight? Not really, but I don't wish to die any more than I wish to fight, so I suppose one must win out over the other. Plus, it's too late to snatch the question from the air.

"Only if you want to, and it isn't a terrible inconvenience. I don't think I could manage a sword. Or a bow. I knew a boy who used to hunt squirrels; horrible pastime if you ask me, but he used a slingshot. Surprisingly, a deadly weapon, against squirrels at least. I did stun one of those beetles with a rock so maybe there's something to it—"

Neith holds up a hand, effectively stalling my rant. "I'll teach ye. Everyone should have th'basic knowledge t'defend themselves."

"Thank you! I promise to be a good pupil!"

She laughs. "I dinnae doubt it. Let's wait until we stop in Astervale. I'll pick up a few things for yer lessons."

Lessons. How fun!

"What are you doing?" Cadoc's laugh erupts through the camp, and my hackles raise. If he wishes to ridicule me for wanting to learn—

—but he isn't looking at me. He's looking at some strange man, covered from head to toe with mud.

"I'm concealing my human nature!" Aeron's jovial voice rings out, and I groan. The man has literally rubbed mud over every inch of his body, even slicking it through his hair.

"The book said to do this? Where did you get it from again?" I can't tell what Aeron's expression is since it's hidden beneath five layers of mud.

"I purchased it from a trader back in Vizia. He swore his stock came from scholarly articles; all peer reviewed."

Jaromir shakes his head. "Sounds like a charlatan."

Aeron lets out a frustrated whine. "He was not. Now, if you'll excuse me. I'm going to prove to you just how effective my concealment is." He stomps off, muddy boots squelching with every step. "Don't come crying to me the next time we disturb a nest. I'll be invisible."

I can't halt the laugh that rips from my throat. Well, 'can't' is the wrong word. I don't even bother trying. "Should I include this part in your ballad?"

Aeron ignores me but pauses, bending to examine a gnarled branch with smaller branches jutting off it in curls. "This is perfect!" He's off again, striding for the road.

I'm still smiling when we climb onto our mounts. Without asking, I'm already waiting by Jaromir's horse, allowing him to lift me into the saddle. He offers no objections, only settles in behind me, like we've done this a thousand times. I'm sure the way my body vibrates with excitement has everything to do with my amusement over Aeron's *survival tactics,* and nothing to do with the way Jaromir's muscled thighs feel against my backside.

Maybe it's a little of both. The man might be an utter bore most of the time, but I can appreciate a well-honed physique as much as the next person.

I'm half-convinced I'll end the day with a sore jaw if I can't wipe this silly grin off my face, but I don't even care.

"Can you help me? These keep slipping." Aeron holds the branches to his head like a pair of antlers.

"Absolutely not." Cadoc is the most affronted by Aeron's *creative* interpretation of the survival text. I can't imagine it actually states to tie branches upon one's head in the shape of antlers, but, here we are.

Aeron tugs a leather wrap from his pack and winds it around his skull, flattening his previously red hair to his face. Now he's just a wall of mud with sticks.

Our hero immerses himself in the wild freedom of the forest, casting off human trappings of civilization in favor of blending in with his surroundings.

I suppose I could write that. But really, the man who rolls around in shit and mud and ties branches to his head is far more compelling, if for the wrong reasons. My laughter echoes in the quiet forest.

Jaromir has been silent this entire trek which is strange even for him. I've come to expect his gusty sighs and low growls.

"You're awfully quiet. Quieter than usual, that is." Why can't I let anything go? If the man wanted to talk, he'd talk.

"If you wanted stimulating conversation, you chose the wrong person to ride with."

Do not make a joke about the word *stimulating*.

"I never asked for philosophical debate, but we might chat here and there to pass the time."

Jaromir hums, and the sound vibrates against my back. "You'll say what you will regardless of what I think, so what's stopping you?"

Nothing, really, but I can recognize an evasion when I hear one. "Tell me about Astervale."

When he shrugs, his arms graze my elbows. "Nothing to tell. Decent enough city. A few establishments offer rooms, so we'll likely find a place to sleep. There are shops, a smithy for repairs." He adjusts in the saddle, and I'm hyper aware of the way his thighs burn against mine. "They've laid stones for the roads, so it's a smooth ride."

"Roads! See, and you thought you couldn't hold your own

with idle chit-chat. Telling me about the roads, well done. You almost sound like a normal person!"

Jaromir makes a noise halfway between a groan and a laugh. My stomach flutters at the sound. Perhaps earning more than a scowl and a grunt from Jaromir is a learned task, and I'm a quick study. It's utterly ridiculous how light that makes me feel, so I turn my attention to Aeron.

He has left his horse with our group and is scouting ahead, moving with exaggerated care as if his footfalls will alert every predator in the forest. He looks utterly ridiculous, yet somehow still adorable. One of his branches, excuse me, his antlers, is drooping.

"Aeron," Cadoc calls out, "if a doe is feelin' frisky, don't break character. Do what you gotta do!"

Aeron ignores him and continues creeping up ahead, carving around the bend of the path until he's out of sight.

"Should we worry about him?" Neith asks, turning to Cadoc.

"Nah, he won't go far so long as he stays on the road."

But will he stay on the road? Aeron seems to have an abundance to prove and a meager supply of wits to achieve that end. If they aren't worried, I won't worry either. Although should anything happen to him... what does that mean for me? I can't imagine the others would want to keep me along. Would they even escort me home, or just leave me at the nearest town? I'd no longer be their problem, and they would have no obligation to me.

"It's eerie for you to be silent," Jaromir rumbles behind me.

I force a lightness to my voice I don't actually feel. "I was just calculating the odds of Aeron surviving this journey."

"We'll keep him alive. If for no other reason than to collect the second half of our payment."

When all else fails, I can place trust in coin.

Despite Aeron's foolishness, he has admirably bright determination. Optimism and careless abandon. Too often, the world hardens what once was soft. A river erodes stone until it is smoother than glass, but people are not carved into smoothness. They push back against the river, and their once soft surface becomes rough as if they could cut the water's edge as it washes over them.

I, too, am determined to go down in history as a great storyteller, but I'm realistic enough to know it's the story that lives on, not the teller. If the story I tell can last the ages, that's enough. I don't need my name to withstand history. Names and faces fade. They shift and reform to match whomever the hero needs to be. But a story passed down? This is the legacy I can leave behind and it's more than someone like me can hope for.

A cry rings out from up ahead, and Jaromir freezes behind me. It's the sound of agony, and it's unmistakably human.

Jaromir urges our horse to gallop, riding past Cadoc and Neith with ease. The wind whips through my hair, and my eyes water. His heart bludgeons against my back, and I count each pulse.

There's a mound of dirt and leaves in the middle of the road. A low groan seeps from the pile. Not a mound. A person.

Aeron.

Jaromir skids his horse to a halt, and I slide down without thought, tripping over my own feet. Aeron is lying far too still. I land beside him, and Jaromir turns him over. An arrow juts from his chest. Blood and dirt mingle to create a thick, dark pool across his filthy tunic.

A man dressed in calf-leather breeches and a dark green cloak stumbles out to the road. He hovers over Aeron's body, and a hand flies to his mouth in horror. His blond hair hangs against his jaw, and his eyes are wide with fear. "I—I didn't know," he stammers. "I was tracking a deer and lost its trail.

When I saw the antlers..." He gestures feebly at our unconscious leader.

Jaromir inspects the entry point, ignoring the hunter.

"Is he..." I don't dare finish the thought. It's a silly thing, believing that voicing my fear will make it real. Up close, he looks so young, even beneath all the mud, his skin is smooth. I gently push the leather wrap from his forehead, freeing his hair and loosening the branches to fall against the earth.

Aeron groans again. He's alive! I reach for him but hesitate. Jaromir's mouth is pulled in a frown as he studies the wound. The arrowhead hasn't made it through. Only the shaft is visible from Aeron's chest. Can we get it out? Do we need a surgeon? If we pull it free, will he bleed out?

"It missed his anything vital, but I don't dare cut this out. Not here." Jaromir murmurs, almost as if he can hear my thoughts. Or maybe I did think aloud.

"What do we do?" What do *I* do? Apart from panic and try not to vomit.

"Cadoc knows enough about medicinal herbs for basic use, but we need a specialist. We're near Astervale. We'll take him to Henry." Jaromir lifts Aeron into his arms and carries him smoothly, gentler than I thought him capable of.

"I'll follow. It's the least I can do," the hunter says, stashing his bow and giving an ear-piercing whistle.

Jaromir grunts at him. He has yet to say a single word to the man.

I haven't spoken to him either. What do you say to someone who accidentally shot your friend? *"No worries, no harm done. We've all wanted to shoot Aeron at one point or another."*

I wipe my wet cheeks, smearing something thick against my skin. Must be mud. Or Aeron's blood. My stomach hollows, and I force my feet to move.

Chapter Eight

I've known fear. I've been afraid I won't find my next meal. Afraid the men at the docks will examine too closely and find something they like. That someone will hate my ears enough to do more than insult me. That I won't survive the night to see the dawn.

I've been afraid I'll disappear as if I never existed, too insignificant for anyone to remember.

But I've never known this type of fear that settles beneath one's skin like a slow-creeping dread. The spike of my rapid pulse has waned, and my limbs are heavy. But something itches inside me. A worry refusing to settle. It's a numbing sort of fear that's quiet and waits in the dark.

I don't much like the quiet. Or the dark.

The town of Astervale is still a bit of a mystery to me. Apart from the healer living above the apothecary, I haven't had a chance to survey our surroundings. The moon was tucked behind a thick swath of clouds when we arrived, so all I saw was the sleepy face of a man, shadows etched along his features as candlelight danced over his surprised expression. He had quickly let us in and showed us to his private rooms where he could examine Aeron fully. I wanted to suggest he wake up more first, but he seemed to snap into awareness upon catching sight of the arrow. Jaromir had carried Aeron into a room behind the healer, and the door shut with a finality. Once Aeron's lodging was secure, the hunter fled our company. It's just as well. What could he really do other than serve as a reminder not to don branches like antlers lest you be shot with an arrow?

Here I sit, back against the wall in a dark corridor, while Cadoc paces the floor, and Neith rests against the spindles at the top step.

I won't pretend there's honor in the tightness of my chest. Of course I don't wish any ill will toward Aeron. He's sweet and has a good heart. His smile alone is enough inspiration to write a swoon-worthy ballad. But I don't know him well enough to mourn the idea of his loss.

The loss of my adventure, though. This is a thorn in my mind, refusing to let my thoughts turn elsewhere.

I'm a terrible person.

The door opens, and I jolt to my feet. The healer wipes blood from his hands with a rag, heaving a deep sigh. "He's stable for the moment. His body is fighting off an infection, thus the fever."

I nod as if I knew about the fever.

"I'll keep him here for a few days for observation. When I'm satisfied with his progress, he'll be free to go." The healer has a gravelly voice I find oddly soothing. A frown forms on his weathered face. "You may all spend the night, but on the morn, you'll need to arrange lodging elsewhere. I can't house the lot of you—I've a business to run."

"Yes, of course. Thank you for all you've done." Cadoc reaches to shake the man's hand. "M___ we see him?"

The healer ___________ ___s rest. But ___

Cadoc and Neith rush through, leaving me in the hallway with the man who may or may not have saved Aeron's life. I should thank him. He could have turned us away. Welkin knows, it must have been quite a shock to receive callers in the middle of the night and his kindness is not lost on me.

"How much will this cost?"

His brow raises, and I curse my tongue as my cheeks flame. But I know better than most, nothing is free, and an unnamed debt is a terrible thing to owe.

"It has been handled. Your friend in there—"

"Henry," Jaromir's voice calls out as he appears in the doorway, clapping the healer's back, "you've done enough for one night. You deserve rest more than any of us."

Henry nods, rubbing his forehead. "You remember where I keep the spare linens?"

"Under the stairs where Lyla could never find them." Jaromir smiles, and it isn't like Aeron's smile, which brightens a dim room with the strength of a high sun. It's an ember in the dark—a soft warmth I want to bask in. "I'll never understand purposely picking a fight with your wife."

"That's because you've never had makeup sex."

I cringe. I'm sure Henry is very spry for his age, but good goddess, I don't want to picture that.

Henry shuffles off, presumably to bed.

Jaromir and I are alone in the darkened hallway. Flickering candlelight spills out of Aeron's room and bathes the side of Jaromir's face. His dark eyes are unreadable, and his mouth tightens.

"He'll be okay," he says, his voice soft as a caress. He clears his throat. "I know you were worried, but Henry is the best in the business. So long as Aeron rests and hydrates, he'll recover fully."

Neith, but my feet won't seem to move. I'm frozen beneath the weight of his stare.

Jaromir reaches out, his touch ghosting against my hair, and I suck in a breath. A gentle tug, and he removes his hand, a small green leaf tucked between his fingers. Right. I haven't checked a looking glass yet. I'm sure I'm in quite a state. He's still holding that blasted leaf, as if unsure what to do with it. Finally, he tucks it in his pocket, burying his hand along with it.

"You just stole my hair accessory." My words are wooden, stilted by the lack of air behind them. I wait for his grunted reply or some sort of insult.

His gaze runs over my face. Once. Twice. His lips part as if he's waiting for the words to come. With a nod, he turns away, descending the stairs to the front door and disappearing into the night.

I exhale a shaky breath, and step into Aeron's room, finally able to move.

"ANOTHER ROUND, then I swear on my honor, I will go see Aeron again." Cadoc places a hand in the middle of his broad chest, his solemn expression lasting a mere moment before a languid grin spills across his face.

"Ye have nae honor." Neith elbows him and sips from her tankard.

The tavern is a riot of color. Red banners hang from wood beams and yellow ribbons wrap around poles. Off-key songs of harvest and feasting fill the room, and the scent of sweat and sweet wine is intoxicatingly thick. I can't believe I forgot it was First Fruits Day. Everyone is well into their cups, and a revelatory spirit permeates the already heady air.

It's glorious.

I adjust the strap of my lute across my chest. No one has asked me to play... yet. My head is hot beneath my red cap, but it's worth it to finally be exactly where I belong. There's no stage, but that won't stop me. I shall not end this night without singing at least one tune—on the bar if I have to.

A busty lass with red curls and a salacious grin keeps eying Jaromir with interest. He doesn't seem to notice as he sips from his mug and nods at mine where it remains atop the table, untouched.

"Something wrong with your ale?"

"Not at all, apart from it being ale." I don't like to drink before a performance. A drunk audience—that I can work with. But a drunk performer? I never know which chance will yield the launch of my dreams, so it's best to treat each one like my last.

Jaromir frowns as if I've insulted his taste. "Suit yourself."

The balance of our group is off without Aeron. He's always quick to come to my defense, and his unyielding optimism is the perfect counter to Jaromir's surliness.

"Do you think Aeron is disappointed he's missing this?"

Neith shrugs. "Dinnae ken he's aware o' much right now."

Jaromir watches me, the furrow in his brow deepening. I nudge my ale toward him in case he thinks me wasteful.

He pushes away from the table, striding to the bar.

That was strange, but I have neither the energy nor the desire to analyze Jaromir's actions. Everything I do annoys the man, and it's exhausting trying to keep up with his reactions.

"Summat else ye'd prefer?" Neith leans over, snagging my cup for her own consumption.

"Oh, no! I find I'm most parched *after* a performance."

A brilliant smile lifts Cadoc's handsome face. "You begin tonight then? Tales of our exploits! The magnificent noble and his motley crew of brave adventurers!" He jumps atop his chair, only slightly swaying. "Hear ye, hear ye. In honor of First Fruits Day, we have a special guest in our midst."

Neith hisses and grabs Cadoc to yank him down, but he leaps onto our table and dances out of her reach.

"The songbird of the east has migrated west to grace us with her tales!" He loses his footing and slips, landing in Jaromir's empty chair and crossing his legs as if it was all part of the performance.

Cheers and drunken hollers ring out, along with a few ear-piercing whistles.

Energy lights up my chest. My mouth tugs into a grin as I stand.

"Ignore him," Neith says, glaring at Cadoc. "Ye needn't do this just because some drunk idiot announced it."

Cadoc blows her a kiss.

I adjust my cap and pull my lute into ready position. "But Neith, I wouldn't waste a warmed-up audience." A simple plucking tune dances from my fingers as effortless as breathing.

This is what I am meant to do.

I haven't written Aeron's ballad, not fully, but I can take advantage of this moment.

"Ladies and gentlemen, I'm honored to tell you the tale of the man who shines brighter than the sun. A man who once spent a year in darkness to better appreciate the sight of dawn setting the sky aflame." I announce in a clear, ringing voice as I continue to pluck my way through an upbeat melody. Weaving my way through the tavern, around stools and patrons as I meet as many watery eyes as I can. A true storyteller connects with their audience.

"He's a man of unparalleled courage, untainted honor, and unmatched virility." I add that last part with a wink, and a few howls and whistles respond. "He embarks on a perilous quest, against unbeatable odds, to face a foe who casts a shadow taller than this very establishment."

A few gasps ring out, and I smother my smile into a solemn expression.

Time to bring it home.

"When deeds fall short of history, what must we do?" My voice booms with authority that isn't mine, and yet I command it. My gaze travels over my rapt audience, sweeping over sticky tabletops, cluttered floors, and ruddy-faces brightened by drink. When my stare falls to the bar, my heart plummets to the pit of my stomach.

Jaromir leans against the bar, his broad body twisted away from me. But he isn't alone. The woman from before—the red-haired beauty he'd previously ignored, now claims his attention. His face is half hidden behind the gentle curve of her jaw. Her auburn curls conceal whatever expression he makes as he whispers against her skin, his chin skimming her pale neck. Her eyes are glazed as her cheeks redden even more. Tangling slender fingers into his dark curtain of hair, she angles his head, seeking his lips.

I can't feel my hands. Everything's gone cold. I can only hope my fingers still dance over the strings of my lute as the floor falls away from me.

Clearing my throat, I force my lips to smile. It feels more like I'm baring my teeth. Strength I don't possess steadies my voice. "My good people, we make history."

I leap into a heavy-handed strum, infusing every ounce of emotion I have into a major key. Cheers erupt and applause rings out, deafening the roar in my ears. As the crowd blurs before my eyes, I blink, clearing away unnecessary distractions.

After all, the show must go on.

THE FLAME of my cheeks hasn't abated, but I sing with gusto, dancing on numb feet about the room as if I feel as merry as the tune promises. Never mind the fact that my chest aches with every breath.

Between my renditions of While the Fisherman's Away and What's in a Dwarven Whiskey, I could have sworn I heard someone yell out 'filthy whore,' but whoever it was, they were silenced quickly enough not to interrupt my performance. But that doesn't trouble me. I've been called worse, and I hardly notice anymore.

If only I could ignore everything so easily.

Why Jaromir and his companion haven't retired for the night is beyond me. Perhaps she must finish her shift before she's free to indulge in the giant, growling oaf for the evening. She flits from table to table, while Jaromir orders another drink at the bar. His jaw is a tight line of disapproval, and I can practically feel his glower. Whenever our eyes meet, I quickly find something safer to gaze upon. Like that drooling man with the bushy blond beard and bloodshot eyes.

My treacherous periphery reveals pale hands sliding over Jaromir's shoulders again. The woman is back, and her appetite hasn't been sated.

Perhaps I can help. I am, after all, a storyteller.

"Have you ever heard of Sir Aeron Fowler's kind nature?" I continue without waiting for a response. Most of my audience is too drunk to follow my lead. "He's a man too big for merely one tale. His heart knows no bounds, and his honor remains unblemished. For in bravery, coin, and friends is he the richest man of all. He's a collector of wayward souls, offering charity wherever he goes."

Jaromir's gaze burns my skin like a brand.

"I once accompanied him on a ride-along as a spectator of his good nature. Would you all like to hear of it?"

I don't care that half of the patrons have retired for the

evening. I don't care that Cadoc is propped up against Neith's shoulders, softly snoring while she continues to drink without showing signs of drunkenness—seriously, where is it all going?

I don't even care that my callouses have ripped open. I pluck a pretty tune and clear my throat.

"*Once we were but specters in the night,*
Once we came to the truth of the light,
In the abyss or in Eden, it matters not.
For this nobleman, Aeron, gives more than he's got.

He found a pitiful beast, alone by the road,
In a puddle of piss, and blood, and soiled.
I shrank away, what a frightful sight.
But Aeron held out his hand, and said, stay for the night.

The creature was no creature but actually a man
Who sniveled and snuffled and begged for a hand
A fae lass had b'witched him, cast a spell on his mind
His condition wouldn't lessen until the end of time

His tented trousers removed all doubt
I gasped, and shrieked, and threw up in my mouth
But he wept and howled and begged for aid
Said, 'I'd rather die than live another day of this ache.'

Aeron wouldn't oblige, not even a mercy kill
For this poor soul had such strength of will
Instead he paid for with coin from his own pocket
All the company of every wench, from here until Denmarket

And when at last Jaromir collapsed and sighed
His condition had fled him, and he was still alive
Jaromir swore an oath, upon the blade of his sword

He'd never touch another woman, he gave his word

If he did, may the fae who bespelled her trick
Once again seek vengeance and remove his prick."

A few murmurs ripple through the crowd. Somewhere, a deep voice calls out, "Any man who'd pay for another man to whet his sword is a hero!"

A rumble of laughter answers his outburst.

Does Jaromir deserve it?

Well, it made me feel better.

Neith shakes her head with a small smile and raises a brow in my direction. A quick cut of her glance Jaromir's way, and I know I must face the music.

I can't avoid his gaze any longer.

The air thickens, and any breath I have flees my chest in a rough exhale.

His dark eyes are so wide, it's comical. His lips are parted, and the stiffness of his jaw is momentarily abated. As ridiculous as he looks, there's almost a vulnerability there in the way his brows are lifted in surprise. The auburn-haired beauty who has run her hands over him all night tracks the tension between us with knowing eyes and backs away.

Jaromir stands and takes a step toward the stage.

And that's my cue! "Well, thank you for being a beautiful audience! Afraid I must go; you can donate to my tab with the barkeep!" I bolt for the door.

In all my haste, I've forgotten my room is directly over the tavern, but it's too late now. Perhaps I can sleep in a barrel somewhere. Wouldn't be the first time.

Humiliation burns its reminder against my cheeks and neck. Why did I sing that song? Why should I care if he finds company for the night? He could marry her and have a million glowering babies and it would still be *none of my business.*

Though it is my business to make everything my business, so I wasn't entirely out of line...

Something grips the back of my collar, wrenching me to a halt. Rough hands spin me and press my shoulder blades against the brick wall of the narrow alley. Jaromir looms over me, crowding my space and making it hard to breathe. I grip my lute tighter and keep it safely between our bodies.

"What in the blazing abyss was that?" His voice is dangerously low, and I resist the urge to shiver.

"That was a song. I believe you've heard one before."

"That was immature and childish."

I should stick my tongue out at him just to show him how immature I can be. "Not as childish as practically having sex on the bar."

Jaromir rears back, his brows lifting in confusion. "What—"

"Why couldn't you go to your room like a normal person to enjoy her company? No one wished to witness that display." Why am I saying this out loud?

His confusion melts into something sharper. His nostrils flare, and a reddish hue steals across his face. "I stayed to ensure you received no further harassment. You seem incapable of taking care of yourself so—"

"Incapable?" Slinging my lute to hang at my side, I shove my hands against his chest. He doesn't budge. "I'll have you know I've done just fine on my own without you. I don't need, nor do I want, anything from you, so stop pretending to care what happens to me."

This doesn't feel like our fun prodding to irritation. My throat is tight, and my treacherous eyes blur with what I'm sure couldn't be tears.

I don't want to feel whatever this is—this confusing, irrational mix of emotions that bears no justification.

His expression softens to one of contemplation. Like he's trying to sort out what to do with me.

"Sylvaine."

The sound of my name on his lips does funny things to my stomach.

I blink any lingering moisture away and fake a smile. It feels tight, like shoes I've outgrown.

"Go. I'm sure she's waiting to assist your cursed prick." My cheeks begin to ache.

Without waiting for a response, I push past him, back toward the tavern. Neith will probably find her way to our shared room soon, and I need to make sure I appear asleep before she does.

Chapter Nine

Despite the stone that's made a home in my belly, sleep finds me. It releases me from its clutches before the first rays of dawn break across the sky. A hint of light smudges the horizon, and I needn't wake for hours, yet I pull myself from my cot and creep across the floor. I didn't bother changing out of my clothes last night, but for once, I leave my cap behind and grab my boots from their spot by the door, sneaking out with slow, careful movements. It's more of a courtesy. I'm sure Neith heard me the moment I stirred.

Yanking my boots into place, I tip-toe down the hall and stairs. The tavern is not yet open for patrons, but that's not my destination.

Once I'm outside, summer's cool morning blasts me in the face. It's thick and damp with the promise of a humid day, but for now the darkened sky keeps the sun's heat at bay.

I make my way across the quiet square, heading for the apothecary. For Aeron. I still haven't had the chance to see him conscious, a fact that shames me almost as much as my performance last night.

My gut twists at the thought. I have nothing to be ashamed

of. I gave a spirited performance, bringing honor to Aeron's name as I promised I would. So what if a touch of pettiness laced my verses? Jaromir is no saint, and I don't need his good opinion.

The door to the apothecary is locked, but Henry left the backdoor unlocked for us to come visit Aeron at any hour. He's either very trusting, or this village leaves little room for paranoia. We haven't been here long enough for me to form an opinion, but in my experience, even "good" people fall prey to bad impulses. Still, I'm grateful for the chance to check on Aeron without the others.

When I reach his room, the door's been left open a crack, warm light spilling out. I poke my head in, finding Aeron leaning against his pillows, studying the book in his hand. His chest is bare, but bandages cover him from his shoulders to just below his ribs. His red hair is tied back in a knot, and concentration creases his forehead.

All the tension leaves my body in a rush. "You're awake."

He peers over his book, and that damnable smile lights up his face. "I was wondering when I'd see my favorite bard."

Taking that as invitation enough, I slip in and find my way to the chair by his bed. "How do you feel?"

He shrugs, then grimaces at the action. "Better and worse. I think I preferred it when I was unconscious and didn't have to feel my wound."

"Well, *I* certainly didn't prefer that," I say. "You scared us all with that stunt."

He places a hand over his heart. "Deepest apologies, my lady. Consider it a one-time offense."

I sniff as if affronted by the whole ordeal like a proper lady. "Very well." I glance at the book resting on his bunched-up coverlet. "So long as you aren't still reading that survival guide."

He laughs, one of his full chested ones that fills the too-quiet room. "I assure you, I'm not. This is more of a comfort read."

Now I must know what it is. It's a fascinating business, the variances in what brings comfort. I slide the book from his grasp and flip it open to the first page. The familiar words, words I've read nearly a dozen times, leap out from the page.

"Whispers of Time," I say with a smile. "This is my absolute favorite story. Favorite not penned by me, I should say."

Aeron grins. "Truly? It's my favorite, too. I've read it over and over since I was just a boy."

I can see it. Young Aeron with long, unbound hair lounging in the grass, book in hand, and absently chewing a piece of straw while a cloudless sky hovers above.

The first time I read this book was out loud to a kind woman who had lost her sight to age. For a week, I read to her, and she paid me with baked potatoes, hot enough to warm me from the inside out. I'd clutch my daily potato, eager to sate the gnawing in my belly, but hesitant to lose the warmth in my dirty palms. On the day I read to her for the last time, I tripped over words that never gave me trouble before and had to slow my pace to read each word carefully. She let me keep the book and gave me two potatoes that day, with the promise to find more books I could read to her. But winter was harsh that year, and she didn't live to see the spring.

Two years, I carried that book around with me. Until one night, when I strayed down the wrong alley. I didn't mourn the loss of my tattered cloak, nor the few coins I'd stolen from unsuspecting pockets. But that book—a light in the dark—I missed its comfort something fierce.

I hand the book back, clearing my throat. "Everyone should read this story as many times as their life allows."

Aeron lowers his head, running his finger along the book's spine. "On this, we agree. Though my father wouldn't say the same."

"On the choice of book or revisiting a favorite for pleasure?"

Aeron snorts. "Pleasure is not a word my father used. He thought of pleasure as listlessness or indulgence. Though, to be honest, I don't think there's much he and I ever saw eye to eye on."

I raise a brow in question. In my experience, one can freely comment on the shortcomings of their own kin, but if I were to chime in, he might take offense. It's best if I let him carry on this conversation without much input.

He takes the hint to continue. "As the youngest of five brothers, I'm the epitome of *the spare*. The unnecessary addition to a long line of heirs." He gives me a weak smile that stretches his dry lips. "For a time, I relished the freedom it brought me. You understand, I was unburdened by the mantle of responsibility. And with my family's fortune at my disposal..." He sighs, his shoulders slumping. "I pursued any venture I liked. Any passion, leisure, or interest that struck my fancy. Did you know I once decided I'd be the next great painter?"

I shake my head. "You paint?"

"I wanted to. Badly enough, I told my father it was my life's calling, boarded the next ship to Lindale, and spent the spring season proving I hadn't the focus nor the talent." He laughs, and it's a thick wheezing sound. "I was fortunate, there's no denying that. But somewhere down the road, I played the part of the fool so well, I negated any trust or good opinion my family might have formed of me."

I reach out to grab his hand, and he squeezes back. "For what it's worth, I see no fault in pursuing passions, even if they're fleeting in nature. Passion is the first ember of creation. Without art, what are we?"

"Are you a bard or a philosopher?"

"You jest to deflect my question. Perhaps I'll write that

into your ballad. 'Aeron Fowler couldn't take the discomfort of someone agreeing with him.' It has a ring to it."

His answering smile softly lingers before the crease returns to his brow. "I'm tired of being the family punchline. The burden." He meets my gaze with an intensity I've never seen in his eyes. "I'm meant for more."

The fervor in his voice and the grip of his hand clenches something in my chest. I know this feeling all too well.

"Yes, you are, and you'll have it." I lean forward. "And I'll make damn sure the world knows you."

A creak of the floorboard makes us both jump. I spin around to see Jaromir hovering in the doorway, an unreadable storm on his face. He is likely still sore about the ballad. His gaze drops to where Aeron's and my hand remain joined, and I quickly pull away.

"I see you're awake." Jaromir's voice is thick and gruff, and his eyes are everywhere but on me now.

"That I am," Aeron says, sitting up taller. "I was just about to regale Syl with the details of where I heard of the dragon."

Now this snags my attention.

"Oh, do tell! I could work some of these details into your ballad."

Jaromir groans, and at Aeron's confused expression, I explain.

"I began my work last night."

"Slander. She began her slander." Jaromir glares at me.

Aeron shifts his attention between the two of us. "I'm afraid I don't understand."

"I was singing your praises, and Jaromir didn't appreciate the artistic license I took with a few details."

"You dragged my name into it."

"Now you're famous."

"You gave me a cursed prick."

"Yes, but Aeron did lift the curse in the end."

To Aeron's credit, he tightens his mouth against the smile threatening to spread. "I need to heal and get out of this bed. It sounds like I'm missing an awful lot of excitement." He pats the space on the quilt next to him because I've taken the chair, and with a huff, Jaromir stomps over and sits. The bed compresses under his weight. I angle away from him so I can't tell if he smells like a perfumed woman has been pressed against him all night.

"Now, do you want to hear how I learned about the dragon?"

"I don't need to be here for this," Jaromir says quickly.

"I want my friend by my side."

At this, Jaromir stops huffing.

"Now, where was I?" Aeron taps his chin thoughtfully. "Oh yes. A traveling merchant came to town selling old maps..."

By the time Aeron finishes his story and curls up to rest once more, the sun is high in the sky, and a headache has made a home behind my eyes. Jaromir also seems worn from his night of debauchery or whatever he got up to once I fled his sight. It's surprising when he walks me out of Aeron's room, softly shutting the door and leaving us alone in the hall.

Glancing over at him, I note the dark circles etched beneath his bloodshot eyes. I'd wager he didn't get a wink of sleep. People know when they look tired; they don't need to hear it.

"You look like shit."

Unfortunately, I care little for what he needs.

"I feel worse."

"I doubt that." I begin descending the steps to the apothecary. The little bell tinkles above the door, indicating customers are already shopping. Judging by Aeron's state, we have at least another night before he's fit enough to travel. Maybe more. Itching restlessness burns the back of my collar. I want back on the road. Stars overhead and forest at my back.

I should use this time to compose the first part of Aeron's ballad. Yes! That shall be my task today. I can even include that bit about the merchant selling him his quest. Wait... no. That sounds less heroic and more foolish.

As skeptical as I am over his acquisition of this quest, something about the map tells me the merchant didn't know the value of what he was selling. Though if you listen to Aeron tell the story, it sounds like he was swindled.

That's the magic of a story. It has the power to shape our heroes, our hopes, our futures.

But right now, his story has the power to spawn ridicule.

I'm following this man... I'm hitching my cart to his wagon, so to speak. So, if he's the fool, what does that make me?

The wishful fool.

"Where are you going?"

Jaromir's irritated voice rips me from my thoughts. I didn't realize he still walked with me. We stand outside the apothecary, beside the fogged crosshatch windows and beneath the hanging wooden sign that reads *Tricks for What Afflicts.*

"I was going to find a quiet place to write." My stomach gurgles, reminding me I haven't had breakfast yet. Food first, then writing.

"I'll go with you." At first, I'm not quite sure I've heard him correctly. But then he adds, "After we get something wrapped up to bring with us."

"All due respect, I think not. I can't imagine I'll get much done with you glowering over my shoulder the whole time. Furthermore, isn't there a certain red-haired woman you might wish to speak to? You joined me in Aeron's room early enough I can guess you snuck out of there like a coward. It's none of my business, to each his own, but if we are to patron the only tavern in town again tonight, it would be wise not to burn our bridges just yet. In fact, had you informed me of your aims to bed one of their employees, I might have saved you the grief by reminding you not to piss where we drink or however the saying goes."

Jaromir's finger presses firmly against my lips, and his touch burns. He shakes his head, eyes widening. "Do you not breathe when you launch into these tirades?"

I shove his hand away, mouth tingling. "Don't touch me. Just because you get by with a few grunts and growls masquerading as conversation, doesn't mean the rest of the world lacks the art of speaking."

His mouth twitches. "It was becoming a safety concern. Wouldn't want you to swoon from lack of oxygen."

He's jesting with me. Damn him, and damn the corner of my mouth when it lifts without my permission.

"Your crusade to keep chivalry alive is a most admirable goal." I step closer to his warmth, I don't know why I do it, but it feels appropriate. Like I need to see how far we can push or pull without us setting one another off. I revel in the fact that he doesn't retreat; he stands his ground while I invade his space. His scent is both clean and earthy. He must have washed her perfume from his skin.

"I don't know about chivalry." His voice is rough. "But I know the sound of your stomach is going to keep you from concentrating." His gaze dips to my mouth. "And you talk entirely too much."

I roll my eyes and push past him, trying my best to ignore the way my skin ignites at the contact. I don't need his good opinion or validation. I need a sweet roll and a quiet spot to write.

He keeps pace beside me, much to my everlasting annoyance.

The bakery has opened its doors, and the scent of sugar and dough reaches my nose. Whatever reaction Jaromir hopes for, I won't give him the satisfaction.

Neith and Cadoc agree to stay in town with Aeron, taking turns sitting with him while I venture to the outskirts and find a quiet field to write. Wildflowers dot the brow of the green hill in blue, violet, yellow, and white. The sun is warm, and the air is heavy with summer's embrace.

And I can't write a single word.

It's like all the inspiration has abandoned me, and nothing sounds right.

I cross out the nonsensical words I've written over and over, and rip yet another page from my book, crumpling it up and shoving it in my satchel.

A soft crinkle is the only indication that Jaromir has slipped the discarded parchment from my bag and smoothed it out to read. He clears his throat pointedly.

I glance up to find he's holding it out for me to examine, a dark brow arched in silent question. My angrily scrawled words glare up at me.

Why has the muse forsaken me?

"It's an honest question," I say with a shrug.

Jaromir crumples it again and shoves it in my bag. "This isn't working."

He reaches a hand down to me, and I smack it away without thinking. He is not the expert on my process, and if he plans to condescendingly lecture me on it, I'll stab him with the point of my quill.

"Let's find shade. You won't be able to think straight if you boil from overheating."

That's sensible. Reasonable, even. Annoying, most of all.

I shut my book with a firm thud and follow him to the nearby copse of trees at the edge of the woods. It doesn't take long to find a spot to rest my back against a thick trunk, and I gaze up at the sun filtering through impossibly green leaves. A deep breath, and I sigh. The thick scent of overturned earth fills my senses, and I run my hand through the beams of light illuminating my empty page. Cicadas call out their humming song, and it's like something out of a dream, a mystical forest where wishes are granted.

And yet... I still can't make the words come.

Jaromir leans against a tree, watching me with an unreadable expression. "Maybe this is penance for the ballad you sang last night."

Now he has my attention. "You want me to apologize? Fine, I apologize for temporarily interrupting what I'm sure was a scholarly debate with your companion."

"That isn't—"

"A right cerebral discussion of carnal exchange."

He moves so quickly, I don't have time to react, not that I could go far with a tree against my back. But he invades my space, crouching to meet me at eye level, and my notebook is all that creates distance between our chests. His dark eyes rove over my face, greedy in their intent.

"Listen to me." His breath ghosts against my lips, and it's all I can do not to lean in closer. "I haven't the faintest idea why you seem fixated on this, but nothing else happened last night."

I swallow, and the action is tight in my throat. "I don't care."

"No, of course not. That's why you sang of my cock and continue to berate me."

I'm too stunned at the way my stomach flips hearing that word in the rough rasp of his voice to properly articulate a response.

"After you ran off, I sat at the bar alone, until I retired to my room *alone*."

My head spins, and I take a deep breath, only to realize what a mistake that is because I breathe in more of his scent. "It's none of my business." My voice is shaky and pathetic.

He laughs, and it's a low, cruel sound. "And yet, you meddle. Is it so sordid that someone might find comfort in another for a night? That when you live your life on the road, sometimes stolen moments with strangers are the closest thing to intimacy you can have? Does it offend your sensibility? Or is it just me you find so loathsome?"

My cheeks burn. I can't think straight with him this close, so I say the only thing I think will throw him off guard. "Is that all then? If anyone will do, why didn't you ask me?"

His eyes flare, and he rears back in shock, the sudden distance both a blessing and a curse. A fresh breath of air untangles the mess of my mind, and finally, I can think clearly again. I knew he was all bluster—trying to overwhelm and outplay me. But I will not be toyed with. It takes more than a handsome face and a broad set of shoulders to intimidate me. He's all talk and no—

His hand tips my chin and his mouth is on mine before I can gasp out a startled breath.

Chapter Ten

I'm no blushing virgin, and in my experience, something as simple as a kiss has never been anything to incite much passion.

But Welkin's eternal goddess, the feel of Jaromir's lips on mine has heat pooling in my gut and a tingle along the base of my spine. I open beneath his kiss immediately, and he sweeps in, groaning into my mouth. A low hum leaves my throat at the sensation, and my eyes flutter closed. He tastes intoxicatingly sweet, and I want to write a damn sonnet to this moment. I want to write romantic, filthy verses and find out if he tastes this good everywhere. I want to relive this feeling over and over until it's all I know, and time ceases to exist. My hands slide from his broad leather-clad shoulders up into his hair, fisting possessively. He presses me against the tree, his hand cradling the back of my head, and it feels perfectly natural to slide into his lap and wrap myself around his waist. He stands, lifting me into his arms, as he fills the space between my legs perfectly. Blazing heat erupts across my skin and... other parts.

"Fuck." His voice is rough as he places harsh kisses down my neck, his beard scratching against delicate skin. I'm trapped between the tree and his firm body, and I don't think there's anywhere I'd rather be. I might pitch a marker and claim this spot as my eternal resting place. His hardness presses against me, and I squirm, seeking friction. His hips move, and he groans into my ear. Stars burst across my vision. I'm quite certain I'll go mad, perhaps even die, if I can't get his hands beneath my clothes.

I grab the back of his neck, and his skin is hot. I've never felt this needy desperation, and it's both thrilling and terrifying. Claiming his mouth, I gently scrape my teeth along his bottom lip, coaxing another sound of need and distress from his chest. It's a heady thing, this power. I want to see how far it extends.

Somewhere in the lust-addled recesses of my foggy mind, a whisper of logic takes root. We shouldn't do this. If it bothered me to see him with another when we were nothing more than travel companions, how much will this complicate things? I only goaded him to make him back off, not to volunteer myself as his personal sheath. That's what started this, isn't it? I essentially asked him to use me for the physical needs he experiences.

What is wrong with me?

I let my legs fall, and my feet hit the ground with a finality. Jaromir presses his lips to my forehead, his hands running down my sides. His thorough gaze searches my face, and the hint of a smile curves against his mouth. He presses another kiss to my lips, softer this time, before he follows the trail of his kiss with the pad of his thumb. I shiver and lean into his touch, but unfortunately, I'm stronger than my impulse.

"We can't do this."

Jaromir's brows pinch, and he visibly swallows.

"I shouldn't do this." I loathe my words. Part of me screams, *yes you should!* But I came here with a job to do, and I can't afford the distraction this entanglement would cause. If my mind is turned to thoughts of him, of possible regret and pain, how can I hope to write Aeron's ballad? How can I hope to make a name for myself?

No distraction is worth the cost of my future success. Of assuring my life here was worth everything it cost to get me this far. I will be more than that scared little elf starving in the gutter. I will matter, and no one will have the power to take my renown from me.

For once... Jaromir looks unsure. He nods almost to himself, running a hand through his dark hair that's come loose from its knot. My hands are already itching to dive back in again.

Why couldn't I have had my epiphany ten, no, fifteen minutes later?

He runs his tongue along his bottom lip, and the twisted part of me hopes he's savoring my taste. I want to catch his mouth with mine and show him how much the instinctive part of me wants this.

Instead, I watch him back away, and the distance between us only grows.

"Three silvers says I make this shot." Cadoc closes one eye as he aims at the empty mug on the bar top. He's finally found a suitable distraction from the fact we're remaining in town until Aeron heals. I've never known a fellow so averse to sitting still, but Neith says he's always been this way.

The air is thick and heavy. The tavern is crowded, but not as rowdy as it was last night. First Fruits Day has come and gone, leaving a sea of hangovers in its wake. I can't say I'm faring much better with the way my stomach dips each time Jaromir moves, blinks, or breathes.

I didn't even bring my lute tonight.

From across the room, the beautiful red-haired woman clears tables, occasionally glancing over at Jaromir. He never meets her stare, and although it's awful of me all things considered, I'm glad for it.

"Ye haven't got any coin left," Neith says, elbowing Cadoc and throwing him off balance.

"I won't need it if I make this shot. My winnings will fund my drinks the rest of the night."

Neith snorts as she sips from her tankard, and it creates a metallic echo. "I won't take advantage of a drunken fool." Ignoring his grunt of displeasure, she turns to me. "Aeron was in a jovial mood."

I trace the knots in the table, glancing anywhere but at Jaromir, though his presence is hard to ignore. The memory of our kiss burns against my lips, and it takes every shred of control not to touch them. I turn my attention to the half-melted candle atop our table. The wax has bubbled and spilled down the side as the flame dances.

"Will he be ready for travel?" I'm almost impressed by how casual I sound.

"Gods, I hope so," Cadoc says with a groan before attempting another throw. "We've tarried long enough."

Neith nods. "He seems t'think he will be. A sudden affliction o' blind optimism has taken hold."

Jaromir rolls his neck, and I fight a losing battle with the heat creeping up my cheeks.

"He's like that, isn't he?" Bright and larger than life, like his ridiculous armor. Even lying in a bed, recovering from an arrow wound of his own stupidity, he shines with the force of his hope.

"Aye, though he seemed down last night, didnae he, Cadoc?"

Cadoc looks up from where he's been aiming his collection of acorns at the lone tankard across the way. "I don't recall."

"Yes, ye do. There was even talk o' abandoning his quest. But he changed his mind. Said summat about Syl's performance."

Jaromir openly studies me now. It's unavoidable, I must meet his gaze, and I find a perfectly formed puzzle meant to elude my best guess at its meaning.

"He even wanted to send a raven t'his brother asking t'come home."

This pulls me back to Neith's conversation.

"He what?"

Neith takes a slow sip of her ale, watching me carefully over the rim of her mug before lowering it to the table with a thud. "He asked me t'pen it for him. O' course, this mornin' Aeron asked me t'rip it up and write another, boastin' of our new bard."

My head spins at her words. But I'm still latched on to the initial revelation. "He needs permission to return home?"

"He didnae tell ye? Oh, why would he when ye're meant t'write of his heroics? His father cast 'im off their lands years ago, and he wasn't even permitted t'return for th'man's funeral rites when he passed."

His father is dead? I really don't know a damn thing about Aeron. Here I thought he was nothing more than a sweet though ultimately misguided fool, seeking glory and even more wealth. I had no idea the hurts he's suffered.

"He's hoping his eldest brother will give 'im leave t'return if he makes a name for himself."

This changes nothing, I was always going to help him and by proxy help me. But how dare his brother keep him from returning home? I don't care what he's done to lose their favor, he deserved a chance to say goodbye or grieve or whatever he needed to do.

I snatch up Neith's ale and take a deep drink. It's thick and bitter, but it blooms something warm in my belly.

Tonight, I begin writing the most epic tale in Aeron's name, muse be damned.

IT TAKES three more days for Aeron to recover enough to travel. Three days of Cadoc grumbling his boredom at being trapped in this town. Of Neith testing the balance and weight of each blade with the weaponsmith. Three days of finding crushed buttercups I don't remember picking in the bottom of my satchel and pressing them between the pages of my book for safekeeping. Three days of writing by daylight, and strumming my lute when night claims the sky, and both drink and coin flow freely. Of singing to Aeron's good name, his honor, his gods, and his heart... without mentioning a certain someone.

It makes no difference. Jaromir barely acknowledges my existence. Though blessedly, he hasn't taken up with any partners in front of me. That's a courtesy I hadn't expected.

I visit Aeron each day and night. Each time, his smile is damn near searing to look upon. Earnest glee crinkles his eyes, and I find myself grinning back. It's an easy thing, this friendship. He's sheer warmth, and I still can't reconcile what Neith shared about his life with the man before me.

He gets stronger each day, and on the third day he even ventures to the tavern with us for dinner. No drinks for him since it doesn't sit well with the medicinal herbs Henry has him on, but he dutifully holds his tankard and watches me sing with a glimmer of pride in his eyes.

Jaromir is actually friendly. With Aeron, that is. He smiles and nods along with his jokes all the while ignoring me. The only indicator that he can hear me is how he tightens his grip on his drink when I start to sing... not that I'm watching or anything.

With daybreak comes the continuation of our journey. Cadoc's smiles come easier, a spring to his step now that we're moving on. Neith carries the weapon she selected for me until we can begin training. Bags are packed, horses are watered and loaded, and we're off.

Jaromir slides into place at my back. I haven't felt his warmth since that day in the woods when we exchanged breathless kisses punctuated by painstaking distance. Every nerve in my body reacts, flaring to life at his proximity, and I bite back a sigh. Aeron gives me an apologetic shrug, as if he detects my discomfort.

If only he knew my discomfort is from the way my skin sings at Jaromir's touch and the reckless wish for more.

I turn in the saddle, glancing over Jaromir's shoulder to watch the town of Astervale disappear from the dusty road, until the cover of trees and over-filled branches blanket the sky.

New verses to Aeron's ballad come to me, and I don't have the energy to fight for my notebook to jot them down.

Farewell is not farewell, in the end
But a promise to meet once more
For where stories end, they begin anew
So instead of farewell, I'll say to you

Until we meet again.

Chapter Eleven

"Tell us another one, Syl," Aeron's mouth pulls in a lazy grin, and it's almost a parody of his usual smile. "I could listen to you spin your tales for hours."

Drink has loosened his tongue and glazed his eyes, so I don't put much stock in that statement. Jaromir clenches his jaw and glares at the fire.

"First of all," I begin with a wave of my hand, "you needn't flatter me to hear me speak. I'll talk whether you want it or not. Second of all, I'm not telling you yarns I've spun. These are either handed down or eyewitness accounts."

"Really?" Cadoc laughs into the bottle of wine we've been passing around the fire. "You actually saw a werewolf?"

"Technically I saw a wolf wearing a nightgown, I merely followed the path of logic."

Neith spits out whatever she'd been drinking from her personal flagon. It smells strong enough to burn a hole in my stomach, so I haven't tasted it to find out.

I accept the wine bottle from Cadoc and tip it between my lips. It's my favorite Hawthokian vintage. Deep notes of citrus and berry slide over my tongue. The wine sits warm in my belly, and my cheeks burn with it.

A hand reaches out, beckoning for the wine.

Jaromir.

I pass him the bottle, allowing our fingers to touch. If he notices, he doesn't let on. He makes a show of slowly sipping from it, and curse my traitorous thoughts, I'm stuck on the fact that he's putting his mouth where mine's just been, and why can't I forget the way he tastes—

"Syl?" Aeron calls from across the fire. "Another tale?"

I could tell him The Bard's Final Tale. It seems fitting since it involves a bard and a dragon.

"This is a tale of betrayal and redemption. A loss of passion before finding the strength to feel again. It begins with a man—"

"Was he handsome?" Cadoc leans heavily on his hand, fluttering his eyelashes at me.

"That isn't the point of this story." I don't want them to fixate on his face. I want them to feel his terror, the way his heart batters against his ribs as he faces down a dragon.

"I'm a visual person," Cadoc insists.

"Fine! He's quite striking. Red hair, green eyes, and a freckled nose. So the man is a disgraced bard who hasn't had the ability to perform for an audience for five years. He takes a job hunting a dragon, but when the rest of his company is slain, he must rely on his wits and storytelling to distract the dragon long enough to—"

"But why would talking distract a dragon?"

Neith glares at Cadoc and lightly swats the back of his head. "If ye'd shut yer gob, ye might find out."

I laugh, and my gaze meets Jaromir's. For once, he doesn't look away. He holds my stare, and something about the way the firelight flashes in his eyes makes the space between us both too close and achingly far. Images of how he pressed me against a tree flood my mind. The rough scrape of his beard, the low hum in his throat, the liquid slide of his mouth. My head spins as my skin heats. The wine sits heavily in my belly, and I'm not sure if I can remain upright.

"I'll continue in just a moment." My voice is breathless, and I only slightly sway when I stand. "Afraid the wine's gone to my head."

I step away with as much dignity and grace as I can muster, seeking the nearby river to cool the fire in my cheeks. Plopping down by the riverbank, I cup the cold, fresh water in my hands and splash my face. I need to find a way to be around the man without losing all sense. I'm supposed to be avoiding distraction, not welcoming it. And yet...

My thoughts loop on a constant refrain. He's a never ceasing shadow I can't seem to shake.

Footsteps approach, not even bothering to be quiet. It's a fool's hope to expect Neith or Cadoc has followed me.

I glance up to find Jaromir, his dark eyes narrowed in disapproval. "Are you going to be sick?"

Gazing back down at the water rushing over smooth stones, I steady my breath. "I'm not sick. The heat of the fire mixed with the wine. I just needed to cool off."

Jaromir crouches beside me, placing a large hand into the water. He brings it back out again, dripping cooling relief against my hairline, the back of my neck, and when he reaches my throat, I let out a treacherous moan.

He freezes, hand in midair, while I wish I could sink into the earth. His throat bobs, and he's cupping more water—this time bringing it to my mouth. It seems too intimate, downright uncouth for me to drink it from his hand, and yet I do—all under his watchful gaze gradually increasing in heat and intensity.

Perhaps the wine emboldens my tongue, but I let it scrape against his palm, if only to see what he'll do. His eyes flick to mine, a silent question in them. An unnamed emotion I daresay resembles a commingling of heat and hope.

Jaromir clears his throat, glancing away. "Should I fetch Aeron for you?"

My mind stutters on the absurdly random question he poses. "Why would I want Aeron?"

He tilts his head so he's only half looking at me. His chest rises and falls with each breath. "If there is anything between the two of you, I will not get in the middle."

My cheeks flush even deeper at the accusation. He thinks... *he actually thinks* I have a secret romantic entanglement with Aeron, even after our little frolic in the woods?

"I would never involve myself with multiple parties, and I certainly wouldn't hide it. Admittedly, it's flattering you think I possess such skills at multitasking, but rest assured, my relationship with Aeron is strictly professional."

I'm tasked with writing his story. No one would ever believe a lover's word of his exploits, and I have no interest in being his lover. He's handsome and ridiculous, but I don't feel that pull toward him. The one that starts low in my belly and fills me with a frantic sense of urgency.

The pull I feel to Jaromir.

I study his reaction, searching for signs of doubt. But Jaromir studies me right back, his gaze arresting on my mouth. His own lips part, and I can practically taste them from memory.

The last time, he kissed me. He took my mouth with a bruising intensity, it only seems fair I return the favor.

Before I can question this line of thought, my hand is grabbing the back of his neck and hauling him toward me. He could resist—he's far stronger than I am—but he seems so startled by this, he loses his balance.

One thing I've failed to remember—

We're beside the river.

Our teeth clack from my hurried assault just as we tip over the edge and into the water. Frigid cold clings to my clothes, seeps into my skin, and freezes my blood. I flail wildly, only sinking beneath the surface where the pressure against my ears blocks out all sound save for the gurgle of the river and the distant, muffled sound of my scream. Strong hands pull me up, and I'm pressed against his firm chest, eagerly gulping down air.

"Gods, Syl. Are you all right?"

I blink the water from my eyes to see his wet hair dripping down his face, concern etched on his impossibly handsome face.

I laugh. What else can one do when they attack someone and utterly fail at seduction. His brows draw together as he examines me before a smile starts to tug at his mouth. A small laugh escapes his lips until it builds, rich and deep, filling me with its baritone sound. His laugh makes something warm and soft curl in my chest, like a comfort I never knew I wanted. It begins as a guarded sound, almost rusty, until he loses himself in earnest at the ridiculousness of the situation. Now, we're both dripping wet and laughing like lunatics.

I knew his laugh was worth earning. If I thought he was handsome before, I'm positively blown away by the way he looks when his joy is an unfettered thing, and the clouds that seem to permeate his expression part to reveal a sight more stunning than the sun.

"That wasn't supposed to happen," I finally say. My mirth has died down to a grin I can't seem to wipe off my face despite the soreness of my cheeks.

"What was supposed to happen?"

It occurs to me, I'm still pressed against him, with nothing but soaking wet clothes between us. Heat pools low in my belly, and my blood warms beneath my pebbled skin.

"I was supposed to ravish you, obviously," I say with a tight laugh. And if I was stupid enough to believe that might lessen some of the tension between us, I'm sorely mistaken. It only coils tighter, tauter, as his gaze darts to my mouth. "I could try again." I wet my lips, reveling in the way he follows the movement. "If that sounds agreeable."

"I'd be disappointed if you accepted defeat so easily." His voice is barely above a whisper, but it feels like a deafening challenge. I tip my chin, seeking his mouth, and he lowers his to mine—

"Why are you in the river?"

I freeze, and glance around Jaromir to find Aeron standing there, blinking with wide-eyed confusion.

"I fell in," I say quickly, "and accidentally pulled Jaromir in with me." I smile up at Jaromir, expecting to find traces of his amusement—

But his mouth is a tight line, his eyes anywhere but meeting mine.

Jaromir lifts me to the riverbank, setting me down before putting far too much distance between us. "We should get dry clothes and sit by the fire. Don't want to catch sickness."

Sickness from the river in summer? Horse shit. But Aeron nods emphatically, even sweeping out a hand to help me. It seems appropriate to accept that hand, but when I turn back, Jaromir's glower has returned in full force.

Whatever the reason, he doesn't want Aeron to know about us. About whatever keeps almost happening. I can't say if it's because he doesn't believe me that Aeron and I are colleagues and nothing more, or because he's ashamed of me.

I swallow the sudden lump in my throat. He's taken no issue with me being an elf, but perhaps this is one step too far.

Pushing the thought away, I make my way back to camp, pretending to listen to whatever Aeron is saying.

THE POUNDING headache that greets me at dawn is more than I deserve. The wine churns uneasily in my gut as we plod along the path. Jaromir still hasn't deigned to speak to me or look at me, which is impressive since I'm pressed against his chest and thighs as we ride. Something has changed in him since last night. I saw a glimpse of that passion when he held me in the river and nearly picked up where we left off that day in the woods, but after Aeron's arrival and our quick return to camp, he's been distant ever since.

Aeron looks ready to pitch sideways off his horse, and he's forgone his heavy plated armor. A blessing, too, for the blinding light off steel would be enough to make me lean over and retch. Cadoc isn't fairing much better, and a sheen of sweat dots the back of his neck. Both appear to be valiantly fighting the battle of will and stomach contents, while Neith— who outdrank everyone and with that rancid swill she refused to name—is the picture of health and comfort. She rides high in her saddle with a smug smile dusting her mouth.

I admire this. Her unapologetic air. Too often, us women can dim ourselves for the sake of other's comfort.

It's this thought that sharpens a sense of boldness in my chest.

"Why do you seem to want nothing to do with me after what happened by the river?" In the river, really.

Jaromir stiffens before offering his hushed response. "I didn't think you wanted everyone to know your business."

By everyone, he means Aeron.

I'm no fool. Jaromir feels something for me, even if there's an unspoken line in the sand. I can't quite remember who put it there, but I wish to cross it and see what happens. Why should I deny myself what I want? At first, I thought to save myself the distraction, but now I'm sure the distraction is in the unknown. Denying myself hasn't saved my thoughts from being plagued with him. Once we complete our quest, I doubt

I'll ever see him again, so what's the harm in having a fair bit of fun while we travel? I got caught up in the idea that I would want more from him than that. It isn't as if we're forging emotional bonds here.

And if he needs further encouragement to trust I want him, not Aeron, I can provide that.

I steel my nerve and run my fingers lightly over Jaromir's knuckles. He inhales a sharp breath at the contact, so I do it again.

"What are you doing?" he murmurs against my ear, and oh, I shiver at that.

I turn my head to whisper against his skin. "I'm wondering what it will take for you to find your way to my tent tonight." My cheeks burn at my choice of words, but I can't bring myself to regret them. Not when he tightens his arms around my waist, pressing me even closer against him.

"To what end?" His voice has a playful edge, but I can recognize the real question behind it.

Now is not the time for declarations. I run the risk of scaring him off if I play this too heavily. "Hopefully we both find our end, otherwise I'll think you a most selfish bedmate."

One of his hands splays across my thigh, and his touch is an exquisite torture. "I've never been accused of being selfish by anyone I've ever lain with."

I ignore the stab of jealousy at the thought of him with others. That sentiment will ruin the game. Instead, I let out a dark laugh. "I'll be the judge of that."

He makes a noise suspiciously close to a growl. "I'll have to earn your good opinion."

His fingers trace my inner thigh. It's a good thing we're taking up the flank, but all it would take is one of our travel companions to look behind to see the state I'm in.

It's this vulnerability I hope he recognizes. Here we are in broad daylight, and I'm propositioning him into this game of brazen pursuit. Of who will pull back first. It won't be me, not even if Aeron glances back at us.

Everything is so much simpler when you admit the things you want without fear or shame.

When he finds the spot between my thighs, all strength flees my body. All he's doing is caressing me through the layers of my trousers and smallclothes, and fire lances through my blood. Images of what it will be like when he sneaks into my tent, into my bedroll, flood my mind. When we have nothing between us, and he can show me how generous a lover he supposedly is.

Welkin above, we should have done this days ago.

I let my head fall back against his shoulder, and his lips find my temple. This feels more intimate than the teasing hand between my thighs, and I turn my face, seeking his mouth. He lets me barely kiss him before he's angling his head away and whispering in my ear.

"Later. For now, just let me touch you."

I'm molten liquid at his words and his touch, but up ahead, the sound of Cadoc whistling carries back to us. Neith says something undecipherable, and Aeron lets out a loud laugh. No one has turned around, but if they did, I'm sure my face would give us away. I whisper back to Jaromir, praying to the goddess the others don't check on how far behind we've let ourselves fall.

"Is this why you were so mean to me? Because you were *aching* to touch me? What a needy, wanton thing you've turned out to be, Jaromir."

He laughs as his hand finds the laces to my trousers, loosening them enough to slip in, and now only a thin layer of cloth separates his thick fingers from the spot I desperately want him to focus on. "You never stop talking, do you? I can't tell if tonight I should gag you or make you scream so everyone hears you."

I bite my lip with a groan, and he laughs again.

His voice and his fingers are all I hear and feel, save for the heat crawling up my spine and neck. Nothing else exists outside this moment, where his hand mercilessly draws a gasp from my chest.

I almost miss the sharp whistle as it flies past us, a blur of movement sailing into the thicket. Another *whoosh*, this time with a *thunk* as an arrow sinks into our horse's ribs. When it rears up, I fall back, and the ground rushes up to meet me.

Chapter Twelve

I squint against the dirt in my eyes and the pounding in my head. All around me is a great commotion, but I can't seem to make sense of any of it. Jaromir hovers above me, and relief softens his features when he sees me, even as a trickle of blood trails from his eyebrow. He hauls me up. When I wince, his jaw clenches.

"Are you hurt?" His voice is demanding as he searches with gentle hands to find any injuries.

Everything sharpens into focus.

Cadoc whispers to our horse, running a soothing hand down her back, avoiding the spot where the arrow is still lodged in her side. Aeron holds up his hands in a calming posture, while Neith is alarmingly still.

A group of unfamiliar warriors, heavily armed and armored, block the narrow road. I count seven of them total; three of their group have dismounted and now form a stand-off. The trees suddenly feel too close, surrounding our parties on this too-small road. Tension crackles in the air. Swords are drawn. Everyone has a sharp line to their postures.

Everyone except for Aeron and the man standing within arm's reach of him.

I realize Jaromir is still waiting for an answer.

"Nothing's broken. I'm just shaken, I think."

He nods and keeps a firm grip on my wrist, leading me closer to the group and positioning himself in front of me.

From where I'm standing, I can see my lute fully intact on Jaromir's back, and despite whatever danger lies ahead, a surge of relief rushes through me.

I peer around his broad frame.

"It was an honest mistake," the man at the head of the group, the leader, I assume, says with a shrug. I can't detect the details of his face from back here, but his brown hair is cropped close to the scalp, and he stands a full head taller than Aeron. "Bollen over here is our greenest member." He shakes a man beside him affectionately. "He has shit for aim, but the intent was to get your attention not to hit your horse."

Aeron's smile is tight on his face. "Perhaps, in the future, you might select an alternative means for communication."

The leader grins, sliding his gaze to me with a predatory stare. "Perhaps he was distracted by their performance."

My cheeks burn, and I clench my hands into fists. That bastard had been watching us while they took their shot and aimed for our horse.

Jaromir's hand remains on the hilt of his sword as he angles his body to block me even more. "State your purpose."

The man laughs. "The name's Danion. And as for my purpose?" He snaps his fingers, and one of his men pulls a rolled-up parchment from his pack. Danion unrolls it and clears his throat. "Wanted: Any who crave adventure, travel, and unimaginable wealth. I, Sir Aeron Fowler, do swear that any and all who wish to join my team will be offered fair compensation, team building exercises, and the chance of a lifetime. We will travel the merchant roads as far as Gilbrock where we will then venture to uncharted terrain in search of a secret cache. Requirements to join my quest include, but are not limited to: courage, loyalty, fighting skills, survival skills, willingness to share with others, and leadership potential. I look forward to meeting you."

Danion rolls it back up with a sneer, while Aeron looks sick to his stomach. "We all fit your criteria, do we not, *Sir Aeron?*"

Cadoc hisses a curse, still tirelessly working to keep our horse calm. "I thought I tore all those notices down. I told you not to state your travel route!"

Aeron winces. "Hindsight, I suppose, is the greatest teacher of all."

Neith flexes her hand on the hilt of her sword, and Jaromir still hasn't allowed me to pass him. I lean around him to address their leader.

"You can't really expect us to believe you want to join up."

A slow grin creeps across Danion's face. His gaze darts between Jaromir and me. "Are you part of the compensation? Are we to *share* you when we grow bored?"

Jaromir yanks his sword from his sheath.

Danion's eyes flash, eager and hungry for a fight, as he pulls his sword from his belt.

This is the part where I should stay silent, shrink back, and hope Jaromir's threats are enough to deter this group.

Problem is, that doesn't sit too well with me, this idle business. It makes me appear an easy target, and in a world such as this, I can't allow myself to become that.

I scoff and step out from behind the safety of Jaromir's body. "Is that any way to address whom you hope to work with? We're going to need a lot more team-building exercises to rectify this rift between us."

Danion relaxes his stance, keeping his weapon light in his

grip. "What would you suggest? I'd hate to ruin this burgeoning relationship." He grins at Jaromir.

"Well," I say, "trust is a big issue for us at the moment, and you just shot our horse. Perhaps a show of good faith would be for you to give us one of your horses and be on your way. Perhaps we can agree to meet for a drink in a few days."

I'm not a fool, what I offer him is shit. But if I can distract him long enough for the others to form a plan, I have to try.

Jaromir reaches for me but I shrug him off. He needs to stop making me a target. Men who crave a fight are gluttonous the moment they find a weakness.

I edge closer, keeping my steps light and unhurried.

Before I know it, I'm standing before Danion. He isn't so formidable up close. He has a splattering of freckles across the bridge of his slender nose, pale green eyes, and short brown hair. He has the sort of face you'd imagine a lovelorn farmhand might have, one that harbors deep affections for the landowner's daughter in a romance tale.

But there is something about the sharpness of his gaze, something that speaks of cruelty and malice.

Danion circles the sword in his hand, the metallic rush of every swing sings through the air, blowing the hair back from my face for how close he taunts me.

"I've got a better idea," Danion says. "How's about we join *Sir Aeron's* crew and take care of this venture ourselves. Think you might be of use to us?" He's openly leering now, and my skin crawls under his thorough stare.

I glare at him—at his disgustingly arrogant face. Keep the tone light; do *not* incite violence.

"I'd rather fuck a fire iron."

Whoops.

Aeron chokes, and Neith lets out a sharp exhale.

But Danion returns my glare. "That can be arranged."

Aeron clears his throat and steps closer, until he's right

beside me. "I believe we got off on the wrong foot—my fault, of course." He places a hand over his unarmored chest. Just this morning, I was grateful for his lack of armor, but now the icy grip of panic clenches in my gut. "I penned this flyer when I was without a crew. Now that I have one, I find we've become somewhat of a tight unit. I appreciate your interest, but the positions have all been filled." He gives his dazzling smile, the one that's all heroic charm. I almost believe his blind optimism. That false bravado and good manners are formidable weapons against steel.

For several heartbeats, no one moves or so much as utters a sound.

Finally, Danion speaks. "A right shame."

His sword cuts through the air, and I don't have time to register the impact. I don't have a chance to cringe or leap out of the way, and yet, I'm falling.

My body hits the earth with a resounding thud, rattling my teeth and sending stars exploding through my vision. My head pounds, and when I place my fingers to the spot, they come away coated with blood. Somehow, I've fallen sideways and knocked my head against a large stone.

No. I didn't just fall. I was pushed.

I glance up, a scream building in my throat.

Aeron stands where I stood not seconds ago, Danion's sword is embedded through his back, and the bloody tip juts from his chest. He yanks it free with a swift pull, and Aeron sways on his feet before sinking to his knees.

Aeron's lips are already stained red. A soft expression claims his face, almost one of disbelief as if he doesn't understand what's just happened. He slumps forward, and a scream rips from my throat.

I crawl to him, ignoring the clashing of steel and the shouts of pain. Arrows whistle through the air, and a responding groan sounds before the heavy *thump* of a body hitting the earth. But I refuse to look. Instead, I turn Aeron over so he can face the sky, and I can see the light remaining in his blue eyes. They're growing hazier by the second. The fight continues, and I can't find it in me to care. Everything narrows to this moment.

"Aeron," I murmur, "stay with me."

His lungs rattle with each wet inhale, and his fingers twitch at his side. Without thought, I grab his hand and press it against my cheek.

"Neith." Blood spurts from his lips, and a crushing despair presses in my chest.

He is dying. He is going to die. What do I do? How can I stop this?

I can't.

I can't.

"Neith," he repeats. "Neith... I need..."

"Neith!" Her name screeches through my lips.

"Home..." A tear escapes the corner of Aeron's eye, trailing down his temple and carving a path through the dirt on his skin. "Wanna go home." His eyes are losing focus, and I squeeze his hand as if I can hold on to his spirit just a little longer. He's looking past me now, and a soft smile curves his bloody mouth. "Neith," he breathes.

It is his last word. His last breath, and the last time I see life in those eyes before they usher in the void of death.

There's a sharp inhale above me. I glance up to find Neith fisting a hand in her hair as she backs away.

I place Aeron's hand against his chest as gently as I can before I raise onto unsteady feet. All around us is a massacre. Bloodied bodies decorate the road, and utter stillness fills the air. Cadoc leans heavily against a tree, his nose bleeding and his face crumpled in pain as he regards Aeron's corpse.

Jaromir stands nearby, chest heaving and face painted with blood. I can already tell, it isn't his own. Our gazes meet, and his stare thoroughly assesses me head to toe before finding my eyes again. There's a flicker of something. Relief? Longing? But it's smothered when he drops his attention to where Aeron lies entirely too still.

The words come to me again, the ones I thought of but never wrote down.

For where stories end, they begin anew
So instead of farewell, I'll say to you

Until we meet again.

Chapter Thirteen

"Home... *Wanna go home.*"

Aeron's words echo in the back of my mind, over and over like the ostinato of a song. I hear them in the stillness of the unbearable quiet. These words remain while Aeron is gone.

This night is darker than the last—than any night before it.

We've long since left that bloodied patch of road behind, along with the corpses of our attackers. But the smell of burning flesh stays with me, acrid and stomach turning, reminding me of how we piled the remains of our felled enemies and lit them ablaze. When I asked why we were bothering, Cadoc answered, "Because worse things are drawn to the dead."

No one has spoken since.

Except Aeron. His memory is an unrelenting whisper in my head, scratching against my skull.

His body had been carefully prepared by Neith. Wrapped and placed on a pyre Jaromir built. I wonder if his family honors that practice or if they would have wanted him buried on their soil. He can't even return to his father's resting place now, but Cadoc was right. We couldn't bring his body with us.

His armor sits in a neat pile beside his pack, his sword and belongings all carefully placed as if at any moment he'll return.

Neith glares into the fire, shadows dancing along the scar on her face, and she takes another deep drink of her flagon. She hasn't shown her tears, but the way her eyes have that sunken-in look, I can assume she's hiding her weeping as she hides most things.

Cadoc sniffs, wiping his nose with the back of his hand. He tosses a fistful of dirt into the fire.

Jaromir has cleaned and sharpened every blade in our camp. His broad shoulders carry a tight line of tension, and the urge to reach out to him overcomes me—

I smother it down and rub my eyes instead.

Aeron is gone.

It seems like a poorly timed joke. That someone whose light burns so bright could be snuffed out in the blink of an eye.

A throat clears across the fire—Cadoc—and it ruptures the careful quiet of our camp.

"What now?"

It's a question that's plagued me, and I'm eternally grateful for Cadoc asking it.

"What do you mean?" Jaromir's voice, the first time I've heard it in hours, is thick and rough.

"Without Aeron..." Cadoc trails off. We all catch his meaning. Without Aeron, there's no sense in continuing. No funding for the trip, no reward when we finish. We still don't even know what we'll find at our destination. Though I've translated the map, that doesn't serve as proof the map itself is real or that anything awaits us at the end of the journey. Even my part in this is rendered useless. Aeron hired me to sing of his exploits, and now it seems the only thing I have occasion to write is a eulogy.

"We turn back, take Syl home," Jaromir says, and even though I knew this, my heart plummets. He scrubs a hand down his face, squeezing his eyes shut. When he opens them again, he wears a tight expression. "Then... I suppose we return to whatever we left waiting for us."

His words sink like a stone in my gut. What, or whom, did he leave behind? Surely, he's unattached if he freely seeks his pleasure on the road, but did he say as much? No... he's merely remarked on the loneliness.

"At first light, then." Cadoc wipes his cheeks, nodding his head with grim determination.

Neith still hasn't spoken.

I want to fight them on this. I don't want to go home, not yet. I don't know what I want... but I can't pretend things will go back to normal, not after this.

SLEEP EVADES ME, and I find myself wandering out of my tent long before the sun is due to rise. The fire is spent, and darkness covers the quiet camp. A familiar form sits against a fallen log.

Jaromir.

We haven't spoken since the attack, and without my permission, my footsteps propel me toward him. He watches my approach, but I can't see his expression.

I don't ask if I can sit. I claim the spot at his side, allowing the full warmth of his leg to settle against mine.

"Couldn't sleep?" These are the first words I've spoken to him.

"Not tonight," he says, and despite my pain at the prospect

of returning to Hollowden, just hearing his voice soothes some of the ache.

My thoughts turn to his words by the fire, of returning to whatever waited for them. He doesn't owe me anything. He's merely a travel companion, a colleague I've kissed twice and... well, he did shove his hand between my legs but we had no understanding or commitment to imply he had someone waiting for him. I should just let it be, since we're parting ways soon anyway, and it's none of my business—

"Who awaits your return?"

I don't even regret the words, even if they leap from my tongue without my consent.

"My brother's wife and my two nieces," Jaromir says this with a resigned sigh. "I owe them much."

It's clear he doesn't want to delve into details.

"Where is your brother?" My eyes have adjusted to the dark, and I catch the way he grimaces.

"Damir died last summer season."

Oh. Perhaps I shouldn't have asked. I can recognize burying old hurts beneath a shallow grave when I see it. If speaking of it still brings him pain, it would be best to let the conversation end here.

"What happened to him?"

Trouble is, I want to know everything there is to learn about Jaromir, including the pain he'd rather mask.

"I asked him to help me complete a contract—easy money; the only true threat was imprisonment. It was a land squabble, and the previous owners claimed their property had been cut in half by their neighbor. Something about a garden they'd planted years ago and the town magistrate calling squatter's rights. Our job was to set fire to their garden in exchange for decent coin. Damir's wife was pregnant with the twins, and they could use any extra scrap they could get." Jaromir releases a heavy sigh. "I didn't need his help, but I couldn't get him to accept the money for free; his pride wouldn't allow it.

We were almost to the designated spot when we uncovered an arachnida nest. Damir took a barb to the heart and died before I could even carry him back into town."

I've heard tales of arachnida nests. In general, the giant spider-like creatures left you alone if you steered clear of their nesting grounds. But step too close…

Jaromir's breathing has quickened, taking an edge of desperation, and without thought, I grab his hand.

"Oh, Jaromir. I'm so sorry."

His fingers gently lace with mine, so instead of a comforting touch, it's more of an intimate hold.

"The past is set in stone," he says with a note of finality. "All I can do now is make sure his wife and daughters want for nothing. That's what this trip was meant to achieve. I was going to tend to the needs they now face in his absence; it wouldn't cover the debt, not by leagues, but it would lessen their burden. The loss they suffered at my hands."

I grab his chin and turn him to face me. That familiar crease in his brow has returned, so I run my thumb over it before cupping his cheek. "What happened to your brother was awful, but it wasn't your fault. Life is hard enough without bearing the guilt of living when others fall. You've done right by Damir's family, and that's more than enough."

When I go to pull my hand away, he catches it and holds it in place.

No wonder he had no patience for me at first. If he remotely perceived me as a means to delay his care and return for them, that would be reason enough. But still… it's such a shame to come all this way only to return home.

Home.

An ideal forever destined to remain out of grasp. I mean, I'm used to Hollowden, and it was harder to leave than I thought it would be, but the idea of returning fills me with dread. I miss Kingsley and Brigitta something fierce, but I can't go back to being the oddity of the village. Until I make a name for myself, something bigger than the sharpness of my ears, there's nothing for me there. Maybe there never will be.

"Why must you bring me back?" I should have spoken up over the fire, with Cadoc and Neith to weigh in, but something held my tongue. Something that doesn't halt my words now.

Jaromir's brows raise. "Because it's your home."

I shake my head and run my hands over my hair to hide my ears. "No, it isn't."

His hand catches mine, gently pulling it away. With a featherlight touch, he tucks my hair behind my pointed ear, lingering at the most sensitive spot. "Where is home?"

"I'll let you know when I find it." I cringe away from him, discomfort warring with a foreign shivery feeling.

No one has ever touched my ears.

The sudden memory of my journey across the sea, of hiding below deck, in the cargo hold and crying myself to sleep, takes shape. Fear of the unknown, grief of loss, it was all an overwhelming swell like the waves against the ship. But more than anything, it was the loneliness. I didn't quite understand it as such. It took the shape of missing the safety of sitting on Da's shoulders. It was curling in on myself, thoughts screaming, *I want my Mama,* over and over.

I've long since grown from that scared little elfling, braving the great wide world on my own, but that pulse of loneliness always remains.

I allow a practiced smirk to curl against my mouth. "Perhaps when I become a world-famous bard, I'll have a home on every continent."

"I have no doubt of this."

Perhaps it's selfish for me to think this now, but this trip, this shot... it was supposed to be my chance. It feels like a loss, like a broken promise. Does it feel that way to Jaromir? He was counting on this payment, this chance to care for his brother's family. And with the ill-timed thrust of a sword, it's over.

I hug my knees, but it does nothing to quell the weight in my stomach. Aeron is gone. His life was cut short and my chances along with it. If only we'd stayed another day in Astervale. If only he hadn't been shot in the first place. If only he hadn't posted those foolish flyers.

If only.

If only.

If only.

"Is there anywhere else you'd prefer to go?" Jaromir's voice snags my attention. "If Hollowden is so loathsome, where would you choose?"

If I could go anywhere? That list is unbearably long and unattainable, so I offer the quickest answer I can give. "I'd continue on our quest to find the dragon."

Something clicks in me, and the rightness of it all sings in my veins. It courses through my blood until I have no recourse but to leap to my feet and stroll to where my lute rests in my tent. I snatch it up and return to Jaromir's side. His curious gaze burns against my skin, but I need a moment to think before I can answer the questions begging for release.

I pluck a soft tune, quietly enough I shouldn't disturb the others, and familiar enough I don't need to think on what my fingers are doing. Muscle memory takes over, and the comforting ambience helps clear my spinning thoughts.

Jaromir's large hand clamps over the neck of my lute, silencing my playing. I glare at him and peel his fingers off.

"Don't touch my lute." I quickly resume plucking. In order for this to work, I need everyone on board. Well, *need* is a strong word. But I've grown fond of everyone, and the loss of Aeron is more than I wish to bear already. Cadoc is useful for basic wound care, Neith for her blades and her wits, Jaromir for his fighting skills and knowledge of the land.

We can do this.

"Jaromir," I say, finally putting down my instrument and facing him with my most winning smile, "I have a proposition for you."

His blank stare must hide his eager anticipation. A practiced mask, I should think.

"We carry on and see the end of this journey. We complete Aeron's quest, everyone gets paid, you can still offer this to your sister-in-law and nieces. I can still bring eternal glory to Aeron's name, thus fulfilling his life's greatest wish."

He's still staring at me, no revealing expression even hinting its approach. Despite the heat crawling up my neck, I continue.

"We already have the supplies, the destination, and the funding." I avoid glancing at Aeron's pack where his coin purse still resides. We divided up the coin we found on the bodies of the mercenaries, but I know it pales in comparison to what Aeron carried. We weren't going to touch it, but if it's in pursuit of his mission, it isn't stealing, is it?

"You want to pretend he's still alive. For coin."

"No. I want to bring him honor even after death for glory... and coin." There's a distinction there, I'm sure of it. "Tell me, and be honest, knowing Aeron... what would he want?"

Jaromir hesitates, a strange look coming over him before a tolerant smile claims his mouth. "He'd want us to forge on. Come fire and brimstone or torrential flood, he'd want this done." He glances past my shoulder, to where Neith's tent sits. "And he'd want her comfortably taken care of for life."

I nod, grinning. "So, it's settled. We'll find the dragon, restore honor to Aeron's name, rub his brother's face in it, and find riches beyond our wildest dreams."

"I don't know who you think is paying us the second half, but none of us will walk away rich."

"There's always a kernel of truth to be found in legends. If there's a fabled hoard, even if it isn't in treasure, it's going to be something valuable. Plus, if we're all heroes, I doubt there's a tavern in the country where we won't be offered free drink."

Jaromir shakes his head, wearing an indulgent smile. "That alone is worth the trip."

IF JAROMIR THINKS I'll have a change of heart in the cold light of day, he is dead wrong. Morning ushers in a renewed determination, and by the time Neith and Cadoc rise from their bedrolls, I'm practically vibrating with nerves.

Excitement. Vibrating with excitement.

Cadoc wordlessly tosses a golden pear to Neith and sets to work packing up camp. That won't do. I was hoping to have their attention over breakfast to ease them in.

I clear my throat. "I had a thought last night. One that Jaromir whole-heartedly supports." This earns me a grunt of disapproval, but I ignore it. "I've been thinking about our next course of action."

At this, Cadoc stills. Neith pulls a knife from her boot and slices into the flesh of her pear.

"Next course of action?" Cadoc asks, brow lifting.

"It would be a mistake to quit now. Aeron... he wanted this. Wanted to restore honor to his name and earn his rightful place in history. In his family's legacy." My throat tightens. "We owe him that much."

Neith's eyes flash. "Aeron is dead because of 'is silly pursuit. Why should we sully his memory further?"

I expected her anger, but still my cheeks burn. "It isn't sullying his memory. We're honoring his wishes." He wanted to go home. To be welcomed home. He deserves a hero's welcome.

"Not to state the obvious," Cadoc cuts in, "but how can a dead man slay a dragon?"

I wet my lips, my speech already prepared. "We carry on as if he still lives. I write and sing ballads in his name, lifting him higher beyond measure. We stay in as many inns and taverns as we can, spreading news of his exploits. Maybe we even pick up a few contracts along the way and complete them in his name. No one knows what he looks like, and we can always come up with excuses as to why he isn't physically in the tavern with us. All the while, his name will gain traction until his brother is forced to restore his honor, and then at the very end of our journey..."

I take a deep breath. This is the riskiest part of my argument, and I don't know how they'll react.

"At the very end... he will die bravely, taking the dragon down with him."

Stunned silence descends over the camp.

The urge to lower my gaze from their scrutinizing stares is overwhelming, but I keep my head high, taking whatever judgment they pass on the chin.

Cadoc is the first to break the silence. "How do we get paid?"

"Aeron was fully outfitted with the budget for this journey, along with the first half of our compensation." I remember these terms because I objected to not getting the first half upfront, and the latter half when we finish, but he was insistent that he didn't wish to carry that much coin on him. "Our second half, we'll collect when we bring news of his heroic death to his brother." This is the biggest stretch in my plan. We have no promise that his family will honor a bargain struck in Aeron's name, but that's where my optimism bridges the gap.

Cadoc winces and Neith shakes her head. "I dinnae ken if Arnorr will give us a copper. But... I agree with ye on everything else." A muscle feathers in her jaw, and her gaze drops to the ground. "Aeron would want this."

I nod emphatically, thanking my lucky stars she was quick to sway, before I turn to Cadoc.

His lip curls, and he whines. "Another month on the road. I can't stomach staying in these small towns for more than a night, you know."

"But, Cadoc," I say, "when we visit every town and tavern from here to Kalinia, you'll be famous from my ballads. It won't feel like vagrancy, oh no; it'll be more like you're a visiting nobleman." I arch a brow meaningfully. "And I can be *very* generous with some of my descriptions."

A broad grin stretches across his handsome face, dimples creasing his dark cheeks. "Well... when you put it that way..."

"Is that a yes?"

His grin only widens before it falters. "Wait, what do you mean generous? You think I need fictionalized accounts of my prowess? I'll pull it out right now, I don't even care." He reaches for his trousers, but Jaromir clears his throat pointedly.

"Don't. We've all seen it. We know."

"Truly, we're all in accord?" I ignore the exchange, even as Cadoc keeps arguing with Jaromir about the lengths at which he'll go to defend his honor. Neith finds my gaze and gives an almost imperceptible nod.

It's more than enough. It's a plan and a promise—

I will bring Aeron honor. And I will fight his dragon.

Chapter Fourteen

"I'll have another ale," Cadoc calls out with a wink. Jaromir dutifully ignores him in favor of studying his cards with far more interest than they warrant. The four of us arrived in Bucklebrook earlier this evening and claimed a table at The Laughing Goat Tavern. We began a game of Sinners and Saints—a truly loathsome card game if you ask me. No one has asked, but I make my displeasure known.

"I still don't understand why the supposed Saints cards carry more value. If anything, my Thief here should defeat an Errant Knight in cunning alone."

Cadoc groans. This isn't the first time I've complained this round nor the last. It's far too enjoyable witnessing the corner of Jaromir's mouth lift each time I provide much-needed commentary.

"True enough," Neith says in a somber tone, "but things never work out th'way they should."

I fall silent at that. Neith hasn't discussed Aeron directly, but I feel the weight of his presence over every word both spoken and unspoken. Part of me longs to take her aside and push her to share everything she's thinking and feeling. But I know it wouldn't be welcomed.

Not yet anyway.

Two tables to my left sits the man who was kind enough to purchase Jaromir's horse, at a steep discount, of course. Cadoc patched the horse up the best he could and assured Jaromir she would live. But we couldn't bring her on our journey, not after the injury she sustained. It was only when Jaromir whispered a brief goodbye to the horse that I learned her name: Chessa.

I let my gaze fall to the boisterous room around us. Heavy posts and beams, all etched with goats in various poses, adorn the space. How did they add such detail in the strangest places? Unless they designed the wood before reinforcing the structure. Either way, an odd if not delightful choice. I can already guess what Kingsley's reaction would be if I suggested such a thing. It would start with a laugh and end with a stern reprimand. Always so averse to change. Someone at The Laughing Goat Tavern had some interesting ideas and enough pull to see them through. Above the bar, a row of clay tankards, painted dark green against a silhouette of a goat, hang from hooks. They appear firmly held in place, but I can't help imagining a strong gust of wind knocking them all to shatter against the polished bar top.

Jaromir clears his throat, pulling my attention from the precarious mugs and back to the furrow of concentration between his dark brows.

"So, now that I know you hold a Thief in your hand, my Errant Knight calls to arms." Jaromir tosses his card onto the table with a flick of his wrist. The armored figure framed in embellished filigree stares up at me.

I glare at him and whip my card toward his chest. "Have it then, but know I accept defeat under protest, for this is a silly game with unrealistic outcomes."

Massaging my temples, I debate the likelihood they'd notice if I just slipped out the door. It's too hot. And loud. And crowded. All conditions I normally enjoy in a tavern, but this night it makes my skin feel too tight for my body.

Jaromir eyes me and frowns. "You all right?"

I don't want his scrutiny. So with a theatrical sigh, I roll my eyes. "I'd be better if I didn't play with lousy cheats."

"You're just sore you lost." He collects the rest of the cards and begins shuffling them with practiced ease. "It's your turn to get the next round."

"But I've had to get every round."

"Mmhmm." He cuts the deck and begins tossing us each our seven card hands.

I shove my chair back and stomp my way over to the bar. Cadoc calls out about his ale again.

I'm clipped by a broad shoulder, and it jerks my head to the side. My hands are over my cap before I can think, checking and holding. The man grunts his apology before shuffling off. My chest is still tight, my heart a battering ram against my ribs. I need to relax. And watch where I'm walking.

I glance behind me. Jaromir is watching with a steady gaze, and I offer what I'm sure is a feeble wave. I'm fine. Twitchy, but fine.

The barkeep pops up from where he must have been crouching below the bar, and I jump at his sudden appearance. He has a head of messy auburn hair, some of it hanging in his green eyes. His skin is warm in tone, far deeper than I'd expect of a red-haired fellow. He's younger than I thought. A teasing smile curls his mouth, dimpling his bronze skin.

"Sorry," he says quickly, pulling the towel off his shoulder and wiping down the wood surface between us. "I didn't expect you back so soon."

I'm still trying to calm the prestissimo tempo of my heart. "I didn't expect to lose so quickly."

The barkeep chuckles, flinging the cloth back in place over his shoulder. The action is so like Kingsley, my stomach lurches.

I remember when I first stumbled into Hollowden. Travel had been... rough. I'd just up and left Birchfield where the sleazy owner of the Red Wyvern Tavern had tried to bribe me into trading sex for food when he found me scraping half eaten food off dirty plates to fill my belly. I hadn't thought or planned; I'd just run. Nothing but my lute, the few coins I'd earned from my set, and my gorgeous cap crammed down over my ears. When I showed up days later at The Rusty Nail, I could barely stand. But I convinced Kingsley to let me sing, and a woman I'd come to realize was his wife, Brigitta, asked me to sample a few dishes for their Winter Solstice celebration.

Now I know, they were looking out for me.

I blink away the unwelcome emotion blurring my vision and fix my gaze on the barkeep before me. I hadn't paid much attention to him before, eager in my pursuit to return to the table. But I'm tired of losing, and Cadoc can wait for his damned ale. The barkeep is a stockier build, all thick shoulders on a wide frame. It's only upon closer inspection I realize he might be of dwarven descent. His mouth quirks, wrinkling the wide cut of his square jaw.

It isn't strange to see a barkeep of dwarven descent. Now if he were elven, the easy air of camaraderie would likely be replaced with tension and vaguely hostile threats amongst the rowdier drunkards. Perhaps this is due to the Hawthokian alliance with the humans during The Unification, otherwise known as *An Call Mòr*, The Great Loss, among elves. There was dissent and infighting amongst the dwarves, but those that took up arms were rewarded with land and minor titles in Targgein. Both human and dwarven history has been archived throughout time, painting them as the heroes against the ancient elves—beings of power and malice. Even though a tenuous peace existed for over a century, the uprising of fear and distrust of elves was a seed sown long ago and brought to fruition during the raids. Elven texts were destroyed along with our most sacrosanct structures. Our history has only survived through spoken word. That my da passed down knowledge of the ancient elven alphabet and our history is a rebellion in and of itself.

"Were you going to order anything?"

"Soon. Right now, I'm leading a lesson on delaying gratification."

"Your name is Syl, right?"

I blink, then nod. "Right. Short for Sylvaine, and you are...?"

"Tomas." He leans his elbows on the bar, and I find myself leaning in, too, as if we're in each other's confidence. "So, Syl, short for Sylvaine, what are you doing with a group of hired swords?" His gaze darts beyond my shoulder, a glimmer of excitement in his eyes, while his cheeks and the tips of his ears flush bright red.

This is just the opener I need. The barkeep, Tomas, is practically begging for me to launch into a performance. My lute rests against Jaromir's seat, ready and waiting. This is my chance, the first opportunity to prove to the others and myself that this is the right path. That even though Aeron is gone, we can carry on his legacy.

Blood rushes in my ears, and the din of noise muffles to an inaudible garble.

"Home... Wanna go home."

His words echo in my mind, and images of blood filling the cracks in his dry lips assault me. I squeeze my eyes shut tight as if that will expel the memory of his death.

I can do this. I'm stronger than this.

But the words don't come. They stall on my tongue, and a

shaky panic grips my chest. It stretches and fills until I'm sure something is bound to break. Something wobbly climbs up my throat, and if I didn't know any better, I'd suspect the pricking in my eyes might be tears.

Tomas' face flashes in alarm, and before I can protest, he's rounded the bar to stand before me.

"Are you well?" His hands find my arms, and though it's harmless comfort he offers, it only serves to heighten the panic clutching my chest.

I can't catch my breath. I can't utter a word. So, I shake my head as his face blurs before me. I want to reach up and pull his hands away. I want to fix my hat and make sure my ears are hidden. But my arms remain heavy at my sides as the pressure tightens my throat.

My stomach rolls, and I'm on that ship again. Alone. I'm hunting rats in the gutter to fill my cramping belly while avoiding the lampposts so the city guard doesn't find me. I'm trapped in the possessive grasp of the tavern owner after he found me eating from the garbage.

I can't think. Can't breathe. The room spins, and my knees threaten to buckle. My heart pounds so fast I fear it might leap from my chest. Something terrible is happening, and I can't stop it.

"Don't touch her." The deep rasp of Jaromir's voice skitters down my spine. I can't even bring myself to turn and look at him, but every nerve in my body is aware of his presence.

Tomas' hands vanish from my arms, and the weight in my chest slightly lifts. Stronger hands cover the spots that still itch. Jaromir's chest is at my back, and I almost sag into him. I'm steered through the room, tripping over my feet as blurred faces pass. A constant stream of voices surrounds me, but it's like my ears have popped and everything is muffled save for the rapid pulse in my head. He continues his steady march, large hands gripping me and keeping me upright. But it doesn't feel rough or threatening. He doesn't stop even when the night air blasts me in the face. He keeps us moving until my feet find their way onto slick grass, and a round moon blankets the field with a silvery glow.

I sink to my knees, and finally, *finally*, inhale a ragged breath. A choked noise escapes my chest, and my next breath is a pathetic stuttered thing.

Jaromir's arms come around me, but he doesn't say a word. He just holds me while the tremors gradually stop and my breathing returns to normal. Bracketed between his thighs, I press into his warmth. My heart is no longer trying to break free from my chest, and the throbbing in my ears fades until the sound of crickets and peeper frogs in the distance fills the silence.

I don't know how long we sit there. Long enough the heat leaves my skin and my trousers are damp from the grass.

Jaromir hasn't said a word. Hasn't asked me what was wrong or sought any answers. It's a comfort because I'm not sure I could offer any.

I lean into him, resting my head on his chest and filling my lungs with fresh air carrying his scent. He seems in no hurry to move as he rubs slow circles against my back. There's no intent in this other than to soothe, and goddess, I haven't been held like this in over a decade. He offers no words, but I feel what he doesn't say in every stroke of his palm.

I'm here. You're safe. Breathe.

It's a strange thing, his silence. I once loathed him for it—found it mocking and cruel—but now I can't help but wonder if he learned to communicate best without speaking.

I, on the other hand, can't stay silent a moment longer.

"Thank you." My voice sounds small, but it lands heavily in the quiet.

Jaromir rumbles a soft grunt of acknowledgement but keeps rubbing my back.

"I don't know what happened in there." I know what I felt physically, but it makes no sense.

"My brother used to get caught in these panics," Jaromir murmurs against my hair. "It happened more when he was stressed. But there was no predicting when or where it would happen or what might set him off." He's still rubbing circles against my back, and his voice is a pleasant vibration against my cheek. "He used to say it felt like death that never comes."

I nod against his chest. That's exactly what it felt like. "I don't understand why it happened though."

"You've been through a lot in these few days."

"We've all been through a lot."

Jaromir tips my chin up to look at him, and it's only when he wipes his thumb against my cheeks I even realize I'd been crying. "Don't diminish what you feel. There is no shame in this."

His eyes search my face, not with the intensity I've come to expect from him but with something much softer. I squirm as something unpleasant coils in my gut, and I pull away suddenly needing the distance.

"I'm stronger than this, and I don't know why my body betrayed me like that. Perhaps it was something I ate. Or rancid ale. Did the ale taste funny to you? I don't drink enough to pass judgment, but it certainly had a strange flavor to me. In fact, I have half a mind to demand recompense for my near poisoning—"

"Syl." Jaromir's hand finds my neck, his thumb brushing over my pulse. "You are strong. This does not counter that truth. There is no shame." He repeats himself, and something about those words makes my throat constrict.

"You said... you said when we first started our journey I shouldn't be coming. And you were right. If I'm too weak to handle—" I bite my lip to keep it from trembling.

Anger flashes across his face. "You are *not* weak. And I was a sodding prick to make you feel unwelcome." With slow, careful movements, he pulls the cap from my head. Cool air hits my sweaty hairline, and I shiver. He tucks my hair behind my ear, lingering against my skin. "I'm sorry."

His apology washes over me, and damn him, it fills every ache I didn't know was there. I lean into his touch, gasping when the full sensation of his fingers against my ear lights a tingle throughout my body.

I crawl back into the safety of his arms, resting my head against his chest. I can't bring myself to acknowledge what his words mean to me, but I suspect he can understand. I want to stay right here, in this very spot, for as long as I'm able. But my lute yet remains in that tavern, as do Cadoc and Neith. "The others will wonder where we are."

Jaromir whispers against my hair. "Let them wonder a little while longer."

Chapter Fifteen

I tune my lute, gently twisting its pegs while plucking each string. We have a full house again, and this time, I'll make use of it.

I can't even bring myself to regret last evening. In the place where I might keep a hefty supply of shame, only a pleasant warmth remains. After several more moments of relishing the safety of Jaromir's embrace, he snuck me into my room so I wouldn't have to face the crowded tavern. Who knew climbing outer walls could be so fun? He even let me stand atop his shoulders, a fact I most delighted in.

Now he sits at the center table, beneath a goat-adorned beam, arms crossed, and watching me with his signature furrowed brow. But what I once assumed was disapproval, I now recognize as concentration. His mouth twitches, and it's all the invitation I need to flash him my signature stage smile. The one that's all teeth and charm.

Neith stands toward the back, leaning against the support post and sipping from her tankard.

Cadoc remains at the bar, his hand gently gripping his

tankard while he chats with Tomas. Tomas doesn't dare glance at me, which is a shame since I need the barkeep to pay attention when I sing so he might collect my stories and pass them on to future patrons. No matter, the show must go on.

Everyone is positioned accordingly. Once word spreads, it'll be easier to allow my ballad to speak for itself. But in its fledgling state, some extra help can't hurt.

I begin to pluck, and it fails to carry over the din of noise— of dozens of conversations and boisterous laughter. Jaromir frowns, and I give him an almost imperceptible shake of my head.

This is how it begins. I blend with the sound of the tavern, as if I was always there, and then once I've woven myself into the fabric of the energy, I demand their attention.

I don't bother singing, not yet. But I pluck a few tunes, some folk songs from the continent and one I picked up from Kingsley about a boar who stalks a hunter. When finally it seems like I've joined the general noise, and earned a few curious glances, I stand and kick my stool away, jumping straight into a heavy-handed strum.

The tavern quiets enough I'm sure I'll be heard.

This is it.

"Ladies and Gentlemen, allow me to guide you on your journey tonight. I'll shed light on the path to certain peril and nefarious villains. Leading you on an epic quest that will test your mettle and measure the contents of your heart!"

With a quick toss of my head, I double check that my cap is positioned just right and in no danger of falling. I can feel the feather bounce with the movement, and a few gazes follow the action.

This is the first time I'll share some of what I wrote of Aeron's ballad, but first, the prelude which went over so well in the last tavern. Jaromir even suggested it, claiming he could weather some embarrassment if it meant earning Aeron some good will for rescuing his cursed prick.

A true grin dawns my face, and I begin.

WHEN THE CROWD has accepted me as their main source of entertainment, hanging on to my every word and cheering at all the correct prompts, I know it's time.

Jaromir only winced once or twice during my introductory ballad, and perhaps I should change the name of the poor sod afflicted by the curse.

No matter. That's a question for another day.

I pluck an uplifting tune. It reminds me of the first day we set out on our adventure. Of how the horizon was a promise of destiny fulfilled, and how bright the dawn seemed. Bright and gleaming like Aeron's armor.

A dull ache settles in my chest, and I clear my throat.

"Sir Aeron has the heart of a warrior and the mercy of a saint

With warmth that rivals the sun and drives darkness away

Man or beast of evil intent will fall to his sword, fall to his sword

He'll bring us deliverance, mark my words, mark my words

He fells poisonous creatures of malicious intent

Spares no killer, and no earthly threat

I rode along by his side, saw with my own eyes

The depth of his courage and the strength inside

The tale of our quest is not one that's short

So if you've the patience, and offer no retort

I'll recount to you our journey though it stretches on

For we are not finished, we've adventures beyond

But here is a taste of what's passed so far."

I slow my plucking a touch and shift to a minor key. This part isn't sung but spoken word against the backdrop of my playing. I can feel Jaromir's gaze on me like a brand. My ballad is not yet finished, but we decided I'd share what I had so far, and each performance add a little more.

"The road-wary adventurers found a secluded spot to make camp. Unbeknownst to them, they weren't the only ones in the shadowy forest that night.

The creatures of the forest were drawn to the band of travelers like moths to a flame..."

When I end part one of Aeron's ballad, I've told the tale of how he vanquished the monstrous beetles, and with help from his loyal crew, slew the entire nest. My forehead drips sweat into my eyes. My fingers ache from new calluses, and my neck is burning.

But goddess, it feels so good to play. To slip into the role of storyteller. I seek out Jaromir in the audience, and I can practically feel each clap of his hands as he smirks at me with warmth brimming his dark eyes. Neith applauds from her spot, where a table of miners, if the soot on their clothes is proof, raise their tankards in her direction. She dips her chin, grabbing one of their drinks and slugging it back with practiced ease.

Cadoc claps Tomas on the back with a broad grin on his handsome face. The stools beside him are suddenly occupied by two comely lasses, their cheeks flushed with laughter and spirits. But he only has eyes for Tomas, who is returning his smile with a blatant appraisal I can only assume means we won't be seeing Cadoc again until morning.

Good for him. And I hope he spills all the details. To enhance the ballad, obviously.

"Thank you for being such a marvelous audience! Be sure to tip your server!" I bow and then sling my lute onto my back.

My body is alive with excitement, riding the high of a performance.

Jaromir pulls out a chair and slides an ale my way. I wave away the drink and hesitate over the chair.

"I'm too restless to sit," I say, bouncing on my heels.

Jaromir nods, rising to his feet. He towers over me, and I find myself tipping my head back to look him in the eye. His dark hair is tied back in its signature knot, and since we've stayed in town for an additional night, he had the chance to trim his beard, highlighting the sharpness of his jaw.

"What do you wish to do?" His deep, gravelly voice does funny things to my stomach. Even in an overcrowded tavern that reeks of spilled ale and sweat.

"I wish to be outside. Howling at the moon or running around stark naked. I don't know. Something ridiculous."

He nods as if this is a perfectly reasonable response and gently takes my hand, pulling me behind him. His palm is rough against my skin, and his calluses only make me want to know how his hands would feel everywhere else.

I beckon Neith just before we cross the threshold. I can't get Cadoc's attention with how far across the bar he's leaning to whisper in Tomas' ear. Tomas' cheeks flush, and he bites his lip.

Neith bids farewell to her new friends and follows us into the night.

The sky is muted by clouds, but every so often, the moon dips into view.

"I'd say 'at was a success," Neith says with a soft huff.

I nod, and the feather on my cap bobs in response. Pulling it from my head, I rake my fingers through my sweaty hair. "The crowd was very responsive. And no one threw anything at me."

Jaromir grunts his agreement, but his stare is firmly locked on where I comb my tangled hair.

"The folks near me enjoyed it," Neith says. "But they want t'see Aeron. Right now, ye're creating 'is fabled hero who sounds too good t'be true."

My fingers snag on a particularly thick knot, and I give up on my hair. "I embellished with my phrasing, but nothing I said was *untrue.*"

Neith's gaze finds the ground, and it's only just now I realize she's frowning. "I ken," she says.

Whatever did or didn't transpire between her and Aeron, she's mourning his loss in a way I'll never be able to fix. Not with pretty words or songs sung with good intent.

"You make a good point, though. If this becomes a regular occurrence, people wishing to see the hero in the flesh, we'll have to do something about that."

The power of a story casts a wide net. But we can help it along even further. People want to believe in the extraordinary; they crave it. If we give them a taste of something tangible, it will feed that belief, that hope for more in a dreary world of boundaries.

"What do you have in mind?" Jaromir asks.

"Well," I say as I begin pacing. I do my best thinking through movement of either my body or my fingers across my lute. Since my fingers ache, it's easier to walk through my thoughts. "We'll need someone to pose as Aeron."

"Are ye suggesting hiring someone?" Neith raises a brow.

"I don't like letting anyone else in on this," Jaromir says, frowning. "What's to stop them from running their mouths or blackmailing us?"

I wave my hands. "Not what I'm saying. I wouldn't tell anyone else what we're doing." I resume pacing. "But we're all to be trusted..."

We have everything and everyone we need to facilitate this.

Jaromir's expression melts into one of amusement. "You can't be serious."

But I'm already nodding. "You and Cadoc will have to take turns donning Aeron's armor."

Jaromir shakes his head, but Neith cuts in. "Aye," she says, "It could work."

Chapter Sixteen

When Cadoc returns from his night with Tomas, wearing a smile that refuses to wilt, we hit the road. For once, he doesn't voice his relief to be traveling.

We agreed to camp earlier in the day to grant us more daylight before dusk falls. The warmth of a low sun trickles through the trees, and the symphony of the night is just beginning its call.

Jaromir has most of the weapons splayed before him while he sharpens and oils the blades. All save for two of Neith's... we haven't finished with them yet.

"Th'first thing ye'll want t'do is get comfortable holding a weapon." Neith swings her sword with effortless finesse, circling and spinning before she holds the hilt toward me.

I tie my hair back with a leather strap and wipe my sweaty palm on my trousers before reaching tentatively to grasp the handle. She hasn't forgotten her promise to train me, and now more than ever, it seems imperative that I learn basic combat.

No one has spoken of the circumstances of Aeron's death. How if I hadn't been too close, he wouldn't have had to push me out of the way and take a blade through the back.

They don't speak of this, but they all know. I can't be a liability.

I force a smile and begin clumsily swinging her sword. It's shorter than the one she straps to her back but still heavier than I thought it would be.

"Like this?" I ask between labored breaths.

Neith offers a patient smile and holds her hands out to signal me to stop. "Less movement until it's firm in yer grasp. Ye have strong hands from playing yer lute, aye?"

"I do, in fact! Quickest fingers in the land. I'm sure there's an innuendo in there somewhere..."

"Never mind that." She comes to stand behind me, her hands clamping my wrists to remain strong and taut. "Keep yer hold firm, and work on slow control." She guides my arm as she speaks, performing a series of slashes, jabs, and parries.

Jaromir watches with his creased brow and assessing gaze. My cheeks do not burn under the weight of his scrutiny; no, they certainly don't. I turn my attention to my instructor.

"Where did you learn to fight?"

Neith releases my arms, stepping back to watch my form as I complete the circuit she's just taught me. "Mostly maself. I didnae have anyone around t'teach me." Her dark eyes are unflinching. "I didnae live up to ma family's expectations."

"What sort of expectations?" My arms are stronger than I thought, and once I get the coordination down, it's easier to swipe the blade faster.

Neith waves her hand for me to continue the series of moves as she perches on a nearby log. "I hail from th'Western Isles, where yer birth order determines yer role."

I pause my movements, holding the sword out straight, sun glinting across steel. The Western Isles is a beautiful region of rolling moors and rocky cliffs. I've learned ballads of the Isles, and its natural features are their own magic. Magic steeped in tradition. But alongside tradition there comes confinement. To be caged by convention and bound by it. Women are still not considered title holders in the Isles. Granted, here in Targgein, women are only landowners in certain regions that have parted with the old ways. Each city has its own magistrate and under the rule of Queen Dhara has been given leave to break with tradition or uphold it. But in the Isles, women are hardly considered citizens. Their duty remains to their fathers and then to their husbands.

I examine Neith, with her half-shorn hair revealing the thick scar running down the side of her face. "You were the eldest daughter."

She nods. "Aye, and my advantageous marriage had been planned since birth." Bitterness coats her words, and I can hear the weight of everything she doesn't say.

"When did you leave?" It seems the safest question.

"Ten summers past." She reaches for the short sword I still hold, trading it for her heavier broadsword. Already the difference in its weight tugs on my arms, and I dread the task before me.

"Whit are ye waiting for?" she asks with a quirked brow. "Show me th'series."

NIGHT CHASES AWAY THE SUN, but the fire keeps us warm. I lounge with a satisfying soreness throughout my arms and back. It helps that Cadoc roasted herbed potatoes for dinner tonight, and my belly is full and happy.

An embarrassing groan escapes my lips as I reach for my lute. Jaromir's mouth twitches at the sound. He's restringing Cadoc's bow, but he has a way of seeming fully engrossed in his task while catching every slight change around him. The only time I've ever seen him truly distracted was when his hand was busy between my thighs—

A flare of heat burns across my cheeks and deep in my belly. We haven't gone there again, not since Aeron. But the memory of his touch, of the taste of his kiss, resurfaces with the flush on my skin.

"You going to serenade us tonight, Syl?" Cadoc flashes me a dimpled grin. He's whittling away at a piece of wood. I can't tell what shape he's making, but it looks... interesting.

"I can. I could even sing a love song if it would land on appreciative ears."

His hands still, and the color on his cheeks deepens. Ah. Looks like I struck a nerve. He recovers quickly.

"I haven't the faintest clue what you're talking about."

"No?" I shoot Neith a conspiratorial look, and she wears one to match. "Not even if I sang about a handsome barkeep?"

Cadoc chokes but masks it with a cough. "Why—" His voice cracks on the word, and he clears his throat before continuing. "Why would I care to hear that?"

Neith prods him with the toe of her boot. "Does Tomas own Th'Laughing Goat?"

"His uncle owns the place, but Tomas handles most of the work. He's promised him the deed upon his passing, perhaps even sooner. If you ask me, I'd say Tomas deserves it. You know he rises before the sun to ensure they're well stocked and everything is accounted for. He even had to cover the work of one of the serving girls he fired when he caught her sneezing into the hunter's pot. Don't even get me started on how hard it is to keep good help—"

Cadoc seems to realize he's incriminating himself and promptly clamps his mouth shut.

Silence falls over the camp, and both Neith and I restrain ourselves from pushing him to share more. Jaromir finishes Cadoc's bow with a satisfied grunt and lays it beside him.

I begin plucking my lute, swaying with the beat.

"There once was a barkeep with hair of fire and gold—"

"No. You, stop it." Cadoc's voice is pained, so I take pity on him and cease my singing.

I keep plucking the tune I've decided will be designated to the ballad of Tomas and Cadoc; it's a working title. I'll workshop it later.

When Cadoc and Neith retire for the night, and only Jaromir and his pile of weapons remain, I set my lute down and stretch.

Jaromir laughs when I make a strangled groan. "Sore?"

I shake out my hands. "A bit. But I've felt worse." No need to go into specifics about that. I'd much rather not speak of life when I first docked in this country.

Jaromir reaches for his pack and hands me a wineskin. I take a sip, smiling when deep notes of citrus and berry spill over my tongue. We haven't found a tavern that carries this Hawthokian wine since Cadoc purchased that bottle in Astervale.

"This is my favorite." I hold up the wineskin, daring him to reveal his secrets.

"Is it?" Jaromir is suspiciously interested in the ground rather than in meeting my gaze.

I swallow another mouthful and pass it back to him. His fingers graze mine, a touch that lasts longer than necessary, and my body hums.

Must be the wine.

"When will we reach the next town?"

Jaromir frowns. "Our next stop isn't for three more days."

"Ah." I focus on the dwindling embers. On the residual smoke still rising from the ashes. Three days of travel means three days of writing. More or less. Sometimes the words come easily. Sometimes they elude me. It's maddening, really. How fickle the nature of the muse can be. But I've since learned to push through, to pen words when they aren't inspired almost in spite of my mental blocks.

Some days.

"That bothers you?" Jaromir watches me carefully. "Missing the comfort of a soft bed?"

I laugh at that. Don't get me wrong, I love a soft bed. The softer the better, with enough plush pillows to suffocate me. But I've spent most of my life sleeping wherever I can safely rest my head.

"No," I say, "that doesn't bother me at all."

He gives a short grunt of acceptance. I'm learning to speak Jaromir!

"What about you?" I scoot closer to him because it's silly to whisper from across the dying fire when we're the only ones still up. His gaze tracks the movement, and he gently pushes the bow and leftover blades he'd been working on further away. "What will you do now that you've sharpened every sword, restrung Cadoc's bow, and fletched a few arrows? Will these days of traveling drive you mad without purposeful distraction?"

I realize I've practically climbed into his lap at this point, and my voice is doing that breathless thing it does when I can't seem to get enough air.

His gaze darkens, and his jaw tightens. "Purposeful distraction?" He says the words so carefully.

Suddenly my intent is so clear to me, it's ridiculous. My body seems to move faster than my mind, which is shocking, really, but I won't dismiss the wisdom of my instincts.

"Yes," I whisper, leaning in even closer. "I've found that a worthy distraction can lend purpose to one's day." I breathe in his scent, and it makes something warm flip in my stomach. "And I find you terribly distracting."

"Do you, now?" Jaromir's hand flexes by his side, and more than anything, I want him to grab me and kiss me hard the way he did the first time. But he waits, adopting utter stillness. Like *I'm* the predator.

Well, maybe I am.

I close the distance, finally tasting his mouth again. He tastes sweet and warm, and all notions of gentleness are lost when I climb into his lap fully. He lets out a soft moan, and finally, *finally*, those hands are gripping my hips, pulling me roughly against his arousal. Directing and grinding me down upon him until I'm practically seeing stars.

His beard scratches my jaw, and I shiver, clutching his broad shoulders for dear life.

"Syl," he murmurs against my neck; the scrape of his teeth sets my nerves alight. "We should—"

But whatever he was going to say is lost in another heated kiss. He parts my lips, sweeping his tongue into my mouth, and I can't think, I can only feel. He breaks away with a ragged exhale, holding my face in his large hands.

"Wait." The desperation in his voice is almost my undoing. "I'm sorry. Do you wish to stop?"

"*Gods*, no," he says. "My tent is right there."

I glance over my shoulder to his tent and bedroll not ten paces away. "But that's so far."

He laughs, standing while still holding me. I yelp and wrap my legs around his waist. "I'll make it up to you."

Anticipation trembles through me. "I'll hold you to that."

He rips open the flaps to his tent and lowers me gently inside. Crawling over me, his large body overcrowds the tiny space. I revel in feeling him everywhere, and yank him down to press against me.

He claims my mouth again, and I'm eagerly tugging at the laces to his trousers. A strong grip pries my hands away, pressing my wrists to the bedroll beside my head. I fight to pull free, but he only tightens his hold.

"Be still," he growls in my ear, and heat shoots through my blood. His hands release their hold to run down my arms, leaving chills in their wake.

I nod as if I'm going to obey his command, but I have no intention of doing so. My hand snakes down to grasp him through his trousers, and I delight in the hiss I receive at the contact.

"Gods, Syl. Give me a moment." His voice is strained and needy, and in this moment, the most glorious sound I've ever heard.

"Jaromir." It's meant to sound chiding, but it comes out as a desperate plea.

He kisses me again, tugging my trousers and smallclothes down. Cool air hits my wet heat, and I try to close my legs, but his hand is so much faster, so much stronger. His fingers slide down with gentle precision, and sparks fly through my veins.

He groans against my neck. "*Fuck*, you're so wet for me already."

I make a choked sound in response.

"Good?" He tucks a lock of hair behind my ear, caressing my skin as his other hand plays music against me.

"Good," I whisper back. When his finger fills me, I gasp. Pleasure shoots through my body, and my hips begin to move in time with his motions.

His mouth falls open, his gaze searing. "Look at you," he says, adding another finger. "You're a fucking masterpiece."

I can't seem to form words. Every part of me tingles, and my blood is on fire. He leans over me, kissing me with slow languid movements of his mouth, and then his thumb is rubbing at the juncture of my thighs. The place that makes my vision blur and my skin feel too tight.

I claw at his arm, and suddenly I'm clenching, waves and waves of pulsing heat shuddering all the way down to my toes.

He works me through the last wave, until I shove him away with a trembling hand.

I'm shaky and sweaty, and it feels like every bone in my body has turned to liquid.

Jaromir brings his fingers to his mouth, tasting them with a ravenous enjoyment, watching me with a challenge in his eyes. I laugh because what else can I do after having my mind melted and my body turned to a puddle.

He grins and sits up. It's only then that I realize we never actually got my boots off, so my trousers and smallclothes have been hastily shoved to my ankles. Jaromir yanks them back up over my hips, ignoring my protests.

"It's late, and Cadoc is due to wake for his watch soon."

Damn Jaromir, his magic hands, and his penchant for logic.

I suck in a breath. "I'll have you know, it's poor manners to leave a lady's clothing in disarray while getting her off. And all without the courtesy of giving her leave to touch you! I have half a mind to write a ballad about this. And don't you think for a moment I won't, because I will. These are the risks of falling into bed, or in this case, onto a bedroll with a bard—"

Jaromir kisses me senseless, stalling my tirade. When he releases my mouth, he's grinning. "You were awfully quiet when I was touching you. Is that what it takes to get some peace? Must I dedicate myself to your pleasure if only to keep your mouth from getting you into trouble?"

I actually need to think about this. On the one hand, he's offering to touch me again, an outcome I'm highly in favor of. On the other hand, he's being a right prick, and maybe I should write that ballad just to spite him.

"Perhaps I was quiet because you didn't do a very good job."

His grin turns wolfish, and he presses me down against the bedroll. "Sounds like I need more practice."

A breathless laugh escapes my chest. "I won't object to that."

Chapter Seventeen

The dull light from an early morning spills across the tent. I stretch, wincing at the pain in my arms and back—

My elbow brushes against a solid warm body beside me. The night before comes flooding back to my awareness. Jaromir. His soft but assured touches as he drove me within an inch of my sanity with nothing but his hands and his kisses. At one point, he'd disappeared for his shift to watch the camp, but when he returned, he woke me with a kiss and his hand between my legs.

He hadn't let me touch him, not yet, but now something hard and unwilling to be ignored is pressing into my backside.

All it will take is slowly slipping my hand down—

Jaromir groans, engulfing my roaming hand with his own. He brings it up to his mouth, threading our fingers and pressing kisses to my knuckles that feel anything but chaste.

"Morning." His voice is a rough, thick sound that fills me with heat.

"You're interrupting my search."

"Am I? Perhaps your wandering hands should stay to themselves."

I pull, but he keeps his grip firm. "You're one to talk about wandering hands."

"Mm," he says, rubbing his thumb against my wrist. "I could spend every night touching you. Even if it means that when I try to sleep, you keep me awake with your incessant chattering while you dream."

"Excuse me, I do not chatter."

"You do." He rakes his teeth against my hand, sparking tingles in his wake. "And you even sing."

Now I know he's making that up. I glare at him, and he laughs, pulling me to sit astride him. I'm still fully clothed—the bastard insisted on it—but I circle my hips, reveling in the sound it pulls from his chest.

"Syl... I'm too tired for self-restraint."

"I care very little for your restraint." I press down harder, and he hisses.

"Not so hard. I haven't pissed yet."

I laugh and mentally debate pressing down even harder on him... but I have no interest in emptying his bladder all over me.

"Have it your way. But the next time you invite a lady to share your tent, perhaps you should make your expectations and boundaries clearer." Something about my voice must give him pause, because as soon as I roll off him, he bundles me against him, wrapping his thick arms around me and pressing my back to his chest.

"Just wait until we aren't three steps away from the others. I won't let you leave my bed the entire time we're in Stoneridge."

I grin, ducking my burning face into the bedroll. "You don't have to do that. Last night was... I don't expect you to do more than you're comfortable with."

I don't know why I'm voicing this aloud. But so far, he only seems keen to touch me, and what if there's something wrong with me? I hadn't let my mind wander to the thought that he might be repulsed by my being an elf. Anatomically, elves weren't so different from humans. Besides the ears and predisposition for smaller builds, there is no great discrepancy. But elven blood is enough to earn disgust and maltreatment in some regions of the world. Jaromir has never given me reason to believe he'd fall into that category, but if the thought of bedding an elf made him uneasy...

"If I wasn't what you thought I might be, that's all right. I'd hate for you to feel obligated to pursue a physical relationship with me simply because I made myself available. If you have clear preferences I don't fit, you shouldn't feel that you have to use your body to make me happy. I was perfectly fine having no intimate touch. I mean, if I had to label the span of time since my last *encounter,* I'd say it lands somewhere in the realm between one to two years. Three to four years. Fine it was four years. Five years. It's been five years. Let's add it to the ballad—"

Jaromir yanks me to face him. His glower has returned, and where I once thought it obnoxious and rude, now I'm stunned into silence as more of that liquid heat unfurls within me.

"Stop," he says, his eyes narrowing, "You are *perfect.* Not because you're available or out of obligation. I'm only halting our progress because I don't want to stop once we start unless *you* want to. That's why not here, not in camp. Because once I bury my face between these thighs"—he runs a hand down my leg, and I gasp—"I'm not coming up for air until you tell me to stop."

My head spins, and I think my blood is rushing to the wrong places. If I were upright, I'd likely keel over. But if he thinks he can scandalize me into silence...

"That is... wildly lewd. You're a bit of a lecher, aren't you?"

Jaromir laughs and tips my chin to press his lips to mine. I sink into the kiss, gently rolling him onto his back so I can climb over him once more.

He lets out a grunt and lifts me off him. "I wasn't jesting. I need to piss." He hurries out of the tent, and I watch him go, admiring the view.

I can wait for Stoneridge for us to pursue this any further. Three days isn't so long.

Three days is an entire century.

I'm certain three days is the longest unit of measurement I've ever encountered. We don't even share a horse anymore, since we stole two of the mercenaries' horses, but I feel Jaromir's eyes on me, and whenever I turn in my saddle to glance his way, the heat I find in his stare is impossible to bear.

It can't be done. I shall surely perish.

I steal another glance over my shoulder, and sure enough, there he is watching me with a shameless thoroughness in his assessment. Jaromir's mouth curves in a suggestive smile as if he knows what I'm thinking, the smug bastard. I turn back, adjust my hat, and ride without giving him the satisfaction of knowing how much he affects me.

Maybe one more look, just to be sure he sees how much he doesn't affect me.

Jaromir meets my gaze with a heated promise in his dark eyes, and I swear I'm about to fall off my horse. What was the horse's name? Turnip? I'm about to fall off Turnip.

"We should make camp here," Cadoc calls back, unaware that I'm slowly melting into a puddle on poor Turnip. "We can make up the time tomorrow, if you're feeling up for training."

He angles his head in Neith's direction, and she responds with a short nod.

"I'm up for it," I say, because stopping now means I'm that much closer to getting Jaromir alone, even if we can't get naked. But *something* to dull the ache.

"Ye say that now," Neith says with a grin, "but today we're running endurance drills."

I slide off Turnip and only sort of land wrong, nearly falling. "What are endurance drills?"

Cadoc laughs, shaking his head and blatantly refusing to answer my question. Jaromir slips by me, gently taking the reins from my hand.

"A crucial facet o' training." Neith starts unpacking her gear and waves me over. She hands me her waterskin. "Drink up. Ye're going t'need it."

I have a very bad feeling about endurance drills.

My instincts are sharp as ever. This is a new pit of eternal torment.

A stabbing sensation lights up my side, and I stagger the remaining steps back to camp. Neith jogs behind me, not because I was faster but because she's been circling me as she corrals me on foot through the forest. *Running.* A vile punishment I've done nothing to deserve.

She passes me with ease, pulling her waterskin out and handing it to me wordlessly. I gulp it down, precious water spilling over my chin and down my tunic. There's a twinge in my lungs, one I answer with a barking cough.

Panting, I glance over at Neith to find she doesn't even have a bead of sweat, and her breathing is even and measured.

I'll take that to mean she is terribly intimidated by my stamina and thus hiding her exertion.

"Ye all right?" she asks. Even her voice is calm and steady.

"I'm fine," I wheeze. "How are you?"

Her brow lifts as her mouth twitches. "Are ye up for some sparring?"

"Never. I plan to sleep for a few decades as if I command immortality like the ancient elves of old."

She says nothing, allowing me to exhaust myself in my half-hearted tirade.

I limp my way over to sit by the circle of stones that will house our fire. I don't even have the energy to be embarrassed by my lack of physical endurance. There was once a time I ran through the forests of Smarighad, leaping atop overgrown roots blanketed by moss without pausing for breath—but that was long ago. I left that life on the other side of the ocean.

I take another sip of water, slower this time. My breathing is almost normal again, just my heart still bludgeons in my chest. I should find a river to dunk in. My hair's been tied back with a leather strap but the back of my neck still drips with sweat, as does my brow. And my arse.

Neith watches me with a wary expression. "We needn't if ye're too winded, but there is value in learning t'find strength when there's none left. It's often then, when we need it most."

That's a clever manipulation if I've ever heard one, but she's right. I stand, emitting an embarrassing groan. "Fine, let's have at it then. But I'm keeping that line. It's a good one."

Neith beams at me, and I think it might be the brightest smile I've seen on her face since before Aeron's passing. She hands me my short sword and a small dagger. "Put this in yer boot. I don't want ye t'rely on it. I want you t'ken it's always there as a last resort."

I examine the small blade. It's a simple piece, handle carved from wood. Closing my fingers around it, I like the way it feels in my hand. "But this would be so much easier to wield."

"Easier to wield at dangerously close range." She points the tip of her sword in my direction. "Yer job is t'stay out of range."

I nod, tucking the dagger into my boot and swinging the short sword to ready my already sore arms. "First to bleed?"

"First t'bleed."

Neith advances, slower than I know her capable, but it's still a shock when our blades clash. The force of the blow reverberates up my arm. "Follow th'series," she says, before twisting her sword free.

We fall into the familiar rhythm like a choreographed dance. I meet each strike—because she lets me—and I deflect each blow.

Finally, she nods her approval. "Good. Now turn th'blade."

"What?" I barely have time to react when she's striking once more, harder, faster. My heart leaps into my throat with each pass of her sword.

"Turn th'blade," she repeats. "For every strike, I want ye t'turn me away and force me on th'defensive."

My body is drenched with sweat, my head pounds, and the muscles in my arms are cramping. "I... can't," I say through gritted teeth.

She pushes even harder. "Ye've learned th'movements. Now adapt t'meet my strike. Strike me for once!"

I can't tell if she's angry, and my stomach burns. I catch the next strike before she lands a cut to my thigh, and I spin her sword away, launching to slice her arm—

But she's much too fast, and catches my sword before nicking her blade against the side of my neck. A small sting, and when I touch two fingers to the spot, they come away bloodied. Between labored breaths, I smile. "Goddess, Neith. You deserve your own ballad."

Neith snorts, sheathing her blade and clapping me on the

back. "Ye're getting stronger, Syl. Perhaps one day ye might draw blood first, aye?"

"We both know you allowed me to last as long as I did," I say, dabbing my hand against my neck. It's a shallow cut, but I don't wish to stain this tunic.

"Even still. Ye're learning."

I can't argue with that. But I can call it quits for the evening. I've done my best and now I've earned a few comforts. Namely, a dunk in the river and a hot meal in my belly.

"I see you survived." Jaromir's voice cuts through my thoughts, and its low timbre is enough to turn my admittedly melted state into that much more of a liquid.

The entire expanse of his well-formed chest and abdomen is on display. Some of his dark hair has fallen loose from the knot he ties it in, framing his severe yet handsome face. Dewy sweat clings to every hardened edge of muscle, and a thin trail of dark hair leads down into his low slung trousers. My mouth goes dry, and I brazenly drink in every inch of him with ravenous eyes. Goddess, what does he do to achieve this form? I've never seen him train his muscles with the care and attention his physique implies. Unless he does so in secret.

I still haven't spoken, and the look on his face is positively smug with a familiar heat in his eyes. His smirk holds both a challenge and an appreciation for my attention.

"Why are you sweaty?"

He mops the back of his neck with a rag before yanking on a loose white tunic. "I figured if you were suffering Neith's drills, it was only fair I completed my own training." An uncertain smile returns to his face, and something about it is so endearing. His gaze travels over my face before dipping lower —to my neck. His eyes harden. "First to bleed?"

"Ah, yes. I lost valiantly."

"On the neck, Neith?" His words are sharp, and he glares

in her direction. She merely shrugs, continuing her task of draining and cleaning the quails Cadoc hunted for dinner.

"Cadoc?" Jaromir calls out. "Assistance?"

Cadoc strides over, examining the minor cut. "I barely see it," he says, squinting.

"Any open wound can get infected."

"Open wound? Oh, for the love of—" Cadoc cuts himself off, rolling his eyes and stalking off to his tent. When he returns, he's holding a salve in his palm. With one finger, he gingerly rubs it against the soreness on my neck. The smile he gives me is warm but amused. "There, satisfied?"

Jaromir nods as if Cadoc isn't using sarcasm, and his face relaxes. He demanded Cadoc treat the wound? The tiny, insignificant little thing that, well, it did bleed but it wasn't terrible.

That's... surprisingly sweet.

"You seem to know a great deal about Neith's style of training. From personal experience?"

"Yes. I was cocky and arrogant when I first met her." Jaromir leads us to sit by the fire. "She put me in my place."

Neith flashes him a knowing smile. "That I did. He stumbled through th'drills, learning that strength doesn't equate t'speed. Syl here kept better pace than ye did your first run with me."

"Did she now?" Jaromir studies me with blatant admiration, and my already heated cheeks burn even hotter.

"Well, it sounds like it wasn't exactly stiff competition if you were as bad as Neith claims. Obviously, I'm far lighter than you, so your own bodyweight would have served as an anchor, dragging you down. Although, your strength would counter that, so perhaps we are on even footing where that is concerned. And let us not forget, this is still my first venture in quite some time, and as such, it takes a certain level of acclimation before one feels accustomed to the 'wear-and-tear' of life on the road. But perhaps your pride was your greatest down-fall, and thus your heaviest accoutrement to carry."

Jaromir is still staring at me with that warmth in his eyes. "All in one breath. Your lung capacity is impressive."

I can't help but grin, all notions of embarrassment vanishing. "Wait 'til I really get going."

His gaze darkens, and his smile turns predatory. "I eagerly await anything you would show me."

There's another challenge—an invitation that I wouldn't have thought he'd extend, not yet anyway. We're still two days off from Stoneridge.

I clear my throat. "I should go wash up." It's my responding challenge, my counteroffer, and I don't dare breathe while I await his answer.

Jaromir's stare never wavers from mine. He wets his lips, and I swear I'll combust if he makes me wait any longer.

"We need firewood." Cadoc's cheerful voice breaks the tension filled moment. "So when you come back, you can warm up."

Jaromir wears a strange expression. Almost... calculating.

"I already split some wood we could use, but that's a good point," he says, glancing at me. "I'll take you to the river. I'll give you privacy while I fetch some kindling."

THE SOUND of rushing water greets me just before the river comes into view. It's a shallow stream, burbling as it rushes over large rocks. The trees thin, and the ground is claimed by soft, spongy moss. The sun sits lower now, painting the river-bank with pink and orange light. The sweat has dried against my skin, leaving a filmy residue that's part dirt. I had wondered why we didn't camp closer to our water source, but now I recognize the gift of privacy.

I approach the riverbank and shiver in anticipation, yanking my boots off then moving to my trousers and tunic. When I stand bare in the last of the day's light, I slowly sink into the water. Welkin's grace! Freezing, indeed. My skin instantly pebbles, and I quickly scrub my body with the soap Kingsley made me. Dunking my head beneath the surface, I emerge and squeeze the excess water from my hair, before climbing back out. Shivering, I yank my smallclothes and breastband over my wet skin. Footsteps approach, the snap of a twig alerting me. I turn my back to the river, keeping my vulnerable side hidden, and tug my tunic over my head. When I'm dressed, I lift my gaze.

Jaromir leans against a tree, arms crossed, with that damnable assessing stare.

I refuse to be intimidated by that gaze anymore. Especially knowing the effect I have on him. I crook my finger at him.

He grins and approaches. Once he is towering over me, he hesitates. An adorable flush rises on his cheeks, and I'm at a loss for why. We've already crossed the line of intimacy once; what does he have to feel bashful over?

He rubs the back of his neck, while the other hand procures something from pocket.

"Here." Jaromir shoves something soft and slightly wet into my palm, his eyes fixed over my shoulder. I open my hand to find a small yellow flower.

He picked me a buttercup. Welkin above, he picked my favorite flower.

I clear my throat and smooth out the crumpled buttercup's delicate petals. "It's beautiful."

"You mentioned liking these..." Jaromir runs a hand over his jaw, and the rough scrape of bristles against his palm punctuates his words.

"I did. Even crushed as it is, the poor thing, it's my favorite."

"Ah. Sorry. I—"

I reach up on tiptoes to silence his apology with a kiss. The tension in his body melts away with my touch, and his arms come around me, pressing me closer. "Thank you," I whisper against his mouth, before deepening the kiss.

His hands skim down my back, gripping my hips. When I gently bite his lip, he makes a rough sound and runs his knuckles along the skin above my trousers.

"May I?" He speaks this as a question, but it doesn't feel like one. It feels like a confession, and I can't bring myself to respond. I nod, knowing I need whatever he's willing to give, and I don't care how pathetic that makes me.

He angles me to sit beside the river, gently pushing me to lie flat on my back. Making quick work of my laces, he yanks my pants and smallclothes down. I gasp, somehow surprised by how suddenly I'm exposed. My skin is still damp and cool to the touch, but that's not why I shiver. He tugs my feet free of my clothes.

Last time, the dark covered most of me from his thorough stare. But now there's nowhere to hide.

Jaromir groans. "Let me look at you."

His hands run from my ankles up to my thighs, gently tugging them apart. I squirm beneath his rapt attention, and heat spreads across my skin. He leans over me, burying his face against my neck. The feel of his beard against my skin makes me shiver, and his mouth skims my pulse point.

"You smell so fucking good."

Reminder to oneself: Send Kingsley a muffin basket in thanks for his black currant soap.

Jaromir's lips scrape against my jaw, slowly teasing their way to my mouth. The first touch of his lips to mine, and my back arches beneath him. His fingers find that aching place between my legs, his touch gentle but certain, and my response is strangled in my throat. I crush my flower in my fist, hoping it survives, hoping I survive his merciless teasing.

"You're *perfect*, Syl. Everything about you commands me." He works his way down, over my damp clothing, and brings his face, *goddess his mouth*, a hair's breadth from where his fingers are. "Gods, you're beautiful."

A needy desperate noise leaves my chest, and *oh*, his tongue is there—*there*—and he groans.

"I knew you'd taste sweet." He seals his mouth over me, working his lips, his tongue in earnest, and I swear, I see stars. My breath stutters as he devours me like a man starved. My skin feels stretched over my body, and a tingling sensation starts low in my belly. He brings my thighs over his shoulders, and suddenly his tongue is hitting deeper. My hands fist in his hair, and he hums against me, his eyes finding mine and holding me arrested at the sight.

His gaze is a smoldering blaze of want, his mouth moving with languor, almost decadent in his pursuit. As if he's actually *enjoying* this. His hand snakes down to reach something, and oh goddess, he's adjusting himself.

I let the next noise, an indulgent little moan, leave my lips with abandon. Smug approval shines in his eyes, and he doubles down on his efforts. Licking, tasting, savoring.

My stomach flutters, and my vision blurs just as something inside me stretches taut—before it breaks in waves of liquid clenching pleasure. He groans and lazily snakes his tongue against me until I finally push his head away. My thighs tremble, and when I catch sight of his glistening mouth and beard, another clench pulses through me.

His gaze is half-lidded, eyes dazed and unfocused.

Something about that, about me reducing him to this, it makes me surge forward and claim his mouth, and I taste myself on his lips. I claw at his tunic, yanking him atop me.

"Fuck," he murmurs against me, allowing me to taste every

bit of him, every bit of me. "I was only going to touch you, but I couldn't stop."

"Good"—I pant against his mouth—"don't stop."

He cups the back of my neck, while his other hand reaches down to his laces. I want to weep with relief at the motion. I smile against his mouth, his chest pressing against my damp tunic. I need to feel his skin against mine. I need—

A low humming sound carries through the trees. A hum punctuated by a *click-click*. Jaromir freezes, tensing in my arms.

Two beats pass, and the humming grows louder.

He yanks my smallclothes and pants back in place, passing me my boots with a frantic edge to his movements. I hurry to dress, still not quite understanding what we're hearing, but recognizing his urgency.

Jaromir grabs his sword belt I hadn't noticed he'd unbuckled from his waist and yanks his sword free. "Run back to camp."

"Obviously there's danger. I'm not running away and leaving you—"

"Without the added danger of worrying over you. Yes, you are. Send Neith or Cadoc if you can. *Not* both. I want someone with you."

"Just come with me." The humming is growing louder, and the clicking now sounds like the snapping of jaws. "Come back to camp with me."

"I can't," he snarls. "If they've caught our scent, I'm not leading them there."

That's ridiculous. "All of us against whatever you're hearing is better odds than—"

"Syl, just go!"

His bellow echoes through the trees, and I flinch. But before I can either argue or acquiesce, a swarm of creatures appear in the not-so-distant clearing. Dozens of monsters the size of ponies. Bile rises in my throat as terror churns in my gut.

They move like giant spiders, but their bodies are armored with a sort of bluish-black shell that shines like a black moonstone. Their tails are long and spiked, flicking with deadly intent.

Click-click. Their pincers snap in a rhythmic threat.

My head spins, and I nearly lose my footing.

Jaromir raises his sword and moves to stand in front of me.

"Please"—his voice is ragged—"run. I can't hold them off forever."

I take an uncertain step back, and then another, heart fracturing with the action. I can't leave him. I can't stay. I'll only get in the way and get him hurt or killed. But I can't abandon him, he doesn't stand a chance against these creatures on his own. Camp isn't far, but it's too far to promise his survival; I'll never make it there and back in time.

I can't leave. I can't stay. I can't. I can't.

My vision blurs with unshed tears as I turn and run.

Chapter Eighteen

Tears roll down my cheeks as I run.

I'm leaving him behind. I'm leaving Jaromir to face those things on his own.

I slow my pace, a strangled cry ripping free from my chest.

I know what he said. I know he thinks he's right, and maybe he is. But I can't take another step if it means leaving him to face certain death alone. I'm not much of a fighter, so perhaps this is me signing my own death warrant, but I'd rather die now than live with the weight of choosing to run.

I turn back, racing to the side of the river with all those stones the size of my fist. When I land on my knees by the rushing water, I shove as many stones as I can into my pockets and tuck a few more under my arm. Heart pounding, I hurry to the nearest tree. It's sturdy, with plenty of close hanging branches.

One thing I'm decent at: climbing trees.

I leap and grasp at the tallest branch I can catch, swinging my leg over to pull myself up fully. I climb slowly, one-handed and burdened with all these rocks, but I climb.

I haven't dared glance Jaromir's way, not yet. But I hear

him. I hear the clang of his sword against their shell-like armor. I hear the snap and *click-click* of pincers desperately aiming for his vulnerable flesh. The shrill squeals of those things I can only assume are cries of pain. I hope they are.

When I reach a thick branch halfway up, high enough I feel safe from those creatures climbing after me but close enough I'm confident in my aim, I stop. One of the rocks sits square in my palm, heavy and warm from my tight grip.

Finally, I look. Jaromir is a thing of beauty when he fights. All power and precision. He spins and slashes with expert finesse, narrowly avoiding the heavy flick of a spiked tail. A few of the creatures are felled, but the rest are slowly closing in. I haul back and aim for the beast creeping on Jaromir's flank. The rock lands hard, and an ear-splitting scream echoes back.

Jaromir shouts in frustration, probably at me for not leaving, but I don't care. I aim again for another of those black-moonstone-colored beasts. The last of the sun glints on its shining armor, almost creating a rainbow against its exoskeleton. I launch my crude weapon, and another shriek responds.

"Neith! Cadoc!" They have to hear me. They have to. Jaromir can't hold them off, and I can't keep throwing rocks from up here. I lob another one, biting back tears as another swipe of a tail comes far too close to Jaromir. I scream their names until my throat goes hoarse.

I'm all out of rocks. My hands shake, so I close them into fists.

Jaromir cries out, and I'm climbing down the tree fast enough to scrape my knees and palms.

He's standing in the river now, chest heaving with every labored breath. Four more of those creatures remain.

A wide gash stretches across his thigh, blood blooming and dispersing in the rushing water. His stance is all wrong, like he's favoring his leg and struggling to stay upright. His eyes find mine, and they widen. He shakes his head, the motion jerky.

As if I'd leave him now.

"Hey!" I shout, even as my lungs threaten to burst. "This way!"

The creatures turn at the sound, clicking their pincers and flicking their tails.

It's all the distraction Jaromir needs.

He brings his sword down, fast and without mercy, cleaving the tails from two of the beasts before him. Their cries of agony fill my head, and I cover my ears even as I run to him.

I snag another rock from the ground and haul it with every last bit of my dwindling strength. The shot goes wide and lands to the earth with a thud. Two creatures still stand, and Jaromir looks ready to keel over. A cry threatens to escape my lips, but I hurtle over the edge of the riverbank, landing in the water beside him.

This close I can see every muscle in his body trembles. Water drips from his hair into his blinking eyes but they're glassy and unfocused.

The sword slips from Jaromir's grasp as his knees buckle. I snag the handle before it's hidden at the bottom of the river, and I catch him, barely keeping him upright. Tremors wrack his body, his muscles fighting to remain standing. If he lets his full weight fall, there's no chance I can hold him up. I lead him to the opposite edge of the river, setting him down half on the bank, half in the shallow water.

"Stay with me," I say because I'm selfish, and I don't want to be alone. I raise his sword—a sword far too heavy for me to train with. The blade trembles, my arms shaking with the force of keeping it high above my shoulder.

I need the momentum it will create when it falls. It's my only chance against one of those things. If I thought the river would afford me safety, I was wrong. The spider-like creatures are large enough, the water fails to deter them. Spindly limbs stroke against the current.

Their tales are sharply curled, flicking back and forth.

The two creatures float to us, clicking and snapping. My fear is a visceral thing, like a knife in my belly.

I'm not a fighter. Not a warrior. I'm not strong or brave.

I'm just a bard. My destiny is to entertain, and I do so by believing in the truth of my tales.

Perhaps if I believe I have courage, it will grow.

One of the creatures advances, a hissing sound escaping its mandibles. I cry out, dredging the last of my will to heave the sword until it lands with a sickening crunch of steel breaking through black-moonstone armor. The piercing scream of the wounded beast makes my ears ring, and wetness trickles down the side of my neck.

I yank Jaromir's sword free from its body and raise it high, but a sharp twinge in my elbow sucks the breath from my lungs and the strength from my grasp. The sword falls from my hands, splashing into the water.

Sweeping my hands through the water, I blindly search for my last hope. I crouch to reach the river bottom, and cold water rushes up my nose and down my throat.

Coughing, I wipe my eyes and back away from the snap of pincers.

I have no weapon. No way to stop them from advancing. But I angle my body in front of Jaromir, shielding him.

There's a ballad in this moment. A shame I can't write it.

The hum of a whistle sings through the air before a hard *thwack* sounds. An arrow protrudes from the spot where the creature's neck must be, and Neith and Cadoc appear, racing toward us. Cadoc raises his bow, the one Jaromir spent so much time caring for, and looses another arrow. It lands true, between the sheets of armor lining its back.

A splash, and Neith is in the water, her lovely face twisted in a grimace. She spins her sword, before slamming it hard through the last creature's skull, pinning it to the bottom of the river.

My body is numb, but soon relief should come, yes? I spin around to find Jaromir, still laying on the riverbank. I land beside him, taking his face in my hands and his eyes roll back.

"What's wrong with him?" Panic sharpens my voice, pitching it high and demanding.

Neith sheaths her sword, wading through the water to us. She gently grabs his chin and tilts his head.

"Cadoc," she calls, "he's been hit."

"Fuck." Cadoc has already stashed his bow on his back and is pulling two vials out of his satchel. "Do we have time to make it back?"

"I dinnae ken." Neith's jaw clenches around her answer. I look between the two of them before glancing down at Jaromir's increasingly pale face.

"What do you mean by *time*? Is he going to..." I don't say the last word. I don't say it, but it hangs there, perfectly poised and threatening to crush the air from my lungs.

"He'll be fine, but this won't be pleasant." Cadoc bites the cork free from one of the vials, the stout round one filled with amber liquid. He pushes Jaromir fully onto the riverbank. Lifting one eyelid, then the other.

"Pupils are dilated... breathing is slowed... yes his body is shutting down, we need to be quick."

"You just said he was going to be"—my throat constricts on the last word, and I have to swallow my panic before I can say —"fine."

Cadoc nods at Neith, who rips Jaromir's pant leg wide enough to see the gash on his thigh. The skin surrounding it is yellowish purple, like a fading bruise. But that isn't possible since he just received the wound.

"Sorry for this, friend." Cadoc actually seems regretful as

he pours the amber liquid over the gash in his leg. It steams and hisses when it makes contact with his skin as if Cadoc is pouring molten ore into his flesh.

Jaromir's eyes flutter open, and his muffled growl behind a clenched jaw rips through me. I scramble to kneel above him, placing my hands at either side of his head.

"Shhh... It's all right..."

Jaromir's fevered gaze finds mine, and he doesn't look away. He stares up at me with desperate intent, and I find myself unable, unwilling, to look away. His thick dark hair is matted with sweat and blood, and I card my fingers through it, pushing it away from his burning forehead. He relaxes, the fight finally leaving his body.

"Now for the venom already in his bloodstream." Cadoc brings a thin vial of pale gray liquid to Jaromir's lips. But Jaromir thrashes against it. With a sigh, Cadoc wordlessly hands it to me, and I know what I need to do.

"Jaromir," I say as softly as I can. That gaze snaps right back to my face. "You have to drink this." I gently tip the vial against his lips, and he parts them, allowing whatever Cadoc concocted to slip in. "Good. That's so good."

I rub soothing circles against his shoulder, unsure if this is helping or not. When he's emptied the vial, I pass it back to Cadoc, who quickly tucks it away.

"We should head back t'camp," Neith says. "Afore th'fever dreams set in."

The memory of when Neith was hit and suffered the venom-induced fever floods me. As if following my thoughts, she continues.

"We'd have more than nightmares t'worry about, were it not for Cadoc. It's a blessing he brewed th'sepsis oil prior to our need for it."

Cadoc nods, looking uncharacteristically solemn. "I wish I'd been prepared when it was you suffering."

A smile wavers at the corner of her mouth. "Ye can't anticipate everything." Before he can argue, she turns to me. "We need t'get Jaromir in dry clothes, and by th'fire."

I brush a stubborn lock of dark hair from his forehead and place a quick kiss against his filmy skin. I don't care what they make of it. I care that he is yet alive.

I won't leave him.

THE CAMP IS WRAPPED in the gloaming, darkness pushing the faint light from the sky. The fire stretches tall into the impending night, reaching for the first hints of stars. Jaromir is bundled in numerous blankets beside the fire, but violent shivers wrack his body.

He hasn't spoken, and a distant glazed look has transformed his normally attentive gaze. It's a helpless feeling, watching someone else hurt. When you can't take the pain away. When you're cursed to bear witness—a useless bystander while they suffer.

"We heard ye, by th'way." Neith hasn't looked up from where she's stitching Jaromir's pants back together, but her voice disrupts my spinning thoughts. "When ye called for us... I thought it was more mercenaries."

There's something in her voice when she says this—something that gives me courage to finally speak of what transpired. "Aeron... in his last moments, he said your name. He said it like you were his last hope, the one person he could trust to take him home even as death claimed him."

Her hands still, but she doesn't look up. "Aeron was an old friend."

That doesn't answer my unasked question. If she'd rather not speak of it, I should respect that.

But she'll tell me if I push too far, and I'm itching to know more.

"How did you two know one another?"

She sets Jaromir's pants aside, finally meeting my gaze across the fire. "When we were children, his family offered mine his betrothal."

Well. I certainly wasn't expecting that. But I'm far too learned in schooling my expressions to let my shock show.

Neith laughs. "I've scandalized ye."

Apparently, I'm out of practice at hiding my reactions.

"So, what did they say?"

"No, o' course. They had their sights set on his older brother, th'heir to the Fowler fortune. Alas, I wasn't nearly worthy of their firstborn." Neith rolls her eyes. "But it wasn't all for naught. Aeron and I exchanged letters every few months. More often when I grew older and right before I left. I gained a friend, which I sorely needed."

I nod. For all of Aeron's silly and ridiculous traits, there was one thing about him that stood without measure.

One was lucky to count him as a friend.

"I miss him," Neith says softly. "He had a way of making everything feel lighter. Life is heavy, is it nae? It's a rare thing t'find someone who lightens yer load."

Jaromir stares with unseeing eyes into the fire. Cadoc watches him with a healer's focus.

"You told me Cadoc was the reason you took this job under Aeron."

Neith smiles. "He was, but I've known Aeron for years. We tried to maintain correspondence. I even told Cadoc t'keep an eye out for him, when Aeron's last letter explained a plan to hire a crew t'hunt a dragon." She grabs the bottle near her feet, taking a swig. "We were both at the port when Aeron stumbled into the Rutting Goose searching for his crew. I was never going t'join Cadoc on the Jaunty Loon, but he had every intention of convincing me. Captain Torrick is notorious for hiring anyone from the ports willing to travel, which doesn't make for th'best crew. My plan was t'stick around the port in case Aeron showed, and at th'very least, keep him from getting himself killed on th'first step of his grand adventure. It was sheer luck Cadoc decided last minute t'forgo travel and happened t'be in the tavern when Aeron appeared." Neith shakes her head, brow furrowing. "Once Cadoc got th'details, I couldn't let Aeron go without"—her voice stalls, and she swallows as if the next word has gotten stuck in her throat—"protection."

Her grief is a palpable thing. It isn't weeping or wailing, at least not from where I can see. It isn't crying out or screaming to the skies. It's a quiet pain that sneaks its way into conversations around the fire. It tinges old memories with a layer of regret and burrows deep enough she carries it without anyone noticing.

But I see it. I feel it.

"He loved you." I don't say these words for comfort, for I don't think there is any comfort in them. I say them because they were Aeron's last thoughts, last moments on this earth.

She was his safety and a piece of home.

Neith smiles, and it's such a beautiful, broken thing. "I ken."

Chapter Nineteen

When the fire dies down, Cadoc offers to stay with Jaromir, but I won't leave his side.

"Do you need to observe in case his condition worsens?"

"No," Cadoc says with a shrug. "But after the day you've had, I figured you'd want the rest."

"Honestly? I won't be able to sleep until I know he's well."

He helps me bring Jaromir into his tent, and I crawl in beside him.

Cadoc pokes his head through the flaps. "The fever should break by morning, and we'll wait an additional day before travel so you can catch up on rest then." His mouth tightens. "You're sure you want to stay with him?"

"Of course." I'm good at reading people, and his raised shoulders show discomfort. Not in my staying awake—that makes no sense—but in my desire to sit by his side.

I'd rather change the subject than suffer his scrutiny.

"Are we in danger here?" Staying another day... it must leave us vulnerable to another attack.

Cadoc's expression resumes its casual nature. "Doubtful.

I'll restore the fire and keep it burning tonight. You guys disrupted what appeared to be a nest. It's no one's fault, none of us could have known, but if there was a nest here in camp, we'd know it by now."

I nod, finding little comfort in that.

Cadoc gives me one last reassuring smile before letting the tent flaps close behind his departure. I debate tying them closed, but in case Jaromir needs Cadoc's assistance, it's best to leave them undone. From what I understand, Cadoc has already done what he can, and the venom needs to run its course. But I'd rather err on the side of caution. I don't know how much time passes, but soon Jaromir is tossing and turning. His face tightens.

"Damir," he cries out. "Damir, no."

I gently place my hand against his burning forehead. Cadoc left me a lantern so I might observe Jaromir. The small flame dances against the glass and illuminates the tent. Beads of sweat dot his forehead, and his dark brows are pulled together as if he's in pain.

"Damir!" He jolts awake, sitting up and reaching for nothing. I rub his back, hoping he can feel my presence in any way and hoping it helps. He glances around as if taking in his surroundings.

Would it have been better to allow Cadoc to watch over him? Am I being presumptuous? We've had our physical encounters, and I'd call us friends. He's shared enough with me; I know what nightmares plague him in this feverish state. But do I have any claim over him in this way? To take the role of nursemaid when he's sick?

It suddenly feels far too intimate.

Jaromir turns, finally looking at me. Not through me, *at* me. "It's you," he says, his voice soft. "I thought I'd never see you again."

"It's me," I say with a little flourish, as if it will lessen any lingering tension.

But he answers with a broad grin that crinkles his eyes. "I thought I imagined it all."

I laugh and resist the urge to push the hair from his face. The notion that I've been doing this, and all while he's been semi-unconscious, is wildly disturbing.

"No such luck. I'm real, and so is the nasty gash you received. Also, the venom coursing through your blood, that's real, too! Been a bit of a shite day, if you ask me. But at least you're alive and likely never to attempt to take a woman out in nature again. What would you call it? Coitus interruptus? A clever narrative can use this plot device sparingly, but in real life I find it rather obnoxious—"

I clamp my mouth shut. His grin, though amused, has turned increasingly baffled at my tangent.

"That's... a lot," he says. He lies back down and pinches the bridge of his nose. "My head... it feels like my skull is on fire."

"It kind of is." See, this is why I'd never make it as a healer. I lack the fundamentals of bedside manner. Jaromir's eyes are clearer now, and I take it as a good sign that the worst is over. "I never did get a chance to thank you for saving me."

Jaromir studies me with that intent look I've missed so damn much. "Thank you for saving me, too."

An unwilling smile tugs my mouth. "Remembered that, did you? How was my form?"

He laughs, but it's tight and weak. "It was excellent considering my sword is almost larger than you."

That's an exaggeration. There's a sexual implication somewhere in there, I just know it.

"And of course, I remember. I remember everything about you." He threads his fingers through mine, and his hand is like an oven. "I remember the way your voice sounds as I fall asleep. How I've never seen eyes so green 'til I saw yours. How you have sunlight in your hair. The way you never stop speaking." A wicked curve of a smirk transforms his sweet expression into something positively roguish. "I remember the noises you make when my tongue is buried between your thighs."

"Jaromir!" My cheeks burn even as something warm and slippery pools in my stomach. I'm ignoring all the pretty things he says about me—the things I'm sure he'll blame the fever for. This is the most chatty he's ever been, so he's clearly not in his right mind. "Keep it in your pants until you heal, at least."

He only grins at me, rubbing his thumb in circles against the top of my hand. "I remember how much you hated me."

"Hate is such a strong word. I prefer 'consciously made it my mission to annoy you.' It has a ring to it."

"You are gifted at getting under my skin. Always have been." His smile is all fond indulgence, and I take that compliment proudly. "I remember the first time I heard you sing."

I snort, shaking my head. "I remember that, too. You were decidedly unimpressed."

His eyes widen. "I watched you the entire night like a transfixed fool. And months later, I still couldn't get your voice out of my head."

That doesn't sound right. We haven't even been on the road for months. "Jaromir, I think that's the fever talking. It's only been a few weeks since Hollowden."

He shakes his head. "No, it was two years ago. I was at the Red Wyvern in Birchfield, and when you sang"—his eyes drift closed as if reliving the memory—"it was like I was finally awake."

Two years ago; that timeline for my stint in Birchfield lines up. That was right before I was driven away by that handsy owner who stank of onions and goat cheese. It was how I ended up in Hollowden with Kingsley and Brigitta. I wrack my brain, searching for Jaromir's face in my memory of nights in that crowded tavern, but all I recall is my hands shaking with hunger. The uneven stool that rocked under me when I played. The gnawing in the pit of my stomach.

The final night in Birchfield comes to me. I remember stumbling my way through a jig before settling on a lullaby my mama used to hum whenever I was scared. The words were always both my comfort and my sorrow, and I let myself feel it all that night. Every ache. Every lament. Every forlorn wish for a better future. I remember my empty cup, how no one deigned to toss a coin apart from one man—

Large build, dark hair, and a glower on his face. He threw five silvers in my cup, and I nearly wept with joy. It allowed me to eat. To escape. To live.

Jaromir is fading back into slumber again. His eyes stay relaxed, shut softly against the warm light of the tent and the weight of the truth he just dropped in my lap.

He heard me sing two years ago? He thought of me?

"Syl," he grunts as if trying to prevent himself from falling asleep. "Sing to me?"

Something warm fills my chest. A comforting swell of affection for this man.

"Of course." I lean over and give him a kiss on his forehead, pushing the hair away. I'd say I have leave to do so.

"My love waits past the heather and o'er the moor,
Oh how I wish I were there,

'Neath the tall, branching oak,
My love sits alone and waits for me.
I cannot follow where she goes, save for my heart.
It's always with she, always with she.

I am the lyre, she is the strings;
But no music sounds, not without my beloved
I cannot follow where she goes, save for my heart.
It haunts her steps, even as she leaves me behind."

Chapter Twenty

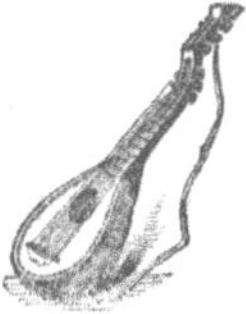

"A drink for the lass!" The boisterous voice of the tavern patron, a man with a bushy blond beard and heavy brow ridge, calls out. He told us his name but between the din of noise and his tongue softened by drink, I couldn't catch it.

This is one of the finest taverns I've ever been in. Suspended from the rafters, flickering lanterns swing each time someone opens the door and the summer breeze blows through. Beneath the bar, it's as if wild roots have sprung from the ground, wrapping their way up to frame each edge. A delicate arch of white wisteria hangs above the bar, filling the air with a sweet floral scent. It's far too lovely a detail amidst a crowd of drunken hollers and competing conversations.

I love it.

We arrived in Stoneridge a few hours ago, ready to hit the ground running. The days we spent traveling after Jaromir's fever broke were a blur. Mostly because he insisted on no delays, even going so far as to ride Turnip with me so I might sleep in the saddle.

I'm not complaining.

I flash Jaromir a grin and earn that smile I've decided

belongs solely to me. The one that's all warmth and fondness. Even if I tend to quickly chase it away with a joke that earns me his famous scowl.

Neith is chatting up a group of dwarven merchants who have been traveling the main roads to Bridgebarrow. Clever to make friends with those who might spread word of our exploits.

I even added a few lines to my ballad detailing the arachnida fight. Of Aeron's dauntless attack on those beasts, armed with nothing but river rocks and a refusal to accept defeat.

It's funny how the same story featuring different people can sound so different. When I imagine myself, all I see is my fear, my weakness.

An elven woman, the first I've seen in this town, places a tankard in front of me. Her hair is bound beneath a patchwork kerchief, and her blue eyes shine with the brilliance of a mountain lake. Her ears have also been tucked beneath her kerchief, but their shape against the thin fabric is unmistakable.

The blond man claps me on the back, spilling the drink he'd just purchased me. I think it's ale. Goddess, that smell, I hope it's ale.

"You're a good kid," he says, ruffling my hat atop my head. "You've got a bright future ahead of you."

"How do you know I'm not your elder?" I ask, adjusting my cap and pretending to sip my drink. Jaromir angles his body to stand closer, and I want to tell him to relax but that's too obvious. In my experience, towns like Stoneridge are protective of their own. Many travelers come through, but outsiders can ruffle more than a few feathers.

"You're tiny! Like a child!"

I laugh even as something cold settles in my gut. I hate appearing an easy target. I'm not tiny, not by elvish standards. But I suppose I'm slight of build and on the shorter side.

I gesture to him. "And you're large which makes you ancient, is that how we equate age now?"

He snorts into his drink, spurting foam over the side. "Fair enough."

The tension flees Jaromir's body, and he leans against the bar. I reach out to grab his hand, reveling in the easy affection we've come to share. His thumb runs circles against my knuckle, and he smiles down at me.

We still haven't spoken of what was said—of when the fever spilled confessions from his lips I'm not sure he wanted to share. But I haven't caught a whiff of shame or regret from him.

Unless he doesn't remember. That would be unfortunate.

As if sensing my thoughts, he places a quick kiss to my knuckle, much to the disappointment of a nearby brunette who'd been valiantly attempting to ensnare him with her charms.

A right shame.

"Are you ready?" Jaromir's gaze darts to the door, and I catch his meaning.

Tonight is the night Cadoc will don Aeron's armor. I will take to the stage once more, to sing an encore no one asked for when he makes his grand entrance.

I slide my questionable ale in front of him and give a short nod. "I'm always ready to put on a show." I fasten my brightest smile to my face. He hands me my lute, letting his fingers linger on mine before he lets go.

I take the stage, head held high and feather bouncing with each step. I wish I hadn't worn my thickest stockings. The night is sweltering, humidity thickening the air, and within this crowded tavern, there is no reprieve. But there are worse things than sweating.

I pluck a jaunty little tune, glancing about the room until I get the general sense people are quieting down to listen.

There's power in this, the ability to command the attention of a room filled with strangers. I knew even when I was little more than a gutter rat, I would never allow myself to exist powerless forever.

"Ladies and gentlemen... and the reprobates in the corner!" A hearty chorus of cheers call out from where Neith has been rubbing elbows with those merchants, and a real smile forms on my lips. "Did you think I was finished? Nay, there aren't enough songs in Common Tongue to lend our hero's exploits justice!"

I launch into a strum, allowing ample wait time for some of the rowdier patrons.

It's a dance, really. A give and take between entertainer and audience. Alienate your audience, and don't be surprised when they turn on you.

It's happened many times. Rotting fruit takes ages to wash out.

My gaze passes over laughing faces, clinking of tankards, and the occasional couple expressing their passions in a very public way. But closest to the stage, a table filled with unfriendly faces snags my attention. There's nothing remarkable about the five people seated nearest me, save for the coldness of their expressions. One man in particular glares daggers at me. His dark hair is shaved on the sides, and the longer top portion is tied back in a knot. His ruddy face, from either drink or heat, is twisted in disapproval, and his eyes... it's too dark to make out their color, but the anger reflected in them is clear as day.

Perhaps he doesn't like bards. Or music. Or fun. It's no matter to me. Can't dazzle everyone with my brilliance.

I shift my focus to find the only face that holds my interest.

Jaromir.

He watches me with his penetrating gaze, a twitch of his mouth revealing his amusement.

I leap to stand atop my stool, showing off a little.

*"Sir Aeron has the heart of a warrior and the mercy of a
saint*
With warmth that rivals the sun and drives darkness away
*Man or beast of evil intent will fall to his sword, fall to his
sword*
*He'll bring us deliverance, mark my words, mark my
words"*

At his cue, Cadoc strides in, decked out in Aeron's armor.
We took painstaking attention polishing it to a high sheen, and
in the candlelight, he looks like a fierce guardian descended
from the Welkin.

"Ah, fair lass! You've sung of me long enough, I should
think." Cadoc turns to survey the room, a proud smile on his
handsome face. Ideally, we wouldn't have revealed anyone's
face in Aeron's armor, but since it's illogical for him to wear a
helm in the tavern, especially if we're to have him mingle with
the patrons, we'll make do. Since both he and Jaromir will
show their faces, eyewitness accounts won't align.

Drunk eyewitnesses are most preferable.

All the quicker to make him the mythic hero he deserves
to be.

"Come! Let us all have a round of drinks on me!"

The erupting cheers and howls are deafening, but this is
almost as important as my ballad. Nothing says hero quite like
a man willing to part with his own coin to get a stranger drunk.

Two things that bring people together: pain and drinking.

I stash my lute upon my back, leaping down from my stool
to join Jaromir at the bar. Cadoc has already been flooded with
admirers and thirsty friends. The crowd thickens, blocking my
way. I pull the cap from my head, fanning myself before
replacing it. It's boiling in here, and no one is really noticing

me anymore. I've done my part, and now it's Cadoc's turn. He's to charm everyone in the establishment, already halfway there, and I am to escape the sweaty tavern and sit beneath the stars. Preferably with a certain scowl-wearing man and a thick slice of bread. With a side of custard. And a bottle of wine because, dammit, I earned it.

My eager steps land me smack into a giant wall of a man. I bounce off his chest as if I'm a bird flying into a glass window.

"Apologies," I say quickly, skirting around his massive form—

A strong hand clamps around my upper arm, holding me locked in place. I glance up to find the man who seemed to loathe my performance. This close I can count the pores on his nose as he glares down at me. Fear grips my chest in a suffocating embrace.

This has nothing to do with my performance. I can feel it in the way my muscles freeze. This is an anger I've spent my life fearing.

But I can't let him know that.

I try to yank out of his bruising grip as a cold sweat erupts across my palms. "Etiquette dictates we speak with our words, not with our hands."

He doesn't relent. "I called you over and you ignored me."

"What a perfectly logical response! Well, you have my attention. Unhand me and speak your piece."

It takes every shred of my control to keep my voice even. The last thing we need is to cause a scene. I glance around, searching for Jaromir, but the tavern is crowded. I can't see him beyond the mass of bodies flooding the bar.

"We want another round for the table."

"Ah. Not a server so I'm afraid you're tapping the wrong tree, so to speak. But I'm sure you heard, my very generous friend over there is happy to pay for your drinks at the bar—"

He yanks me hard, and my shoulder twinges with the

motion. His hateful stare fills my vision, and my stomach churns. "Listen up, knife-ear. You're lucky we even let you into this tavern. Go get our drinks before I show you what your kind really deserves."

I'm sure I have a retort ready. It's on the tip of my tongue awaiting release. But my throat squeezes, and a fluttering cold fills my chest. My legs go numb, and I'm not sure how I'm still standing. My head spins, and I swear, if the panics set in again—

"Get your fucking hands off her."

Jaromir's voice is a low rumble of darkness. He steps between us, slow and deliberate, but there's nothing gentle about how calm he seems.

The man staggers back, a flash of fear in his eyes, but he quickly masks it with a sneer.

Jaromir's hand flexes against the pommel of his sword. He turns to me, ignoring the man completely and leveling me with the full force of his assessing stare. "Did he hurt you?"

I almost rub the spot where his hand squeezed my arm. I can already feel the telltale bruise forming. There's no sense in lying, but I won't fan the flame of Jaromir's anger. "Not enough to warrant retaliation."

Jaromir raises a brow in silent question as if to ask, *are you sure?*

My hand finds his, and I gently tug him toward me. "He isn't worth ruining the night." This answer is loaded with meaning. We have a greater purpose, a greater aim in coming here.

He nods, giving my hand a squeeze. If we can just get outside, get some air, we can forget all about this unpleasantness and celebrate tonight's win. After everything, we deserve—

"Get the other knife-ear over here. I'm fucking thirsty."

Jaromir freezes, his nostrils flaring and his jaw clenching.

Oh, but the door is right there, we were so close.

Jaromir turns back to face the idiot who can't keep his mouth shut. "Is that what you called her?"

The bastard actually looks confused. Jaromir drops my hand, shoving into the man's space. His hand is around his throat faster than I can blink.

"Jaromir," I call out, "he isn't worth it." *Shit. Fuck. Tits.* "Please, let's just go."

Neith appears, placing a hand on Jaromir's shoulder. Reluctantly, he steps away. "Peace, friend. I'm sure it's a misunderstanding." She looks down her nose at the ruddy-faced man. "If ye apologize, we can all return t'our evening."

Disheveled and gasping for air, the man's eyes widen in shock. "Apologize? You're lucky I didn't cut her little rabbit ears off for running her mou—"

Neith punches him in the throat, and whatever he was about to say is lost to a gurgling noise. She tackles the man to the ground and wails on him blow after blow. His companions dive after her, but Jaromir blocks, landing a punch that sends a stray tooth flying. A battle cry blended from a group of voices rings out, as the dwarven merchants Neith had been sitting with leap into the fray. Tossing bottles and tankards at anyone who attacks her flank.

Cadoc appears, holding a wooden club, and beats back a few stragglers. Neith is still bashing her fist against the man on the floor, strike after strike to his already bloodied and mottled face. A rage has taken over her features.

Someone breaks a chair over a man's back, and splinters fly. The crunch of broken glass under boots and grunts of pain fill the air in a brutal song. If this wasn't the worst outcome for tonight, it might make a thrilling ballad.

Jaromir pulls Neith off the man, shoving her toward Cadoc who leads her out of the tavern. Cadoc tosses the club and a full coin purse toward the barkeep as he passes. The barkeep catches both, giving a short nod of acknowledgement.

Jaromir leans down to grip the battered man by the hair— the man who started it all. He whispers something in his ear, slamming his fist into his bloodied face one last time. He stands and winds his arm around my shoulders, steering me around broken glass and splintered wood.

I allow him to guide me to the door, tripping on overturned chairs. The noise of the tavern fades to a dissonant ringing of angry voices.

The night is still oppressive in its heat, but the open sky offers sanctuary. When we're far enough away, Neith shrugs out of Cadoc's hold, cracking her knuckles.

Jaromir rubs my shoulder. "Are you all right?"

I exhale a harsh breath. "Let's see. All the goodwill we earned in that tavern? Gone. Do you think they'll remember us fondly after this? No. We'll be remembered as the group that brought the knife-ear into the tavern, causing a bloody riot."

His face hardens. "Don't call yourself that."

"Why not?" I give a brittle laugh that aches in my chest. "It's what I am, isn't it? Do you really think that was the first time I've had to deal with this? Or even the worst encounter I've had?"

I'm dangerously close to hitting a note of hysteria I'm not ready to face. I take a few calming breaths, anchoring myself to my surroundings. I am safe. I am not alone.

Jaromir reaches out, tucking a tendril of hair behind my pointed ear. "I can't erase the past or whatever you've faced. But I will not allow anyone to treat you thus." He glances over at Neith. "Neither will she."

"Nor I," Cadoc says. I'd nearly forgotten he was here, which seems impossible to do with how much Aeron's armor shines even in the night. "And to address your concerns, I spoke to the barkeep before our little scuffle even broke out.

He said that lot has been causing trouble for months. He was practically begging us to do something about it, us being heroes and all." A crooked smile tugs at his mouth, dimpling his cheek. "I paid him off, but I don't get the sense anyone viewed us as the offending party so"—he twists his mouth to the side—"no harm done?"

It may have worked out this time, but we need to come to an accord on how we deal with this type of thing.

It won't be the last.

I bury my face in Jaromir's chest, muffling a particularly colorful stream of curses even amidst my relief. When I pull away, Neith has stepped closer, and if I thought I'd find any remorse on her stunning face, I was sorely mistaken. She stretches, flashing a satisfied smile.

"Thank you," I say, "for defending my honor."

As much as I wished for a peaceful resolution, one that ended in less fanfare and dislodged teeth, there's a comfort in knowing I have someone who'll tackle a man to the floor and beat him senseless for wounding me.

And I have three of these people in my life now.

Neith glances down at her torn and bloodied knuckles. "It was my pleasure."

Chapter Twenty-One

The Cunning Fox Inn holds our reservations, granting us rooms for the night.

Two rooms—Cadoc bunking with Neith and Jaromir staying with me—a deliberate choice that has me trembling with anticipation.

Neith flashes us a knowing grin, but Cadoc pauses, a furrow to his brow as he studies the two of us. Neith drags him away and bids farewell for the night.

Jaromir leads me by the hand to our room. I stumble over eager feet, wondering if he still remembers the promise he made days ago in the safety of his tent. When we reach the door, he ushers us in, quickly lighting candles and placing the lantern on the bedside table. The room is filled with the soft orange glow of fire light. A bed large enough for the both of us is against the far wall, a chair is tucked in the corner, and my heart leaps at what sits in the center of the room. A large wooden bath, ready and waiting to be filled.

I spin around to find him already grabbing the nearby bucket.

"I get to bathe?" I grin and bounce on my heels.

"We get to bathe," he says, laughing.

A shiver of delight races up my spine. The only thing more enticing than a bath, is a bath with him.

"I'll fill the tub and then we can light the coals."

"I get to take a warm bath?!"

His answering grin floods me with heat as if I've already stepped into a basin of hot water.

It takes longer than I prefer, him running back and forth to fill the tub, but it's better than asking someone else to do it and awkwardly waiting and watching. I busy myself by quickly washing with the tabletop basin, ewer of water, and my soap. I know I'm about to soak in a bath, but I'd rather not stew in my own filth. I'd much prefer to laze in the water for as long as it holds heat, and that will be far more relaxing if I know the water is somewhat clean. I fumble with the package Kingsley sent with me when I first departed on my journey. I shrug off my doublet and lift my tunic over my head. Then I pull down my short pants and stockings. I scrub my skin until it's raw, and reach for the white tunic I wear to bed and a fresh pair of short pants. My hair still needs washing, but at least my body feels clean. The comforting scent of black currant envelops me, and for reasons I can't quite name, tears blur my vision.

I don't want to go back to Hollowden. Not anytime soon, at least. I'm happy with my life on the road, with this quest, with Jaromir. Yet, I ache for my narrow cot in the corner of my small room, the one Kingsley and Brigitta set up for me. I miss the shitty ale and wine we served and my nights of badgering Kingsley with big ideas while waiting for Petey to wake up and head home.

I've always known I needed more than that town, than a life graced by charity. And I have that now. I have purpose, adventure, and people who care for me, not out of pity but out of mutual understanding.

So why are my eyes burning?

Jaromir appears, and I quickly clear my throat and wipe my nose. He frowns, dumping the last bucket of water into the large tub, striking the flint to light the coals before shutting and locking our door. In three strides, he's before me, studying me with that penetrating intensity. "You're upset."

"No," I say, "I just wasn't prepared for how memory is triggered by scent." I give a theatrical sniff of his clothes. "See? Now it's as if I'm on the road, rubbing up against the horses."

He steps back to pull his tunic over his head.

Any notion of wistfulness is gone as I drink in his imposing form. He's all hard lines and sharp edges. Heat pools in my stomach, and I want nothing more than to feel every inch of him against me.

"Tell me your thoughts." His voice has taken an even rougher quality.

"I was thinking I'm ready to make some new memories." It sounded cleverer in my head.

His mouth tips up in a soft smile, before he frowns at the tabletop basin behind me. "You couldn't wait for your bath?"

"I'd rather not see leaves and dirt floating in the water. I plan on relaxing in there until my skin is wrinkled like a prune."

His baritone laugh makes my stomach flutter. "I'll do the same." He stalks over to the basin, and dips a nearby cloth into the water. Welkin above, I swear the way he wrings the water out is damn near obscene. So is the way he runs the cloth over his rippling muscles, down his abdomen, and dipping into his low slung trousers.

When he begins to unlace them, he nods toward me, an unmistakable command even without words. I tug my tunic over my head, revealing my upper half. A strip of cloth—my breastband—is all that remains. Jaromir sucks in a sharp breath. His eyes greedily rake down my form, his throat bobbing. When his stare finally meets mine again, his mouth is slightly parted.

"Why did you stop?"

I shiver and pull down my short pants until I'm clad in nothing but my smallclothes. Jaromir lets out a groan, pushing his laces open and shoving his trousers down low enough to free his hardening length. My skin buzzes with anticipation, and my stomach dips. I'd only ever seen him in the dark tent, but watching him run the cloth against himself, take himself in hand while candlelight dances across his magnificent form makes my blood heat and my vision spin.

He advances on me, and I freeze, awaiting the relief of his touch. When it comes, when he slides his rough palms down my bared arms, leaving goose pebbles in their wake, I want to weep.

He sinks to his knees, placing reverent kisses against the plane of my stomach, my hips, my thighs. It's dizzying, and I grab ahold of his shoulders to keep myself upright. His hands roam the expanse of skin at the back of my legs, up over the curve of my backside, and he squeezes possessively. I'm a panting mess as his hands venture higher, higher. So lost in the feel of his touch, I don't think to stop him.

When his hands reach the small of my back, he freezes. I'm paralyzed in place, my hands fisted in his hair as he runs cautious fingers against the spots that never see the light of day.

"What are these?" His voice is soft, careful.

I clear my throat, keeping my eyes trained on the wall. "Scars. Have you none of your own? What a sheltered life you lead."

"Show me."

This feels like a trap. "Only if you intend on picking up where we left off immediately after."

Finally, I chance a glance down where he kneels staring up

at me. He nods, and slowly stands. I keep as still as possible while he circles to my backside, the side I've always carefully kept from view. He doesn't make a sound, only gently runs his hands over each one. My eyes slip closed, and I try to stay here in this moment with the sensation of his tentative touch.

I was a mere elfling when I docked at the port. Alone. Starving. It didn't take long for me to resort to desperation. The first time I swiped an apple from the fruit cart in the market, I was giddy. It was my stake in an unfamiliar world, one that perhaps didn't even notice the point of my ears, and nothing had ever tasted so sweet.

I grew bolder. Swiping breads, and once even a mincemeat pie. It was freedom—it was life. Gone were the days when my ears meant I was hunted for sport. I could appear and disappear at will, and no one paid me any mind. My parents—their sacrifice to see me safe and out of harm's way, in a new world where I might *thrive* wasn't in vain. I had living proof in the food filling my belly and my eagerness to greet each dawn.

The day I went after a braided sugar cake, I was careless. I never thought what might happen if I was caught. I never thought they'd strap me to a post in the middle of town and whip me until I screamed and bled and vomited. I never thought they'd spit on me and call me a thieving knife-ear. That even though so much had changed, in a way, everything was still the same. I was still nothing.

They left me tied to that post, covered in blood, vomit, and tears for the night before they cut me loose. The aim was to teach me that stealing is a sin.

All it taught me was the importance of not getting caught.

Jaromir's touch brings me back to this moment. He places a soft kiss against my scarred flesh, the heat of his breath chasing a shiver through me. His words, too, are soft as he murmurs against my skin. "Whoever did this, do they live?"

I can hardly focus on his words, so lost in the feel of him.

"Um, I think so? I haven't ventured to Bridgebarrow in years." The guards all looked alike to a small, terrified child. I don't think I could picture their faces even if I wished to.

"Anyone who hurts you, I'll light their pyre myself. I don't care how long ago it was."

Before his words can settle in my fog-addled brain, he exhales against my skin, yanking my small clothes down to my ankles and freeing my legs one at a time. He stands, towering over me once more. A hand slides in my hair, tilting my face up, and his mouth descends, brutal and thorough in its pursuit. His kiss is ravenous, angry, before it melts into a soft caress.

There's a tug at my back, and my breastband falls away. Jaromir kisses his way down my neck, my collarbone, my chest. His tongue is hot and eager, worshiping me until my sanity is fraying. My entire body, naked and flushed, is pressed against his half-clothed one.

That seems unfair.

I tug at his hair, hard. "You're overdressed," I say breathlessly. "It's woefully poor manners."

He grunts his agreement, lifting me, and carrying me over to the bed. He lowers me to the soft coverlet with heart breaking gentleness, before dropping to his knees. Yanking me to the edge, he deftly maneuvers my legs over his shoulders.

"What are you—the bath is that way!"

He bites my inner thigh, and I gasp at the sudden influx of heat pooling between my legs. "After," he says darkly.

"But the water will get—*oh*."

His tongue parts me with soft, slick precision, and pleasure jolts through me. Sealing his mouth over my heat, he kisses me, deeply, thoroughly, leisurely. Propping myself on my elbows, I gaze down at him. His eyes are all consuming, holding me trapped in his thrall as he obliterates me with each slide of his tongue and the wet movements of his mouth.

I could die like this and be utterly content.

When his finger presses in, I keen. My body feels stretched taut like a too tight string of a lute, and he masterfully plays me as if he already knows my body by heart. When he groans, the vibration is too much for me to bear, and a sharp spike of pleasure floods through me, crashing and clenching in seemingly endless waves.

He presses one last kiss to me, earning a soft cry, before he pushes me back on the bed and climbs up, covering my body with his.

"No... fair," I say weakly.

Jaromir presses a wet kiss to my mouth. "Forgive me for being selfish. But I waited years to taste you. It's only fair I make up for lost time."

Selfish. Only Jaromir could stare down at me, his face still glistening from devouring the space between my thighs, and call it *selfish.* That, and the fact that he so casually mentioned the confession he made when he was suffering the venom-induced fever. It's an offering—a way of showing he remembers what he told me and suffers no shame of it. Something about my expression must amuse him because he grins and places a quick kiss to the tip of my nose.

"The water is still hot. The heating stones will keep its temperature." He moves to slide down the bed, and I seize the opportunity and flip our positions. He must allow this, because there's no way I'm stronger, but the flare of surprise in his eyes is genuine.

I make quick work of his trousers since they're already unlaced.

If he can take what he pleases, so can I.

Dropping between his legs, I lower my mouth over him, his thickness spreading my lips and making something coil deep in my gut. He cries out, I'm not sure if it's meant to be a word, but it's more of a guttural sound. I swallow down his length before he can think to object.

"Fuck." His hands tangle in my hair, brushing against my ears, and I'm lost in the feel of him stretching my mouth, the salty taste of him on my tongue.

It's addictive.

Jaromir watches me with his heavy gaze, groaning each time I punch him deeper into my throat. An attractive flush creeps up the hard expanse of his chest, and a tingle starts low in my belly. There's a vulnerability in this, a trust both received and given, and my head spins from the dizzying pleasure of that.

"Syl, you should—I'm going to—"

I take him deeper, needing to see, to feel, to taste this. His trust. His loss of control.

Jaromir's head falls back, and I swallow down the spill of his release. When he pops free of my mouth, he yanks me up, crushing me to his chest, and sweeping his greedy tongue into my mouth as if he wants to taste himself on me. He practically tackles me to the bed, running possessive hands all over my body.

"You are, without a doubt"—he punctuates his words with another languid kiss—"going to be the death of me."

I slap his chest with no real strength behind it. "What a horrid thing to say after acquainting yourself with my mouth. I have half a mind to write a scathing song about this if only to teach you some manners."

He laughs but it melts into a pained groan. "Gods, your mouth. What am I going to do with you?"

Mark me. Fill me. Love me. Promise to never stop.

"How about that bath?" Much safer request.

He shakes his head. "It's much too late for that now. I told you I wouldn't let you leave my bed once I had you."

Pleasure trembles up my spine as wet heat spreads between my legs. I rub my thighs together, as if it will quell my ache. "What a teasing degenerate you are. Did you ever intend to let me soak in the bath? I have a special diffusing soap I'd very much like to try. You pop it in, and it makes the water thick with its scent. It even spouts little bubbles. Let's be honest, there are certain places that only come clean with a good, honest, soak. And if you think I'm going to forget the comforts of a long bath—"

Jaromir cuts me off with another bruising kiss. "Syl, you'll get your bath. First let me make you filthy."

I can't help my grin at the promise. I wrap my legs around his hips, pressing my feet to the backs of his powerful thighs. With a slow, deliberate movement, I rub my heat against his increasing hardness, pulling a strangled groan from his chest. I gasp at the way pleasure jolts from the contact.

I wasn't jesting when I said it had been years. When youth first blended into the early age of adulthood, there was a boy who'd meet me in the barn behind the butcher shop where he worked. He'd never speak to me in public—this was Elmwood, where my ears put 'respectable' people on edge—but we shared clumsy kisses and poorly rhythmic motions, following the call of instinct.

But this. Jaromir isn't even in me, and this is already so much more.

"Sylvaine." Jaromir's voice is a soft caress, and I find myself held captive by the emotion in his dark eyes. The unspoken promise, the assurance of care. He gazes down at me as if I'm something precious, something to be cherished, and part of my heart breaks that I never imagined anyone looking at me this way.

He tucks a sweaty lock of hair behind my ear, running his touch down the length, as he always does. "Are you sure you want this?"

There's something in the way he asks this. It doesn't feel as if he's asking me if I want to continue, as I'm rubbing my naked self against him with wanton abandon. It feels like he's asking if I really want *him*.

It dissipates any snarky response I might have made. "More than anything."

Unnamed emotion fills his eyes as he nods once. "This isn't going to sound very romantic, but I asked Cadoc for a thorough inspection, and you needn't worry about... consequences of this."

Now I'm confused.

"I'm healthy. There's no risk of you contracting any sort of infection."

Oh. My gut squirms. Not because of the conversation; the man is responsible and thoughtful. I find it utterly endearing he thought this through, and I can't even laugh at what I'm sure was an uncomfortable exchange between him and Cadoc when he asked for such an inspection.

No, my discomfort comes from my impetuousness. I didn't think to ask after that. Here I am rubbing up against him like a cat in heat, and any good sense I might have had disappears entirely.

"And there's no chance we'll conceive."

"That hadn't even crossed my mind. What a foolishly impractical lecher I've turned out to be."

Jaromir huffs a laugh. "Cadoc brews something for me. Something to ensure I won't put anyone in the position of facing any repercussions."

It's irrational, but I can't help my reaction. Jealousy flares in my gut, a cold sinking feeling. He's been taking this long before we had a chance to explore our attraction, and yes, he is practical, and it is sweet that he would think to address this rather than expect the woman to. But the fact that this gesture existed before I was even a thought to receive it only sharpens the reminder that just a few short weeks ago, he likely was having this same conversation with another woman. He has no shortage of admirers, as is evidenced by the fact that hungry eyes seem to follow him wherever he goes. And he's only in this position with me because I all but begged him to use me for his physical comforts. And why am I thinking of this right now? I'm going to ruin every—

"Syl, look at me." His voice interrupts my inner tirade, and I blink up at him, clearing my blurred vision. "Where did your thoughts go?"

"I—" It would be easier to lie. Likely protect his good opinion of me, too. But I'm not in the business of lying. I might stretch the truth for a good story, but that's for show.

And I'm sick of performing.

"I was remembering you had a life before me, that's all."

Understanding dawns his face, and he cups my jaw. "Yes, I did. And I won't pretend I've never felt affection for another woman." Before I can spin another mental spiral on that thought, he continues. "But you... Syl, you change *everything*." He kisses me, a featherlight touch. One of quiet reverence. "You're more than I ever thought I'd find in this lifetime. More than I deserve."

My throat tightens, and I exhale a shaky breath, letting a soft laugh escape. "You're very good with words when you want to be."

He touches his nose to mine, and my heart swells. "I'm trying to learn to use words. I've been told I rely too much on grunting and growling."

"But I was just becoming fluent in Jaromir."

He laughs, and I'm entranced by how beautiful he is like this. I kiss him, slowly. Trying to pour everything I feel and wish for in that kiss.

"So," I say, "you've told me how you feel. Care to show me?"

Chapter Twenty-Two

Jaromir's mouth descends once more. His kiss is soft, exploring—judging and weighing the strength of my feelings. He offered me a precious gift when he spoke so freely, knowing I needed to hear these things.

But Jaromir speaks best with his actions.

His thick hardness rubs against me, and he deepens his kiss with a groan. My skin is on fire, and I'm about to drown. Somehow, these opposing feelings coexist in the strength of his embrace. In the spark of his touch.

He lines himself up, watching with his intent stare as he slowly stretches me and sinks in. When I cry out, he stills, studying my face for any sign of discomfort. I nod and try to push him deeper with my feet against the backs of his thighs. His dark eyes drift back to where we're joined, where he's splitting me, achingly slow.

"Fuck," he says, still watching the sight with rapt attention.

"*Jaromir.*" His name is a needy whine in my throat, and he actually smirks at me.

"Slowly," he says. "Don't... want to hurt you."

But I'm lost in the liquid slide of him filling me with such care and devotion. I can't wait. I need more. I grab at his firm backside, trying to pull him to me, and he scrapes out a stuttered laugh. He bottoms out, groaning as the last of him fills me.

Sharp pleasure sparks in my belly. It's a fuller feeling than I've ever experienced, and I'm dizzy with the sensation. I've never given much thought to our difference in size, but the sheer fullness of our joining, and the way his body engulfs mine, makes me realize how much larger he is. I don't feel vulnerable, I feel cared for. That thought makes my body clench with liquid pleasure, ripping a deep moan from his chest. When he begins to withdraw, I whimper, and he shoves back in with a firm thrust.

Oh.

He doesn't withdraw too far, just enough to make me mourn the depth of his length, and with each plunge he punctuates the strength of his pleasure.

Settling into a beautifully tortuous rhythm, he circles his hips each time he drives all the way in. Canting my hips to meet his, my vision blurs from the onslaught. Every nerve in my body sings. I rake my nails down his back, seeking relief from the exquisite torment of his ministrations.

He bites my neck before soothing the spot with his tongue.

There's something so pure about the unfiltered pleasure stealing my vision and hardening every line of his body. A song untainted by the pressures of the world and the expectations of life. It's nothing but his body responding to mine, and mine lost in the instinctive rightness of our joining.

I couldn't possibly write a ballad to match the beauty of this raw moment.

My mouth finds his in a messy kiss, sliding down to his jaw, his neck. The sting of his beard only sends my nerves alight. Nothing exists outside of this need, this pleasure. Jaromir lets out a guttural groan, lifting to his knees and pulling my body with him. He slams me down hard on him, circling deep until I see stars. There's a brutality in this. A desperate cry of need, of life, of love, and I'm falling.

His hands, his mouth, his tongue, his teeth. They're everywhere. Everywhere as he fills me and drives in deeper, deeper. My heart squeezes, and my stomach clenches.

"Jaromir," I sob, unable to articulate how I'm drowning in pleasure, in need.

His thumb finds the spot that makes me clench as waves of euphoria crash over me again, and again. With a shout, he slams deep, holding himself within me as his release empties and fills. Warm, wet heat floods me as he slowly lays us back on the bed, back down to earth, back into the rapid beating of my heart.

Gentle kisses caress my face as he leans over me, still inside, and brushes my hair out of my eyes. His thumbs wipe my cheeks, and I sigh into his touch.

Words are my life. My calling. And there are no words for what I just experienced. Maybe the best things can't be described in spoken or written word. Maybe they can only be felt.

Jaromir watches me, hovering above as if waiting for my reaction.

"That... was..." My words stall because there are none.

He exhales a breath of a laugh. "Yes, it was."

Finally, he withdraws, lying beside me and pulling me to rest my head against his chest. His fingers card through my hair, sending shivery comfort through my head.

"Is it normal to feel... drunk?"

I don't need to see his face to know he's smiling. I can hear it when he says, "That's a good way to put it."

I snuggle deeper against his sweat-slicked skin, placing a kiss against his collarbone.

"Don't sleep yet." His low voice is hypnotic against my ear. "I promised you a hot bath."

I'd almost forgotten about the hot basin of water in our room.

I leap up, collapsing almost immediately, since my bones are now liquid. Jaromir scoops me up and carries me over to the tub. I lean my head against his shoulder, unable to name the emotion that fills my chest.

It's remarkable how much joy one can find in a hot bath. Especially when a handsome man who just pleasured you to near insanity is washing your hair.

This is a luxury I could get used to.

The familiar scent of black currant fills the tub, as I lean against Jaromir's naked chest. The basin is large enough for us both to fit, me caged between his knees. There's a domestic intimacy to this. It's less urgent than the animalistic coupling from earlier, but it fills my body with a humming sense of pleasure, of safety. He rinses the soap from my hair, massaging my head, neck, and shoulders as I slowly fade to a blissful oblivion.

I've just finished describing the forests in Smarighad, where I used to run and play as a child. Where the trees grow taller than the eye can see and giant oyster mushrooms hover above, wider than the roof of a house and perfect for climbing.

"My childhood was a thing of magic... until it wasn't. My parents tried to shield me as best they could, but one by one, everyone I'd grown up with seemed to disappear. My friends... our neighbors... everyone just left. No goodbyes, no explanations." I tilt my head to the side as Jaromir finds a particular tense knot in my shoulder. His attentions and the weightlessness of my body give me courage to continue. "It was as if something sucked them into the sky, and they floated away. I didn't understand at the time, how we could go from trusting the forest and playing freely to hiding in fear."

"The elven raids," Jaromir murmurs solemnly.

I nod. It was a bloodbath. After The Great Loss, elves fell to the lowest rank of society, and an uneasy peace had settled over the land. But for generations, the distrust of elves had been building. There had always been stories of elven magic and how dangerous it was. It was our belief that, centuries ago, the ancient elves possessed great power, but no echoes of this power had trickled through to the elves of present day.

It didn't stop the humans from telling their tales. How an elf could control thoughts with the mere sound of their voice, or how they drank the blood of innocent human children. It was ridiculous, and for a time, we relied on logic and rational thinking to keep us from harm. No one of sound mind would truly believe those things, so it went ignored.

Until enough dissent was sown, and any peace we thought we had, vanished. It started with land disputes. It was easy enough for town magistrates to side with a human on their word over an elf's, because elves were forbidden to speak in official councils, just in case the stories were true, and they could sway their minds with magic.

Then came the accusations. *An elf hypnotized me into bedding them. I never would have traded that fabric for so cheap, she must have wielded her elven magic.*

The raids weren't far off after that. Elves lost the right to hold titles, including land. Those who refused to relinquish property and move into the cities where we would be subject to searches and curfews were branded as fugitives. And for a taxation fee, humans were given license to hunt fugitive elves for sport. Some of the hunters even wore ears on a chain around their necks like trophies.

Though we were tied to the land, with memories and generations of ancestors laying our claim, it was no longer home. Those who could, left, fleeing our land to find safer shores. But the price to escape was steep, and there weren't many vessels willing to transport elves to the continent.

We could only afford one boarding pass. I had to leave my parents behind, knowing a life of imprisonment faced them, or worse.

Here, the hate and mistrust of elves isn't so blatant. I don't fear for my life simply walking down the road. But I double check my cap before every performance to make sure my ears are covered. I never know how widespread that fear has traveled or when it might strike again. Fear is a powerful thing, capable of making monsters of us all.

I don't wish to think of this. I don't even know why it came to me now.

I lean into Jaromir's touch, grateful that he seems to always know when to push and when to let me take control of what I share. It's hard to believe we've only known each other a month.

Well... *I've* only known *him* for a month.

"So," I say, "you really carried a torch for me for two years?"

He doesn't pause his attention, bless him, as he answers. "I did."

"Then why did you hate me at first?" The memory of the day he, Aeron, Cadoc, and Neith waltzed into The Rusty Nail fills my mind. I've come to learn scowling is his face's natural disposition. But Jaromir wouldn't even look at me, his fists clenching as if he was in physical pain. He was rude and didn't even toss a coin in my cup.

"I wasn't expecting to ever see or hear you again."

"But wouldn't you be happy? I mean if you were madly in love with me for two years, and fate brought you into my tavern whilst I was giving a wonderful performance."

"I was caught off guard."

Relief and disappointment war for dominance at his casual ignoring of my dropping the word love. "You didn't seem off guard. You seemed angry."

He presses his thumb into the base of my neck, and a groan slips loose from my mouth. "Perhaps I was a little. Seeing you tormented me with what I couldn't have. Doesn't excuse my behavior, though."

It still feels like I'm missing something vital to understand his initial reaction that day, but what do I know? My beautifully hulking, scowling man emotes in strange ways.

"Jaromir?"

"Hm?"

"Are you... mine?"

It occurs to me, we've exchanged no vows or promises, only shared mind-blowing pleasures and moments of intimacy. Whatever we are, it started as a challenge for physical touch, one I leveled as an insult, but it's always been more. I'm not sure if it's unfair to ask, if he'll feel pressured to answer contrary to what he feels because of what we've just shared. But I need to know so I can stop thinking of him as my anything. If he isn't really mine, I need to disentangle before I grow any more attached.

His mouth finds the curve of my neck, placing an achingly soft kiss and exhaling against my skin. "For as long as you'll have me."

Chapter Twenty-Three

"Aiming should be instinctive, not exact. You won't have time to line up every shot for precision." Cadoc paces behind me, remarking on my form and offering adjustments. Day three back on the road, and I have to admit, it's been wildly more enjoyable than I ever expected.

"Did you know the earliest bow was of elven make?" Maybe I can distract Cadoc long enough he abandons our lesson. My neck and shoulders ache, and a cramp is working its way into my palm. It is true that bows are an elven design, not that anyone remembers such history.

"Shoot now. History lesson later."

Rats.

Neith still trains me in endurance and sword fighting each evening, and in the morning, while Jaromir packs up camp, Cadoc teaches me to shoot with a recurve.

This was Jaromir's idea to keep me out of close quarter combat and capitalize on my 'impressive aim with rocks.'

He whittled the bow I wield, claiming it was a project for idle hands early in the journey when he took watch.

We have two more villages to sing of Aeron's deeds and

spread his name, before we venture off the roads to find our dragon.

Once our adventure is complete, I suppose I'll have to head back to Hollowden, for nothing else than to bid farewell to Kingsley and Brigitta. I promised I would, but perhaps he knew not to expect me. That I was destined for fame and glory and everything that seemed so important not so long ago.

I'll finally be what I always wanted. A bard who wrote the epic tale of a great hero. I could probably gain access to any concert hall, sing in any tavern, and earn the respected title I've always deserved.

But why does this ring so hollow?

"How's your arm? You sore yet?" Cadoc stares at me expectantly.

I give a theatrical roll of my eyes so he doesn't suspect I was lost in thought. "I'm always sore."

"Good." He grins. "Shoot again."

I grit my teeth and nock another arrow. I've been informed the pull weight of my bow is *embarrassingly* low. Cadoc's words, not mine. But I have to start somewhere. "Honestly, wouldn't it be safer if I just throw rocks? I seem to have success with that."

"What do you think, Jaromir?"

Jaromir finishes loading the last saddlebag and comes to stand behind me. Every nerve in my body responds to his proximity. After our night at the inn, there aren't enough stolen moments in each day or night to sate my hunger for him.

Cadoc seems to have passed the role of instructor on to Jaromir, stepping away to examine his pack.

"How does the bow feel?" Jaromir is all calculated scrutiny, his perusal far too clinical for my taste.

"Awkward."

He hums to himself. "Noted. But I admit"—he leans close,

whispering in my ear—"you look stunning armed with a weapon."

My shot goes wide, and my arrow launches between the trees, lost forever. I glare at him. "That was your fault. Cadoc won't be happy."

He pulls me in for a kiss. "I'll fletch him a new one."

THE CLEAR NIGHT is a blanket of stars, and when my belly is stuffed with spit-roasted quail and fried apples, I lean back and sigh. I never realized how easy it is to starve in the city and thrive in the forest.

"Cadoc, my friend, you have a gift." I pat my full stomach. "Do you know how much coin people spend on meals like this?"

He grins, flashing his dimples and appearing utterly pleased with himself.

Neith smiles, too, gently kicking his foot. "Does Tomas know what a credit you'd be to the tavern?"

Cadoc kicks her back harder, biting his lip to hide how his grin widens at her comment.

Across the fire, Jaromir is whittling something small enough he keeps hiding it from view. No matter how many times I crane my neck to catch a glimpse, he snatches it away and tucks it in his arm.

"What's he got over there?" I nod my head in Jaromir's direction, aiming my question at Cadoc.

He leans up to get a better look, and Jaromir once again, tucks his secret project away. "Maybe he's making you a wood carving of his prick so he might get some sleep."

I toss a leftover quail bone in his direction. "What a grievous insult! It's far too small for that."

Neith chokes on her wine.

"Maybe it's a decorative piece to adorn the tavern when you and Tomas inherit the place," I say.

"Maybe," Jaromir cuts in, "it's my private business until I say otherwise."

"If you wanted it secret, why would you work on it where we can all see?" Cadoc leans back, lacing his hands behind his head.

"Because then he has th'perfect excuse t'glare at us for asking," Neith says with a laugh.

"I need the firelight." Jaromir frowns down at whatever is in his hand.

I lean over to grab my lute, plucking a soft melody. Neith and Cadoc reminisce about old jobs completed. The gentle sound of fire crackling, the scrapes of Jaromir's whittling, the hushed tones of conversation punctuated by bursts of laughter, and the tune to my song blend and weave to create the atmosphere of the night.

When Neith and Cadoc retire, leaving Jaromir to take first watch, I tuck my lute away and scoot closer to his side. Wordlessly, he lifts his arm to pull me to him, and I breathe in his familiar scent. Already the urge to shove him down and climb atop him is mounting, but we've decided it's best to wait until Cadoc's watch. Responsible, even. Jaromir doesn't wish to be *distracted*. Especially after the arachnida debacle.

"Would you be terribly distracted if you kept watch while I was free to do what I wish?" It's an innocent question.

Maybe not so innocent from the way he stares at me. "Like what?"

"I don't know," I say, casually slipping out of his hold to kneel in front of him, walking my fingers across his thighs. "Would it be too much of a distraction if I used my hand? My mouth?"

His hand closes over mine, halting my reach.

"Don't tempt me." His voice is a warning, and I want

nothing more than to see how far that warning extends until he breaks. He releases me, clearing his throat. "I have something for you."

"Is it more buttercups?" After he gave me my flower by the riverbank, they kept appearing in odd places, tucked behind my lute strings, carefully arranged outside my tent. And each time, I'd find Jaromir refusing to meet my eye.

I even suspect him of slipping them into my satchel those times I couldn't remember picking them.

Jaromir grins, shaking his head. "Not this time. It's, ugh, more of a present."

A present? I love presents. Not that I have much experience with receiving them. I jump back to my seat by his side.

"For me? Oh, Jaromir, you shouldn't have!" I stretch my eager hand out, wiggling my fingers in excitement.

He gives me a strange look, almost one of uncertainty, before placing something solid in my waiting palm. I close my fingers around it, bringing it to my face for closer inspection, while Jaromir watches me with a careful readiness as if I'm about to bolt.

It's a wooden handle with two arms reaching up and a leather strap with a stretching band attached to each limb.

He carved me a slingshot.

My very own slingshot.

It's utterly perfect.

I run my fingers over the delicate craftsmanship, sucking in a breath at each deliberate groove and marking. He carved a few music notes and a phrase I have to squint to read. The familiar letter shapes of a forgotten human language peers up at me.

Vis leaenae.

I'm eight summers old, writing my alphabets in the dirt. My da is laughing when I spell out a word that would earn me a swat from my mama. The same alphabets I practiced on the dust-covered deck on the boat to Targgein as I cried myself to sleep. A swell of emotion fills my chest, tightens my throat, and I cough out a watery laugh.

Strength of a lioness.

It's a ridiculous thing to carve into a slingshot handle, but somehow, it fits.

"You don't have to use it," he says, scowling at the ground.

"But I want to." I reach for him, lifting his chin to meet my eye. "Thank you."

He clears his throat, plucking the slingshot out of my grasp to turn it over in his hands. "It's a fine weapon. Don't laugh, I mean it."

I smother my laughter and wait for him to continue.

"It's a shepherd's sling, and I can forge you lead sling-bullets, or you can use acorns or rocks, as you are known to do." He hands it back to me. "Just don't hit any of us with it, and you'll be set."

I quit fighting my losing battle against my smile and throw my arms around his neck. "I love it! It's perfect."

When I pull away, he settles his arm around my shoulder, kissing the top of my head. "I'm glad you like it. But if you prefer the bow—"

"I hate the bow."

Jaromir laughs. "I thought you might. This is just as helpful in a fight, you know." He studies me intently. "A well-placed shot or two can turn the tide in any battle."

I nuzzle into his neck. "Well, consider your flank guarded."

He rests his chin against the top of my head. "You watch my back, I watch yours."

"Deal."

"Good," he says, "and tomorrow we work on your close quarter combat."

I tilt my head to examine his expression, only to find his serious resolve. "What? Neith has that covered."

"Neith is a skilled fighter, and her training methods are suitable."

I laugh and steal a quick kiss. "There's a 'but' coming, isn't there? That sounded nearly complimentary."

"But"—Jaromir smiles against my mouth—"I would feel more comfortable if I could train you, too."

I want to tease him. I want to threaten to tattle on him to Neith and laugh when she makes him run endurance drills. But something about the quiet contemplation in his eyes gives me pause. So, instead I ask, "Why?"

He bundles me closer to his chest. "Because, if something ever happened, and I wasn't there, I want to ensure you come back to me."

Oh.

I lay my head back down against his chest, breathing in his scent.

I can't find anything funny about that answer.

"Tell me again, what are my advantages?" Jaromir faces me, his dark hair tied back in a knot and his stance relaxed.

After I'd agreed to let him train me in hand-to-hand combat, he had insisted we begin first thing in the morning. But his mornings start so much earlier than mine.

He watches me with a severe expression, the one that's all cold stoicism. As if we hadn't spent the night before tangled in each other's arms, gasping against each other's skin.

"You're larger, stronger, and the aggressing party—so your intent is aimed on control and overpowering."

He nods once. "And your advantages?"

"My lady bits can be used for distraction."

He tuts a disapproving noise, his frown deepening. Guess we're not in the mood for jests.

"I'm smaller, faster, and my aim is escape," I amend.

"How is your objective an advantage?"

"So long as I can get far enough away from you, you're no longer a threat. You're reliant on incapacitating me, I just need to evade you. If that fails, I go for the easiest kill."

Warmth and approval glimmers in stare. "Good."

I'm not even ashamed of the ripple of pleasure that runs down my spine at his praise.

So far, we've spent our time practicing basic holds and defensive maneuvers, repeating attacks and evasions with slow precision so I master the techniques. Jaromir has proven to be a most patient instructor, and I'd be lying if I said I didn't enjoy playing at escaping his grasp.

"This time, we won't go at half speed," Jaromir says, stalking toward me. "And I won't go easy on you."

I'm practically vibrating with excitement. "All right, have at me, then."

He lunges, his massive hands gripping my throat and applying just enough pressure to make me panic. His earlier instructions float through my memory, and I tuck my chin to keep his grip from tightening against my air supply. Grabbing his wrists, I yank him toward me—slamming my knee into his stomach.

Jaromir grunts against the blow, smiling. "Good, but you haven't taken me out yet."

I bring my elbow across his face, before driving my palm into his nose. He releases, stepping back with a cough. I hesitate, waiting to see if he's all right—a mistake. He's already advancing.

I take off running, leaping over roots and fallen logs. His strides aren't far behind me, and his every exhale is harsh but measured. For a moment, I'm transported to when I would run through the forest as a child, all unchecked energy and bursts of speed. I revel in how strong my body is after a month and a half on the road and eating three nourishing meals a day. The wind I create with my speed tousles my hair and pricks my eyes. My path is winding, ever changing and impossible to predict—whatever it takes to throw him off my trail.

A memory returns, unbidden. Something curls in my stomach and a trembling dread steals the strength of my limbs. Suddenly, I'm nine summers old, playing with Mama's sister— my ahntan Elothwyn. She's braided my hair into a crown and adorned it with bluebells. She hears something—something that makes her grasp my wrist and yank me off the moss-covered stone I'd been using as a throne. *'Want to play chase? Run as fast as you can. Don't stop until you cross the river.'*

Heart pounding in my chest, a familiar panic starts to grip my throat.

'Faster, stóirín. Don't let me catch you.'

Pain stabs through my ribs, and my eyes blur. I push my pace harder, weaving around trees and avoiding rolling my ankle.

This isn't real. This is meant to prepare me. I trust Jaromir. And yet, a shaky fear spreads through my body as I propel my legs harder. Leaves and bracken soften my footfalls, but I'm running so hard, each step vibrates through my thighs.

His labored breathing comes faster. He's gaining on me.

I don't dare look behind me. Never look back. Keep your head forward. Aim for safety.

I pass a large tree, and for a millisecond, I debate climbing it. I doubt he's as strong a climber, the man is huge. But I'd be trapped with no way down and at his mercy.

My deliberation costs me.

Jaromir's large body crashes into me, dragging me down to the forest floor and somehow absorbing the fall. He straddles me, his thick thighs on either side of my legs, and his hands wind around my throat again.

My muscles tense. I can't fight my way free. He's stronger,

and I'm flailing on the ground, pressed into the dirt. Every nerve fires, buzzing beneath my skin. It's too loud. It's too quiet. My pulse is deafening in my ears.

What do I do? How do I escape?

He has me.

He has me.

Jaromir's instructions float back to the surface. I push every thought away, save for the memory of his spoken word again and again as we practiced the movements.

I grab his arm with both hands—one at his wrist, the other at his elbow—locking him in tight to my body. Bracing my foot beside his leg, I roll, tumbling his body beneath me. I yank the dagger from my boot—the one Neith gave me for safekeeping—and press it against his throat.

Jaromir stares up at me, eyes widening and a soft smile claiming his mouth. "I yield."

My hand is shaking, everything is shaking, when I roll off him to sit on the ground. I sheath the small blade, and drag a hand through my hair, trying to catch my breath.

Jaromir keeps a safe distance between us, but he leans toward me. "Are you all right?"

I don't know how to answer that question. It's difficult to assess how I am right now. But rather than respond in vague riddles, I give him the easiest answer.

"Of course," I say between heavy breaths. "Just need to do more endurance training with Neith."

He nods, accepting my lie. Well, it isn't quite a lie, I do need to work on my running stamina. But we both know this playacting scenario has left me rattled.

The memory of ahntan Elothwyn flutters against the edge of my mind. I don't want to think about that day. I've spent years burying it and there's no sense in dredging it up now.

"In fact," I continue, "I'd say we both could use a little work. I know I have much room for improvement, but at least I have a good excuse. I'm too busy changing the world with my brilliant songs and epic ballads. *You*, on the other hand, should have had no trouble catching me. It's almost as if you wanted me to evade you, which makes for a terrible attacker. My word, you should invest in schooling for nefarious intent, because you are utterly abysmal at catching your prey."

He watches me with that damnably probing stare, seeing every crack and flaw in the rapid spewing of my nonsense. Finally, he nods. "You're faster than you think, which sets me at ease."

That's right... this whole venture was meant to arm me with more skills should I need to call on them.

Because he's afraid for me.

I don't know why, but for some reason, that helps me tuck away my fear. Almost as if I'm sharing the burden of it all.

Jaromir tugs me against his chest, wrapping me in the safety of his arms.

Chapter Twenty-Four

"Ladies and gentlemen! It gives me immeasurable pleasure to spread the word of the greatest hero of this age! His ancestors, sired by the actual gods! His virility is unmatched, and his generosity knows no bounds!" I holler into the crowd of the Golden Selkie, giving everything I have to this performance. I've learned that talk of the goddess or her guardians alienates my audience, so I've calibrated my speech. The town of Greenfell is our second-to-last stop before we venture off the beaten path.

Tonight, Jaromir is on display in Aeron's armor. Well, the chest plate, at least. The greaves were too short, and seeing Jaromir try to walk around in armor too small was a sight that sent us all into tears of laughter. Well, everyone except Jaromir.

I've always appreciated the way he looks in his armor: his aged and hardened leather cuirass, with those thick arms on display—his dark hair falling free from its knot, and his perpetual scowl. He always looks a little bit wild, a little bit dangerous.

But tonight, his hair is swept back from his face, he's

trimmed and tightened his beard, and the chest plate he sports gleams like a beacon calling to me.

He's undeniably handsome.

Seeing him step into the tavern during my over-the-top introduction nearly causes my fingers to trip over my pluck pattern. Beneath the warm light of the suspended circlet of candles, he carries himself with an air of authority, and a friendly demeanor he rarely shows in public. I want to leap off the stage and land in his arms, but that would raise too many questions about Aeron's private life. We need him accessible. The man other men want to be and the man women dream of.

He pauses at a table filled with men playing Sinners and Saints, and murmurs something low only for their ears. The table erupts into boisterous laughter. He saunters to the bar, leaning toward the barkeep to quietly extend his offer to pay for everyone's drinks. When the barkeep announces it loud for all to hear, it's Aeron's name they cheer but Jaromir they flood with their adoration.

He's playing his role quite nicely. Where Cadoc was all flair and attention stealing, Jaromir has a quiet charm, as if he's too modest and humble for acclaim as he orchestrates everyone around him to heap it at his feet.

He's charming and alluring.

And I'm not the only one who notices.

He answers unsubtle flirtations with ease, seemingly encouraging the attentions of a comely blonde with his crooked smile.

It doesn't matter. I know he's mine, and this is all for show. The shepherd's sling I now keep in my back pocket reminds me of this. I continue playing, softly singing songs of the heroes of old, trying to match Jaromir's subtle performance. A group of women fawn over him, and he's all soft smiles and genteel manners. But across the crowded tavern, his eyes lock on mine, and the fierce longing reflected there is all I need.

I play through a few songs. A few old favorites and one I made up based on Cadoc's archery instructions.

I don't even notice when I start to play the old lullaby my Mama used to sing.

"My love waits past the heather and o'er the moor,
Oh how I wish I were there,

'Neath the tall, branching oak,
My love sits alone and waits for me.
I cannot follow where she goes, save for my heart.
It's always with she, always with she.

I am the lyre, she is the strings;
But no music sounds, not without my beloved
I cannot follow where she goes, save for my heart.
It haunts her steps, even as she leaves me behind."

Jaromir finds me over the crowd. I fall into the ending refrain of the tune, flashing him my most brilliant smile—

He immediately drops my gaze, focusing on the ground instead of meeting my eye. When finally, he lifts his chin once more, he wears a harried expression. Something is wrong. Something leaving that haunted look on his face. I end the song, tuck my lute on my back, and approach the edge of the stage.

In a blink, his face smooths back into his open expression as he chats with the barkeep. Whatever storm is brewing in his head, we'll discuss it later. When he can be Jaromir instead of Aeron.

Rather than approach him, I find my way to Neith.

"He's doing quite well, isn't he?"

She nods. "I half expected him t'stomp and growl his way through yer set."

A light laugh bursts from my lips. "I would have had to amend a few lines of his ballad. 'Sir Aeron Fowler has both the strength and patience of a mother bear.' And then he could snarl for effect."

"A mother bear?"

"I hear they're ornery."

Neith's mouth twitches, and she takes a quick sip from her tankard. Glancing about the room, I notice a woman drinking alone. No one pays her any mind as she sips from her tankard. Her dark hair is cut short, and the ends sprout over her pointed ears. I approach her.

She doesn't spare me a glance until I'm already tugging a chair out, its wooden legs scraping against the floorboard. Her gaze is sharp, narrowed in suspicion.

"What do you want?" Her voice is low and throaty, as if she spends her days inhaling smoke. It isn't unbecoming, quite the opposite. I long to know how it would sound if she sang.

"I thought you might wish for some company."

Her brows bunch together, confusion twisting her sharp features. Her gaze drifts pointedly to my hat. "You're that bard."

I yank my cap from my head, holding it in my lap. My hair is probably a laughable mess, and I can feel the sweat along my forehead. "Sylvaine Abelan, at your service." I sketch a half-bow, as low as I can while perched in a chair, and tuck my hair behind my ear.

Understanding dawns on her face before she sneers. "Oh, I get it. You're one of those. Thinkin' we'll be thick as thieves with nothin' in common save for both bein' elves?"

She doesn't mince words and cares little for my good opinion. This tells me two things: she's had a rough go of it, whether now or earlier in her life, and she's dealt with this before. In any case, I hardly need a warm welcome.

"Not at all. I thought we'd become lifelong friends over our common taste in"—my gaze finds the intricate leather braiding of her cuirass, the woven detailing—"fine craftsmanship."

She glances down at her chest piece, scoffing. "You like my armor?"

"Like it? I *love* it! I don't know if you know this, but it's hard on the road. You never know when a fellow might start feeling a bit stabby. Where can I purchase a piece like this?"

Her smile fades, a cool anger claiming her expression. "There was a leather armorer in town. Had a pretty decent shop, too." She lifts her tankard to her mouth, slowly sipping.

I watch, reading the tightness in her movements. "What happened?"

"What's it matter? It's gone. Everythin' is gone." She slams her tankard down on the table. "Look, Sylvaine? We're not friends. I don't even know you, and I'm really not good company tonight. Let me drink in peace."

"Of course." I push out my chair as I stand. Cramming my cap back over my head, I turn to leave.

"I liked the last one you played," she says softly.

My mama's lullaby. The one from back home.

"It's one of my favorites, too." I flash her a smile. "Look, if this armorer ever finds themselves open for commissions"—I lean closer to whisper the last part—"I'd pay handsomely for the quality they offer. The quality one can't normally find on this side of the sea."

Without waiting for her response, I slip away, back toward where Jaromir is holding court. He's surrounded by admirers, all hanging on to every word like he's the second coming of the goddess. The tightness in Jaromir's eyes is the only tell of his discomfort.

I glance around the tavern until my gaze falls on someone set apart from the rest.

There's a man watching Jaromir from afar. His dark hair is short on the sides, longer on the top, but his eyes are the greenest I've ever seen on a human. Greener than Kingsley's bottles of Bjovian wine. The man makes no move to approach

Jaromir, but he wears a strange expression as he stares at him. I consider introducing myself, but Jaromir catches my gaze, smiling at me. It's a distracted and distant sort of thing.

A trio of men in the corner let out a peal of boisterous laughter, one of them even falling off his seat. He jumps up, bowing to more laughter. When they catch me staring, they eagerly wave me over.

Shaking my head, I offer an apologetic smile. They've had more than enough entertainment for the evening.

I saddle up to an empty stool, flagging down the barkeep.

MOST OF THE tavern has cleared out, and I can call this a success. No one attacked me. No fights broke out. It went... smoothly.

Cadoc and Neith bid farewell to the group of farmers they'd been chatting up, and Jaromir pays the tab. We head for the door, Cadoc and Neith leading the way. Jaromir still hasn't spoken to me, and I'm trying not to read into it.

"You did well, *Aeron*," I say as we step through the threshold.

Jaromir gives me a soft smile, but it's almost an afterthought. Like he had to remind himself to do so.

The night sky is cloudy, not a single star in sight. The moon is even tucked behind a thick swath of clouds. Summer is coming to an end, and I can feel autumn creeping into each night. I shiver, and Jaromir wraps an arm around me. But his armor is so cold, I shrug him off.

"How did you fare under so much flattery?"

Jaromir cringes, reaching for the buckles of Aeron's armor. "I'd rather talk of more pleasant things."

"Such as?"

He grabs me by the hips, pulling me to him. It's terribly

uncomfortable, being pressed against the steel of his chest plate. "Such as, spending the night between your thighs."

I laugh and spin away, though it's a comfort to witness his playful side. He's been tense all night, hating the attention, I'm sure. "You can't ignore me all night and then expect to worm your way into my bed! That's madness! You'll need to beg for my favor—"

"I'm not opposed to begging."

He is already tugging me back into his embrace again, and the foggy part of my brain wants to let him. Let him have me right here on this road should he wish it. But the memory of the elven armorer in the tavern douses my impulses like a bucket of cold water.

"I think something bad happened here."

At this, Jaromir freezes. "What do you mean? Did someone threaten you?"

"No, nothing like that. I just spoke with someone who's fallen onto hard times."

He waits patiently for me to continue.

"An elven woman who shapes leather armor."

"She's being harassed?"

I pull off my cap to run my hand through my hair. "I don't know. But if someone is threatening her business, maybe we can spare some time to help her."

Jaromir's eyes soften. "Of course."

He cups my jaw, running his thumb along my skin. In a few short words and the barest of touches, he assures me of more than I dare to voice. He recognizes how much this means to me and answers in kind. This matters to him, too, and he'll always have my back.

It's a comforting thought, one that has me leaning into his touch.

Before he can continue, a man darts out of the tavern—the

dark-haired man with bottle green eyes. He staggers up to us, his gait labored by drink but his grin easy and wide.

"Someone is coming," I say.

Jaromir turns in time for the man to clap him on the back.

"I thought that was you!" He pulls Jaromir in a half-hug, much to my utter shock.

Jaromir's eyes are wide with panic, and I don't understand why. "Thalon," he says, "why are you here?"

Thalon shrugs. "Needed a change of scenery. I took a small carpentry job in town. Building a new barn for my wife's cousin after a fire took out most of his structure."

Thalon makes no mention of Jaromir going by Aeron's name. Perhaps he's too drunk to notice?

"Guess it took out a small leather shop next door, too. Bad luck, I'm afraid, but it's all good for business. My business, that is."

He keeps talking as if I'm not there, something about structural integrity, but I'm still stuck on what I've just learned. The armorer. Welkin's guardians, her shop caught fire. Whether it was an accident or not, her losses must have been terrible.

"You swinging through Kalinia soon? Avalie and Rhosyn have been in full planning mode."

"I'm not sure," Jaromir says, frowning at me.

I catch this part of the conversation, and I'm positively befuddled. Kalinia is our next stop, is it not? And Thalon speaks as if Jaromir regularly passes through there. "I fear I'm missing something important. How do you know Jaromir?"

"Forgive me! I've only been married two years and already I've forgotten how to properly address a lady." Thalon offers me a low bow and kisses my hand, lingering long enough I pry myself free. I try to discreetly wipe the wetness off on the back of my vest, but by the way he smirks at me, I'm sure he knows.

"I've known Jaromir since before his balls dropped! I grew up with him, Damir, and even his betrothed!"

Something about the way he phrases that hits the ear wrong. "I'm sorry, whose betrothed?"

Thalon laughs, elbowing Jaromir, and losing his balance. Jaromir is watching me with that haunted look again. Like he's about to be sick all over his boots.

"Why, Jaromir's betrothed, of course."

Chapter Twenty-Five

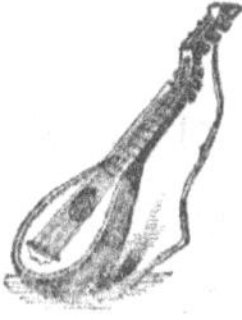

Jaromir's betrothed.

I laugh, for what else can one do when their heart shatters in their chest? I laugh, and it's a cold, brutal sound. The chipping of ice. A broken sound of anger and pain.

"That's just... that's brilliant." I shake my head. My knees wobble, and I'm certain the world is slowly shifting so the ground might leap up to me.

Jaromir appears before me, a pained expression on his face. "I'm sorry, it's not—please let me explain."

I pull away from him, his touch searing now that I know he isn't mine.

He isn't mine.

He never was.

Thalon darts terrified glances between the two of us.

Neith and Cadoc haven't waited for us. And why would they? For all they know we've already retired to our room, ripping each other's clothes off exploring the depths of our pleasures. But no, we stand frozen on the road, frozen in time.

Did they know of his betrothal? Cadoc's uneasy expression flits through my memory. When we first shared a room at the inn, and when I stayed with Jaromir during his fever.

Of course they knew. I'm the only one who was left in the dark.

Goddess, what a fool I am. A dimwitted, gullible fool.

I press my palms against my eyes, shoving every image of his smile, his intent stare, out of my mind. The memories of heated kisses and soft touches. Of buttercups tucked in my bag, in my lute. Every time he ran his fingers along my ear, loving every part of me. But they creep back in, and each stolen moment we shared is tinged with betrayal.

"How could you... to her? If you're betrothed to another—" I take a deep breath, calming myself, even as the sharp pain in my chest remains. "How could you betray someone you're planning to marry?"

Jaromir shakes his head, reaching for me. But I can't stomach his touch. Not for one instant. He lets his hands fall, fists clenching at his side. "It isn't like that."

"It is, though. You've sworn vows to another and betrayed those vows each night with me."

His face twists, and I swear my stomach twists alongside the visceral pain reflected there. "What we share is not a betrayal. It's the most truth I've had in—"

"Truth?" I laugh again, but it comes out as a sob. "You withheld your truth. You can't tell me otherwise while confirming your attachment to another."

Thalon tries to step between us, but at Jaromir's glare, he scurries back. "I didn't mean to—"

"Not now, Thalon." Jaromir's voice carries the threatening rumble of thunder, and Thalon has the good sense to shut his mouth and nod as he puts more and more distance between himself and the storm of this revelation. I might feel sorry for the man as he slowly retreats with the caution of skittish prey, but right now I only have room to feel the betrayal Jaromir has committed against me. Against her. Against every moment he whispered lies in my ear and upon my skin, making me think I could actually have this.

"I have no attachment to anyone but you," Jaromir says. "My agreement with Rhosyn is not based on anything deeper than paperwork."

My heart is a battering ram, and I'm sure it'll bust through my chest soon. Just hearing her name on his lips is enough to twist the knife in my gut. "That doesn't make it any less so. You. Are. Pledged."

"I never wanted this! I was prepared to live with it. To do what's right, after how much I've failed." Jaromir reaches for me again, and I step back. "But then there was you. And I've made a mess of everything. Had I known what I'd find with you, honor and duty to Damir be damned, I *never* would have sworn any vows to her."

Something clicks into place. The last piece of a puzzle, finally fitting. I'm normally so good at reading people. I should have picked up on it when he told me of his brother. "Damir's widow?"

Jaromir nods.

That makes this so much worse. And even if he didn't know what we'd turn into, he was openly seeking his pleasures before me. All while knowing he was bound to another. That day in the forest, when I pushed, and he met me with eager hunger, floats into the back of my mind. He could have said no. He could have told me then, but he didn't. Rage roils in me, bubbling up until I can't stay silent anymore.

"So, what? You figured you'd have your fun before you settled down? Have a little tryst with the knife-ear before you had to attend to your *honorable* duties?"

His brows draw together, anger finally stealing the defeated look from his face. "Don't say that. You know that isn't true."

"Don't I? You said yourself there was something about me two years ago, the first time you saw me play. Was this your chance to play out your little fetish before marrying the human like a man ought to?"

"No!" He cuts his hand through the air. "I know I can't atone for what I've done. For the hurt I've caused. But don't you dare downplay what we have."

"What we have?" I laugh again, and the brittle sound echoes through the night. "We have nothing, Jaromir. You're marrying your brother's widow."

Just speaking the words aloud pierces deep in my chest, and tears spring to my eyes. I can't seem to catch my breath, and I swear, if the panics set in now—

I shove past him, needing movement. My jaw aches from clenching my teeth, and I can't stand being near him right now.

"Syl, wait."

I turn long enough to say, "Just, leave me be. I need—" My voice cracks, and damn him for making me speak when all I want is to get away. "I need you out of my sight."

He nods, hands clenched into fists at his side.

I turn back and walk down the road to the fields.

He doesn't follow.

With each step, my anger dims, and something dangerously close to despair sets in. It's a dull sort of pain, spreading like ice through my chest and hollowing my legs. Without my anger, the night is quieter. Colder. I wrap my arms around my shoulders as the tears finally fall. They skirt down my cheeks, settling into the crook of my neck beneath my collar.

It was always borrowed time, wasn't it? How foolish I was to think it was real. And when I asked him if he was mine... he said for as long as I'd have him. Was that another joke? A clever dodge of my question? The easy answer after a night spent exploring each other's bodies?

Ice spears through me at the memory. It was more than carnal attraction, wasn't it? It felt like more. It felt like it was the beginning, a promise, and finally coming home.

I sniff, wiping my nose.

But it had to be real. On some level. And maybe I took him by surprise. Maybe what we felt wasn't part of the plan, and he hadn't realized until he had already fallen in deep with me. Tangled in where his feelings began, and his duty ended.

He should have told me. There is no excusing that. He lied to me and hid something so important—and yet I feel like the dirty secret. A mistaken detour. The side quest before he starts his real adventure.

I hate him. I hate him. I fucking hate him.

And what hurts the most is, even now, I can't wholly hate him. It's intertwined with so many other feelings. Most inconvenient of all is how much I... how I've come to...

Damn it all the deepest pits of the shades.

I love the way he studies everything with impossible focus. How attentive he is when one speaks to him. How quiet and surly he seems, only to surprise you with a quick retort. How thoughtful, and strong, and selfless he is. I love how generous a lover he is, and how he saw me, understood me, beyond the showmanship I hide behind.

And he's going to be hers.

I never should have come on this journey. Aeron is gone. I can't stomach being around Jaromir. How will we ever finish what we started?

I slump to the ground, finally spent from every gut-wrenching emotion. I've wandered into a nearby pasture, and one lone oak, ancient and towering, stands vigil over the field. I pull my lute off my back, and lean against the thick trunk, wiping my wet cheeks.

In the quiet of a lonely night, I can't even find it in me to play a single note.

VOICES ROUSE ME, and I jolt awake.

Has Jaromir had enough of waiting for my anger to cool? Fresh despair rips through my chest anew at the mere thought of him. At the mere thought that his presence no longer offers me joy and relief.

Multiple voices float over to where I sit against the tree. None of them are Jaromir. None of them are even familiar.

"I pissed through last month's wages."

"You know you can always ask me for help."

"I know, but I don't want it to be strange. Never borrow nor lend coin."

"Sure, but if you need it—"

"You never offer me coin when my pockets are empty."

"That's because you never pay anyone back."

Their voices carry, growing closer and closer. I'm not paranoid, but the idea of being caught alone in a field in the middle of the night with strangers seems a terrible idea. I can't run, not if I don't want them to see me. So, I sling my lute on my back and climb. Higher and higher, until I reach a thick branch hidden by leaves.

Three men stride into view. They look like some of the patrons from the tavern. The rowdy ones in the corner. They hadn't caused any trouble, but groups of loud men always put me on edge. Normally, I make it a point not to be caught alone and far from any witnesses. It's a wretched truth I've come to accept, even as it fills me with bitterness.

I touch a hand to the short sword Neith insisted I carry, and the shepherd's sling in my pocket.

The men tarry beneath my tree, showing no signs of leaving. From up here I can study each of them. The one with a stocky build wears a linen coif atop his head. At his side, he carries a wooden haft. Though he lacks the head of an axe or the tip of a spear, the fact that he still carries the useless lumber tells me only one thing—it's a bludgeon. The tallest one wears his blond hair loose, barely touching the top of his narrow shoulders. Though I'm above, I can make out the sharp line of his prominent nose. Lastly, is a dark-haired fellow decked out in a crushed velvet doublet.

"You see how quickly Oliver's barn is coming along?"

"Bit dodgy that he hired that fellow from Kalinia, though, innit?"

"Nah. That's family. You do right by your family so when they croak, they remember you in their wills."

"Shame about that armorer, though. I heard she lost everything."

"You couldn't afford her elfy leather pieces anyway."

"True. But she was pretty in places."

The coif wearing fellow—the one carrying a haft—pulls out his prick and starts urinating on the tree. The tallest one bumps into him.

"Fuck, Aiden. You made me piss on my shoe."

Laughter breaks out, and the sound sets my teeth on edge.

I shouldn't have to hide. I shouldn't fear a group of friends out for a walk.

But I'm alone. I'm alone and outnumbered, and even if they're perfectly pleasant—I don't like being an easy target.

The pissing man tilts his head back, gazing up into the tree.

I don't move. I don't breathe. Goddess and guardians willing, he's too drunk and it's too dark for him to make out my shape.

I catch the precise moment he sees me. A confused smile lights up his face. "What have we got here?" He shakes himself, his grin only widening. "You're that bard, yeah? Havin' a peek at me, are ya?"

Perhaps the goddess doesn't hear the silent prayers of elves.

Bile rises in my throat, and a freezing panic constricts in my chest.

The others step to the base of the tree, craning their necks to get a good look.

I know what it looks like when a group of bastards get a rotten idea at the same time. In this case, it's a trio of sharp smiles and narrowed eyes.

I project my voice, lacing it with as much confidence I can muster. "I was merely out for a stroll and took a nap. You be on your way, and I'll be on mine."

The three of them seem to exchange confused glances, before they all break out into laughter.

"An elfy lass sleeping in a tree? Sounds about right!"

I grind my teeth. Momentary anger takes the edge off my fear, but I'm no fool.

They are not the vulnerable party.

I squeeze my eyes shut, scraping my reserves for courage and strength. I'm not a helpless child.

And I am armed.

I pull the shepherd's sling from my pocket, careful not to drop it, and yank the small bag of stones I've collected. There aren't many—only six. I wasn't planning on needing them tonight. Tears burn my eyes, and I quickly blink them away.

"How's about the lot of you head on back to the tavern. Have a drink on Aeron's tab." One last chance at peace. One last chance.

"Tavern's closed, girlie. Come on down, I'll teach you all about what it means to be human."

I shake my head, loading the first stone with shaking fingers.

"Guess I'm climbin' a tree tonight."

The sound of muffled grunts rise to where I'm waiting as

the pissing drunk climbs up. Cadoc's instructions from the day he spent teaching me to shoot echo in my head.

Aiming should be instinctive, not exact.

I yank back the leather strap, the groan of the stretching bands filling the air. My aim is a guess—where I anticipate him to appear. His coif-covered head jumps into view, and I release. The stone strikes him square between the eyes, and he falls back, his body landing on the ground with a heavy thud.

Silence.

Then shouting.

"Donnick!"

"You filthy knife-ear!"

Two men start climbing, the branches shaking under their weight and leaves shivering. I load another stone, yanking back just enough to feel tension. The tall blond with the sharp nose comes into view, and I pull back hard before releasing. Blood blooms from his nose before he howls and falls, disappearing from view.

A sharp tug against my back—my lute—and I'm ripped out of my spot. My cap flies off my head, and I scream, falling, falling until I land hard on my back. The shocking sensation of snapping wood and strings shudders through me. Coughing, I roll away, freeing my short sword at my side. But hands are already on me, yanking me back. I claw at the earth, dirt filling my nails, my mouth, as I scream and kick.

Neith's voice rings in my head.

Turn th'blade.

I slice at the grip on my ankle, pulling free when he lets go and cries out in pain. A burst of pain erupts against my back, and I turn, catching the next blow from the haft with my sword. His strikes are messy, tactless, but the strength and anger of his attack makes my arms tremble against the force.

I block, parrying and disarming. His haft goes sailing

through the air, and I want to cheer. To jump for joy and shout.

But there are still three of them and one of me.

I want to ensure you come back to me.

The lesson of Jaromir's training session springs to mind. They're larger, stronger, and the aggressing party—so their intent is aimed on control and overpowering.

I run. Faster than I've ever run before. There are no trees, no obstacles for me to leap over. Only a wide, open expanse. My ruined lute bounces against my back, and still I run. My lungs burn, sharp pinpricks lighting up my sides as I begin to cramp.

And still I run.

'*Faster, stóirín. Don't let me catch you.*'

The day my ahntan chased me through the forest. The day I laughed and ran and leapt over fallen trees and moss softened ground. When I made it past the river and turned to boast— she wasn't there. I'd thought her tricky and still playing our game. It wasn't until later, when I found Mama sobbing into Da's chest, falling into his arms and sinking to the floor, that I even knew something was wrong. It wasn't until Tanniv told me his da had found her, her ears cut off and her innards on the forest floor, that I even knew she was dead.

Tears roll down my face, and still I run. My legs tighten, aches rippling all the way down to the soles of my feet. The road isn't far. It isn't far. If I can make it within shouting range, I can call for Neith, for Cadoc, for Jaromir. I can shout for help. I can—

Something hard collides with the back of my head, and I land hard on the ground. Grass and dirt fill my mouth, and my skull throbs. Pushing myself up onto my shaking arms, I try to stand—

Three sets of hands seize me. Tugging and ripping and grasping. My sword is twisted free from my grip.

Someone grabs my chin, and I pull free and bite down on his hand hard, spitting his blood on the ground. A sharp crack against my cheek, and hot pain blooms against my skin, my eyes watering.

My vision spots, and nausea rolls through me.

"Hold still," someone hisses. I shake my head, screaming and biting and clawing and kicking. The world tilts, and my stomach churns with the movement. The sharp edges of my broken lute stab into my back. My cap appears, crumpled in a tight fist, and he stuffs it into my mouth. The feather tickles the inside of my nose. The blond man looms above me, shoving my legs apart. He glares down at me, down his bloodied prominent nose. I try to brace my feet outside his legs, to prepare to flip him—

Someone grabs my feet, holding them apart. I'm clawing, punching and aiming the heel of my palm for his wounded nose—

Hands find my wrists, holding them down against the ground.

This isn't happening. This isn't happening.

The back of my head feels wet. Someone tugs at my trousers, and I almost wish to lose consciousness.

I have nothing left in me. My lungs burn from exertion, and a hazy oblivion awaits along the edges of my vision.

My mind cleaves itself from my body, distancing from what is about to happen. If part of me can float away, I can survive this.

There is value in learning t'find strength when there's none left. It's often then, when we need it most.

Neith's words ring in my memory, beckoning.

My dagger. The one I was never meant to rely on. They haven't found it yet.

I twist, angling toward my ankle, spreading my legs even wider to help me reach it—a move they don't anticipate.

Clawing at the edge of my boot, I rip my dagger free and thrash with every shred of fight I can dredge from the bottom of my reserves. The edge of my blade slices through his cheek. A howl of pain, and the man trying to force his way between my thighs lets go to staunch the bleeding. His fist flies faster than I can react, and pain explodes along my mouth and jaw. My vision spots, and the coppery taste of blood coats my tongue. The tight grip returns to circle my wrist, dragging my arm out to free the dagger from my grasp.

My eyes squeeze shut as I tighten my hold on the last weapon I have, a noise I hardly recognize escaping my chest. It's the sound of anger, of enough anger to last two lifetimes. Of all the pain I hide behind smiles and jokes and songs and fuck this world that would let bastards like this survive while those I love are gone.

Another animalistic noise of rage, muffled by my hat, slips free.

I will not go gently.

I open my eyes just in time to see the sharp tip of a sword protruding from the blond man's chest above me. It pushes through, skewering him, and we both stare dumbly at the sight. In the span of two heartbeats, he is dragged away from me, and the gurgling sounds of his last bloody breaths fill the air.

The rapid pounding in my chest nearly drowns out the shouts of my remaining attackers. I don't even bother glancing over to see who they're fighting. I can't tear my eyes away from the convulsing man on the ground. As if I need to witness his final breath to be sure he won't leap up and attack me again.

Gentle hands graze my chin, pulling my hat from my mouth. Jaromir's face fills my vision. His dark eyes survey me with a mixture of rage and heartbreaking sadness.

"Syl." His voice breaks on my name. At once, the anger flees my body like it was barely held by a thread. The dagger slips from my shaking hand and falls to the earth. I sob and slump into his arms, burying my face in his chest. Seeing him doesn't spark a fresh reminder of pain, not in this instant. There is only a flood of relief. He holds me tightly to him, his body vibrating.

"Syl, look at me."

I lift my gaze, only to find Jaromir's brows drawn together. He runs his stare over my face. Again and again.

Neith and Cadoc hover above, their swords aimed at where two men wait on their knees, their hands behind their heads. The one in the coif and the one in the doublet. I wipe my cheeks, and rise on unsteady feet. Jaromir's touch gradually falls away. Despite the tremors, I stand tall over the men in the dirt.

Jaromir is a storm of rage. He unsheathes his sword, kicking the one in the velvet doublet to lay flat on his back. Without hesitating, he drives his blade home in the center of his gut, twisting before yanking it free. He moves on to the next one, and I touch a hand to his arm.

"Wait," I say before he can object. I grab my short sword from the wet grass and approach the man. The one who first spotted me when I hid in the tree. The one who refused to walk away.

Crouching, I make sure to catch his wide-eyed stare. Of course he's afraid. He never thought there might be consequences for his actions.

My fear is still with me. I still fear what almost happened. I fear that I was right to hide when they appeared. That I'll never know safety.

I wet my lips, flinching when my tongue touches a tender spot where they hit me. "Your name is Donnick."

He nods, tears staining his cheeks.

"What did you say when I asked you to leave me alone? To go your separate way and allow me to go mine, what did you say, Donnick?"

His gaze darts around wildly, as if searching each face for help, compassion.

He will find none.

"You told me," I say, "you would teach me what it means to be human." My voice cracks, and I blink back the threat of tears.

Behind me, Jaromir hisses.

"I'm s-sorry. We were only foolin' around."

I nod. I'm still afraid. My anger is far safer, but the fear always creeps back in. I'm holding the sword; he kneels in the dirt. He sobs and whimpers, his breath stuttering as fresh tears roll down his filthy cheeks—and yet I'm still afraid. Something writhes in my gut, burning and twisting. My pulse pounds in my head, and all I want is to not be afraid anymore. To live and trust that this won't happen again.

But it can. It can, and I'll always fear men like him.

For this one, fleeting moment, I have the power. I've lived powerless for so long, but now is my chance. I have the blade poised at his pulse. I can end his life knowing it was my turn to command fear in the heart of another.

I aim my sword lower and press deeper, nearly burrowing into the soft skin of his belly—

But I halt.

This is not the way. I wish it was, and a small voice still whispers in the back of my mind to push the blade through.

I don't want to be afraid. I want his blood on my hands even less.

I will not keep his death as my constant companion.

"I'm not human," I say, swallowing against a tight throat. "Nor do I want to be."

I slowly back away, and something dips in my stomach.

Shame.

It threatens to make me heave, the weakness in my muscles that stays my hand when I could easily take his life.

But I don't have it in me, the strength of the final inches between mercy and justice.

Jaromir and the others make it look so easy, their swords parting flesh like a hot knife through butter. The weight of death, a negligible thing.

But I cannot bring myself to test the lengths of my anger.

"Does that mean"—Donnick sniffles—"you're lettin' me go?"

Jaromir angles his body to block mine, a low growl escaping his chest. "Not in this fucking life."

His sword meets Donnick's chest in a violent thrust.

The noises Donnick makes should frighten me. I should feel remorse from the way he cries, before he slumps over, eyes glassing over. But I can't find it in me to regret his death.

I only wonder if the others recognize my weakness. If they finally realize what a liability I am in all my failures thus far.

I lay down my sword on the dewy grass. I have no right to carry it.

Chapter Twenty-Six

Dirt and blood disperse into the water. Spreading and sinking, disappearing, into the shadows of the large tub. Thick mist rises from the heated water, coiling against the cool air of the room. I run my hand against the surface. Ripples form beneath my touch before it stills again.

My broken lute rests against the far side of the wall. Its lacquered cherry wood body is caved in, strings snapped and curled.

Jaromir sits on the floor, leaning his head against the flat of the door. His eyes are squeezed shut, his face twisted in pain.

There's a strange finality of it all. Jaromir will marry another. We killed three men. Our quest is lost the instant someone realizes they're missing. The violence will follow Aeron's name, rendering his legacy tarnished.

I splash my face, wincing when my lip and cheek burn.

Jaromir is at my side in an instant.

"Is there pain?"

Is there pain?

There's nothing but pain.

I shrug, disturbing the water once more. "It could have been worse. I am grateful you appeared when you did."

"As am I." His words are softened, but the murderous glare in his eyes suggests anything other than the gentleness in his tone. I'm sure he's imagining everything that transpired before he arrived and everything that could have been. "Their deaths were too peaceful for what they deserved."

I don't want to spend any more time thinking on them. Thinking on the way I couldn't answer their call for violence with violence of my own. A swift justice, a means to an end. But I'm alive while those men no longer breathe. I taunted him—Donnick, that was his name. I taunted him before Jaromir ended his life, throwing his own words back in his face. The elven bard who got the last laugh. There's a ballad in there somewhere, I'm sure of it.

But I have no interest in writing it.

It's done. No use checking over my shoulder to search the road taken for regret. All we have is the way forward. If you had asked me yesterday what my next steps would be, I'd have known without pausing for thought. Sure, there was always the question of *after*, but that was a question for the future.

Now, everything is shrouded in doubt. The path is without light. We could push forward, risk word traveling of our crime, sully Aeron's name, and end up behind bars or worse. It wouldn't take long to connect the dots. Unfamiliar travelers blow through town, an elven bard in their company, and three of their locals go missing. The arrest warrant practically writes itself.

We could disband, returning to whatever corners of the world we call home. My throat tightens at the thought. I thought I found something like home with Jaromir, but that chance has been destroyed.

Maybe some small part of me needs to hear its decimation confirmed.

"What happens with us now?" I search my well of strength to speak the truth I always long to hear. The truth I deserve to hear. No games, no falsehoods. If this is to be the closing page of our story, I would not have it end with *what if?* "What happens to you... to us?"

Jaromir lifts his hand as if to touch me, but he lowers it before he can. "Whatever you choose."

I laugh. "Strange to think it's all up to me."

"I told you, I was yours for however long you'd have me."

Something akin to anger forces its way through my numbing calm. How dare he? *How dare he?* I want his truth, not pretty words he offers as comfort. He gave me those once already, and look where that brought us? "Would I keep you as master and be your pet?"

His nostrils flare as his face flushes. "No!"

"No? Would I be your mistress? Waiting for you to slip away from your wife to warm my bed when the urge arises?"

A small part of me, a cruel, terribly selfish part, wants to hear that he was never going to marry her. That it was a false promise he made and regretted. That he was already in pursuit of severing this vow *before* he met me, so I'd find enough space to dismiss the lies I'd swallowed.

"I offered my hand to her in title only. To ensure she was taken care of should I fall. My brother's land, his farm, his house, it passed to *me.* Not to her. If I die, she has no claim to her home, her property. Rhosyn has tried to petition for the right to bypass the inheritance laws, to establish a binding contract as steward of the inheritance, to buy out the deed, whatever the cost, but the magistrate refuses. Even in these circumstances." His words are laced with bitterness, and I know he's thinking of the way Damir died. "He's already threatening to call for the deed in my absence. I promised Rhosyn I wouldn't let her lose their home. She is my family. I had a duty to uphold."

His words land like heavy blows, weakening my resolve. If the inheritance passes to Jaromir, and he has no heirs, his property would go to the town magistrate. They must have planned to bear a son of their own. He's right. He's right. He had to take care of them, I know this, but my anger is so much safer to feel.

"And what of your duty to me? Do I not matter enough for a piece of that honor you so revere in yourself?" I don't remember standing, but water sluices down my body, dripping into the tub.

His eyes darken as he gazes up at me, his hands clenching at his sides. "You matter more than everything. I was going to call it off when we got there." He stands, his shoulders taut.

"Were you?" Something treacherous stutters in my heart at this admission, but I know better. It's an easy promise to make in the aftermath, after it's too late to follow through on. It's a confirmation that he chose to lie, that he was always going to marry her, and my involvement was a complication to his plan.

I step over the side, dripping water on the floor, on his boots, and prod my finger against his firm chest, hard. "And were you ever going to tell me of your arrangement? Or were you going to lead me to your betrothed's door, like some ignorant, lovesick girl?"

Jaromir grabs me by the shoulders, his touch searing. "No. I was never going to tell you—" I fight against his hold, but he only tightens his grip. "I wasn't going to tell you because it would be my shame to bear. You would have demanded me to honor my vow. And I couldn't bear losing your respect when I chose you over my family."

The fight leaves my body, and it's a struggle to remain upright.

I'd never want him to abandon his vow, not for me. I'd never want to live with the guilt of knowing he chose me over his family. I just wish... I wish everything was different. That I could hold on to this, on to him, and carve out a space in this life that's *mine*.

I have memories. And I have anger. I have all too much in my head, in my chest, in my heart. Nothing I can keep from slipping through my fingers, even as it yet remains in my thoughts.

And maybe it's anger or pain that fuels my next choice.

My hands curl in his tunic, pulling rather than pushing. I yank him closer, and when our lips meet, there's no gentleness. It's a rough and desperate descent. We don't even make it to the bed, I shove him down to the wet floor, yanking his laces open and gripping him with a possessiveness I'll never have over him. His hand twists in my hair, pressing my bruised mouth harder against his. Our teeth collide with a *clack*, and his beard chafes my chin raw, but I need this. I need him. I'm angry and I need him.

Pushing him to lay flat, I rise over him and sink onto his length. He hisses, his grip on my hip painful. I slam down, forcing his entry far too quickly so the stretch of him carries a sharp burn.

But I don't care. I don't wait to adjust. I'm already moving above him. He gazes up at me, vulnerability and adoration in his eyes, meeting my brutal movements as if he's accepting whatever punishment I deem fitting.

Somehow that makes it so much worse.

I bite down on my sore lip, circling my hips and trying not to cry.

He's not mine. He could have been, but it would have been a lie. This is a lie. It rings like truth in my blood, in my bones, in the roughness of our joining, but it isn't mine. It's a stolen wish and when it disappears, I'll be left alone again.

Jaromir leans up, kissing my abused mouth. We slow our movements, and the first of my traitorous tears begin to fall.

"What do you need?" he murmurs against my lips, pressing shallow thrusts into me even as he asks.

I shake my head, unable to speak. He kisses me again, moving in me with heartbreaking gentleness. His thumbs catch my tears, and his lips follow his touch. Slowly, he stands, lifting me even as he pulls free. I cry out at the achingly empty feeling.

He presses a kiss to my temple as he carries me to the bed, laying me flat against the mattress. "Do you wish to stop?"

"No." I find my voice and tangle my fingers in his tunic, twisting and yanking. "Please."

He's sinking in slowly, but I frantically shake my head. Understanding dawns on his face, and wordlessly, he flips me to my hands and knees, pressing his palm against my back. I arch into his touch, trying to force myself back onto him.

"Is this what you need?" His voice is raw and guttural, he slams into me with enough force to rattle my teeth. "Is this what you wish for?"

"*Yes*. Please, Jaromir." I sob as relief floods me. He pulls back, and drives into me with a brutal force, and I gasp, clenching around him. His hands are rough on my hips, yanking me back to meet each punishing thrust.

"Tell me I'm still yours." His rough voice grinds out between the harsh slapping of flesh, the angry sounds of our coupling.

Another sob gets stuck in my throat, and I squeeze my eyes shut against the onslaught of pleasure and despair.

"Please." His voice is so broken; it breaks me, too.

He doesn't finish the thought, but we both feel it. *Please. Even if it's a lie.*

"You are mine," I cry out. "You're mine, and I'm yours."

Jaromir makes a stuttered sound of pain, angling his hips to drive into me even harder, deeper. He yanks me up so my back is pressed against his chest, and the friction of his tunic against my skin reminds me that he's still clothed while I'm completely naked. He pulls my head to the side, covering my mouth with his in a messy kiss. When we part, his dark eyes are all agony and pleasure-induced madness.

My release crashes into me without warning. Hurtling, careening off a cliff. I cry out, my vision blurring as the violent force of my pleasure steals the breath from my lungs. Jaromir pumps into me once, twice, before flooding me with his own end. It's a commingling of soreness and liquid satisfaction.

Slowly, he lays me down beside him. When he withdraws, it feels as though he's tugging at my heart before he flips me to face him. The expression on his face is utter wreckage—desolation and hazy pleasure. His cheeks are wet, and each breath is a labored effort. He pushes the sweaty hair back from my face, lingering upon my ear.

"My heart is yours. Always."

That's all he can offer me. Somehow, it's both too much and not enough.

Chapter Twenty-Seven

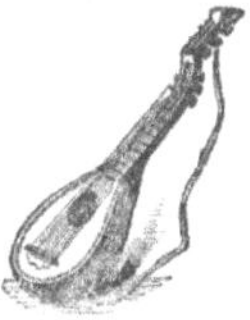

I pack my things with a detached numbness. I refuse to glance at Jaromir or my ruined lute in the corner.

Dawn threatens its approach on the horizon, and we best be gone before anyone reports those men as missing. I'll go back to Hollowden. There's nothing else for me out here. I'll work in Kingsley's tavern, washing dishes or serving, until I earn enough coin for a new lute... however long that may take. The fabled hoard sits unclaimed, if it ever even existed in the first place. The dragon of stories remains undefeated, while I try my best not to count my losses. Folding my short pants, I tuck them into my pack. I've swapped my brightly colored stockings for a pair of sensible trousers.

I reach for my bright red cap, running my fingers over the crumpled plume.

We all have our armor. Whether it's a brightly polished chest plate or the hat of a bard. We guard ourselves against dangers both blatant and hidden, building our impregnable fortresses, and just trying our best to survive. But something always gets in. There is no such thing as infallibility. I thought, perhaps in stories I could create the invincible hero. The one who lives on while everyone else falls. But eventually, we all fall. To time, to the nature of life. There is no life without death, and the death of a dream—

I shove my hat into my pack. There's no use waxing poetic about this. It's done. I shoulder my pack, and I walk out the door, leaving Jaromir and my broken lute behind.

NEITH WAITS JUST outside the inn door, leaning against the stone cladding, and picking her nails with her dagger. When she catches sight of my face, her expression turns murderous. Reaching out, she tilts my chin and examines my cheek.

"If only we could put them in th'ground twice."

I pull away. "Could be worse. It appears no one has found them yet. We should probably hit the road before they do."

Neith's brows draw together. "Whit do ye mean?"

I keep my voice low, though the street remains empty. "Even if you hid the corpses well, someone's bound to find their remains eventually, and even if they don't, their disappearance is bad enough. It's suspicious that three of their men die after newcomers arrive in town." I don't mention that I'm sure I'll be blamed first. Any excuse to paint elves as the monsters of ancient tales.

Neith leans in close. "Cadoc and I burned th'bodies last night. There's nothing t'find." At my astonished expression, she continues, "We couldnae risk luring th'corpse-eaters. Once they find food, it's difficult t'get rid o' them." Her hand falls onto my shoulder in an uncharacteristic show of affection. "And we willnae let that trace back t'ye."

I don't know which idea I'm more stunned by. The casual mentioning of something called a 'corpse-eater' or how far their care for me extends.

"Corpse-eaters?"

Neith cringes. "Nasty blighters, but dinnae fash over them. It's done." She gives my shoulder a squeeze before releasing me.

"Those men still disappeared. They'll know something happened to them, and they'll blame us. Aeron." *Me.*

Giving me a funny look, Neith shakes her head. "Aye, they'll ken somethin' happened all right. We left their shoes and valuables by th'lake. People will assume th'drunk fellas drowned."

"Oh." I try and fail to come up with a proper response. It was fast thinking on their part to devise a strategy of proper disposal and plausible cause of death.

Why didn't I think of something like that?

Neith glances over my shoulder. "I was wonderin' where ye were."

I can feel Jaromir's overwhelming presence at my back. He grunts some noncommittal noise before stalking past. His presence washes over me as he steps far too close, setting every nerve alight. I want nothing more than to reach for him—but there's no use in prolonging what can't be. Whatever passed between us last night, it's over. The final thread severed until all that remains is regret and an echo of longing.

Neith misses nothing. Her eyes flick between my face and his retreating form. She doesn't press.

"Cadoc readied our mounts. We should make it t'Kalinia by nightfall tomorrow." She's already turning away to follow Jaromir to the stables.

"We're still continuing on?" *Even after everything?* After I foolishly allowed myself to want something that wasn't mine? After we murdered those men? I refuse to regret it, they deserved what they got, but I won't call it something other than what it is. I won't dress it in pretty trappings and call us heroes. It was an execution. There was nothing heroic about it. I may not have held the sword, but I didn't defend them either.

Nor did I want to.

Neith stills, studying me with careful consideration. "Do ye wish t'turn back?"

All last night, I didn't think I had a choice. I took it as fact, one I already mourned. The rest of the journey will be painful, Jaromir's presence a constant reminder. My lute is destroyed, and where I once found strength, a gaping hole has made its home. It would be easier to slink back to Hollowden, tail tucked between my legs. Kingsley would never judge me. He might even be glad to see me. Everything could go back to the way it was before.

Except I'm not really that foolish. Things can never go back, can they?

"Just say th'word." Neith is still waiting for my answer. "No one would fault ye for it."

But I would.

I might not have much left, but dammit, Aeron deserves this. He deserves whatever I can give him.

His ballad will be finished. And I will be the bard to write it.

There it is. The only truth I need. Not Jaromir's promises, or a hope for a fairer, better world. But the truth of who and what I am.

I am a storyteller, and Aeron's story will be told.

How strange, that in the cold light of a new morning, what once seemed so lost might still be found.

"Absolutely not," I say, dropping to one knee and yanking my familiar velvet cap from my pack. I pull it on, blowing the low-hanging feather out of my face. "We have a dragon to slay."

Cadoc gazes thoughtfully at the sky, rubbing my quill against the underside of his chin. I lent him some spare vellum, and he's been working on something terribly mysterious for most of the evening.

"Syl, how would you phrase, 'I miss your tight hole' but in a romantic way?"

Jaromir chokes on his water—he's filled everyone's water-skins without asking—and launches into a full-bodied cough.

"I would say," I begin, trying to ignore Jaromir as he recovers, "something that goes beyond the immediate of what you're communicating. Something like, 'I miss how perfectly we fit.' It gets the message across while offering a bit of restraint for interpretation."

Cadoc scribbles furiously.

"What about, 'I miss how you whimper my name?'" His expression is so earnest as he awaits my response.

"Perhaps you should write in your own voice, so it sounds like you. There's nothing more romantic than hearing unbridled truths from the one you trust."

He nods, his brow furrowing as the quill dances across his parchment.

I don't have to glance at Jaromir to know he's staring. I feel it in the way the back of my neck prickles. My hands itch to pluck my lute, but the memory of its ruined body sagging in my room at the inn dashes my impulse, and a fresh wave of regret washes over me.

I should have brought it with me, even if it is broken.

"So... Tomas finally wrote t'ye?" Neith tosses a knowing grin at Cadoc.

"He"—Cadoc's tongue pokes out the corner of his mouth while he scribbles another line or so—"did."

That explains much. His chipper moods, his request for my writing materials, even his incessant humming.

If I still had my lute, I'd play the tune I wrote to represent him and Tomas while I draft their ballad. Even if I'm a touch bitter that I have no occasion to write my own love sonnet.

"Arnorr still hasnae answered any o' Aeron's letters," Neith says. "My letters."

This snags my attention. I hadn't given Aeron's brother much thought lately... any thought, really. "You've been writing him?"

"Each town we stop at, I send off a message from Aeron." Neith shrugs. "He used t'have me pen his letters t'his brother anyway."

"What have you told him?"

A sad smile crosses her face. "Just assuring him that I, Aeron, am still alive. I tell him of our adventures, th'ones ye write, so he has nae reason t'believe Aeron has fallen. Nae 'til it's time."

We all fall silent at that. I wonder what Aeron would make of all this. He never got to truly bask in any measure of fame. He spent one night, early on, in the tavern after I sang his praises while he was still recovering. But he never had the chance to reap the benefits of what we set out to do. He would have liked the attention, but most of all, he would have loved how he brought us together. He was easy to love, an easy friend to make. I didn't know him very long, and yet I feel his loss. Cadoc and Neith—they cared for him greatly. And Jaromir—

Jaromir never told me how he met Aeron. They seemed true friends, but I have no idea how that came to be.

I clear my throat and force my gaze to the man I've been avoiding for hours.

It shouldn't shock me when I find he's already watching me, but it leaves me stunned. His dark hair is tied back save for a few strands that hang in his face. His brows are drawn together, and his mouth is tight beneath his beard. The top laces of his tunic are loose, and the firelight dances along the firm edges of the top of his chest.

He's searing to look at, but I keep my stare trained on him, even as it hurts.

"How did you meet Aeron?"

Jaromir's eyes widen, likely because these are the first words I've spoken to him since I poured all my anger into his body back at the inn. He sits up as if he's going to stand, and if he did, what would I do? If he stood and offered me his hand, I would surely take it, and lose every ounce of control I've tried so hard to maintain. I would fall into his arms and forget everything that hurts and focus on how the rightness of his touch sings in my veins. Or would I retreat? Would I flee from his touch and protect myself, guarding my heart and my sanity until we complete this quest and I am forever free of his dark stare?

These questions go unanswered. He doesn't stand, or come to me, or offer me his hand. He clears his throat and says, "He hired me to train him with a sword, about two weeks before he posted for recruits. He paid for each session with coin, so I could send..." He trails off, a crease forming between his brows.

Right. To his betrothed.

"That makes sense." I hear myself say the words. "And then he asked you to come along?"

Jaromir nods, his eyes devouring every reaction I try to hide. "Initially, I declined, but when I caught sight of his ridiculous notice calling for recruits, I changed my mind. It was a good way to make quick money."

Fast coin, faster route to marriage.

"Well," I force myself to say, "good thing we're seeing this job through, huh?"

His face shutters, and his chest hitches.

The night is too quiet. Only the crackle of the fire and the distant hum of crickets fill the air. For what feels like the hundredth time, I wish for my lute.

"I'm tired." I stand, refusing to meet anyone's eyes. I retreat to my tent like the coward I am, grateful that sleep finds me before any tears can fall.

WE REACH our destination when the sun is high in the sky. Beneath its glow, my clothing is hot against my skin, but when I shove my sleeves to my elbows, a light breeze instantly cools me. I normally love this time of year when the seasons duel for dominance. Autumn claims the night, but under the hot sun, summer has not relinquished its grip.

I shove my sleeves up again, knowing it's only a matter of moments before I'll tug them down to cover my arms once more.

The town of Kalinia is a bustle of activity. When we arrive, all the shops are open, people milling about. The market overflows with vendors, fruit stands, even a bard performing for the crowded square. He wears a black oversized muffin cap, strumming away on his lute as he croons about a lost love. I pause to watch, fascinated at being in the audience for once. He catches my attention, and winks, pulling a laugh from my lips.

Jaromir tenses beside me.

I angle my head to address Cadoc. "Is that what I look like?"

Cadoc studies the bard, who is delighted at our attentions. "Yes. It's eerie, actually. A perfect mirror image—especially the mustache."

I laugh again, and *goddess,* it feels good to laugh. Even if it's a fleeting sensation that remains surface level before evaporating almost instantly.

Jaromir watches me with an unreadable expression. Unreadable, because I refuse to glance back at him, so I must rely on my periphery.

I stare at the bard, clapping in time with his playing. He's begun to bounce along with his song.

Not bad. Not bad at all. Although, I can dance circles around him without losing the rhythm of my playing—

The memory of my broken lute interrupts my thoughts. No... I won't be impressing anyone with my playing for a while. I still haven't sorted how I'm to gain an audience without my instrument. I suppose spoken word and acapella singing will have to suffice. I could potentially stomp out a tune while I sing. It would be dreadfully amateur compared to what I normally perform, but desperate times and all that.

I bow and toss a silver into his cup.

"Much obliged, fair one," he says with a grin, completely dropping the pretense of his song and his persona. "Your name, my lady?"

I flash him my brightest stage smile. "Don't worry, sir. By tonight, you'll know my name."

A bold proclamation from a bard without an instrument, but I've always favored confidence over logic. From the way he grins, I may have accidentally propositioned the man.

"Because everyone here will know my name," I say quickly. "I'll be the talk of this town for some time, and if you don't believe me, just wait and see. I come bearing news of a great hero. The bravest hero of our age—"

"Ugh, you're one of those." The bard ceases playing, slinging his lute to his back, and quickly retrieving his cup of meager coins. His shoulders slump, and he yanks his hat off his head to fan himself. Sweat glimmers off the hairless spot in the center of his head. "Look, sweetheart, this town isn't as impressed by our talents as you seem to think. Save your speech for your performance and have a good stiff drink on hand for when you finish. Better yet, preempt your performance with enough spirits you don't care when they shout at you to play 'Unfettered Wings' for the hundredth time."

I nod as if I'm considering his advice. "Good to know. Well, I best be off. Places to go, hearts of the masses to win over, you understand." I give a short wave and leave him to his work.

Jaromir scowls at him, falling into step behind me.

He rarely walks at my side anymore.

I don't have the space in my mind to examine the meaning of that or how I feel about it. I need to prepare for tonight and try my best not to weigh the likelihood we run into Jaromir's betrothed.

"Shall we settle in, then?" Neith's voice is a welcome distraction from the dangerous turn my thoughts have taken. She and I will share a room tonight. I don't know where Jaromir plans to stay. Likely at his betrothed's home.

I am not faring well with avoiding these thoughts.

One night, and we'll be on our way to the fabled lair of Aeron's dragon. One more night, and then we begin the final leg of our journey before Jaromir can go live out his life and I can claim my place in history.

One more night.

Unwillingly, I turn to find Jaromir's intent stare burning into me. He quickly looks away, but for an instant, that flash of longing slices through me, ripping open my poorly sutured heart.

It's going to be a long night.

Chapter Twenty-Eight

I haven't experienced performance anxiety like this since I snapped a lute string on stage at the Sauntering Duck. Wiping my sweating palms on my blue and white striped trousers, I trudge my way to the stage, nearly catching my foot on the stacked barrels in the corner. I didn't bother requesting permission from the barkeep, who'd likely raise a brow at my lack of instrument. Neith has been tasked with distracting him long enough I can stake my claim and win over my audience before he notices.

Easier said than done.

My heart pounds, and the back of my neck is damp. I straighten my cap, exhale a shaky breath, and try desperately not to meet Jaromir's eye. We agreed Cadoc would playact as Aeron tonight since Jaromir is known in these parts. Already, folks have stopped by his table, offering him a clap on the back, and stealing his attention for a moment or two.

So far, I haven't caught sight of his soon-to-be wife. A small blessing; I can go on pretending it won't pain me to see them together.

I take my spot in the center of the stage, trembling even as the crowd fails to notice me. Again, I check my cap to make sure my ears are safely hidden. I open my mouth—

Silence. I can't make a sound.

My chest tightens, and I dart my gaze around wildly, searching for something, *something*, to anchor me here. My stomach twists in knots, and I'm sure the panics are about to set in. I have no lute, nothing to hide behind. I'm a fraud. I'm a fake. I'm not worth my salt, and this crowd of drunken villagers will be the first to know. Word will travel, the bard who choked on her own tongue.

My face burns, and tears blur my vision. I can't do this. I can't do this. I can't—

As I blink away my shame, Jaromir's face comes into view. He's seated near the stage, watching me with that damnably intense stare. His dark eyes don't leave my face, not for one instant, and I focus on that. On him. On the safety he still represents to me. He might not be mine, but he's here, *he's here*, and I hold on to that thought as I clear my throat.

I stomp out a simple beat, the base rhythm of my song. The sound is lost to the overlapping of conversations and laughter, but I stomp away. My hands find another rhythm, clapping a faster and more intricate beat so it blends and weaves with my steady stomp. Voices hush, and finally, *finally*, I have the initial stirrings of a rapt audience.

"A man there was
By the name of Aeron
All fire and gold
All honor and bold
The first to take a stand

Against the dragon
Seeks the dragon
To claim his hoard
By the tip of his sword

You'll hear his name again, again

How brave he was
And pure and true
The man with honor
through and through

He comes tonight
You'll meet him tonight
He comes to you
Riding the summer air"

By the time I've settled into the familiar verses of Aeron's ballad, a few voices join me. I keep stomping and clapping, and others meet my rhythm, some banging tankards against the flats of their tables, others slapping their knees in time. A broad grin stretches across my face as a buoyant joy fills my chest. Word is spreading. It's working. People know Aeron's name, they know my ballad, *my* ballad.

When I finish my song, an eruption of cheers fills the hall with a deafening triumph, and I sweep my hat from my head to bend in a low bow. When I rise, I find Jaromir's gaze once more. His eyes are all warmth, and part of me wants to tuck away all our pain and take my place in his arms.

I step to the edge of the stage, leap to the floor of the tavern, and stand before him. A table separates us, but by the way our gazes are locked, I'm about ready to climb across it to reach him.

Logical? No. But I'm too invigorated from my performance to care.

Jaromir's face is so damn hopeful, like he's waiting for me to close that distance.

But before I can crawl across the sticky table, or better yet, toss it out of my way, a slender pair of pale hands find his shoulders, then slide up to cover his eyes.

My heart sinks to the bottom of my churning stomach, and the floor falls away from my feet. A beautiful woman with wavy dark hair and sharp hazel eyes studies me curiously, all while whispering something against Jaromir's ear. He pulls her hands away, and his eyes immediately find mine. She lifts her elegantly pointed chin in my direction. By the look of sheer horror claiming his face, my guess is confirmed.

Jaromir's betrothed has made her appearance.

"Your song was delightful," she says, offering me a soft smile.

Damn, even her voice is low and sultry. She stands tall, taller than most women, and certainly towers over my height. Wearing a simple woven dress with a blue linen vest and leather belt, her understated outfit does nothing to hide the feminine curves of her ample body. She's both a true beauty and a hearty looking woman. Her skin is freckled from working in the sun, and she holds herself with an elegant posture that makes me all too aware of how I can't seem to keep still.

Damn. Damn it all.

I respond with a shaky smile. "Thank you, um..." I hold out my hand, gesturing for her to introduce herself.

I know who she is. Of course I know. But I don't trust myself to speak. Who knows what might spill from my tongue?

She glances down at Jaromir, as if waiting for him to cut in. He doesn't. He merely watches me with a pained expression.

"Rhosyn," she says as she darts her calculating stare between the two of us.

"Sylvaine, the bard. Storyteller, occasional apple-thrower, and official keeper of history, or something closely resembling history. There's always wiggle room for a good story." I reach out my sweaty hand to shake hers with frantic enthusiasm. "Well, I'll leave you to it. People to see, drinks to consume. You know how it goes." *Corners to curl up and cry in.*

"Syl, wait," Jaromir says, and his brows pinch together. As if there's any word of comfort he can offer right now.

"I'm sure you have loads to catch up on," I say, waving him off. "Besides, we've been on the road a long, long time, haven't we? Bet it's been ages since the two of you have gotten a chance to shoot twixt wind and water."

Both of them appear horrified, but I can't seem to stop.

"You know, ride below the crupper, make butter with one's tail, make the beast with two backs—"

"Syl!" Jaromir's voice cuts through my tirade, and I'm grateful I've run out of euphemisms.

"Right! It was"—I swallow down the tightness in my throat —"a pleasure to meet you, Rhosyn." I offer a short bow and practically run for the bar—I mean... I make a swift and well-executed retreat. I slip on a wet spot on the floor, punctuating my impeccably smooth introduction to Jaromir's future wife with an equally impressive scuffle with the floor.

I find my footing before anyone can notice, hopefully, and muster as much dignity as I possess to walk to Neith's side. Her eyes are tight as she watches me with an expression that's an even mix of pain and pity.

"Barkeep, I'll have whatever will make me forget that conversation."

He nods as if he knows to what I am referring and slides a dusty looking bottle my way. "Free of charge," he says. "You've put everyone in fine spirits tonight."

I raise the bottle in thanks. "It's what I do. Bringing joy and happiness to the masses. Digging through my pain to bring smiles to their faces."

He walks away to wipe down the other side of the bar, clearly done with me.

I yank the cork out with my teeth the way Cadoc does and tip the bottle back. Bitter, vaporous liquid spills over my tongue, and I choke, tears burning my eyes. Despite assaulting my tongue and throat with the nasty substance, it warms my belly, and already my head feels a touch lighter.

That barkeep is a credit to his profession. I should write him a ballad. I'm trying to choose between calling it The Wizard of Whiskey or If Only All Men Were As Reliable As a Barkeep when Neith finally speaks.

"So," she begins, "that was painful t'watch."

"Ugh." I squeeze my eyes shut, willing the memory away. "I don't wish to talk about it."

She gently takes the bottle from my hands. "Maybe wait on this, until after *Aeron* makes his appearance. Then we can leave and finish it off."

I debate arguing, grabbing the bottle back and, in a display of petulance, downing the entire thing. But she's right. I have a job to do, and as much as I love a drunk audience, I can't control the tide as a drunk performer.

I glance over at Jaromir. Rhosyn sits at his side, and the comfort with which they converse twists something in my gut. Jaromir smiles at something she says, and I'm sure whatever I just drank will make another appearance.

I grab the bottle from Neith to take one last sip before straightening my cap and wiping my mouth. It makes no differ-ence how much I hurt.

The show must go on.

Cadoc's laughter booms through the tavern, his herd of adoring fans surrounding his person. My work is done, and now I'm enjoying the fruits of my labor.

All around me, dozens of conversations flutter in and out

of focus like I'm rising and sinking beneath water in a steady current.

"Should I offer Sir Aeron a discounted tumble?"

"Did you hear about that fire in Greenfell?"

"I thought elves were supposed to be pretty."

"Rumor has it, a certain someone keeps a lady in every major city."

"Was she elvish or dwarven? Don't give me that look, it's an honest question."

"A man who leaves a woman compromised and alone has no business keeping the staff between his legs."

"I bet Sir Aeron would never leave a woman alone to raise his child."

Their words filter in and out of my awareness, and I commit as many secrets and gossip fodder to memory as my addled brain allows. My head buzzes like it's filled with a swarm of honeybees, but it isn't entirely unpleasant. On the contrary, my body is weightless, and the bees in my head are the only fetter I have to this earth.

Or it might be the dwarven whiskey. I like dwarven whiskey. It's one of many things they've mastered. Whiskey, metalworks, and technology. I once heard there was a dwarven fellow who discovered a way to make fire that never burns out. Imagine! Forever fire! Eternal fire? It sounds romantic and worthy of a ballad. But right now, I want to write a song about this whiskey. It stings going down, and I'm sure I've burned my esophagus, but it makes everything feel like I'm underwater. Minus the not being able to breathe bit.

Neith once again takes the bottle from my clumsy fingers, her beautifully lethal face filling my view. Right now, her mouth is tight and that little pucker of concern pinches between her brows. "Ah, shite. Ye're fou as a tipple. Jaromir is going te kill me."

"He won't care," I say with a bright laugh. "I doubt he'll even notice."

I glance over to where he and Rhosyn sit. They've joined a group of locals; all seem friendly and familiar with Jaromir. There's an effortless intimacy amongst his group, in the way they laugh, and all seem to know the same stories. He has a whole life I don't know about.

Neith snorts. "If I wernae lookin' out for ye, he'd have hauled his arse over and slung ye over his shoulder by now."

That is a very specific image, almost romantic. In fact, I think I've read this very phenomenon before when the book-selling merchants traveled through Hollowden and allowed me to peruse their wares.

"Neith," I say with a slow smile, "do you read romance serials?"

Her brows pinch even tighter, and a decidedly discomfited expression crosses her lovely face. "Might have found some o' Aeron's."

I laugh, and the force of it nearly sends me off my stool. Neith grabs my arms, steadying me. "That's brilliant! May I see them?"

She gives me a suspicious look, like she can't decide if I'm teasing or not. "Ye may..."

"Great!" I leap to my feet. Well, leap is a stretch. I stumble into a large blond fellow, catching myself against his back. "Apologies, sir."

I don't let go right away, because my legs are traitorous things, and my stomach roils like an angry sea. *Please, stay down, dwarven whiskey.* Instead, I clutch his tunic, earning a baffled smile from the man.

Before I can launch into a descriptive tirade explaining why I'm still holding on to him and how I mistrust my legs, a large hand grips my wrist.

I'm yanked away, swiftly enough my vision spins, and I collide with the broad form I know by heart. Jaromir's scent fills my senses, and I don't need to lift my gaze to know I'm pressed against his chest. No, I glance up out of need to see his face this close, a position I surely never thought I'd find myself in again.

His eyes are a storm, the union of anger and pain. He tightens his mouth, and goddess, I can't focus on anything else right now. He's so close, and all it would take is for me to lift onto my toes and press my lips just so—

Rhosyn is right over there, I should pull away, and I try to, but my legs won't work. They buckle under the movement, and Jaromir tightens his hold on me.

"Sylvaine." My name on Jaromir's lips does nothing to aid in my struggle to remain upright. I smooth my hand up his chest, my palm finding the space where his heart batters against my touch. His eyes search my face, greedy and thorough in their intent.

"Are you all right?" Rhosyn's smooth voice cuts through the space with the force of a great sword. I immediately fight against Jaromir's hold, and when he releases me, I stumble back, holding myself up against the bar.

"Seems the whiskey has gone to my head," I say with a tight laugh. "I best be off to bed." Oh, that rhymed! "I'm already writing my next song!"

Neith moves to help me, but Rhosyn extends her hand as if to steady me. "She can stay with us."

No. No. Goddess no, that's a terrible idea. The worst idea anyone has ever had in the history of ideas. Please, guardians, no.

"My room is just upstairs, right, Neith? I couldn't possibly—"

"Nonsense. My home is just up the way, and you'll be far more comfortable. The tavern won't quiet down for hours."

Rhosyn has already placed a firm hand beneath my arm, helping me stand.

"Rhosyn," Jaromir's voice grinds out, "what are you doing?"

"I'm showing your *friend* the hospitality you should have extended," she says with a huff. "The girls are staying with Avalie tonight. There's plenty of room." She turns back to me. "Come along, now."

I don't want to. I don't want to see their home, into their life, into their future. I throw Neith a desperate look, and her answering expression is indecisive.

"Look," Rhosyn says, lowering her voice, "you won't get much grief in these parts. But I'd sleep better knowing you weren't vulnerable." She gazes meaningfully at my hat.

Oh.

Not my hat, but what it conceals.

I press my palms against my heated cheeks, cursing my foolishness. How do I appear? A weak, drunk elf.

"No one will harm you," Jaromir says through a clenched jaw. "No one would dare."

"No, they won't," Rhosyn says, "because she'll be with us."

Neith wouldn't let anyone hurt me anyway. But that shouldn't be her burden. I exhale a sharp breath, cursing the clarity of hindsight.

"Thank you," I force out. "I won't forget this kindness." Nor my everlasting shame, but there's room for gratefulness and regret in this overcrowded chest.

Rhosyn nods once, gliding toward the door. I won't be gliding anytime soon. I stare after her, before glancing down at my feet.

"May I?" Jaromir asks.

I nod, not knowing what exactly he's asking permission for, but knowing somehow, I trust him. This man who lied and hid his betrothal from me.

He lifts me into his arms, holding me close to his chest, and carries me out the door. It's not the most dignified position, but I sink into his embrace, reveling in one last chance to feel the warmth of his body against mine.

The night is calm, stars silently watching overhead. I let my eyes slip closed, breathing in Jaromir's scent. The wind has a bite, and I shiver. His lips press against the space between my brows, and it's both a balm and a searing brand.

Chapter Twenty-Nine

I jolt awake to find I'm alone in a dark, unfamiliar room. Flinging the covers off, I stumble from the bed and make my way to the window.

Silvery light peeks through the panes of glass, spilling across the floor, and illuminating the room. I survey the space, trying to remember how I got here and why my head throbs. A small bed sits tucked against the wall, and a clay mug rests on a low table beside my red cap. I'm still in my performance clothes, save for my shoes, which are neatly placed beside the closed door.

This isn't the inn... where is Neith?

Everything floods my memory, pulsing painfully along my skull.

The tavern... performing... meeting Jaromir's betrothed... dwarven whiskey.

I groan, massaging my forehead. I'm in their home because Rhosyn insisted I stay with them. Slipping out of bed, I grab the mug, sniffing for inspection.

Just as I thought. Water. I gulp it down, and already my head feels less foggy. I grab my cap and slip on my shoes. The inn isn't far, or at least it shouldn't be. Neith might still be up, but even if she's fast asleep, I remember which room is ours. I might need help knowing which direction to walk in, but that's a simple matter.

With a careful touch, I pull the door open a crack. Warm light spills in, and two hushed voices slip through. I should quickly close the door or make my presence known. Nothing good ever comes from eavesdropping.

I hold perfectly still, straining my ears to listen.

Just because nothing good will come of it doesn't mean I'm not curious.

"—don't know what you're talking about." Jaromir's voice is low, angry even.

"Don't I? You think Damir never spoke to me? Never told me of your *excursions*. Don't play me for a fool. This isn't one of your dalliances."

I wince, because something in Rhosyn's voice sounds accusing.

"It's none of your business."

"Of course it is, you blasted fool!" A chair scuffs against the floor, and Rhosyn lets out a sharp breath. "Look," she says, gentler this time, "I know you feel responsible. But at some point, you have to decide where your guilt ends and your life begins."

"You know what will happen. You have no claim on this land, this home. Without me—"

"We'll manage. As we always have."

"I don't want you to *manage*. I want you and the girls to be safe and cared for."

"I know, Jaromir. I know. And we are. You'd never turn us out, and we appreciate every bit you send us."

"It's not nearly enough."

"Isn't it?" Rhosyn's voice is softer. "You have given much.

Given all, it appears. Could you really sacrifice so much and still find contentment?"

Jaromir's response isn't immediate, it's a drawn out silence punctuated by a harsh exhale. "I'm sacrificing nothing, since it's already lost to me."

"Surely not—"

"Leave it, Rhosyn." Jaromir's voice is a rough growl. "She will not have me. Not that I even deserve her." Another pause. "She is destined for more, and I would not stand in the way of that. Not when I'm unworthy of a second chance."

"You're just giving up? The land wouldn't fall to me until your death. We have some time—"

"There's no security in this. Magistrate Ridion is already pressuring me to claim ownership before it's considered a desertion of inheritance, and he won't be happy with a verbal agreement of marriage. He's had his eye on this farm since Damir's funeral. I won't have my sister and nieces thrown to the wolves."

"You should stop calling me your sister to make your point about marriage."

Oh, goddess.

"Did you hear that?" Rhosyn's voice rises, her chair scraping the floor again.

I said that out loud, didn't I?

Footsteps stride for the door I hide behind, and I consider ducking for cover, or at the very least appearing casual as if I haven't been eavesdropping, but what's the point?

The door swings open, flooding me in the lamplight from the lantern at the kitchen table. Rhosyn stands over me, a hand on her hip and a warm expression on her face. Jaromir stands so quickly, he knocks his chair back.

I don't know what to say.

"She's right, you know. You shouldn't call your betrothed your sister. It raises a lot of uncomfortable questions."

Well, I shouldn't have said that.

Rhosyn gently tugs my hand, pulling me into her kitchen. "Come," she says, "you and I have much to discuss."

That sounds particularly unpleasant.

"Actually, I was going to go find Neith..."

"Nonsense. Jaromir, out. Sylvaine and I need a chance to speak privately."

This is my nightmare, and the single worst way to spend a hangover.

Jaromir glares at her before turning his eyes on me. A wave of longing, so strong it nearly sends me to my knees, washes over me. And once again, the hopelessness of it all pulses its painful reminder.

But maybe this will be the last prod at the still-healing wound.

Seated across the table from the woman Jaromir is set to marry, I fiddle with my steaming mug. It's dreadfully quiet, and I can't help but wonder if she insisted on our privacy just to make me sweat under the weight of our mutual silence.

Her home is of sturdy build, with little wood carvings of different animals placed throughout. It reminds me of Jaromir's craftsmanship. I've watched his hands whittle a hunk of wood into something beautiful, intentional. Usually weapons, though. Weapons can be lovely.

"You have a charming home," I say. "It's very... homey. Is that the word? There's a word for the cozy charm you've created here. It means something about the significance of family. It's right on the tip of my tongue, and alas, it eludes me. Don't you hate it when that happens? I admit, it doesn't happen to me often, but when it does..." I muster the fortitude to allow my rant to die down.

Rhosyn watches me with a befuddled expression creasing her elegant brows. I gulp down a mouthful of questionably fragrant tea, forgetting it's boiling hot. It scalds my mouth, creating a fuzzy feeling on my tongue and down the back of my throat. "Ah... excellent... tea." I cough, wishing I was never caught eavesdropping.

I wish a lot of things were different, actually.

"You seem nervous," Rhosyn says. "You shouldn't be."

That's interesting coming from the woman who insisted on a private discussion and then followed it up with a staring contest.

"I don't enjoy anticipating a conversation. I'd much rather just have it. Anticipation leads to anxiety which leads to me thoughtlessly spewing words. I'd much rather not fill the silence with incoherent ramblings but it tends to happen anyway." I hope she realizes what a true threat this is. I've been told I have impressive lung capacity, and I'm not afraid to use it.

Her eyes widen, her elegant hands cradling her steaming cup. "You are... not what I expected."

From a bard? An elf? From the woman who has pleasured every nook and cranny of her betrothed? Ugh. *Nook and cranny*. I'm utterly grateful I didn't voice that thought aloud.

"And yet... it makes so much sense why Jaromir loves you. You know, he would have spent the night guarding your door had I let you sleep above the tavern."

Her words halt the breath in my lungs.

I knew this conversation wasn't going to be pleasant, but I certainly didn't expect her to lead with that. Though thrown off guard, I won't lie to her.

"We've made no declarations," I say, flattening my voice. "No promises."

"You're too clever to mistake me for ignorant." She sighs, exasperation elevating the sound. "Jaromir is... difficult. He's always assumed the responsibility of everyone around him. I grew up with him, and I've seen every side of his. Did you know when his father died, Jaromir and Damir were meant to inherit in equal parts? Jaromir didn't want any of the land, had no interest in the farm, wouldn't even let Damir buy out his share. All he wanted were a few sentimental items, his mother's scarf—small tokens. He was always this way. Only accepting the smallest piece while granting the lion's share to someone else. I think... somewhere along the line, he got it in his head that his worth is measured by how much he gives to others. To his detriment." She examines her tea, a brief flash of pain alighting her face. "He's lost so much, we all have, and part of me thinks he truly believes he doesn't deserve to be happy."

I don't know what to say, a rarity for me, and I'm afraid I'll break whatever spell she's under that allows her to speak her truth so freely. So, I take another sip of this awful tea and wait for her to continue.

"I harbor no interest in marrying Jaromir," she says with a shake of her head. "But I don't want my girls to lose their home. Damir built this. It feels like part of him is still with me when I walk these halls. A creak of the floorboard, the nail in the third step he forgot to hammer down all the way. I can't bring my girls' father back. But I've found comfort in knowing his touch is all around us. His father's land, and his father's before him, it's where we dreamed of our future, our life. The life we wanted for our daughters."

"Why are you telling me this?"

Her smile turns wistful. "I've always struggled with Jaromir's insistence on our marriage. We're planning a winter union, and to be honest, I've dreaded the coming days. It was agreed we would live as if we're unattached, he was free to seek his own pleasure as was I, but when we married, we would take the rites seriously. We've known each other our whole lives, and I've only ever thought of him as Damir's brother and my friend. But some small part of me hoped, with time and circumstance, we might grow to love one another. We already have friendship and respect."

Pain rips anew in my chest at her words. Winter. That's only a few short months away. Autumn in the central regions of Targgein is notoriously short. Once we reach Harvest Day, it's practically a matter of weeks until winter.

I bite my cheek, chiding my foolish disappointment. What difference does it make when? I knew it was coming, and the sooner the better, so I might finally be free of the ridiculous idea that anything might change.

"That sounds like a strong foundation for a marriage," I say.

Rhosyn laughs. "But then I saw you. I remembered Damir teasing Jaromir about a bard they'd seen in a tavern in Birchfield. About how he was too nervous to speak to her but watched her all night. About how he hummed her song the entire journey home."

My vision blurs, and I stare at my tea as I blink the moisture away.

"Somehow, you're here now. And watching the way he looks at you..." She trails off, shaking her head. "He'll never look at me like that."

I hate how her words crawl inside the space in my chest. I hate how she's making me feel *guilty* for our feelings. Perhaps I have his affection for now, but she has his future. She'll have her home with him.

I clear my increasingly thick throat. "Give it time. He'll forget me, and you'll live happily ever after or some version of it."

The corner of her mouth downturns. "What usually happens in the stories that end in sacrifice?"

Sacrifice. Isn't everything a sacrifice of some sort?

I rap my knuckles against the table in a steady rhythm. "The stories don't really tell what happens after the big adventure, do they? How after the hero slays the dragon and hangs up their sword, they find a new adventure. A quiet one. How each day brings its own challenges and triumphs. And sometimes, the hero looks back on that one great adventure, and for a moment, they wish they could feel that way again. But ultimately, they know this is the real story. The one forgotten by all but remembered by the people who matter. The story that doesn't exist in songs and tales because it's the life they fought for. And they turn the page, thanking their lucky stars they're right where they belong."

Rhosyn stares at me, her face unreadable.

I cough, uncomfortable by her unrelenting stare. "Or maybe the hero falls into the creek and dies of a terribly boring and inconvenient illness."

She blinks. "You are... delightfully strange, Sylvaine."

I flash her my stage smile, and it's tight against my cheeks. "I take that as the highest compliment. So, if there's nothing else you wish to say—" I stand, eager to escape this conversation and the emotions it's pulling from me.

"If only there was a way to give Jaromir the end to the tale he deserves," she says.

My smile dims, even as I try to keep it firmly in place. *If only*. Those are the words I loathe to write in any story. The words that echo after a great loss. My da once told me those two words are useless. *If only* can yield a thousand outcomes.

If only things were different, but they're not.

"You both will be fine," I say as I pull my cap back atop my head. "I have a nose for good stories, and yours will end in comfort. And really, after the long road to home, isn't that what we all want?"

Chapter Thirty

Neith swings her sword with the practiced moves of a dance. The impossible symmetry of her face is on full display, her thick scar catching the light and highlighting her ruthless beauty. She's braided the hair she wears long so it hangs in a thick plait down her back, swinging with her movements. Each series she performs is a lesson in grace and lethality. She deflects invisible enemies with a swift cut of the blade, steel glimmering in the midmorning sunlight.

I am not as graceful.

Everyone assumes elves have this natural ability, this keen penchant for dance. And don't get me wrong, I've been known to dance a mean jig even whilst playing my lute. But this is awkward and clumsy. Each time the blade passes, I flinch thinking I'm going to cut my thigh.

"Why do ye fear yer own weapon?" Neith doesn't pause her movements, she speaks as fluidly as the journey of her sword.

"Because," I pant, "you made me use the heavy one."

My short sword is safely packed away, along with the rest of my travel gear. Neith insisted we rise before the sun to get some extra training before we depart. She also insisted I use her spare sword, the one she named *Reaper*. A bit of a tall order if you ask me. I'm supposed to be the harbinger of death while I swing a sword I can barely hold steady?

"Ye're no' tryin'."

"Of course I am!" Heat dots my cheeks as my anger rises. I wipe the sweat from my eyes to glare at her. "Look, we both know I'm not some great warrior, and I won't be. So, let's just... call it what it is. I've learned enough to not be completely useless or stab myself. Good enough?"

Our destination is little more than a day's journey away. Perhaps one more night, and we'll reach the valley. The last staircase to the mountaintop. To the dragon's cave. Everything we've worked for will reach its crescendo.

I can't decide if I wish to prolong the end of our journey or hurry up and get it over with. Imagining either outcome leaves a sharp pain in my chest.

"Good enough?" Neith's voice dips to a dangerous decibel, a chilling calm coming over her. Finally, she's halted her movements, and all I want is for her to scoff and keep swinging her sword. She advances on me, and I take a few skittered steps back. *Reaper* drags against the ground, drawing a line in the earth. "Tell me, was it good enough when that mercenary drew his blade, an' Aeron took th'blow knowin' ye couldnae block?"

Her words land their mark, sinking like a stone in my belly. I tighten my grip on the sword, tears stinging my eyes. "Stop it."

"Was it good enough when ye could barely lift Jaromir's sword, when he'd fallen unconscious on th'riverbank, th'only thing standin' between life an' death was ye?"

Her words are another jab I fail to deflect. "I don't need this." I make to brush past her, but Neith angles herself to stand in my way.

"Was it good enough when ye were flat on yer back, legs forced apart?"

"Stop!" I don't remember raising my sword. I don't remember aiming to cut her down, but her sword catches mine, and the force of impact shudders through my arms.

I spin my sword free, but she catches my blade again, forcing me into a defensive stance. Rage blooms in me, like pouring ink into a basin of water, and the only thing that feels right is to lunge, advancing and thrusting with every bit of hot anger coursing through me. Steel meets steel, again and again, and my teeth vibrate against each blow. It isn't fair for her to use these things against me. It isn't fair, and if she isn't planning on sticking with me long enough to ensure those things never happen, then why is she pushing? Everyone is always pushing, always demanding, and when all this is over, what will I have left? I'll have nothing. I have nothing. I am—

Neith pivots, her riposte far stronger than my attack. She knocks the sword from my shaking hand and levels her blade at my throat.

"Syl." Her voice is soft, careful, which is funny considering how harsh she was a moment ago. "I didnae mean t'wound ye."

She lowers her sword, and I wipe my tear-stained cheeks. I want to say, 'you didn't.' But we'd both know that's a lie. She's prodding at poorly healed hurts. Of course it's wounding. I search for the least vulnerable response I can offer, the one that will mask the painful thudding in my chest.

She continues before the words find me.

"But *good enough* doesnae exist for people like—"

"Me?" I laugh, and it's a strangled sound. "Nothing will ever be good enough for people like me? Because there will always be someone who hates me for nothing I've done but for every lie they cling to in their feeble-minded fear? That an elven bard has a target on their back from every idiot who believes I can influence their thoughts with my voice? You think I don't know this? You think this hasn't occurred to me? That even when I stood over my attacker, and he was the one in the dirt while I held the sword, I couldn't fucking do it? Once a victim, always a victim, isn't that right?"

I'm utterly deflated, and a heavy calm pulls over me. Like the rise in anger is balanced with numbing fatigue. I've had everything taken away from me. In the span of a blink, I lost my home, my family, my belief that I could be anything of value in a world such as this. But I clawed my way back up. I saw what happens when the spark of life truly leaves one's eyes—when the finality of death claims a person. When all was lost, I was still *alive.* And when I found my calling, and I realized there was a way for me to carve out my place in this world, I took it. I spun my tales and songs and found a way to get people to listen to me. If only for a moment.

But somewhere along the line, it wasn't enough. Something was missing, and I felt its absence like an ache.

I wanted home.

Not charity. Not Kingsley and Brigitta shouldering the burden of feeding me, like I was a stray cat.

I wanted home.

Somewhere I belonged and with people who understood me.

Aeron... I didn't realize how much he meant until he was gone. He was my *friend.* And not just because we could help each other, but because he understood me.

Neith and Cadoc... they must still blame me for his loss. I doubt they'll ever forgive me, but they looked out for me and watched my back when it would have been easier to turn away.

And Jaromir. My heart squeezes at the thought of his name. I thought I belonged with him. With them. I thought...

It doesn't much matter now.

"Us," Neith says, watching me with a calculating expression. "I was going t'say, people like us." She sheaths her sword with a harsh movement. "I gave up everything, *everything*, t'follow my own path. I've burned so many bridges, it's a wonder I stand on dry land. My family disowned me, in every sense o' th'word, because I knew I was meant t'be more than a transaction."

Her fingers catch on something hanging around her neck. Something I never noticed before. It's a half-circlet of twisted bronze branches, a dark stone nestled in its center. It feels strangely familiar. "I dinnae regret this, and I would do it again. But..." She holds her arms out to the side, gesturing to the world around us. "I'm aimless. I haven't found th'path I'm meant t'walk but I will never stop searchin', stop tryin', stop fightin', until I prove t'myself what I've always known. So, no. I dinnae believe in *good enough*. I believe in good for today. Better tomorrow."

I nod, letting her words sink in. *Good for today, better tomorrow*. Today, I'm a luteless bard with a broken heart and weak arms. Good for today. Tomorrow, I'll be a luteless bard with a broken heart, and weak arms, but I'll be that much closer to the end of Aeron's tale. To the next chapter of my story, and by Welkin's guardians and the goddess' favor, I will have the ending I deserve.

It isn't much, but somehow it's just enough. It's scraping the very dredges of your reserves for the faint pulse of hope. Clawing through the pain of disappointment to endure when the world screams at you to yield.

And maybe this surge in focus and determination is a pathetically fleeting thing. Maybe I'll wake up tomorrow, and the weight of it all will threaten to crush me once more. I'll find that hope once more and drag myself to the promise of a better day.

"Ye keep talkin' about the stay of yer hand like it was weakness." Neith's voice is unbearably soft. "Ye dinnae ken how strong tha' makes ye. 'Tis nae easy t'find mercy in th'face of yer anger, but ye did. There's a softness in ye, Syl. One 'is world needs. Dinnae mistake it for weakness. Ye're stronger than ye ken. Stronger than us all in this. A victim? Nae, Syl. Ye're a fighter."

My jolt of disbelief is quickly tempered by warmth unfurling in my belly. In the memory of holding my sword above Donnick, of him shaking with fear beneath my blade, I can't find regret in my inaction. There's shame when I consider what the others must think of me, but I would lower my sword again and again and again. No matter how foolish that makes me. It wasn't a moment of survival, or the final blow against my own death. It was a choice. A moment the world stopped and I had the chance to decide who I wanted to be going forward.

That Neith accepts, even admires this in me?

A squirming feeling dips low in my belly, not wholly unpleasant, but uncomfortable enough I can't allow the weight of this moment to linger.

I clear my throat. "You can be awfully motivational, Neith. Have you ever thought about public speaking?"

Neith studies me a moment and scoffs before she slings an arm around my shoulders, leading us back to camp. "Ye do enough speakin' for th'both o' us. I'll stick t'weapons."

THE AIR IS COOLER, especially after washing in the stream. I shiver beneath my cloak—it's the first time I've had occasion to wear it. My wet hair is twisted in a braid hanging over my shoulder, and the ends drip on my tunic and trousers.

Jaromir is nowhere to be found. When I asked Neith where he'd gone, she shrugged.

So here I sit, waiting for Neith to return from washing in

the stream, and trying desperately not to think about the man who broke my heart. The man betrothed to a woman I can't claim to hate. Not even dislike.

It would be easier if I hated her.

"Syl?"

I glance up to find Cadoc watching me, wringing his hands. He wears a tight expression. "I wanted to talk to you."

"Is this about me singing of your manhood? I thought that line about 'Cadoc's formidable weapon' was subtle without hiding my meaning. Would you prefer I spell it out plainly?"

Cadoc huffs a laugh. "It isn't that." He drops to sit beside me on the log we'd dragged to the center of camp. "I wanted to apologize."

"Whatever for?"

"I knew about Jaromir's betrothal."

Ah. That.

My heart climbs up my throat. "That's... that's all right."

"No, it isn't." Cadoc places a hand on my shoulder, forcing me to look at him. His brows gather in a pinched expression. "I understood his situation, and why he wasn't dishonoring Rhosyn, not with the understanding they shared. But that you got caught up in this, that you were hurt." His eyes fall closed, and he shakes his head. "I should have voiced my concerns. To both of you. I wasn't sure about the nature of your attachment... but I had a feeling it was more than physical. And seeing the way both of you are hurting... I'm sorry."

My eyes sting, and I blink the threat of tears away. "Nothing to be sorry for." It's my own fault for getting swept up in the fantasy. Did I really think it would end in a *happily ever after*? That we would spend our days traveling together, me performing in every tavern on the continent, him seeking adventure at my side?

Life isn't a story. There are no neat and tidy endings.

"I'm sorry he's a stubborn ass who's determined to sacrifice his own happiness out of guilt."

Well. When one puts it that way.

"He'll be fine," I say, because I wish that for him. He can't be mine but that doesn't mean I don't want him to be happy.

Eventually.

"For what it's worth," Cadoc begins, draping an arm around my shoulders, "he's utterly devastated without you."

"Stop." I almost smile, and shrug him off.

"I mean it!" Cadoc grins at me, his dimples on full display. "I even devised my very own drinking game. Every time Jaromir gazes at you longingly, I take a drink. I had to quit playing so I wouldn't purge all that hard-earned alcohol. And that was only after an hour of playing."

I elbow him, and he laughs. "Truly, Syl. The man is gone for you. Anyone with eyes can see that."

I tug my cloak tighter, letting Cadoc pull me into his comforting embrace again. It's the first time someone other than Jaromir has held me, and the warmth and safety of his touch is both familial and solacing.

"Thank you," I say, "but his feelings were never the problem."

THE FIRE BURNS high into the sky, on this last night of our journey. We're half a day from the valley, and as long as this trip has taken, it also feels like if I blink, I'll miss the rest.

The day has passed in a blur while I was lost in my own head, turning Neith's words over and examining every angle. Aeron had been seeking glory, and Neith—she searches for purpose. For meaning in a life she fought for.

Cadoc... I thought his search was for coin above all, and while that's still a driving force, the hazy look of besotted longing he gets every time he brings up Tomas tells me it's no longer his only motivation. Perhaps that's the reason for our heart-to-heart earlier. Love has softened the previously untethered man.

It's a good look for him.

Orange light bathes the side of Jaromir's face, highlighting the silhouette of his angular nose and sharp jaw. He's made no effort to speak to me, not since my conversation with Rhosyn. There's a finality to everything, and as much as it aches, at least it's done. I can stop ripping open the wound and start letting it heal.

"I almost forgot," Neith says, reaching behind her. She holds up a leather bound book, leaning around the fire to pass it to me.

"What is it?" I turn it over in my hands, examining the cover. It's the finest book I've ever held. When I had occasion to read to the kind woman who paid me in potatoes, her book was fraying and falling apart. I never could bring myself to part with coin unless it was to fill my belly, and Kingsley didn't own books. A fierce, aching nostalgia for a life that hasn't been mine for many years slams through my chest.

My da had a library. It was meager compared to the libraries I wasn't allowed to set foot in on account of my *mischievous proclivities*, but it was a single shelf of books handed down through the generations, and some new ones. Once I learned to read, he'd gift me one new book each nameday. I had ambitious plans to fill the house with more books than one could ever read in a lifetime, even invite anyone and everyone to borrow from my collection, because no one should be barred from stories.

But that day never came.

And I never even got a chance to take a single book with me when I boarded that ship.

Flipping the cover open, I peer down at the title page, shadows dancing across the fading ink.

Whispers of Time.

Excitement flutters in my chest, even as my throat squeezes. I find Neith's knowing grin through the flames.

"Aeron said he was going t'give it t'ye at th'end of all 'is. As a thank ye."

I hug the book to my chest. A strange ache fills me, tightening my ribs. I clear my throat against the lump that's formed. I can't begin to explain how much this gift represents to me, and now I'm hit with another wave of regret that Aeron died before I could know him better.

I realize I still haven't responded to Neith's gesture, likely a kindness she felt compelled to reveal after the hard fought day I had. Rather than share the sentiment that is sure to result in my tears, I head for safer waters.

"Did you give me this because it's the only book in Aeron's collection lacking romance?"

Neith blushes, and her eyes narrow. Cadoc's eyes light up like a child's on Feast Day when they find their hidden present.

I guess her penchant for romantic stories wasn't public knowledge.

Jaromir is dutifully paying close attention to whatever new project he's working on, refusing to glance up at Neith. She's still fuming across the fire, and it feels like we're waiting for the first clap of thunder.

Cadoc crosses his legs and leans closer to her, resting his chin on his hand and grinning with ill-restrained delight. "So... how explicit is the romance in these books? I hate it when they skip the good parts."

That'll do it.

Neith kicks his boot hard enough, he loses his balance and

nearly tumbles into the fire. But he merely laughs, swatting at her half-heartedly.

Guilt trickles through my chest. At Aeron's behest, Neith has gifted me my favorite book, and I've rewarded her generosity by sharing her secret indulgence. But there's no shame in reading romance, and the sooner she realizes that, the better.

They dissolve into good-natured ribbing and bickering. The sort that proves how close they are and how long they've been friends. It's a bittersweet thing, being on the outside looking in, but I observe their swift banter and evenly traded remarks.

That's the thing about not having any roots. Nothing has a chance to grow into anything real—into anything that might stand the test of a storm. Cadoc and Neith have roots in one another, even if they don't stay in one place very long. It's beautiful, really, the idea of home not being a fixed point, but the people you love who love you back. I want to say it's safer that way, harder to take your home if it isn't measured in bricks or stones or timber or books in a library.

But people can be taken away just as easily.

I sneak a glance at Jaromir, admiring him even as it hurts. If nothing else, I'm glad he'll be happy.

Tucking my hair behind my ear, I hear a soft melody.

Jaromir hums softly to himself while he works, and the low tone of his voice vibrates through me. By the look on his face, he doesn't even realize he's doing it, but by the Welkin, the deep growl of his hum is the finest music I've ever heard. It floats through me and settles somewhere deep in my chest. When I realize what he's humming, my breath catches.

It's my mama's lullaby.

AFTER THREE DAYS of keeping the sun at our left shoulder through midday travel, the putrid scent of rot and death fills my nose. Tears blur my vision, and I heave. The rising sense of dread that's made a home in the pit of my stomach only confirms the accuracy of my translations. Traveling closer to danger should call to a primordial instinct of survival, shouldn't it?

"We're almost there," Cadoc calls out, his voice muffled by the scarf tied around his nose and mouth. "This must be why no one settles in Death Valley."

"Could be the charming name that deters them," I mumble.

Bealucwelm. When the maps were redrawn, and the Targgein monarchs had the chance to rename this valley, they went with Death Valley?

Foolish.

At first light, we had set off, making good time on the last leg of our journey. Now, I'm wishing we'd tarried so I might have had an empty stomach by the time we arrived. My meager breakfast keeps threatening me with a reappearance.

The air is acrid, and I press my forearm against my nose as bile rises in my throat. As the forest thins, and the valley creeps closer, I'm sure I'll choke on my own vomit if I have to take another step.

A touch to my arm catches my attention. Jaromir holds out another scarf. "I can fasten this for you." His voice is unsure, as if he thinks I can't stomach the idea of him touching me, which is fair. But the truth of it is, every nerve in me screams for his touch, even as it burns.

I nod, lifting my hair off my neck. His calluses graze my skin, and I shiver. His touch is careful, deliberate. Lingering.

When he finally pulls away, I turn to face him.

"Thank you."

He nods, tying his own in place. His dark eyes appraise me over the fabric covering the rest of his face.

I rub the material between my fingers. It's soft to the touch, but strong enough to blot out most of the smell. Gold is woven into the scarlet fabric, intricate knots and patterns adorning the piece. It seems too fine a cloth to use to block out the smell of death and shit. In fact, I haven't seen cloth like this anywhere in these parts.

"Where did you get this?"

"It's from the artisans of Lindale," he says. His eyes hold mine arrested, as if he doesn't dare turn away first.

Lindale... that means... "Is this willow infused samite?"

He doesn't even flinch. "Yes."

"I can't use this!" I quickly try to remove the absurdly expensive piece of thickened silk from my face. The cost of such an item could feed a small family for a month. If he wants to live by his honor and provide for his family, he should not be wasting coin like this and why did he tie such a tight knot—

He stills my movements. All I can see are his dark eyes and the way his brows furrow in concentration. "You worry over its worth?"

"Yes," I spit out. "You should sell this and scrape every coin it fetches to give to Rhosyn and your nieces. Especially, if this proves to be a fruitless journey. We still don't know what we'll find, and if you wasted the trip for nothing, it would be good to have a few fast ventures for coin on hand. The fact that you even parted with coin to procure this is wildly irresponsible given your priorities—"

"I didn't purchase this."

"You stole it?"

Jaromir scoffs, and for a moment it's almost easy to stand here berating him while he takes it in stride.

Almost.

"I didn't steal it." When my expression remains expectant and waiting, he adds with a sigh, "It was my mother's."

Realization hits me square in the gut. His mother's scarf. One of the only pieces of his inheritance he actually claimed. A remembrance of what he's lost. Who he's lost. And he's so quick to hand it over?

"Take it back! I can't use your family heirloom to cough and retch into."

Jaromir's hands close over my shoulders, and I almost sag into his arms. "I wouldn't sell it for anything, but I will insist you use it"—his brow lifts—"to cough and retch into."

A tight laugh leaves my chest, and I thumb the fine fabric circled around my face. Even now, he's still trying to take care of me. Trying to show how much I mean to him. It would be so much easier, for both of us, if I didn't mean much at all.

And maybe it really does pain him as much as it pains me that we're in this situation. Would it have been better if we never felt this way for each other? Part of me wishes to forget, to erase every memory we have together.

But even now, I wouldn't trade them for anything. Even now, with my still-bleeding heart and the way he keeps ripping it open with each reminder of his care, I wouldn't trade what we had. Some stories are cut short, and that's just the way of things.

"Jaromir," I begin, unsure of what traitorous thoughts I'm about to share. "I—"

"Shit! Guys, you need to see this."

We exchange a pointed look, a silent promise to discuss this later, before we jog to catch up with the others. We'd tied our horses a few paces back, on account of the fit I threw at the prospect of a dragon cooking our mounts. Turnip doesn't deserve to go out like that. But now, as my worn boots rub against the blisters on my heels, I wish I hadn't made such a compelling argument.

When we get to the edge of the forest, the pestilential scent of rotting flesh wafts through the samite scarf around my face. My stomach churns, and a wave of panic and nausea ghosts through me.

There are strange beasts with mottled gray flesh, almost humanoid in their appearance but prowling on all fours. Some of them pick at the remains, two of them start fighting each other over what appears to be a deer carcass. I can't tear my eyes away from the large, jagged teeth and sloe-black eyes. They're like the monsters one hears about in tales meant to scare children into behaving—the nightmares one awakes from to find they're in the comfort of their own bed.

"I've never seen an actual nest before." Cadoc's voice is a distant thing while I struggle not to tremble.

My voice is thin and reedy, shaking with fear as I ask, "What are those?"

"Those," Neith says with a shake of her head, "are corpse-eaters."

<h1 style="text-align:center;font-style:italic">Chapter Thirty-One</h1>

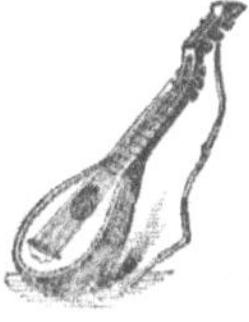

C*orpse-eaters.*

They're more grotesque than I could have ever imagined. Low growls and snorts fill the air as the beasts prowl across the valley. The one nearest us hasn't noticed our presence yet, a blessing and a wonder, since we're only about fifty feet from where it carves up the earth with its bloodied claws. It stalks back and forth, marking each pass with agitated strokes. Despite the graveyard of human remains, this corpse-eater has all the markings of starvation. Its ribs shift with every movement, pressed tightly against sallow skin.

"Why do they not sense us?"

"They're drawn to the scent of death," Cadoc hisses, elbowing me in the side. "Good thing we don't reek like a day-old body left out in the sun, yes?"

Give us a few more days on the road and we'll see.

"They say corpse-eaters were human once," Neith whispers to me. "That a plague claimed th'crops o' an ancient civilization, leaving them starving. They started eating their dead because they had nothin' else to sustain them, and eventually they stopped waitin' for death t'choose their next meal. Whether it was diseased flesh, or th'curse o' eatin' fellow humans, a new monster was born."

A shiver creeps up my spine. Back in Smarighad, we had a similar tale of creatures born from unspeakable acts. How the taste for living flesh alters the soul, inviting darkness to take root. But they are just stories. The very real horrors on our doorstep didn't need the help of magical forces.

Neith continues, "They aren't picky. They'll consume ye where ye stand should they realize ye're nearby. But they're drawn t'the dead who aren't properly buried or burned."

All of the times we carefully disposed of bodies come to mind. Even in Hollowden, burial rites or funeral pyres were swiftly held. As soon as the medic confirmed death, the process began. With or without next of kin. Even in Bridgebarrow, when I'd trip over a poor soul succumbing to disease or starvation, I never stumbled upon the same body twice. The guards always cleared them out without delay. I assumed this was to halt further disease from infesting the populace, but what if it was to prevent attracting the corpse-eaters?

Jaromir leads us deeper into the forest, putting some distance between us and the beast carving up the dirt as it paces the bloody field. "Sylvaine can stay here under the cover of the trees. The three of us will draw them away, closer to the mountain's entrance, and try to pick them off one by one."

I glare at him, even while he refuses to face my ire. There is no way I'm staying back here and *hiding* while they run into danger.

"Care for a wager?" Cadoc asks, tugging his scarf down and grinning. "Whoever slays the most wins an extra ten percent of the share from the two losers."

"I'm not staying behind."

Neith responds to Cadoc as if I haven't spoken. "Make it fifteen percent."

I shake my head, anger tightening my hands into fists.

"Oh? Feeling lucky, are we?"

"I dinnae need luck. I trust my skill."

I pat the short sword strapped to my belt before yanking my shepherd's sling from my pocket and counting each rock bulging in my belt pouch. Twenty. It's a good thing I've taken to collecting round stones when I spot them. Jaromir glances at me, his mouth firming in a disapproving line as I ready myself.

"I'm not hiding. If you wish me to stay back to take up the flank, so be it. But I'm helping. Is there anything I should know about these beasts? Weaknesses? A special way to kill them?" Welkin help us if they require fire. Although, if they did, wouldn't the dragon have slain them all?

Why does the dragon allow their presence?

Neith arches a brow at me. "They dinnae require anything more than a mortal wound. But they are fast. Strong. Unpredictable."

"Nothing about these things is human," Cadoc says with an uncharacteristically solemn expression. "You can't hesitate; you can't reason with it. Your pretty mouth will get you killed if you don't strike first."

I wasn't going to try talking to one, but clearly, I haven't been wholly forgiven for Aeron's death.

"Fine."

Jaromir lets out a low noise before spinning to face me. "You aid us from afar and from a high vantage point. If anything happens to us, you *do not* come down. You either stay put or run back to the horses. Do you understand?"

"I'm not a child."

"So help me, if you do not agree to these terms, I will carry you back, tie you to Turnip, and send you to the next village. Do you understand?" His dark eyes flash, and he grips my shoulders, but a slight tremble gives him away.

His fear means they are downplaying the danger of the situation.

All the more reason for my help.

"I agree to these terms."

"This is a verbally binding contract."

I roll my eyes, hoping to disarm him. "Yes, I know. I'm obligated to keep my word. We both know how much you love your contracts." The words slip from my tongue with far too much ease, and his face tightens.

"Good," he says, before releasing me.

I head for a large oak and leap into one of its many branches, climbing with ease. I've always favored this type of tree for its many thick limbs. It makes leaping to another tree easy. I only hope these creatures can't climb.

Once I'm settled, I glance down to where Jaromir waits, gazing up at me with unreadable eyes. He pulls his sword from its sheath before creeping away. I tiptoe to the furthest point of the branch I can without swaying the limb or popping into view. I yank my slingshot free and balance a few stones in front of me.

I peek out from between the canopy of green leaves because it's far too quiet.

The whisper of a whistle and a hard *thunk* are all I hear before the prowling corpse-eater slumps forward, one of Cadoc's arrows juts from its skull. Jaromir slinks along, keeping low and silent as he stalks another monster. He angles his sword, and thrusts, piercing the space where the head meets the neck.

If they can keep picking them off one by one like this, we'll be in that cave in no time.

But what happens when we enter the cave?

Damn the voice of worry and reason in the back of my head. It's a terrible spoilsport.

A sharp screech fills the air. I snatch a stone from the

branch and line it up in my sling. Neith's sword protrudes from the belly of a corpse-eater, holding it skewered in place while it lets out a warning scream. Neith yanks her dagger from her belt, swiftly cutting its throat and silencing it.

But it's too late.

The beast's cry has echoed through the entire valley.

He's just rung the dinner bell.

Snorts and growls fill the air, as dozens of corpse-eaters run to where Jaromir, Neith, and Cadoc have made a sort of triangular formation so no one's back is exposed.

Shit.

I pull and release, sending a stone flying to the nearest beast. It pegs the corpse-eater in the back of the head, sending it careening to the ground and momentarily stunning it.

I aim another, slinging it into its throat. Black blood oozes from the wound, spilling down its scarred chest. Jaromir takes the opportunity, forcing his blade through its gut.

I can't help like this. Not really. I'm too far out of range for any true damage. I know what Jaromir said, but he's wrong.

With shaky hands, I climb down the tree, landing soft on my feet. I'm already running. Running out of the cover of the forest, running into the field, into where the smell of decaying blood is strongest. Jaromir's cloth still covers my nose and mouth, and the material is damp against my face.

More creatures surround them. Surround Jaromir. He's covered in black blood and showing no signs of fatigue. His eyes lift, widening in horror as he sees me.

I aim for the corpse-eater he hasn't noticed yet, the one barreling for him while he hacks away at another. The stone hits it square in its temple, stunning it and dropping it to the ground. Jaromir glances over his shoulder then back at me with a scowl.

I yank the short sword free from my belt, eager to prove my

mettle, and take up my pace again, running to where Jaromir fights monster after monster.

Cadoc is perched on a tall boulder, aiming his bow with swift and expert finesse.

Neith keeps both sword and dagger constantly in motion, spinning and slashing.

Something knocks into my side, launching me to the ground and rattling my teeth. I roll away, keeping a firm grasp on my sword while avoiding its edge. My vision whirls from the motion, but before I can right myself, a heavy body lands on top of me, pinning me in place.

I gag as the putrid scent of death fills my senses.

The monster is more horrifying up close. Its black eyes glare down at me, lips curling to reveal rows of jagged brown teeth. Where a nose should be, is just open skin and two slits. A low growl rumbles above me, and a trail of saliva spills onto my shoulder.

All strength flees my body, leaving behind quavering terror and spinning thoughts.

I'm dead. I'm going to die. I'm going to be eaten alive, and how much pain can the body withstand before the blessed relief of shock kicks in?

Distantly, the sound of Jaromir's shout pulls me back.

With a cry, I thrust my sword up into its belly, twisting and plunging through flesh and bone and sinew.

Black blood pours over me, and the rotten smell intensifies. I gag, turning my head to the side as my stomach heaves. The beast slumps, falling even heavier over me. With a grunt, I tip it to the side, scrambling to pull myself out from underneath its large body.

A hard grip finds my shoulder. I'm yanked to my feet and spun around. Jaromir's face fills my vision. He's ripped his scarf down below his chin, and panic twists his blood-splattered expression.

"You're all right?"

I don't trust my voice right now, so I nod.

Relief softens the tightness around his eyes. He yanks me into his arms, and I'm hugging him back, resting my head against his chest and leaning into his warmth. His filthy, blood-coated warmth.

His hand finds the back of my head, running gently through my hair in a soothing motion. "Blazing abyss, Syl. If anything happened to you..." He clears his throat, holding me even tighter. "We had an agreement. You were to keep your distance."

I pull back enough to stare up at him. "Yes, well, the problem with verbal contracts is the lack of notary presence to verify such a legal claim. It's a nasty business of 'he said, she said,' don't you think?"

Jaromir's brows lift, and finally the corner of his mouth concedes the fight against his smile. "I'll remember that next time."

He tugs me close again, tucking my head under his chin, and I go willingly, sinking in this stolen moment where nothing exists outside of—

"Wait! The corpse-eaters!" I shove away from him. We can't stand here blissfully unaware of the bloody scene around us and the ever-present threat of death.

Jaromir glances over his shoulder, to where Cadoc and Neith are tallying up their kills. "We broke down the horde, and most of the stragglers ran off. If one or two slink back, we can handle them."

I study the carcass of my single kill, ignoring the queasy feeling in my gut. "So... do I get marks for any assists I made?"

His mouth twitches. "Yes, Syl. You can claim any kill I made with your aid."

"Good." I nod and stumble past him toward Neith and Cadoc. Jaromir makes no sound as he follows me, but I feel his steadying presence at my back. It's awfully dangerous that he remains such a comfort. My heart is a bloody fool and intent on making me suffer all over again. The greedy tart.

I clear my throat as if it will clear my thoughts. "I only want a fair shot at winning the title of most kills."

Chapter Thirty-Two

I didn't win Cadoc's wager, but neither did he. Neith claims the victory, with a death toll of eleven. Jaromir wasn't far behind with nine, and Cadoc counted eight felled by his arrows.

Obviously, I must write this into the ballad. Neith, the bringer of pain, commander of death! Aeron can share some of the glory. By the rotten blood coating her arms and face, and the slight limp she's valiantly trying to hide, I say she's earned it.

The cave's entrance looms above, a dark gaping opening into the heart of the unnamed mountain. Dead grass lines the narrow path as it curves its way up the side of the increasingly steep terrain. The sun fights its way through clouds and mist to dapple along our trail. A few trees still stand, having not yet fallen into waste like Death Valley. A few pines, hearty and unyielding, edge along the side of the rock face, but even they gradually thin, until all that remains is the unforgiving stone and the dormant earth.

My breath is harder to catch, and each step grows heavier.

I tug down the samite scarf, tucking it beneath my chin in search of air.

"Try to keep your breathing even." Jaromir touches my shoulder. "Don't hold your breath, but don't try to breathe too quickly."

I huff in exasperation. "Easy for you to say, with your giant strides."

His mouth twitches. "Think of it like a song and maintain the beat."

Well. That's actually kind of brilliant. Unhelpful, since I'm not trying to breathe *wrong* or whatever, and it isn't as if one loses their breath on purpose, but still, brilliant.

"You should teach something. I'm not sure what, but you're annoyingly patient for a man who only spoke to me in grunts and growls not too long ago."

He offers me his hand, and I'm not even ashamed when I accept his help over a particularly steep part of the path. "Perhaps I'm only patient with people I care for."

My heart gives a little jolt at his words, but that's all they are. Words. I once thought words were the most powerful thing in the world. But now I see how empty they can be when there's nothing to bolster them. A promise hanging like the last leaf of late autumn, only to be blown away by winter's gale.

"Right." I pull my hand from his, ignoring the way my nerves alight at the sensation of my palm sliding against his, and keep my gaze trained ahead. On Neith and Cadoc as we push our way higher. "Shouldn't be much longer."

"It isn't," he says gruffly. "In fact, we're here."

Neith and Cadoc have stilled up ahead, staring into the cave without making any move to enter. The closer I step, the more the details of the cave's entrance sharpen into focus. The stone is marred with scorch marks. A few scattered pieces of rusted old armor are strewn about the floor of the cave. A dull-looking sword here. A blackened helm there.

One very important detail I haven't quite let myself think about this entire trek.

There's a *dragon* inside.

Any doubt has been swiftly erased by the signs that flames have consumed this entrance on more than one occasion.

I run my hand along the stone, cautiously, as if I expect it to be hot to the touch. But, of course, the rock is cool. My finger finds a strange hole, a pipe. Examining the area, I realize a series of thin pipes line the mouth of the cave. A strange hissing sound softly emitting from each one.

"Do any of you hear this?"

Jaromir presses his ear close to mine, and his frown deepens. "I hear it, but I don't understand."

"Just," Neith calls out, slowly stepping around us to enter the cave, "be careful."

"I'll do my best, but I don't think tiptoeing is going to trick a dragon."

The walls of the cave are so neat and... uniform. Almost as if they were carved with great care. More and more rows of those pipes lurk along the stone, nearly invisible to the eye unless one knows to look for them.

My foot finds something smooth and level; even through my boot I can feel the difference, and a metallic *clink* echoes through the cave. I freeze, heart pounding in my chest.

The hissing returns in full force, louder this time. I glance down to find I'm standing on a perfect bronze tile laid into the floor of the cave. Panic grips my throat, and I whip my head to meet Jaromir's alarmed stare.

"What do I do?"

Jaromir holds his hands out, creeping toward me. "I'm going to slowly take your place, and you're going to let off when I tell you."

That makes no sense. All I know is, I step on the square,

and the walls hiss at me, as if they're pissed I didn't watch where I was going. "Jaromir…"

"It looks like you've stepped on a pressure-plate. It's ancient dwarven technology. I'm going to replace the pressure so you can move away safely."

I've read of ancient dwarven technology, of advancement of engineering in Hawthok. But theory is safer than practice.

Jaromir is far heavier than I am. Will the added weight trigger some sort of mechanism? Is this an alarm system? Why is he familiar with ancient dwarven artifacts?

I swallow down my questions along with the hysteria rising in my throat. "Why… why is there a trap in a dragon's cave?"

"I don't know. But as I place my foot, you're going to step away, understand?"

I nod, not at all understanding any of this, but I can follow simple orders. He invades my space as he slowly presses his boot next to mine.

"All right, slowly lift your foot as I place mine."

I do as he says, trusting in the moment that he knows what he's talking about. It's safer than falling to panic over all my unanswered questions.

I step backward, leaving him in my place on the pressure-plate. This isn't a solution exactly, but at least I can take a full breath knowing I'm not about to cause some sort of catastrophe within these cave walls.

"Now what do we do?"

Jaromir glances around, as if it's only just occurred to him he'd be just as stuck as I was. "I'll wait here. Without knowing what this trigger does, I won't risk setting it off."

Of course, Jaromir would trade our positions, placing himself in direct danger without thought.

He'll take good care of Rhosyn. The thought cuts through me before I can stop it, but alongside the accompanying sting, there's a warmth I might even call fondness. Jaromir is many things, good and noble, sometimes downright daft. But I can't claim he's ever faked what we have.

Had.

What we had.

With a sigh, I sit on the ground at his feet, stretching my legs. If he's staying, so am I. The look he gives me is decidedly cross, but he says nothing to counter my decision. Neith and Cadoc move at a glacial pace, clearly not wanting to set off any more surprises.

"What do these triggers tend to do?"

"Spikes, floors falling away, cave-ins." Jaromir gives a shrug as if he's rattling off specials at the tavern.

"Why do you know so much about these?"

"I've explored caves and ruins across the continent. Always on the lookout for a secret hoard."

I can see it. Jaromir's dark hair unbound as he rides off to his next big adventure. The freedom of the great unknown. He might play the part of the hulking grump with aplomb, but he can't fool me. He was made for life on the road. I've seen it in the way he relaxes by the fire, always working on something. How the tension in his shoulders gradually loosens with each step we trek away from civilization. How at home he is amongst the trees.

When I first met him, he was so... harsh. Angry. Perhaps because he knew this was his last adventure before he planted roots. Once he marries Rhosyn, I have no doubt he'll stay close. He'll be the husband she deserves. The father to his nieces.

"Maybe we'll spot a few more places to explore on the way back." Just saying the words, mentioning what comes next after this, spears ice through my chest. But I force myself to smile. "Nothing that would defer you too long, of course."

Jaromir's expression softens. "Syl..."

"Watch out!" Cadoc's voice cuts through the cave, interrupting whatever Jaromir was about to say.

The cave rumbles, a deep angry sound. The floor beneath me trembles its warning, and I freeze, unsure if I move, I'll make it worse.

"It's all right," Jaromir says, holding out a steadying hand. "Neith and Cadoc must have stepped on another pressure plate. If no one moves, we should be fine."

Should.

I don't very much like that word in this context.

Another thundering quake reverberates through the cave as if in rebuttal to his assurances. My heart drops, and I fight the urge to squeeze my eyes shut, as if not seeing the danger will keep me from harm.

When has that ever worked?

The span of several heartbeats grants us blessed silence. Perhaps he was right, and we can assess our next move as soon as—

The floor opens, and like a punch to the gut, my stomach sinks as I'm plunged into darkness. Jaromir's voice calls my name, but soon that, too, is lost to the pitch-black chasm.

Chapter Thirty-Three

Utter blackness. The darkness weighs me down.

A harsh cough rips from my throat, carved from deep in my chest. I cry out as sharp pain jolts through my ribs. Each inhale is wet and crackling, like I'm drowning in my own breath.

Strong hands rub soothing circles against my back, and I flinch, regretting the action because it stabs through my ribs again.

"Are you all right?" Jaromir's voice floods me with relief, and I desperately grapple at his arms, his shoulders, any part of him that eludes my sight in the darkness of the hole we've tumbled into.

"We fell... I fell..." I gasp and break into another coughing fit, gripping the back of his neck with each punctuating bite of pain. "Why are you down here, too?"

Jaromir scoffs, and I'd bet the last coin in my pocket, if I could see his face, I'd find his brows furrowed in disapproval. "I wasn't going to let you out of my sight."

Interesting choice of words, since we can't see a thing, but the sentiment sends a different sort of pain pulsing through my chest.

"But the pressure plate... are Neith and Cadoc safe?"

"I'm sure they're fine." He doesn't sound convinced, but it's not like we can do anything from down here. We need to find a way out, and then we can search for them.

"Do you have a lantern? Something to keep us from stumbling around in the dark?" With how easy it is to set off traps with the aid of sight, I don't trust my ability to survive this cave robbed of it.

"If I did, it would have shattered on impact. I wasn't wearing my pack when I jumped."

A simple no would have sufficed.

"But," he continues, "I do have this." The sound of flint striking, and a spark flies between us, flashing me a glimpse of his handsome face frowning down at his hands. "Hang on, just need—" His words stop short as his fingers find my neck, untying the knot of his mother's samite kerchief where it rests beneath my chin. I shiver against his touch, and his hands still for a space of a heartbeat before he pulls the fabric away from my skin.

Another strike of flint, and a spark illuminates his face once more before catching a small flame on the precious fabric he'd never sell. He's wound it around a wooden haft, a makeshift torch.

The room appears, walls carved into stone to form a perfect circular prison. The air is dank and thick. Shadows dance along the too-smooth rock face, and beyond Jaromir's shoulder, a dark hallway comes into view.

A means of escape or another trap. Who can tell anymore?

Jaromir stands, helping me to my feet. I wince at the movement, and his large hands skirt up my side, seeking the pain. When he finds the expanse in my ribs where it stabs with each breath, he stills.

"This won't burn long, so we need to be quick and find something else to keep the fire going, but I can bind this so you aren't in pain."

I don't think I can handle more pressure on my ribs at this point. "It isn't necessary. We should move on before—"

"Hold this." He's already shoving the small torch in my hand and dropping to one knee. Without hesitation, he pulls his leather jerkin off and tugs his tunic over his head. Ripping the fabric into neat strips, he sets to work wrapping each one around my torso, tying them on tight enough to offer support, but not so tight as to inhibit my breathing.

Well, maybe a little. But it hurts to take full breaths anyway.

"There," he says, rising to his feet, keeping his hands firmly on my waist. His upper body is now clad in only his jerkin, and it must be terribly uncomfortable having nothing between his skin and the hardened leather of his armor.

I'm still holding the torch out to the side, allowing us to stand far too close. I glance up, finding his face mere inches from mine.

"Thank you," I whisper, and my words ghost against his mouth. His brows draw together, and his eyes drop to my lips. Gently, he takes the torch from my numb fingers, claiming my hand in his, and putting much-needed distance between us.

"We haven't much time." His voice is rougher than it was a moment ago as he leads me out of the circular room. As we pass the entryway to the hall, more of that hissing noise fills my ears.

"Does dwarven technology include hissing pipes?"

"Pipes running through stone, yes. I came across an old ruin I believe ran water through the walls, so nobles didn't have to dredge it up from wells. But no, nothing quite like this."

I'm familiar with the theory of running pipes through

walls for water. That particular advancement, along with most dwarven architectures, was banned after the catastrophic failure that led to the death of Lady Margaret, the favored cousin of King Elvard. He'd commissioned a Hawthokian engineer to build his palace out of a cave, like the dwarven kings of old. Complete with mechanical doors, heavy enough to hold back an army. The pipes burst, causing a flood, and no one could get the door open to save Lady Margaret.

I suppose it's a comfort that these pipes hiss instead of carrying water. At least we won't drown.

Jaromir stops short, causing me to collide into his solid wall of a back.

"Here we are." His voice is triumphant, and when he turns to face me, I realize why.

He finds a torch on the wall and lights it; the hall is illuminated with a bright glow. He drops his makeshift torch on the floor as the last of the samite scarf burns away and tugs me along.

"I'm sorry about your mother's kerchief."

Jaromir grunts. "I'm not. We needed light."

A thing is a thing and all the wealth in the world matters naught at the end of it all. Yes, yes, I know and understand all this. But sometimes an item is more than the sum of its parts, and the loss is keenly felt. Not by way of greed, or inconvenience, but the loss of an ideal tied to the item. Sometimes our hopes are too fragile to survive without a sort of conduit for them.

But I don't bother arguing my point. If he wants to pretend he doesn't care about the loss of something important to him, so be it.

The path twists and turns, cutting deeper into the stone. The walls remain smooth, carved with care.

Still no sign of the dragon.

We never did discuss what we would do if this was a dead

end. I was so sure it would at least lead to something worthwhile. That everything we fought for wouldn't be in vain. That this adventure was real, rather than a misguided delusion of our dead friend.

My stomach hollows at my own callousness. But the fact remains.

I convinced everyone to continue on in Aeron's name. To seek our fame and glory at the end of everything. If all our journey yields is an abandoned cave and clever traps, where will that leave us?

Where will that leave me? A failed attempt at staking my claim in a world that doesn't want me.

No. I don't need to languish in these fears a moment longer. The world doesn't need to want me, I'm here to stay. And if this fails, if this amounts to nothing, then I will find another way.

"Is that a door?" Jaromir's voice cuts through my thoughts. He halts, his hand on the latch. "If this is another trap, take the torch, and run back to where we fell. Perhaps Neith will be at the top, and she'll find a way to get you out."

"There you go again, insisting I run away." I tug on his arm, forcing him to face me. "When have I ever listened?"

"Never. But there's a first time for everything." He pushes the door open, a low groan scraping through the thick silence. Jaromir blocks the doorway like a sentry.

"What is it?" I try to elbow him out of the way, but he's frozen in place. I swear, if this is the room to the secret dragon and we get immolated on the spot, I will be terribly angry. Dead, but angry.

Finally, he shifts into the room, bringing the torch with him to reveal what lies beyond.

The room is... nothing I would have expected. Bookcases line the walls floor to ceiling. Glass cases and a large ornate desk occupy the space. A neat stack of parchments sit atop, begging me to rifle through it. Jaromir lights all the candelabras in the room, only adding to the absurdity of what we've found.

The only wall without books is covered in a strange series of pulleys, cables, and mechanisms. The traps. The pressure-plates. Each trigger must be rigged all the way back to here.

Jaromir recovers quicker than me, searching the room and various mechanisms.

Barrels line the far wall, each one marked with a different symbol denoting its contents. Aged dwarven whiskey, wine from the Western Isles, and black powder. Four barrels of black powder are tucked away in this strange room. The use of saltpeter was outlawed after the dwarven alliance with the humans during The Great Loss. The damage caused by the explosive material was deemed inhumane... after it was used to win the war against the elves.

What have we stumbled upon?

I turn back to face the bookcases, and one of the glass cases catches my eye. A black sphere, with streaks of jade marbling its surface. *A prayer stone.* I've heard of these. The goddess' temples used to house them as conduits of prayer and reverence to the goddess and Welkin's guardians. Da told me they were all destroyed over a century ago during the war. When they sacked the temples and structures of elven design, all was lost in the rubble.

Except this one remains.

On numb feet, I cross the room to the desk. A letter written in looping letters and exaggerated flourishes stares up at me.

To whoever this finds,

Congratulations on surviving the tempest trials! I wish I could congratulate you in person, but if you've made it here, I suspect I've already succumbed to the collapsing lung. It's not a glamorous way to go, but at least I didn't have the dancing plague! As I write this, I am in my third year of being "the dragon" as my lungs slowly fail. My physician said to enjoy as many leisure activities as I can in the time I have left, and this has been most diverting! Though, I purposely made the map difficult to translate, and no one seems to survive the trials. Maybe I made them too difficult.

Should you wish to keep the tradition alive, the alchemical formula for dragon fire can be found in the top right-hand drawer. I could have sold the formula to the highest paying nation in search of an incendiary weapon at sea, but I have no use for gold I'll fail to spend before I draw my last breath. The mixture will react with the steam I've sent through these little pipes, lighting any who dares venture into the dragon's cave on fire.

Oh, now I almost feel bad. A lot of people have tried and failed.

No matter! You survived, and now here is your prize! Do with it what you will.

I have no heirs and no interest in leaving my wealth to a kingdom that refuses to grant me a title without noble blood.

I forged my own title and a legacy no one will soon forget.

Enjoy your reward; you've earned it.

-The Dragon, First Fruits Day, 8:54 Wolf

The date... 8:54, Age of the Wolf... that's over one hundred and fifty years ago.

"Well?" Jaromir says from where he's investigating the toggle switch near the bookcase. "What does it say?"

"It says... a lot." The dragon isn't real, or not in the way we thought it was. It's... a clever trick. A story spun by a dying man in pursuit of leaving a lasting legacy a century and a half ago. How did we survive when no one else had? I can only assume a component of his formula has been rendered inactive by time. The corpse-eaters served as a means to ward anyone off from investigating, and soon, the story of the dragon faded into myth. Aeron happened upon an old map from that traveling merchant, a false trail to anyone else, but one we followed and soon began to believe in, because when all seems lost, it's a comfort to find faith in something.

But how long until people stopped venturing to this mountain? Stopped searching for the hoard hidden behind impossible traps and fire and death. How long until his map was lost in a sea of forged copies lacking the true directions? It's horrible, how many lives his scheme has claimed. Horrible, and appalling, and—

A sharp laugh bursts from my lips. Then another. Soon, I'm gripping the table unable to stop the hysterical laughter as tears prick my eyes. My ribs ache, and something twists in my chest as the weight of it all punches through me. But still I laugh. I laugh until the tears in my eyes roll down my cheeks.

Chapter Thirty-Four

Behind the bookcase, there's a secret room. A room only found when one pulls the correct lever and opens the door hidden behind books and stories. Inside is enough gold to fulfill all the promises Aeron made us: fame, glory, a comfortable life cushioned by enough coin to last the rest of our days.

It's everything we hoped for and more. Yet the moment is tinged with an ache of bittersweet disappointment. The end of all that we fought for, and the beginning of the journey home.

I drop to sit at the large desk, leaning my elbows on its dusty surface. A glass case on the opposite wall holds a few ancient relics of bygone eras. Most notably, a few giant teeth I can guess are old remnants of a dragon long lost. Once a great power, raw energy, and unbridled chaos, and now? Nothing more than a memory. A memory of a story trapped behind filmy glass.

In the end, that's what we all become. Someone else's story, preserved in a memory.

I'll need to start blocking the fight scene between Aeron and the dragon in my head, but right now my mind won't cooperate. I'm still stuck in this vicious cycle of relief, disappointment, and disgust.

"So, that's it then."

Jaromir examines a map to all the underground tunnels, exits and secret passages, and how to avoid traps and triggers. He drops the map and glances up, watching me with that intense stare I've come to know as his search for understanding.

"It's more than I dared hope for."

I huff a tight laugh and begin pulling out drawers in search of more stories. Maybe a real name to this moniker of 'the dragon'. I find a messy scrawl of handwriting, numbers, and symbols that are absolute nonsense to me. Must be the formula for dragon fire. My grip tightens, crinkling the parchment in my hand. I want to burn it. I don't care that it's sitting in this dank cave, hundreds of feet beneath the stone. No good can come of this, and I want it stricken from existence.

"Let's find the others."

Jaromir's voice cuts through my thoughts, and I swiftly hold the parchment over the flame of the half-melted candle. The edges glow with bright embers before they curl and disintegrate. I drop the page onto the desk, watching the flames consume the alchemical formula for dragon fire. Something tightens in my throat—I'm destroying something that isn't mine, a memory that isn't mine, but I can't bring myself to regret it. When nothing else remains but a pile of ash, I tear my gaze from the sight.

"Lead the way."

THE BAGS WEIGH A TON, filled to the brim with gold as they are. And an ancient elven prayer stone in mine. Our horses carry saddlebags filled with coins. It seems a foolish way to travel, but we won't be returning. There was some debate as to how to prevent anyone from venturing into the cave again, but ultimately, after looting the place of its treasure, we used the blackpowder to collapse the entrance. Perhaps it was a disservice to a forgotten man's legacy, but I owe no allegiance to the one who calls himself *The Dragon*. The one who led countless to their deaths for his own sport.

We'll burn Aeron's map, along with my translations. Hopefully, that's enough to keep this secret cave hidden. Should people come looking, all they'll find is a corpse-eaters nest and a destroyed cave.

I have confiscated the evidence that "the dragon" was ever there. There are still his furnishings and mechanisms in a room deep in the heart of the cave, buried behind rubble and fallen rock, but the contents of his letter remain burned in my mind. We concocted a story of how the dragon was felled by Aeron's blade, and when the giant body collapsed, as did the cave. How we only just escaped with our lives, having already robbed the dragon of his hoard before the beast awoke to intruders. How Aeron dealt the killing blow, just as he received his own. How we had to drag the brave and mortally wounded Aeron to freedom so he might see the sky one last time before his eyes shuttered closed. The dragon tooth is sharp in my satchel, jabbing its reminder against my thigh.

Lying about Aeron's death, the circumstances, it never struck me as bothersome until now. Perhaps it's exhaustion, or hunger, or the reality of the situation finally sinking in, but guilt gnaws against the pit of my stomach.

If I can immortalize his name in all this, it will all be worth it.

The strap of my bag digs into my neck, the weight of the gold bumping against my hip.

The days we spend traveling are different from before. We're all swimming in riches, and yet there's an emptiness in it all. When we scorch Aeron's armor against the campfire at night, the air is heavy with accusation. Perhaps it was always going to feel this way, dragon or no.

Neith offers to train with me, but I don't have any fight left. None of us do, really. Even Cadoc is quiet, pensive, rather than his boisterous self.

Jaromir keeps to himself, working on something by the fire, and when we all retire, he takes watch. I can see him through the stitches in my tent, his broad shoulders and the way his back ripples with the motions. I turn away from Jaromir and his secrets.

There's much work to do.

In the stillness of a dark night, I pen the conclusion to Aeron's ballad. My throat tightens against the words traveling from my mind to the page, never crossing my lips but promising their return when I will share it with the world. Behind the safety of my tent walls, under dwindling lamplight, I write feverishly. When my fingers are stained with ink, and my hand cramps from pressing my quill too hard, I finish the last line with a flourish.

It is done.

THE TOWN of Kalinia appears on the horizon. A lump lodges in my throat at the sight, at the knowledge that this really is the end. Until Aeron's face fades into myth, and the drunken patrons we charmed have forgotten the smile of the man buying their drinks, we must be careful where Cadoc and Jaromir are seen.

Memory is a funny thing. One day, a stranger's face will hold the familiar resemblance to a hero you once knew, and you'll wonder if you remembered them wrong or if your mind is projecting an old memory onto a new one.

But not today.

Cadoc can't set foot in the town, not since he played as Aeron, and I'm going to sing of his heroic demise tonight, so he and Neith will stay in the forest and bypass the town limits, meeting us a mile or so past the gate.

Not us. Me. Just me. Jaromir will stay behind with his family.

Cadoc ruffles my hat and chucks me on the chin. "I wish I could hear the first time you sing his song." There's a thickness in his voice I don't normally hear.

I flash him my stage smile. "The first performance is a dress rehearsal at best. I'll work out any kinks in time for my next performance, and you'll be there to witness it all."

"I can't wait." Turning to Jaromir, he pulls him into an embrace. "Take care of yourself."

Jaromir claps him on the back. "And you. I'll visit you and Tomas after you've settled a bit."

"I'm holding you to that. I might even offer you a discount."

"You would charge me to drink the swill in your tavern?"

Cadoc laughs. "You can afford it now."

Neith shakes her head, approaching me with an amused expression aimed at Cadoc and Jaromir. "Look," she says, "I'm not going anywhere. We'll get ye wherever ye wish t'go, and I won't leave 'til ye're ready."

How she knew I needed to hear this is a testament to her ability to read people.

Or just how well she knows me.

"Careful. I might keep you forever."

She shrugs, and it doesn't feel like a dismissal so much as an invitation. "Oh, and afore I forget—" She unclasps a bronze chain from behind her neck and tugs the intricate necklace free. Twisted branches and raw amethyst laid in bronze greet me. The strangely beautiful design in all its glory. Something about it calls to me, reminds me of something I can't quite grasp.

"Ye ken what this is?"

I blink at her. "It's a necklace." Does she think I've suffered a head injury?

Neith holds it closer to me, running her thumb over the stone. "A necklace of elven make. In The Western Isles, elven designs are rare commodities, only worn by the elite with th'coin t'pay for such luxuries."

Rare, because even the artisans in Smarighad were forced into hiding.

Neith arches a brow. "I chose this piece because my mother hated it, and it was th'most expensive. I didnae ken why I continued t'wear it. Maybe as a reminder. But over time, I believed it was always meant t'find me. Maybe it was a sign t'take courage and follow my true path even when it hurt."

She slowly lowers it into my palm, closing my fingers over the edge. Bronze branches stab into my fingers. "I want ye t'have it."

"I can't accept this—"

A memory flits unbidden to the surface. My ahntan and her long flowing hair, shimmering gold in the sunlight. Her large green eyes, wide with the silly expressions she'd make because it always made me laugh. Mama always said I favored my ahntan Elothwyn. Her simple homespun dresses, cheaper fabrics we could afford because most of the merchants charged heavily for elves. And around her neck—

She had a necklace like this. It had been in the family for generations. The branches were rounder, and the stone was a dark red garnet, but the design was so similar it gives me a funny feeling in my stomach.

"Ye can. Means more t'me that ye have it than I." Neith watches me patiently, waiting for me to continue my rejection of her gift. But I can't reject something like this.

"Will you help me put it on?"

Her answering smile is broad and unrestrained as she clasps it around my neck. It's surprisingly light and warm against my skin. And worth more than all the gold weighing down my pack.

AFTER CADOC and Neith disappear into the forest, Jaromir and I are finally alone. I'll likely stay in his guest room, under the same roof as him and his betrothed, like an unwanted relative. I'll force a smile through my ballad, then be on my way to find Cadoc and Neith, and never see Jaromir again. A fitting end to our disastrous union, but at least we both survived. A silver lining in an otherwise shit storm if I've ever seen one.

"Syl," Jaromir says, pulling one of his packs off his shoulder gently. "There's something I wanted to give you before we make it into town. Things are... difficult. People know me here; they have certain expectations of my intentions to avoid desertion of inheritance. I still need to handle that and..." His voice trails off as he eyes me with uncertainty.

Before I can respond, he grips me by the jaw, pressing a hard kiss to my lips. It's a punch to the gut, and a gasp gets trapped in my throat as every emotion I've desperately tried to bury rises to the surface. My body reacts before I can think, and I'm gripping his shoulders to keep him from pulling away, deepening the kiss with a sort of urgency that borders on madness.

His arms come around me, surrounding me with his warmth. He invades my senses and leaves my head spinning. Reluctantly, he pulls away, resting his forehead against mine. "That wasn't what I wanted to give you." His voice is ragged, and he huffs a laugh against my lips. "I just needed to feel this one last time."

I step back, already colder without the safety of his body against mine. "Right, you had a present for me, did you?" I aim for a cheerful tone, a great feat since I'm still reeling from the pendulum of emotion resulting in the kiss that still burns against my lips.

Jaromir nods and reaches into his spare pack. "I couldn't let you go without replacing this."

It's a lute. A smaller one than my old one, but the unmistakable body of the gorgeous instrument is enough to catch my breath in my throat. He carved the round shape so perfectly, even whittled tuning pegs attached to gut strings. I pluck a soft tune, blown away by the full sound he's crafted. Sure, I have enough coin to buy the finest lute in creation, a tavern, too, should I wish it. But this is far and away the most beautiful instrument I'll ever have occasion to play.

"If you hate it, I can buy you a new one. I could go to one of the larger markets and get you whichever you see fit to replace the one you lost. I'm sure this isn't nearly as high quality as the one you're used to playing, but I did scrounge up some of the wood from the old body in case it had sentimental value. You don't need to play it tonight, but if you wanted something that could work in a pinch, I think this should do the trick."

Jaromir is rambling. Jaromir doesn't ramble! I turn my incredulous gaze on his handsome face, only to find his stare darts around wildly, and his large hand rubs the back of his neck.

It's perfect. It's the best gift I've ever received in my entire life. And that it's from him makes it even better.

Welkin above, but it hurts how much I care for this man. This time, I welcome the pain and all it means. How deeply it cuts me, my affection for one I can't have. How in another world, another life, we could have been home for each other.

I yank him down to look at me. "I love it, Jaromir. It's perfect." *You're perfect.*

"I'm no master craftsman. I had to make this from memories of watching you play." From the way his cheeks redden, I gather there are a lot of memories.

"It's perfect," I repeat and run my hand down the length of his arm, lingering against his palm. "I can carve Aeron's lasting legacy with this."

If I'm to really sell Aeron's ballad, the story of how he faced down the dragon, I need this lute. I need to pull out every advantage I have to captivate my audience and keep his memory alive. The power of stories is in the telling, and I intend to tell his story with everything I've got.

Jaromir closes his hand over mine. "The story of Aeron's fate was altered by the tales you spun." A sad smile steals across his mouth, and he tugs me against his chest, against his heartbeat, and inhales deeply. "If only our fates could be so easily changed." His arms tighten. "I'm not sure I can let you go, even though I have to."

I'm not certain I'll remain standing when he finally pulls away, so I cling to him tighter, savoring this moment. Once we cross into town, everything will change. He won't be mine, and I can't be his. Did I squander our remaining time with my anger? For the sake of protecting my heart? Should we have pretended we had forever until the very last moment? All I wanted was to build up my defenses and keep my heart from bruising, but the way it squeezes in my chest proves I did nothing of the sort. If anything, I poorly patched the broken thing and now it's being ripped open anew.

If only I could change our fates with the scratch of a quill and a convincing story. Aeron will be immortalized, not as the man who forfeited his life to protect his friend, but as the great hero who defeated a dragon. Perhaps his true story is the better one... but who's to say where the line between truth and fiction lies? 'The dragon' managed to sell the tale of a dragon, all in pursuit of protecting his wealth from the town laws. A well-spun story has the power to change everything.

Yet here we are. Trapped in an impossible situation.

"I'm not marrying her." He says it so softly, I'm not sure I hear him correctly. "Not that it makes any difference, nor would I expect it to. But I can't... not after this. Not after us."

"What about Damir's home? Your family's land?"

"I'll give her my share of the hoard. It will be more than enough to grant her and my nieces a comfortable life. Somewhere." More than a comfortable life, by my estimation. I had mentioned to Rhosyn about paying off the magistrate in exchange for him looking the other way, but she said he'd made false promises before, pocketing coin and feigning ignorance of his bargain with widows in the past. He always refused to sign anything, claiming it a conflict of legality, and leaving anyone who dealt with him vulnerable to his changing whims. The scheming bastard.

"You would live in her home? Work her lands?"

Jaromir grimaces. "Ah. No. After I persuade her to take the gold, I'll sign the deed over to the magistrate. Or sell it. It matters naught." Because he wasn't built for a life tethered to one place, all the memories of his brother echoing against empty walls, or the knowledge that he let Rhosyn and her daughters lose their last piece of Damir. This isn't a resolution to anything.

It feels like a penance.

"And you walk away with nothing?"

"Not nothing. I'll have memories of you, and that's worth more than all the gold in this world." Jaromir's expression is etched in such sorrow. He's throwing everything away and expecting nothing from me. I'm not trying to punish him for lying, but how can I be complicit in tossing Rhosyn out of the home her husband built? The life she and Damir built together?

It would always hang above us, the sharp blade of loss.

"Are you sure there aren't any bastards of yours running around? Someone we can dote on and bond with so Rhosyn wouldn't have to sign her home away? You certainly sowed your wild oats far and wide before I came along." I force a laugh.

Jaromir offers me the barest of smiles. "You know that isn't possible. I made sure of it."

Of course. The brew Cadoc keeps him supplied with. Jaromir would never be so irresponsible as to leave one of his partners facing the consequences of their actions alone. He, unlike some men, has honor and integrity and—

It hits me. The answer to everything.

I can't believe I hadn't thought of it sooner. Welkin above, words can wield all the power of the world, and I plan on seeing how far the power of my words extend.

I grab Jaromir's arm, excitement flooding me like a torrential storm. How did I not think of this sooner? The answer is right in front of me—has been the whole time!

"Jaromir, what if we could protect Rhosyn, grant her ownership of her home, and you didn't have to marry her?"

His eyes widen in alarm, his mouth parting in surprise. "How... what would we do?"

I'm practically vibrating with excitement. "We pay a visit to the town magistrate."

Chapter Thirty-Five

I can appreciate fine craftsmanship when I see it. This desk, for instance, is a gorgeous ebony, carved into intricate shapes and filigrees. I rest my feet atop its surface, crossing my ankles and sinking into the cushioned chair.

Yes, the magistrate has fine taste, indeed.

I debated a more delicate approach to petitioning his lordship when the idea first came to me, but upon verifying my suspicions with Rhosyn, this was the way to go.

She'd already tried petitioning the man numerous times to no avail. He wasn't required to adapt to the new by-laws under Her Majesty the Queen. Each town has their own governing structure with local magistrates enforcing their laws, and the town of Kalinia has yet to yield to the very popular notion of allowing next of kin inheritance laws to include all manner of kin, even by will of testament. No, Kalinia still holds firm to the archaic law of the town absorbing inheritances in the absence of a suitable male heir.

The ornate desk beneath my filthy boots and the silk cushion I'm staining with my road-worn attire offers me all the insight I need to understand The Honorable Magistrate Ridion's hesitance to adapt.

I tuck my hands behind my head, careful not to disturb my cap. For such an expensive room, the magistrate relies on piss-poor locks for security.

Rhosyn adjusts her skirts where she sits in the visitor's chair, flashing me a knowing grin. As soon as I informed her of my plan, her eyes had glimmered with excitement and cunning.

"*He travels most frequently,*" she had said. "*I heard a rumor he got drunk enough to confess he had a companion in every major city.*"

I bet every coin from my share of the hoard his wife doesn't know that. Nor does he take the same pains Jaromir does to ensure no woman he lays with faces lasting develop-ments to their coupling.

Jaromir crosses his arms, leaning a hip against the wall where he waits. He, of course, won't allow Rhosyn or me to confront the magistrate alone. I don't mind. This concerns him as much as Rhosyn, so he should be here.

The added comfort of knowing I have a hulking body-guard is another point in favor of his presence.

Footsteps sound just outside the door. Jaromir tucks deeper into the corner, as much as he can, given his size.

I reach up and adjust my cap. The same fluttering of excitement I get before a performance erupts in my belly.

It's showtime.

The door swings open, and a man in a black chaperon and robes steps into view. He stills, the tippit of his elaborate head-wear fluttering with the movement. His gaze travels along my relaxed posture, with my feet atop his expensive desk, and over to Rhosyn where she sits, the picture of patient elegance. He narrows his eyes, adding more creases to his crow's feet.

"I see you've come to badger me again."

Jaromir firmly shuts the door behind the man, causing him to jump and spin around in surprise. Without uttering a word, Jaromir angles his body to block the exit.

Magistrate Ridion lets out a derisive snort. "And you've hired thugs to threaten me to do your bidding."

Rhosyn rolls her eyes. "We've come to offer a proposal. His presence is merely to ensure you'll listen. Don't you recognize Damir's brother?"

The magistrate takes a cautious step in Jaromir's direction. "Are you here to accept your claim to his inheritance or to sign it over to me? There can be no other legal reason for your visit."

Jaromir's scowl never lessens. "Neither."

I clear my throat. "I'd say have a seat, but as you can see, there are none to be had. You wouldn't expect a lady to relinquish her chair, would you?"

The magistrate has the good sense to bite his tongue against whatever barb he might have had prepared. Probably something about there being no ladies in sight or some such nonsense. Through clenched teeth he utters, "Of course, not."

"Splendid!" I clap my hands together, delighting in the flinch of irritation it earns. "We haven't met, dreadful shame, but allow me to rectify that." I sweep my cap in a flourish. "Sylvaine Abelan. Bard extraordinaire, defender of both written and spoken word. Acting notary in some happenstances. Formidable slinger of stones"—I toss a wink Jaromir's way, reveling in the private smile I receive—"and, at present, your guide for a better tomorrow."

Magistrate Ridion scoffs, eying me with thinly veiled disgust. "An elf who thinks she's more than gutter refuse. How charming."

I laugh at the attempt to disarm me, but Jaromir's hand clamps around his throat.

"Watch your tongue or lose it."

Ridion's eyes bulge from his head as Jaromir's grip tightens, a faint wheeze escaping from his mouth.

"Thank you, but we need his signature," I say.

"His apology first."

Ridion's face is turning a lovely shade of purple. "S-sorry."

Jaromir releases his hold, remaining a close and threatening presence.

Ridion gasps, coughing and rubbing his throat. "You're all animals," he chokes out. "Common beasts."

"Oh, come now! You don't know me well enough for that sort of talk." I lower my feet from his desk, leaning onto my elbows instead. "I know you, though."

"You know nothing—"

"William M. Ridion. Most assume the M stands for Mortimer after your father, but it stands for Margaret to honor your mother's midwife." I pause. "I actually quite like that. It's rather endearing."

I allow him exactly five heartbeats before I continue.

"I know your father had to pay off your exorbitant gambling debts twice before his untimely passing. You and your wife have two lovely daughters and a strapping young son. I know the local healer advised you to watch your intake of spirits and meat due to your heart troubles, and I know you've sired no fewer than four illegitimate children in your travels. Children you've neglected despite your lavish lifestyle." I wave to indicate his furnishings.

William Margaret Ridion gapes at me, a tremble building along his shoulders. "You can't... you can't possibly prove any of these claims..."

"Can't I?" I raise a brow and allow a sly smile to cross my face. "William, I'm a collector of stories. They all came from somewhere."

Like the friendly locals, the serving girls at the tavern, a dwarven healer, a traveling merchant, and the fellow bard I interrogated.

"Besides, I don't need to prove it. All I need to do is what I do best." I lean my chin atop my fist, waiting for him to realize the extent of the destruction I could cause for a man like him and my penchant for writing catchy songs. "Isn't there a vote coming up? I heard something about it. A new town motto? A new trade route?"

He seethes, his narrow chest rising and falling with each breath. "The next magistrate's term, you abominable heathen."

I snap my fingers in triumph. "That's it! I should think you'd want to keep a low profile where scandal is concerned."

Magistrate W. M. Ridion's shoulders lower, collapsing his posture. "What do you want?"

I nod to Rhosyn. This is her demand to make. Her home. Her life.

She rises, dark hair tumbling over her shoulders. All poise and grace as she lifts her chin. "You will dispense with this antiquated inheritance law and make the proper amendments so no person can be thrown from their home in the wake of family tragedy. You will serve the people rather than steal from them when they're most vulnerable. You will enact Queen Dhara's inclusive land and title ownership policies so any person can create a life in Kalinia." She glares down at him; I hadn't realized how much taller she is, but the effect is jarring in the best way. "And you will accomplish this all today. Or Syl will sing of your exploits this night."

His cheeks redden, a vein bulging in his forehead. "It will take time to draw up the proper legal documents. To track down a scribe, and a notary—"

"No need." I flash him my brightest stage smile as I fish the legislative document I penned on Rhosyn's table while she paced around the kitchen. "It's all here, and as a notary, I can witness your signature and the official stamp of your signet ring."

His hands clench as if he'd love nothing more than to wring my neck. Jaromir shoves him toward the desk, a reminder of his presence and a warning.

"Very well," Ridion mutters through a tight mouth.

"Oh, in triplicate." I grab the duplicate documents, fanning them out across his desk and trying not to smear my ink-stained hands across the words. "I'd hate for you to misplace one."

"Indeed." His lips have thinned to almost nonexistent proportions as he flourishes his signature and stamps his ring with more force than necessary.

I stand and immediately hand one copy to Rhosyn, tucking the other under my arm. "Pleasure, William. Do come watch my set tomorrow evening!"

His eyes widen. "You wouldn't still..."

"Not if you behave." I march out of his office, Rhosyn and Jaromir trailing behind. When we finally push through the outer door, dusk has fallen. I exhale a sigh of relief. The faintest hint of the earliest stars glimmer against an increasingly dark sky, and for the first time in weeks, I can appreciate the sight.

I pull the coin purse from my pocket, the one I'd swiped from his desk. Tossing it from hand to hand, I grin. This will go straight to the mothers of his forgotten children. Perhaps I should visit him monthly and pilfer his reserves for familial upkeep. Call it my civic duty.

"I can't believe that worked." Rhosyn's voice is soft as she stares down at the proof of her ownership. "I can't believe it worked!" she repeats, hitting an ear-splitting shriek as she scoops me up into her arms and spins me around. "You absolute seraph! I can't thank you enough!"

Normally, I love praise, especially well-deserved praise. But at her words, my cheeks burn and I have a warm, squirming feeling in my gut. She sets me back on my feet. "I was prepared to invent an heir. What luck he really is a scoundrel. My threats carry the weight of the truth." I'd caught wind of his dalliances that night in the tavern when we were here last. Little tidbits of secrets passed between confidantes. I'd almost forgotten, courtesy of the dwarven whiskey and the broken heart I'd been nursing that night. But what was meant to be Jaromir's goodbye in the middle of the road unearthed the hazy memory.

I glance over to find Jaromir giving me a strange look. His lips are parted, and his eyes are wide as he refuses to break his stare. He gives a slow disbelieving shake of his head as if he's still in shock we pulled it off.

As if he still can't believe his life is wide open again.

I give him a little shrug, and the corner of his mouth lifts. He takes a step toward me, and the air between us is rife with everything we haven't said.

Rhosyn intercepts, pulling him into an embrace and whispering in his ear. He nods and places a chaste kiss to the side of her head. Once again, his gaze finds mine. We have all the time in the world to sort out what this means for us.

"I don't know about you two, but I'm in the mood to celebrate!" Rhosyn glances between us with a knowing grin.

A celebration is undoubtedly due. Something ridiculous. Naked howling at the moon would be a good start.

I glance down at my clothes. Dirt and ash still coat my skin, along with some questionable stains I haven't been able to scrub clean yet. As soon as we ventured into Kalinia, I set to work investigating, and before that we were on the road, fighting corpse-eaters and slaying a fake dragon.

"Yes," I finally say, beaming back at Rhosyn where she's twirling her skirts in glee.

There is much to celebrate, an entire life wide open for the taking, and there is something I must do before I can conquer this newfound destiny of greatness.

"But first a bath."

Chapter Thirty-Six

I pluck my new lute, reveling in its rich sound as I swing my legs hanging off the side of the tall bed. I never got a chance to stay at the inn the last time we were here, and I'm pleasantly surprised to find it's outfitted for comfort. A large wolf pelt drapes across the coverlet, offering my wandering fingers something soft to tangle in.

Droplets of bathwater coat the wooden floor, and my hair hangs loose and wet down my back, dampening my tunic. I've already bathed, scrubbed, and soaked all the parts that seemed destined to remain filthy, and I feel lighter than I have in weeks. Maybe ever.

Jaromir has been... not distant, but cautious. He gave me my privacy when I bathed and has yet to return. Perhaps it was presumptuous of me to assume we'd pick up where we left off as soon as he was a free man.

Or perhaps he never wanted more than the fleeting time we had together.

My fingers dance over the strings, and I feel the falsity in that thought. He's shown me time and time again how much I mean to him, even when he had nothing to give me besides his ruined heart. And maybe I was unfair to him, or maybe love isn't a question of fairness but how far you're willing to go and how much you're willing to hurt. Love can be a selfish act, neglecting all else in favor of your heart's call. But Jaromir doesn't love selfishly. He loves selflessly, giving all he has and more to the ones who earn the space in his heart, expecting nothing in return but the knowledge that he's cared for them.

Even if he doesn't wish to build a life with me, even if he needs to follow his newfound freedom wherever it takes him, I'll love him endlessly for the strength of his heart alone.

I love him.

The rightness of it all sings in my veins.

The door creaks open, and I still both my circling thoughts and my incessant playing. Laden silence claims the room, and my ears prick at the sudden loss of my music. Jaromir fills the doorway and hesitates. His hair is damp and tied back in a knot, his skin cleaned of the road, and he's changed into a linen tunic and a pair of simple trousers. He waits, tension tightening his broad shoulders.

I should tell him to enter, give the man the reassurance he desperately needs to cross the threshold and stay. Stay for as long as he'll give me.

"You bathed."

"Yes," he says, rubbing the back of his neck. "I needed to."

I gently place the lute on the bed, rising to stand. For once, no joke rests on the tip of my tongue. There's too much hope filling my chest, and it aches with the weight of it.

"What else do you need?"

He takes a cautious step forward, slowly shutting the door behind him. *This is it. Say you need me, and I will be forever yours.*

"An answer."

I wasn't expecting that.

"I don't recall hearing a question."

Jaromir runs a hand over his mouth, taking a deep breath as if bracing himself. "I have some things to say, things I should have said a long time ago. Syl, I'm so fucking sorry. I was a selfish coward, and I should have told you about my agreement with Rhosyn before I ever kissed you."

My breath catches in my throat. He isn't being fair to himself, not after everything has been brought to light, but I can't bring myself to contradict him just yet. "That's not a question."

"No, it isn't. I must ask... I must ask, would you still have me? Though I don't deserve you, and I've broken your faith in me. I fucked everything up in every way but even still..." His eyes are pleading, and I can't fathom how he doesn't know I never stopped being his. "Just put me out of my misery and tell me your thoughts."

I pad across the floor, small puddles of water clinging to the bottoms of my feet. I can do this. I've been guarded with him before, and he needs to hear the words especially since I've been so free with my words in the past. His gaze tracks my movements as I edge closer to him, upon the precipice of everything. It's the last step before the plunge, and though hope flits against my ribs, I will accept whatever happens next.

"My thoughts, Jaromir," I say, exhaling a huff of disbelief and shaking my head, "my thoughts are always of you." Wetting my lips, I stare at the center of his broad chest where the tunic ties hang loose and open. It's a safer place to fix my gaze so I can make it through this next part. "I wish to remain at your side. To be your partner in all things. To spend as much time I have in this life showing you how much I love you." I trip over the word, because it's a steep step to take, but I continue despite the trembling in my hands and the heat filling my face. "I love you, and I want to wake beside you each morning, fill my days with your endless scowling and grunting, find new little wooden carvings you've made me—always practical as they are beautiful—write songs that make you blush and laugh, and seek new ways to learn this world with you. Would I still have you?" My voice wavers, and tears prick my eyes as I lay everything bare. "Once you asked me where home was... and I told you I'd let you know when I found it." My vision blurs, and I force the rest of my confession free. "It's you, Jaromir. You are my home."

The last of my resolve crumbles, and the tears I've only just kept at bay roll down my cheeks as I utter the final words of my plea. A warm touch beneath my chin forces me to face Jaromir—his expression has transformed into one of astonishment and wonder, his own eyes shining with emotion. Ghosting his fingertips along the point of my ear, he traces my face before running his thumb against my jaw, lowering his hand to rest against the space between my throat and my neck. My pulse pounds against his touch.

"Syl." His voice is rough, thick. "I've always loved you, and you will always be my home."

The final piece clicks into place, and I surge forward, closing the distance and claiming his mouth. Jaromir lifts me, carrying me to the bed. Winding my arms around his neck, I kiss him with every promise I have in me. His beard is rough against my face, and already my skin is sensitive, but I deepen the kiss to taste the words he's just spoken. A ragged groan leaves his mouth, and I swallow the sound.

I love him. I love him. I love him.

My thoughts are a canticle as my heart expands. He places me on the bed, gingerly moving my lute to the floor before I can protest. I tug his tunic impatiently, dragging it over his head. Jaromir's formidable form is on display for me once more. All hard edges and battle scars, but the bright grin on his face is joy and disbelief.

"Is this real? Tell me I won't awaken to find this has all been a dream."

I pinch his arm playfully, and he grabs my wrist, pressing his mouth against the delicate skin. He smiles against me. "Say it again."

I know what he longs to hear. "I love you."

His lips crash against mine, and he cages me with his large body, holding my hands high above my head. When he pulls back, he shakes his head, gazing down at where he holds me in place. "I love everything about you. I love your mouth and your sweet voice that never ceases even when you sleep." He grinds against me, sending sparks through my body. "I love how sensitive your beautiful ears are." He nips at one, and I shiver. "I love the soft noises you make when your perfect body opens for me." He follows his words with another roll of his hips.

I fight to pull my hands free so I can touch him, but he holds firm.

"I love your mind, your quick tongue, and your cunning. I love your heart, your impossible kindness and joy. The light you cast with your smile. Fuck, I love you, Syl. And you're mine. You'll always be mine." He growls these words against my throat, making me dizzy with want. Making my chest ache with the way my heart fills.

"Welkin above, Jaromir. If you love me so much, let me touch you."

His laugh ghosts against my skin, but finally, he releases my hands.

I fumble with his laces, and he tears off my tunic, ripping the neck in the process. I can't halt the laugh that spills from my lips. Lips that press to his, to every inch of skin I can reach. I'm smiling against his kisses as his hands run over every part of me, greedy in their exploration. When we've nothing left between us, souls and bodies laid bare, he trails his mouth down my stomach. I don't want to wait, there will be time enough to relearn every curve of each other.

Right now, all I need is him.

I yank on his hair, and it falls loose. He glances up at me, amusement in his eyes along with a fierce adoration I've come to recognize.

"Impatient?" he rasps against my hip.

"Prioritizing." I tug his hair again to pull him up to me.

He chuckles against my skin, rising to meet my eager mouth and line himself up with my entrance.

"Gods, I've missed you."

He sinks in slowly, allowing me time to adjust to his size. I claw at his back, twisting my hips to try to force him in faster. With a groan, he plunges in, bottoming out, and ripping a cry from my lungs.

I sink my teeth into his shoulder as the burst of sharp pleasure fills me. The noise he makes is enough to encourage me to do that more often.

"Syl," he growls, "careful, or I'm never letting you leave this bed."

A breathy laugh leaves my chest. "Promise?"

Jaromir slowly unravels me with each thrust, punctuating the motion with a circling of his hips. He whispers filthy and adoring promises in my ear, following his words with the drag of his teeth. I'm forever undone by this man, and when the searing pleasure flutters deep within me, my vision blurs, and I clutch to him even tighter.

Mine. My beloved. My home.

Chapter Thirty-Seven

I breathe in the heady aroma of sweat and ale. The tavern in Astervale is our last stay, our last chance to spread word of Aeron and leave our mark on history. We've come full circle, and it's only appropriate that our final stop is the one place Aeron made it to. Cadoc, Neith, and Jaromir all sit in the center table, watching me with reassuring expressions.

We've done right by him. I've done right by him.

We might not have lost him to a dragon, but it feels that way. We carried him with us each day. Words and memories, there's power in them. It kept Aeron alive enough that this feels like the true goodbye.

First Fruits day has come and gone, along with the summer season. The last time we were here, red banners hung from wood beams and yellow ribbons wrapped around each pole. Now, burgundy fabrics drape delicately above the bar. Small pumpkins and bumpy gourds adorn the tabletops in a bold proclamation of the impending Harvest Day. Outside, the air has more of a bite, but in here the fires are warm and the drinks are flowing. Camaraderie fills the tavern with a generous spirit of belonging, and it doesn't feel like a farewell to summer so much as welcoming the shift in season.

I adjust my cap, and begin to pluck the familiar tune, the one I've been playing in every tavern we stay in, in the privacy of every inn Jaromir and I have paid to sleep in, by the fire of our camp each night.

The ballad of the last dragon. The ballad of Sir Aeron.

"Sir Aeron had the heart of a warrior and the mercy of a saint
With warmth that rivaled the sun and drove darkness away
Man or beast of evil intent fell to his sword, fell to his sword
He brought us deliverance, mark my words, mark my words

He felled poisonous creatures of malicious intent
Spared no killer, and no earthly threat
I rode along by his side and saw with my own eyes
The depth of his courage and the strength inside

The tale of our quest is not one that's short
So if you've the patience, and offer no retort
I'll recount to you our journey though it stretches on
For we are not finished, we've adventures beyond..."

My gaze travels over the crowd, arresting on Jaromir. He offers me a soft smile and a dip of his chin. He's here with me, as are the others. Here in this moment where everything comes to fruition. Cadoc has placed Aeron's scorched armor, the chest plate we held over our very own campfire, on the table. He rests his hand loosely upon it, tracing the grooves bordering its design. Neith lifts her tankard, and my gaze catches on the dragon tooth she wears around her neck. It's fitting that she should be the one to carry it.

"When Aeron stared down the dragon, sword in hand
I saw the glimmer in his eye, and knew his intent
He shot me a wink, and in passing he said
'Sing of me and offer no tears for the dead.'

The dragon roared, erupting its flames
Aeron surged forward, ending life's claim
Taking the dragon to embrace death's arms
Two lives ended, two souls gone

He met his match that fateful day
But his honor lives on if we speak his name
So, drink to his memory if he were here, he would say
The drinks are on me, this joyous day

Through whispers of time, listen for my call
I'll always be with you, you'll hear my song
In the way shadows dance by firelight
Or the sun rises and sets, giving way to night

Farewell is not farewell, in the end
But a promise to meet once more
For where stories end, they begin anew
So instead of farewell, I'll say to you

Until we meet again."

THERE'S a weightlessness in my chest, a joyful buoyancy even
as a glimmer of grief settles in my stomach.

It is done. Aeron's ballad is through. Judging by the teary
expressions in the crowd, and the way some of them sang along
with the familiar parts, we achieved our goal.

Jaromir's arm slips around my shoulder, and he presses a kiss to my sweaty forehead, knocking my hat out of the way. "You were wonderful."

My heart fills at his words, but I toss an aggrieved expression his way. "Wonderful? Is that it? I wasn't spectacular? Life-changing? Stupefying or prodigious?"

He fixes me with his hardest look—the one that used to convince me of his hatred and now only serves the impulse to shove him into a private alcove and ravish him. Judging by the way his eyes darken, I'd wager he senses the turn in my thoughts. "I'll show you how much I enjoyed your performance later. Especially since you didn't sing of my cursed prick again."

Oh... there's an idea. "I've been working on that one, actually. Added a few stanzas I'm sure you'll appreciate."

"Don't make me take you over my knee."

As if that's a threat.

The server bustles over, none other than the red-haired beauty from the last time we were here. I wag my brows at Jaromir, poking and nudging him with conspicuity. He pulls me closer, trapping my wandering hands from making too much of a scene.

The woman smiles softly, no hint of discomfort or ill will, and sets the meat pie down in the middle of our table with four plates and forks.

"It's on the house," she says.

My mouth waters, stomach growling as the smell of corned beef, cabbage, carrots, and potatoes waft on the steam rising from the buttery crust.

"Hmm... I must have left a lasting impression." Jaromir's words rip me from my appreciation of the meal, and I whip my stare to find his face looking far too innocent. His mouth twitches, revealing the amusement he finds in his own joke.

Neith claims her chair, having just ventured to the bar,

and interrupts what I'm sure would have been a worthy retaliation on my part.

"They're putting it up now." She gestures over her shoulder where the barkeep is hammering a large nail into the wall. He reaches for Aeron's chest plate, hanging it and stepping back to examine his work.

We all fall silent, staring at the last piece of Aeron adorning the tavern wall. His bright, and gleaming chest plate, marred by scorch marks and tarnished by the road.

"Should we have polished it?" Cadoc's voice is soft and unsure, almost lost to the din of noise.

I swallow the lump in my throat. "It serves his purpose better that we didn't. It lends credibility to his tale."

Cadoc nods, not tearing his eyes from the sight.

Neith elbows him. "It would have driven Aeron crazy t'see it in such a state."

An unrestrained smile dawns Cadoc's face. "Remember how he used to wake up early just to make the damned thing shine? I told him, it was going to get dirty and not to waste his effort. But each morning, sure as the sun rising, he was out there, polishing away."

Neith laughs into her tankard. "Aye, I remember. He was th'same as a wee bairn. Meticulous with his armor care."

"You should have seen him when I first trained him with the sword," Jaromir says, shaking his head. "He spent more time whetting than thrusting."

"I'm sure there's a filthy joke in there somewhere..." My words dissolve into a shriek when Jaromir's teeth graze my neck in a playful bite.

As Cadoc cuts into the meat pie, steam billowing from where he slices through the brown crust, Neith clears her throat.

"I'm going te write Arnorr about this. About... Aeron's tale, and I'm going te ask him t'put up a memorial for him in their family crypt. I might even venture there maself t'see it done."

I nod, pushing too-hot potato slices around my plate. It's another disappointment in the big picture, the idea that Aeron never had a chance to reunite with his family and reinstate his honor in his lifetime. But if we can give him this posthumously, we've achieved all he wanted. Everything he whispered to me in that sickroom, when he was recovering from the arrow wound in his chest.

I hope by the grace of the goddess he can see everything we've done, everything his name carries, what it means to us all. That he can see he never needed his family's blessing.

"Be sure to stop by The Laughing Goat whenever you swing through Bucklebrook. Tomas and I will be thrilled to see you."

Cadoc's letter writing campaign has forged some impenetrable bonds between the two of them. When we stopped by Bucklebrook, they were inseparable and even ended the visit with a teary goodbye. I'm glad he can return now that our job is done, and never have to worry about leaving Tomas behind again. A strange and beautiful thought, considering his former discomfort with staying in one place very long. Now it seems his wish is to plant roots and forever remain by Tomas' side.

But still... *The Laughing Goat Tavern?*

"You sure you're attached to that name? You have a chance to reinvigorate your venue."

Cadoc gives me a secret smile as he sips from his tankard. "Don't you worry about me and our tavern. We have big plans."

It's as much of an answer I'm going to get for now. I'll have to see it in person. The thought sends a thrill through me. We have no fixed destination anymore, we can go anywhere, do anything. The world has suddenly expanded, limits dissolving into spaces of time in which I can achieve anything.

"What about you?" I turn to Jaromir, spearing one of my steaming potatoes. "What's your next move?"

I thought all I wanted was fame and glory. To be untouchable by any who might deem me lesser. To rise above my status, and never let my ears define me again. My wish has always been accompanied by the fantasy of never going hungry, never wondering where I might rest my head, or what might await me as soon as I let my guard down. But never in my wildest dreams have I imagined this feeling. This trust and hope and want for a lasting life. A simple wish that feels anything but simple. It's everything.

Jaromir's gaze softens, holding me in place as he studies me. "I'll follow you anywhere. Point to a spot on the map, and we'll go." He leans forward, brushing my nose with his. "So long as I'm with you, I'm home."

I press a soft kiss to his perfect mouth, euphoria washing over me. When I pull back, I plop the potato in my mouth and sigh, letting it fill my cheek as I sate my hungry belly.

"Well, then, my heart, I have a few places in mind."

Epilogue

I'm alone onstage at the Rusty Nail, but I bend in a deep bow, and straighten my cap as I've done many times before. Kingsley left my stool right where it has always sat, a fact that makes my throat tight. This time, when I approached my spot center stage, I let my footing find that creak he never fixed, reveling in the familiar sound. The same mismatched chairs, each crafted by Kingsley with leftover scrap wood, sit empty in the tavern. He hasn't decorated for Winter Solstice—no surprise there, since we're riding the tail of the last days of autumn—but part of me wonders if it's because he's been waiting for me.

Jaromir flashes me a knowing grin, my only audience member for the moment, and leans back in his chair, watching me with his intent gaze. He's dashing with half his hair knotted back, sporting his new leather jerkin. The elvish design of intricate braiding and detailing was worth every penny. As was seeing the armorer, Adlanniel, rebuild her shop. We might have greased a few palms and commissioned enough armor to get her business going. And since the heroes who aided the great Aeron in slaying the last dragon choose only her wares, other merchants clamber to work with her.

The ballad of Aeron has followed us far and wide, but there's something I need to do before we venture much farther.

This is the time of year when Kingsley shortens his tavern operations. Less folk travel to Hollowden in the cold season, so it doesn't make sense to open his doors far before supper. But Kingsley should arrive at any moment, and anticipation curls in my belly. I haven't seen him since the day I left, back when the summer season was in full bloom. Now, the sky darkens with night's call, and the threat of the first snowfall hangs in the air.

I begin to pluck "While the Fisherman's Away", and I'm struck with a keen sense of nostalgia. It aches in places I'd forgotten I possess, this memory of what once was good and now is a little lost. But today is a happy occasion, and on happy occasions, we make room for the twinge of sorrow to commingle with joy.

The familiar jangle of Kingsley's iron keyring sounds from outside, and I sit up taller, determined to stay put until the last moment. The door creaks open, carrying a gust of wind, and his massive form fills the frame. The torches and candles we've lit cast a warm glow about the tavern, illuminating his wide eyes and gaping mouth.

Kingsley blinks, frozen in place. "You're... you're here."

At the sound of his gruff voice, I abandon all pretense and leap off the stool, running toward the giant oaf and throwing my arms around him—carefully so as not to damage my favorite lute.

Kingsley lifts me, hugging me tightly to his chest. The very real threat of suffocation further proves my theory that he's killed a man with his bare hands.

"You utter terror," he says in a watery voice. "We thought we'd never see you again."

He and Brigitta. They once made my survival their personal mission and came to think of me as a form of family. But I force out a laugh through the emotion squeezing my throat.

"Petey missed my songs, eh? I can't blame him. I am the best there is and the ambitious force behind themed events we'll host here."

Kingsley lowers me to my feet and all but drags me over to the bar. "You tell me everything, *everything* that happened, and I'll pour the two of us a drink." He glances over my shoulder, spotting Jaromir, and narrows his eyes in suspicion. "I suppose, I'll pour the three of us a drink."

"Deal," I say, waving Jaromir over, "but you must promise not to interrupt. It's a long tale, and you haven't the time to listen to me all night, much as you might enjoy that."

He gives a laugh with his whole body, reaching behind the bar to grab the shittiest wine I've ever tasted.

"It all began when that bright smiling fellow—you remember him? Aeron? When he invited me to ride along to witness him hunt a dragon..."

"THERE HASN'T BEEN a dragon in over a century," Kingsley says when I finally end my story. "And you're telling me, you not only found a dragon, but a gold hoard?"

I pause, shooting him a half-hearted glare. "Well, when you put it like that, it sounds rather ridiculous. Say it better. Use more adjectives."

He lifts his hands in surrender. "I'm sorry, go on."

I poke Jaromir in the shoulder, and he pulls the scroll from my pack.

"Here is your share. I've already paid off food and drink suppliers"—I scrunch my nose at the wine in my glass—"and

I've commissioned a few carpenters and builders to follow your orders and expand the tavern however you wish." A warm satisfaction falls over me as I drop the details into Kingsley's palm.

His eyes bulge, and he rubs his jaw. "This is—"

"A good start. Part one of reciprocating all that you've done for me." I hold up a hand to silence his arguing. "I wouldn't have survived without your kindness. And now"—I gesture around the empty tavern, knowing part two is about to unfold—"I have a way to make sure you and Brigitta want for nothing."

Kingsley swallows hard, pulling me into another crushing bear hug. "You owe us nothing. Nothing but a few letters and maybe visiting occasionally when the wind blows you our way."

I grin and extricate myself from his hold. "Occasional visits? I'm a world-famous bard now, and I will make sure to visit the finest establishments in my circuit regularly. Which is why"—I lean closer and offer him a conspiratorial whisper—"The Rusty Nail will be my favored stomping ground."

As if on cue, all right yes, it was planned and I craved the theatrics of good timing, Cadoc and Neith sweep through the doors, followed closely by a crowd of revelers we may have swayed into joining us this evening with the promise of free drinks.

Kingsley stands, knocking his stool back. "How did you—"

"A bard never reveals her secrets!" I stand and clap him on the back. "Only everyone else's."

I sling my strap over my shoulder and adjust my lute into position. A quick touch of the feather in my cap, and I'm ready to begin.

MY STOMACH HURTS FROM LAUGHING. Cadoc has just finished regaling us with stories of his acting duties as co-owner of the tavern with Tomas.

"How was I to know the room was rented out?" he demands between chortles. "We need a ledger of sorts. I've only just stopped visualizing the oldest arse I've ever witnessed, high in the air, every time I close my eyes."

"Good on him for staying limber with age," Neith says with a laugh.

I wave my tankard, sloshing ale over the side. "Exactly! Jaromir isn't nearly that flexible. He'll be a stiff old man in no time."

Jaromir yanks me onto his lap, threatening to tickle me for such an affront.

"I'm working on the logistics of running a business. Remind me to chat with that Kingsley fellow later," Cadoc says.

We all turn to find Kingsley leaning over the bar to plant an aggressive kiss against Brigitta's lips. Her white-blonde curls spill over her shoulder, as she reaches across to hold him in place. They'll be celebrating later in private. Goddess, I hope they wait for privacy.

"Did you change the ghastly name yet?" I ask, eager to wipe the image of old man arses and Kingsley's robust marital bed from my mind.

"I did!" Cadoc stands, lifting his tankard high and propping his foot on the chair. "You are now looking at the co-owner of... *The Last Dragon.*"

My chest fills, and it's a bittersweet joy. I lift my drink. "Hear, hear. A fine name if I ever heard one."

We all drink from our cups, and though none of us speak for the moment, we're all thinking of Aeron.

"What are you going to do about all the goats?"

Cadoc snorts into his drink, wiping his mouth and chin

with the back of his hand. "I don't want to talk about the goats. All you need to know is we came to an accord, and Tomas is working on adding the dragon detailing above the bar." He returns to examining his cup, done with the conversation.

Tomas was the one to carve goats into the posts and beams throughout the tavern. But they appeared integral to the structure of the place. And if he spent all that time hand crafting those fine details—

"Whit was th'bargain?" Neith asks, connecting the dots quicker than I and fighting a smile.

A casual shrug accompanies Cadoc's answer. "Some of the goats stayed. The ones in high places. The others were... relocated."

Neith and I exchange a glance. Her mouth twitches.

"They're in your home, aren't they?" Jaromir doesn't carry quite as much glee as Neith, but the way the muscle in his cheek feathers, he's holding back a smile. Cadoc answers with a resigned nod, which only sends Neith into a fit of laughter.

Hesitantly, Cadoc begins to chuckle. "I know what you're thinking of. You're remembering the time—"

"Aeron insisted we observe th'mountain goats t'better understand th'way they leap from crag t'crag." Neith wipes her eyes, a few broken laughs fighting free. "Failing t'realize yer intense fear o' th'animal."

"I'm not afraid of goats! I have a healthy respect for them, and just prefer to give them a wide berth."

"Th'way ye shrieked each time we heard a bleat from th'cliffs suggests otherwise."

"I don't remember this," Jaromir says with a befuddled expression.

Cadoc grins. "That's because you spent the night tracking down a courier."

"Remember when Aeron finally realized yer fear and decided t'bleat back even louder?"

Neith and Cadoc laugh and stare at each other, mentally exchanging more of the story than they're willing to voice aloud, and I can't find fault with that. Sometimes, the power of a story is in the telling, spreading it far and wide so it might take on a life of its own. But even rarer is the story protected, guarding key details from public consumption. Apparently, Aeron's goat story is worthy of such protection.

It's so ridiculously him.

"I heard from Arnorr," Neith finally says. "They're building a memorial, as I'd hoped. In a few months, I'll mount a journey t'go see it and pay my respects."

I reach over and grab her hand, even though mine is sticky from spilled ale. "And when you do, I'm going with you."

She nods, a small smile forming on her mouth. The tavern is bright and loud, and through it all, a glimmer of sadness remains. We will always be one man short—strange, since we were without Aeron for most of our journey.

There's also the question of when we will all be together again. This plan was set in stone from the moment of our parting, but now... the future is a wide expanse of the unknown.

"What's next for you?" I ask, needing to know to which corners of the world my friends are venturing.

"I was going te talk t'ye about that," Neith says examining her ale. "I've signed up t'be a member of Cinna's crew. She captains *The Sea Harpy* and offered me an interesting opportunity. She's putting together an elite crew for extractions."

My heart thuds along my ribs. "Where are you extracting from?"

"A few neighboring countries, but namely"—she takes a deep breath—"Smarighad."

"You're rescuing elves?"

She nods, a solemn expression on her face.

I try my best to rein in my emotions, the dizzying tangle

that accompanies the news. Weighing my words carefully, I continue. "What are you charging them for transport?"

Her face softens. "Nothing."

Staggering relief courses through me. They aren't taking advantage of people trying to escape death and dismemberment. They're helping.

"And what safeguards are in place for those who disembark and start their new lives here?"

Neith gives a short shake of her head. "Our goal is extraction and transport. The rest is up t'them."

I nod, head spinning and stomach threatening to revisit the shitty ale I drank. It's a noble goal—one I admire in my friend.

"That's amazing, Neith." I mean it, but too many thoughts and memories duel for dominance.

Jaromir's hand finds my neck, giving a gentle squeeze. "Do you need some air?"

"Yes," I say, standing and shifting the table with my abrupt movement. I dart out the front door into the cold night, not pausing to see if Jaromir follows me.

I know he will.

The air is sharp and still, and a heavy quiet has settled through the trees. The noise from the tavern is muffled, but warm light and soft rumbles of laughter spill through the cross-hatch windows and into the night. The sky above hides the stars from view. My nose stings as I breathe in the fresh air and exhale wisps of steam.

Jaromir's hands find my shoulders, rubbing a soothing path and anchoring me.

"Tell me your thoughts." The rumble of his voice is my safe harbor, and between the fresh air blasting me in the face and the comfort of his presence, I find the thread I wish to follow.

I can do anything. Be anything. The coin and the status I've acquired give me more freedom than I've ever had. I could go to Lindale and continue building my name. I could travel the world, exploring all it has to offer.

Doors that have always remained locked are now wide open.

I glance up at Jaromir, at the man who has given me home no matter where I go. His dark eyes are awash with concern. I lift up onto my toes and press a kiss to his lips, losing myself for a moment in the way he tastes. Something cold lands featherlight on my nose, on the tips of my ears. When I open my eyes, the first snow is falling, and the hush of the forest is like a heavy blanket.

I remember the first time I saw snow in Targgein. It was such a magical, wondrous thing. I'd been on my own for a few months, and already been plagued by fear and hunger of living on the streets as a child with nothing. But that first snow, heavy flakes falling and landing on my eyelashes and coating my hair, was a glimpse of hope. Of magic found in the longest of nights.

Of course, then I had the bitter cold to contend with.

I'd arrived with nothing. Been prepared for *nothing*. And no one was waiting for me.

I cup Jaromir's jaw, kissing him again out of sheer joy for all I have now. "You said you'd follow me anywhere; do you mean it?"

Jaromir presses his brow to mine, inhaling deeply. "Of course, I do. Always."

I nod; I knew that would be his response. Neith is rescuing elves from the life I escaped, but who will guide them and help them to land on their feet in a foreign country with nothing but the grace of the goddess?

And what if... do I dare hope... could I receive news of my da and mama?

"I've been thinking about where my talents would be best utilized."

"Oh?" He bundles me tighter in his arms, his mouth twitching. "Enlighten me."

"Hmm... I do believe a bard such as myself would do quite well in all the major port cities. Perhaps Neith could help me comprise a rotational schedule."

Jaromir grins against my mouth, lifting me off my feet and holding me close to his chest. "I think that's a wonderful idea."

"Only wonderful? Not brilliant? Or genius? Or putting all other thoughts to shame?"

He laughs, and I bask in the sound. In the rich timbre of our shared joy.

I'm home. I've made that impossible dream my reality, and while there's still work to do, and many more who need my help, I can think of no greater purpose than to offer my services to any and all who come searching for refuge. With this wonderful, ridiculous, amazing man by my side.

There's a ballad in this moment somewhere, I'm sure of it. But if I write it, I might just keep it for myself.

Aeron's Ballad

A man there was
      By the name of Aeron
      All fire and gold
      All honor and bold
      The first to take a stand

      Against the dragon
      Seeks the dragon
      To claim his hoard
      By the tip of his sword
      You'll hear his name again, again

      How brave he was
      And pure and true
      The man with honor
      through and through

      He comes tonight
      You'll meet him tonight
      He comes to you

Riding the summer air

Sir Aeron had the heart of a warrior and the mercy of a saint
With warmth that rivaled the sun and drove darkness away
Man or beast of evil intent fell to his sword, fell to his sword
He brought us deliverance, mark my words, mark my words

He felled poisonous creatures of malicious intent
Spared no killer, and no earthly threat
I rode along by his side and saw with my own eyes
The depth of his courage and the strength inside

The tale of our quest is not one that's short
So if you've the patience, and offer no retort
I'll recount to you our journey though it stretches on
For we are not finished, we've adventures beyond...

(This is where the bard uses spoken word to regale any number
of the adventures of Sir Aeron's. Regionally, there are variances
in both stories and styles. After which, a return to the pluck
pattern and song structure ushers in the final verses)

When Aeron stared down the dragon, sword in hand
I saw the glimmer in his eye, and knew his intent
He shot me a wink, and in passing he said
'Sing of me and offer no tears for the dead.'

The dragon roared, erupting its flames
Aeron surged forward, ending life's claim
Taking the dragon to embrace death's arms
Two lives ended, two souls are gone

He met his match that fateful day
But his honor lives on if we speak his name

So, drink to his memory if he were here, he would say
The drinks are on me, this joyous day

Through whispers of time, listen for my call
I'll always be with you, you'll hear my song
In the way shadows dance by firelight
Or the sun rises and sets, giving way to night

Farewell is not farewell, in the end
But a promise to meet once more
For where stories end, they begin anew
So instead of farewell, I'll say to you

Until we meet again.

Acknowledgments

I think it's traditional to save partners for last, but I can't seem to wait another moment to gush about my husband. Lance, you've always believed in me, been my biggest fan, listened to me rant about my plots, and even fanboyed over my characters. I love you more than I can possibly say. Thank you for always helping me physically block scenes, for always being ready for a brain dump, and for not laughing too hard on New Years Eve when I fell down the stairs running to get my elf ears.

My beautiful daughters, my wildling and my elfling. You both bring so much light, joy, laughter, and magic to my life. Being your mom is my greatest adventure. I love you both more than I thought the human heart was capable of.

Friel. You believed in Syl and Jaromir and their imperfect journey. You gave me courage and hope when it was so easy to give up. Then you took my finished book and made it shine with your brilliant edits. My editor, my best friend, my writing soulmate, my sister. I can't believe how lucky I am to have found you. Late night writing sessions, hours of voice chatting, endless Twilight and LOTR memes, monster smut buddy reads, hazy summer days spent dreaming and plotting. It's like I've known you my entire life. I love you, and I'm forever grateful we found each other in the niche writing corner of instagram. Even if you thought I was a tech savvy eighty year old woman.

Elle. I miss you doesn't begin to explain the longing I feel when I think of you and remember I won't have new voice messages waiting for me when I wake up. The Ballad of the

Last Dragon was the last book of mine you read. But you're still with me in every story I write, in every flower and fairy tea party. My writing sister of blood and gore, every star in my sky, I love you.

Devon. Were it not for our summer side quest, this book never would have happened. Here's to our voice message rants, analyzing the greatest literature known, and hobbit energy. I love you and our chaos. It's you, it's me, it's we.

Brit. My darling who tolerates my overly affectionate verbal affirmations. You are a balm to this weary soul. Your kindness and compassion, your all-encompassing friendship is a gift I'll cherish forever. I love you more than apple pie.

Stella and Brandi, you both alpha read this book and not only hyped me up but helped me so much it's unbelievable. Stella, you are the godmother to my mushroom. Brandi, you are my dragon age loving soul sister. I love you both so much!

My beta readers; Tuesday, Kate, Kristin, Kristen, Krystal, McKenzie, Erin, and Kelly (AKA my sex scene midwife) I cannot articulate how much I appreciate you all. You kept me excited while helping me so much, and you treated my story with so much care and respect. Forever grateful to each of you.

Jaime. My love. My Jo. My pookie, or are you my schnookie? Thank you for forgiving me for that sword in the eye misunderstanding, and trusting my offspring to play and grow up with your offspring. Twenty nine years. That's how long we've been gathering blackmail on each other. Seriously, I love you and I'm stupid lucky to have you in my life.

Last, but never least, you, dear reader. You are the one making my dreams come true. Every single person who messages me letting me know they read my book and connected with something on some level, you've made a permanent space in my memory. Thank you for giving my books a chance, and letting me connect with you. If I could send each of you a pie, I would.

About the Author

C. A. Farran is a fantasy author. She's addicted to video games, KitKats, and energy drinks.

Farran grew up by the sea on a steady intake of fairytales, renaissance fairs, and mythology. She's always felt a profound connection to horror and dark fantasy, spending her childhood searching the woods for monsters and magic.

Now, she spends her days photographing nature in Maine with her three cats; Commander, Demon, and River, her husband, and their two wildlings.

This is her third fantasy novel.

To stay up to date on her shenanigans and literary mischief, check out cafarran.com or find her on instagram. She's absurdly friendly, it's rather off-putting.

9 798985 132786